CAREY'S FORTUNE

CAREY'S FORTUNE

ANNE EMERY

THE WESTMINSTER PRESS
Philadelphia

STANDARD BOOK No. 664–32455–X
LIBRARY OF CONGRESS CATALOG CARD No. 72–82412

PUBLISHED BY THE WESTMINSTER PRESS ®
PHILADELPHIA, PENNSYLVANIA

PRINTED IN THE UNITED STATES OF AMERICA

CAREY'S FORTUNE

Chapter 1

AT SEVENTEEN Nancy Carey had almost everything a girl could wish for. She was a popular Annapolis belle, with admirers begging for every dance at the balls. Her family was important—her father, a noted member of the Maryland legislature. She lived in a handsome town house part of the year and spent the summer months on one of the loveliest plantations in Maryland. And a rich and handsome beau had been courting her seriously for the past six months.

With all these advantages, Nancy was hard put to understand why life seemed dull, and she found herself bored much of the time.

She loved Annapolis—a wealthy and sparkling little town, with the gayest social life north of Charleston. Nancy spent the season going to the theater, attending the fortnightly dancing Assemblies, following the horse races in the fall, calling upon her friends in the mornings, going to parties, giving parties, and having fittings on pretty clothes. Her life was exceedingly full. There was no good reason for the fit of the dismals that attacked her at unexpected moments, when she found herself wishing something exciting might happen, wondering what was wrong with herself, and hardly enjoying herself anymore.

She was slim and graceful and pretty, with a certain independence that showed itself in the way she carried her head high, the way she looked at a man, wondering not if she pleased him, but if he pleased her. Such independence troubled her mother.

"You must hide your tendency to argue and disagree with men," Lucy Carey told her daughter more than once. "No man likes a strong-minded female. It's most unwomanly."

Nancy listened to her mother politely and did not believe a word she heard. Roger Tucker had been swearing devotion these six months past, and she had been putting him off, laughing at his protestations, teasing him cruelly, and telling him she was too young. Her mother was afraid she might put Roger off once too often, and both her parents favored his suit strongly.

Roger was the eldest son of a wealthy Federalist family, with one of the finest plantations in Maryland, adjoining the Carey plantation on the Patuxent River. He was both rich and good-looking, and many girls envied Nancy his attentions. And yet Nancy dreamed of being madly in love with someone who would sweep her off her feet. Sometimes she wondered if there really was such a thing as romantic love. Certainly Roger never stirred her to anything like the love she read about in *Clarissa Harlowe* and talked about with her friends.

Now on a golden day in September, 1800, Nancy looked forward to the first Assembly dance with fresh hope. She must meet an unknown someone who would be the answer to all her uncertainties. She had a new gown, in the very latest French fashion, of sheer pink India silk, coming barely to her ankles, with a tiny, high-waisted bodice and a frill edging a low-cut square neck. It was a delicious gown, and, looking at it, she dreamed again about the handsome stranger who would leap to his feet when she arrived at the Assembly Rooms and compete for her favor.

She looked from the silken gown to the note she held crushed in her hand, shaking her head and trying to find it an amusing joke. Her little black maid, Clio, was watching her hopefully. Nancy spun around on her heel and dropped into a flowered chintz chair by her window to read the note again.

My dear Nancy,

I have asked your father for your hand, and he has consented to my suit, with his blessing. I shall ask you tonight, and hope for a kind answer.

Ever your faithful servant,
Roger Tucker

Her throat was dry. The unknown young chevalier of her dreams might appear tonight with his heart in his hand. But she must admit that was unlikely, since it had not happened in all the past year of Assembly dances. And this note from Roger was an ultimatum—he had talked to her father, he was making a serious offer, and Nancy knew quite well that if she refused Roger tonight he would not ask her again.

There was every reason why she should marry Roger. He was part of her own circle of friends. Her parents approved of him. She would have a life filled with money and social importance, like the life she now lived. And she was not in love with anyone else.

She was not in love with Roger either. But was love, after all, as important as ensuring a well-to-do future? Nancy got up and paced back and forth. She looked at the silken gown lying on the bed, ran her fingers over the sheer stuff, unfurled the pink fan and waved it gently. Clio smiled widely, approving her pretty mistress. And Nancy, catching that smile in the mirror, smiled back.

Suddenly the choking sensation took hold of her again,

the feeling of being imprisoned in a web of boredom that, once married, she could never escape.

She turned her back on the mirror and read Roger's note again. If she could find some way to put him off, just a little bit, not enough to make him angry—not too long. Just long enough to give her a chance to think. Perhaps tonight she would know better than she knew at this moment. That would be her signal, she thought, grasping at the same faint old hope. If she saw no one new or interesting at the ball tonight she would tell Roger . . .

Her heart began beating fast again, fast enough to stop her breath. She went slowly downstairs to join her family for the three o'clock dinner, feeling that she could not swallow one bite.

Grandmother Carey, sitting on Father's right, across the table from Nancy, looked at her and said, "What ails you, Nancy? You look like a ghost." Grandmother Carey was pert and plump at seventy-two, with snapping black eyes that seemed to notice more than anyone else in the family. What she noticed she did not hesitate to speak out about. At her age, no one complained about her being strong-minded.

Nancy lifted her eyes reluctantly to her grandmother's question. "I don't know why I should look like that, Grandmother. Perhaps I'm just tired."

Her grandmother munched noisily on a crust of bread. "You should get some rest before the ball tonight, then. A young thing like you should not tire so easily! When I was your age I could dance the night through and be rosier than when I began."

Jonathan Carey looked sharply at his daughter, now that his mother was remarking on her looks. He was a high-tempered man, with a tendency to apoplexy, impatient with differing opinions, and accustomed to telling his family what to do. He had been an officer under General

12

Washington twenty-five years before and had never lost the habit of command. Nancy quailed. She had had words with her father before this over Roger's suit.

"Still mooning about Roger?" he barked. "I don't know why you must be so contrary about a marriage I've given my consent to. If you'd just make up your mind about him, you'd feel better right away. What's so hard about that, I'd like to know?"

It wouldn't be hard at all, if one were in love with the man. Nancy picked at her deviled crab indifferently. The hard part was wondering whether if you refused the man who offered money and land and social position, you would ever get another chance. Or, if you made up your mind to marry him, might you fall madly in love with another later? And what then? She wished someone could answer those questions for her.

She leaned her head on her hand and said mopishly, "I don't know if I can dance tonight or not, Father. I feel a chill coming on, and my head is aching as if it would split."

He recognized all her excuses and ignored them. "Pray be reasonable, Nancy! Not many families today have enough wealth to keep their plantations, and Roger's got enough for his and yours besides." Looking to his mother for support, Jonathan Carey glowered at his family and announced, "The way this country's going now, with taxes and war scares all the time, we're all going to be bankrupt if we aren't careful." He glared at Nancy. "That's why this Tucker alliance will be such a good thing for you, my dear! I can't imagine a girl of good sense having any doubt at all about it! Roger is a fine, upstanding young man, and a good Federalist. What's all this shilly-shallying?"

He drew a deep breath and tucked his napkin back into his coat. His face was quite red, and Nancy felt alarmed and guilty, recalling his last fit of apoplexy.

Everyone finished the deviled crab in silence. The maid took away the dishes and brought in roasted quails with orange sauce. It was a favorite dish of Jonathan Carey's, and the sight of the little brown roasted bird before him calmed his temper somewhat.

"If there was someone else you were in love with, that might make a difference," he told Nancy, as if he were making a great concession. "But you don't seem to have that kind of problem, Nancy. Or is there someone else?" He raised his voice in angry suspicion.

Nancy shook her head and said carefully, controlling her voice so she would not anger him further, "Father, I have to think about it. I can't decide all in a minute. And I'm only seventeen!"

The table was silent again, while Jonathan Carey ate his roast quail with hearty appetite. Then he informed his daughter, "Lots of girls are mothers at seventeen! It's quite a proper time to get married. And you've known Roger all your life. What's so hard to decide about someone you know?"

The maid removed the quail course and brought in lemon cheesecake, while all the Careys waited in silence. When she had left the room, Jonathan Carey plunged his fork into the cheesecake and stuffed a huge portion into his mouth. Nancy looked at her favorite dessert. She could not swallow a morsel of it.

"If you'll excuse me, Father," she said, rising, "I have the headache very badly, and I must lie down, if I'm going to dance tonight."

Nancy fled to her room, flung herself on the bed, and closed her eyes. Her head was aching in truth. She clenched her fists tightly and tried to put her father's words out of her mind. If she married Roger, she would be free of such nagging. Or would she? How much might

14

Roger be like her father? She wished her bother, Tom, could advise her. But Tom was spending the weekend hunting on a friend's plantation.

She reviewed all her reasons for doubt, and all the reasons for certainty, and somewhere in that exercise she fell asleep. When she wakened, the sun was setting, and the long cool shadows of the fir tree outside her window darkened the room.

"Come in," she called to a knock on the door.

"Have you been sleeping, Nancy?" Her mother entered. "It's time to begin dressing for the Assembly."

Lucy Carey was a pretty, older edition of her daughter, plump and rosy and still blond at thirty-nine. She had been a Baltimore belle, just seventeen when she married Jonathan Carey in 1778. He was then a handsome major in the Revolutionary army, and she was so deeply in love that she had eloped from the home of her Tory father with the Patriot officer.

So deeply in love, Nancy thought, watching her mother adjust the shutters at the windows, as to run away with a rebel. What had that life been like? Had it been hard? Had her mother ever been uncertain? At least, she had been in love—

"Honey." Lucy sat down on the side of the bed and put one arm around her daughter. "I just want you to understand how much this offer from Roger means to your father. He's so worried these days about his debts. And the plantation doesn't pay anymore. He's nearly beside himself. This marriage will provide you with a good safe future. And otherwise he may have nothing to leave you. Nancy, a safe future is terribly important for a girl."

"I know, Mother."

She wanted to cry out, Did you worry about a safe future in the middle of the war, Mother? Her Tory father must have been wild! Yet today Mother was talking about the importance of a safe future.

Nancy knew about the unfortunate women who never married, who found themselves with no inheritance, who were forced to work for a living. But she could not believe in poverty for the Careys. Not when there had always been money for beautiful clothes, for new furniture, for carriages ordered from England, for racehorses in the stables.

She got wearily off the bed and sat down at her dressing table to let Clio brush and arrange her hair, while her mother watched.

"I know it's hard to imagine not having any money, when there's always been plenty," she said, as if she had read Nancy's thoughts. "But good friends of ours, wealthier than we were, have gone bankrupt since the war. I don't understand these things either, Nancy. Yet they do happen. And it would make your father feel so much better to know that you were well taken care of."

Nancy met her mother's eyes in the mirror. Her mother's anxious effort to make her understand hit Nancy with the first sense of uncertainty she had ever felt about her family's wealth.

"I know, Mother," she repeated.

Lucy Carey hugged her daughter approvingly and went to dress for the ball herself. An hour later Nancy turned around before the long pier mirror, gazing at her new pink gown, the tiny puffed sleeves just off her shoulders, the soft silk slippers laced with ribbons about her ankles, the silken ribbon tied through the knot of curls on top of her head. She felt pretty in this darling dress. Her spirits lifted. She took a few steps back and sideways, bowed to her reflection with a coy glance above her silk fan, and looked flirtatiously at herself over her shoulder.

Tonight, after all, looked more promising than it had earlier in the afternoon.

Chapter 2

THE ASSEMBLY ROOMS were filled with flowers and lighted with hundreds of candles in crystal chandeliers that refracted the tiny flames in a million dancing lights. A soft west wind blew through the long open windows with the nighttime fragrance of summer's end, and moonlight cast a silver glow upon the formal gardens outside. Nancy's spirits were high for this first dance of the season, and she greeted her friends with the lively mischief of the candlelight.

The rooms were packed with surging people, talking of their summers away from town and gossiping about the newest scandal. Three different ladies told Lucy Carey about Peggy Mason's elopement. "Ran off with that Republican Benjamin Brown just last night! Her mother is distracted! Who ever thought Peggy Mason would do a thing like that?"

"Poor Margaret!" said Mrs. Carey of Peggy's mother. "It must have been a dreadful shock!"

Nancy thought of the Loyalist daughter running away with the rebel officer, years ago. But today was different. She knew Peggy Mason, a quiet, brown-eyed girl whom she had seen at the last Assembly dance in May. Come to remember, Peggy had not seemed interested in any of her dancing partners that night. And of course Benjamin Brown was not a member of the Assembly.

Nancy listened with horrified fascination as the details

began to be known. It was beyond imagination that the aristocratic daughter of one of the richest planters should have run away with a journeyman blacksmith. She kept trying to understand such strange behavior as Mrs. Tucker poured out what she knew of the story.

"To run off with Benjamin Brown, of all people! That is the worst of it. She left a note for her mother, and her parents discovered it early this morning. But no one knows what road they took, and now it's gone too far to be stopped."

"What a pity!" Lucy Carey shook her head in scandalized sympathy. "Young people are so headstrong these days! What did you say the young man does?"

"That's the worst of all!" Nellie Tucker exclaimed, fanning herself vigorously. "Young Mr. Brown is a blacksmith! With no money at all! Mr. Mason called upon his parents, of course, and all his father could say was that young Mr. Brown was planning to go out to the frontier! Such a dangerous life to take a young girl into. And Peggy is only sixteen!"

Her audience gasped with horror, and in spite of wishing to contradict Mrs. Tucker, Nancy could not repress a shudder. The frontier, of all places! So wild and lonely and dangerous. And Peggy, who had been shy and sheltered— How could that poor girl be happy so far from home and family? What tragic mistake had she made?

The fiddles were sounding, and some of the older guests began making their way to the smaller salons at the far ends of the ballroom, where tables were set up for cards. Roger came toward Nancy from across the room.

He was a big, blond young man, with a very serious opinion of his own worth, and no sense of humor. He had been sent home from college six months ago because of a dueling incident and had been calling upon Nancy since then. By now everyone in town knew that Roger Tucker intended to marry Nancy Carey, and Annapolis matrons asked each other in puzzled whispers why the Carey girl kept him dangling.

Roger had no particular ambition, other than hunting, racing, and living at Green Hill, the Tucker plantation, with as little effort as possible. He spoke of getting an appointment with the diplomatic staff in England, since his father sat in the Congress. And because the Tuckers had enough wealth to support a life of leisure, he was admired as a young man of great promise and the most eligible bachelor in town.

His mother watched with fond pride as he presented himself to the ladies sitting together. "I believe we have this dance, Nancy. I've waited all summer for this night."

Molly Tucker watched Nancy with an expression of sour envy. Roger's older sister talked too much in a high, vivacious tone, fanning herself in nervous haste and watching hopefully for someone to invite her to dance. She was a very plain girl who was spiteful about more popular girls. Nancy disliked her at the same time that she felt sorry for her.

Nancy rose to Roger's outstretched hand, smiling at him above her fan, deliberately coy and flirtatious. After the shock of Peggy Mason's disaster, Roger looked more attractive than he ever had before.

They joined the set for the romping country dance, and as Roger caught her around the waist, whirled her about, and sat her down again, Nancy found herself exhilarated and sparkling with enjoyment. He danced away, holding her eyes, and back again, and she thought with surprise that he was more attractive than she had realized.

He returned Nancy to her mother after the first dance, promising to see her for their next dance an hour later, and went off to play cards, deliberately not dancing with anyone else. Nancy accepted other partners, all of them old friends. The evening ran along swiftly to the rhythms of the fiddlers, the fluttering of silk and muslin skirts, the repartee of flirting couples, and the watching eyes of mothers sitting on golden chairs around the wall.

But Nancy saw no new face in the crowd, and looking at all the Annapolis people there, she thought, with the feeling of being very clear-sighted, that there need be no uncertainty about Roger. There was no one in all this party she liked better, and she recalled her earlier panic with some amusement.

When Roger returned for the promised dance, he brought a strange young man with him. Nancy saw him with surprise, wondering how she had missed a stranger tonight, with all her searching. But she had not missed much. He was smaller than Roger, thin and sallow, dressed in the height of fashion, with an elaborately tied cravat, and with a manner of arrogant assurance. Roger presented him to his mother, to Mrs. Carey, and to Nancy, and then to his sister. The stranger eyed Nancy with an appraising stare.

"Molly, Mr. Blaney has asked me if you would honor him with this dance," said Roger.

Mr. Blaney bowed to Molly, who was on her feet in unbecoming haste, with a gratified smile that almost transformed her personality. Nancy rose to take Roger's arm, watching his sister cross the dance floor. If Molly were a happier spirit, she might find someone who would look at her money instead of her receding chin.

"Who is Mr. Blaney?" Nancy asked Roger.

"He's here from New York to study law with Judge Chase. One of the Chase girls presented him to me tonight. He seemed lonesome, and I thought he might like to meet my sister."

"Studying with Judge Chase?" Nancy said. "I wonder if Tom may have met him."

"He only arrived from New York last week. But he seems quite struck with our town."

Roger looked very complacent as he crossed figures in the dance with his sister and Mr. Blaney. When the set was finished, he took Nancy back to her mother and went away to play cards again. Nancy sat on a golden chair, fanning herself gently and thinking—about Mr. Blaney and Molly, about marriage, about Roger.

It was a fact of life in the society of 1800 that any marriage was better than no marriage. But Peggy Mason's marriage? She must have been madly in love. Perhaps Nancy was lucky in never having known that kind of mad love. Peggy probably had had no idea at all how hard life could be on the frontier, in a log hut with hostile Indians lurking in the trees. Nancy felt as if she herself had escaped a dark menace, and a chill ran down her spine. Roger offered security, luxury, wealth.

And someday Roger was going to be Important. Nancy told herself firmly that she would see that he was. If he were with the diplomatic corps in London—how romantic it must be, the social life of the court, a presentation to the queen, court balls, titled friends. She let herself dream of that romantic future while Molly returned to sit beside her and rattle on about how charming Mr. Blaney was, how much he delighted in Annapolis, what pretty compliments he had paid her.

"He asked if he might take me to supper," she cried, "and I swear I was so confused I told him he might!"

Roger came to take Nancy to the supper table an hour later, and after supper asked her to walk in the moonlit garden with him. She took his arm and felt in that romantic hour that he might turn into her knight in armor after all.

They strolled down grassy paths between phlox beds fragrant in the night air toward a private corner hidden behind high hedges. There they sat down on a marble bench.

Roger took Nancy's hand, and she sat very still, her eyes cast down.

"Nancy," he said, sounding very sure of himself. "You received my note today?"

She looked at the spot of silver moonlight on the path beyond them.

"I received it, Roger."

"Will you give me the answer I hope for, Nancy? Will you marry me?"

He sounded so sure of her answer that Nancy found herself beset with doubt again. "Roger—I—don't know what to say—"

He was on his knees, kissing her hand. "Nancy, my love, I can wait no longer for your answer. You have kept me uncertain too long—"

Like a parade of pictures, the thought of Peggy Mason ran across her mind, of Molly Tucker who had never at twenty-three been asked for her hand, of a spinster who must live with her family all her life—it was too much. There was no one other than Roger. There might never be anyone else.

"Yes, Roger, I will marry you."

Without warning he seized her in his arms and kissed her so passionately that she was breathless and struggled to free herself. He released her with an apology for his ardor.

"I've been so impatient to hear you say those words these past weeks, Nancy! I waited only until your birthday was past, and that was hard to do!"

He reached for her again, and after another smothering moment she managed to detach herself.

22

"Roger—" Nancy pulled away in sudden panic at what she had done. "Please—we must go back to the ballroom. We cannot stay here like this—"

She stood up, trembling, and Roger stood at once. He apologized for allowing himself to be so carried away and promised to take her to her mother now and to call upon her parents tomorrow.

"Will you be at Carey's Fortune to hunt with us next week?" he asked.

She had forgotten the hunt. "Oh, yes, I'll be there with my parents."

"We can settle all plans then," he promised.

They walked slowly back along the grassy paths to the ballroom.

"As soon as the settlements are arranged we must set a wedding date," he said. "I have so many plans for us . . ."

Nancy was wondering how long she could put off the wedding day. She must have time to get accustomed to the idea, and already the illusion she had enjoyed in the moonlight was fading. He was so much more impatient than she supposed Roger might be! A quiver ran through her. Marriage was so final.

"Roger, I'll have to think about the wedding day. Where would we live? I don't want to live with either of our families, not even for a little while."

"I have plans for that too," he said. "I began building a house this summer, and it's going to be beautiful. The finest house in this part of Maryland."

They entered the ballroom for the last hour. He raised her hand to his lips as they left the terrace, and they moved sedately across the floor to join the mothers. Nancy wondered if anything of her feelings showed.

Molly was watching her curiously as she took her place with them. Mrs. Tucker raised her eyebrows, with a smile, as if she knew what had happened. Mrs. Carey looked at

Nancy hopefully and settled herself to wait patiently until they reached home to be told the good news. And Nancy watched Roger cross the floor toward the cardrooms, wondering about her own feelings.

She had known all along that she was going to marry Roger. And now she had promised him. Why, then, did she have this uneasy sense that some lovely golden thing was missing? Impatiently she turned her thoughts to the house he was building, a beautiful new house for his bride. She wondered what kind of house Peggy Mason would be living in on the frontier.

Chapter 3

A S THE COACH rolled up the curving drive to the manor house at Carey's Fortune, Nancy watched her grandmother, who always stared in rapt excitement as if she were entering some promised land. She had come to this house a bride, more than fifty years ago, and for her it was tradition and continuity and homeplace, the roots of the Carey family.

Nancy shared that feeling. The hounds were baying in their runs. A cardinal threw a spill of song on the air, and a cat was watching a brown bird on the ground. The old familiar scent of browning pine needles underfoot scented the air.

The coach pulled up before the deep-set white door. The old Negro houseman let down the steps and handed out Grandmother Carey. She stood a minute, shaking out her voluminous skirts, and stepped onto the porch out of the sun. Nancy followed her mother and grandmother into the wide hall of the house, with its pale pink walls and silky Oriental rugs on polished floors. On the right wall a stairway with low steps rose to a landing where the grandfather clock with brass face and dials to show the quarters of the moon sounded the hour with a mellow chime. Beyond the staircase a wide-open door overlooked green lawns running down to the bluffs of the Patuxent River.

Nancy stood in the door, looking beyond the rose garden

where the leaves were turning bronze to the river glistening in the western sun. I'd do *anything* to keep Carey's Fortune! she thought passionately. Nothing must ever spoil this lovely place.

She was seized with a nostalgia for her childhood when there were no problems and life was radiant with wonder and surprise. Life was still radiant at Carey's Fortune. If she must marry Roger Tucker to keep it that way, it was a small price to pay. She wondered how she could ever have questioned that step. It was so obviously reasonable.

Tom was to return from his week of hunting on the Calverts' plantation and join them for dinner. Nancy wondered how he would respond to the announcement of her engagement. Surely, he too must find it reasonable.

He arrived in good time, and as they sat down to dinner soon after three, Nancy thought Tom had never looked better. He had picked up the new styles at the University of Pennsylvania a year or two earlier, and they were most becoming. He wore his brown hair cut fairly short in the back, flying loose instead of neatly clubbed the way his father still wore his, and carefully shaped in casual curls on his forehead. He wore a white stock wrapped high about his throat, with a freshly starched bow above his velvet-collared coat. Nancy smiled at him, feeling quite open-minded to approve his appearance while she disapproved his politics. With the new styles Tom had adopted those impossible Republican principles and had quarreled most of the summer with his father about politics. Lately, however, he had given up the argument, striving to keep peace with his family while he lived at home and read law with Judge Chase.

Jonathan Carey looked excessively old-fashioned, Nancy thought, but of course one could never say that to him. He looked critical every time he saw his son, and tried im-

26

patiently to hold on to his temper until Tom outgrew those outlandish sentiments he had brought home from college. Now as he looked about the table at his family and at Tom's modern garb, Jonathan Carey could not refrain from grumbling, "I'm sure I don't know what's wrong with young people today. When I was young, we fought proudly under General Washington to build a free country. And today young people must all dress like tramps and hoodlums. No pride! No style! I don't know what the country's coming to these days."

Tom caught Nancy's glance, raised one eyebrow, implying that he had heard all this before, and half smiled with a wry twist of his mouth. But he said nothing, and after Jonathan Carey dipped into Ophelia's Scotch barley broth he cheered up rapidly.

"Hah!" he said. "No use complaining while we've got Ophelia to cook for us. Even the situation here at Carey's Fortune doesn't look so bad, now that Nancy is going to marry Roger Tucker."

Tom cast a quick look at Nancy. "No, I daresay it isn't so bad." He seemed very sober as he ate the roast beef and Ophelia's specialty, the light and crunchy Yorkshire pudding. As soon as he could speak to Nancy, when dinner was over, he said, "Shall we walk down and look at the river?"

Sitting with Tom on the bluff, watching the sun sink beyond the woods on the far side of the river, Nancy said wistfully, "This is so beautiful, Tom. I wish nothing ever had to change."

He was staring at the river with a gloomy expression. "You think nothing will change when you marry Roger Tucker?"

"But—" Of course something would change. That was exactly what she feared. Yet on the other hand, what changes might strike if she were not married? "But with

27

Roger I'll live close to Carey's Fortune. We'll have a lovely house between the two places. There won't ever be worries again about money—and things can go on just the way they are now."

"Are you in love with him?"

"Oh, love!" she cried. "How do I know? I've never been in love. And look how many people marry and fall in love afterward."

Tom was staring at the red, sinking sun. "Maybe you'll be lucky if you never do fall in love," he said bitterly.

The sun had set, the mist was rising over the river, and the cool air was beginning to stir. Nancy shivered a little. She knew about Tom's lost love. Polly Moore had been the daughter of a stiff Federalist family in Philadelphia, and she had been unable to resist her family's pressures against the Republican student at the university. Tom had not got over it, although she had married someone else a year ago.

They stood up and walked slowly back to the house, where lamplight and candlelight glowed in the windows. Nancy wondered if she was bowing to family pressure. But when she thought about the home rising near Carey's Fortune, and the wealth that would make it as lovely as this home, she knew the family was not forcing her against her will. To keep Carey's Fortune—she could understand her father on that matter very well indeed. She smiled as she recalled his reaction to her news the day after the ball. He had kissed her so warmly she felt that at last she had done something of which he thoroughly approved.

No, Nancy shook her head, reassuring herself, she had made no mistake about this marriage with Roger Tucker.

The Tuckers were joining the Careys on Monday morning for the hunt breakfast. After the hunt over Carey's Fortune, the party would hunt over Green Hill. Nancy was waiting soon after dawn, in her hunting dress, impatient for the day to begin.

The hunt was stirring as always. Nancy loved the chase beyond anything—riding through the pastures and thickets, the woods and open lands of Fortune, until at the end of the long day the huntsmen rode back to the Careys' manor house for the hunt supper.

Everyone was intent upon the fox, the chase, the hounds. There was little time for any conversation. Kitty Tucker was thrown when her horse balked at a hedge. But by the time Nancy swept by, Tom was already looking after Kitty and waved the rest of the party on, crying, "No harm done."

At last the party gathered where the fox had gone to earth and decided to give up the hunt for the day. Tom and Kitty rode up together after everyone else, and Nancy observed that they rode back to the house side by side.

Roger, riding at her side, remarked, "Tom seems quite taken with Kitty. Wouldn't that be a happy coincidence?"

Nancy nodded, saying nothing. She had never liked Kitty Tucker, who flirted vivaciously with any man in sight. Kitty was much prettier than her sister and had had many beaux. She had always betrayed a special interest in Tom which, Nancy suspected, he had never noticed, though Nancy had seen it clearly. Somehow it would be a match she could not really approve. Surely Tom could do better than Kitty Tucker. And yet after his bitter remark last night about love, she wondered if he might give up the idea and settle for money. As she had, Nancy thought, with a bitter little laugh of her own.

Before they sat down to the hunt supper, Roger told Nancy he wanted her to ride out afterward and see the house he was building for them. She nodded. "My father is giving us two thousand acres of Carey's Fortune, bordering on Green Hill," she told Roger. That part of the settlement pleased her more than anything else about this marriage. Part of Carey's Fortune to go with Roger's money . . .

At the table the two families toasted the engaged couple, offered advice, and talked about the wedding. Nancy listened, eyes cast down, half pleased to be the center of notice, half wondering at herself.

"I told Roger if he can fix this wedding soon, he and Nancy can live at Green Hill until his house is finished," Nellie Tucker announced. She was a domineering woman who was devoted to managing her children's lives. Nancy could not stand her. "After all, they would have the place to themselves most of the time, when we're in town."

"That would be lovely," Lucy Carey agreed cordially. "But I'm not sure how soon we can be prepared for a wedding."

"What's to prepare?" demanded Nellie Tucker. "I'll send some of my own girls over to sew on the linens! I say, when young people are impatient to be married, why wait?"

Nancy said nothing, feeling her cheeks reddening, resenting Mrs. Tucker's taking any voice in her wedding plans, wishing she could be away from both families, and wondering if she could stick out a week of such intimacy with the Tuckers. Under the table Roger's hand rested upon hers. It took all her will power not to pull hers away.

More toasts. The fathers were growing exceedingly cheerful.

"And when this election is over and the new Congress convenes," George Tucker announced, glass in hand, "I'll see that Roger is named to the diplomatic corps in London! Let's drink a toast to the new ambassador!"

They drank that toast, and Nancy brightened a little as she thought of the diplomatic life abroad.

"There shouldn't be much question about the election," Jonathan Carey cried. "A toast to the congressman! The Republicans won't do much damage in Maryland."

The talk turned to politics, the dinner was ended, and

30

they all went into the drawing room to talk about more plans. Roger and Nancy slipped away to ride over and see the new house.

She was half eager to ride out in the early evening, half wishing to forget the dinner-table conversations that kept ringing through her mind. When she recalled that this was her last season in her parents' home at Carey's Fortune, regret stole over her. She was almost mopish as she rode away from the house beside Roger.

The fruit trees were old and gnarled and as pretty as Christmas trees, with red apples and golden pears and blue plums hanging from them. Green Hill was some three miles away. Nancy and Roger rode across pastures, into woods, and out upon a high point on the bank of the river.

There, across the bend in the river, Nancy could see the beginning of the house on a high spot of ground overlooking the water. A handful of men were working at the foundation.

"I set the men to work as soon as I got here today," Roger said. "Told them there was no time to be lost!" He swept his arm in a semicircle from the house back toward the manor house at Fortune. "You can see your home from the house," he pointed out. "I thought you'd like that setting."

She was touched at his thought for her pleasure. "The very spot I should have chosen."

As they rode back, Roger talked about the details he wanted to put into the house, the wood-carver he had discovered who had trained with William Buckland, the outstanding architect he had found who approved all of Roger's own plans.

"Roger, I'd like the house to be ready before we're married." Nancy said. "I don't want to start our life together with either family."

He looked at her, half disagreeing, half questioning.

31

"But that will take six months!" he exclaimed.

"Six months is a very short time to be ready," she said.

"But I hoped we could be married before Christmas!"

She wondered if she heard dictatorial undertones.

"I'm thinking of a spring wedding," she said stubbornly.

She glanced at Roger as they rode back across pasture-land. His mouth was sulky, and he was staring ahead under lowering brows. She had heard some comments before this about Roger's temper, and now she wondered.

"Nancy," he protested, "six months is a long time to wait, when it is not in the least necessary."

"I think June would be a lovely month for a wedding." She smiled persuasively at him.

"June!" He sounded outraged.

"But in June we could have the wedding at Carey's Fortune," she pointed out. "Anyway, when will that house be finished?"

He argued. He begged. He pleaded. She was firm. At last he conceded sulkily that the house would be ready by late March.

"If I have to drive those workers with a whip," he said grimly, "they'll finish the house by then."

"We'll be married March twenty-first," she told him. "The first day of spring. I'm very romantic, Roger."

He gave in. "The first day of spring."

But a little later, when he lifted her down from her horse in the stable yard at Carey's Fortune, he was so ardent that Nancy wondered uneasily how she could make him wait for six months.

The fathers talked about settlements several evenings during the week. At last Jonathan Carey told Nancy she was making a truly inspired alliance.

"Mr. Tucker is giving Roger three thousand acres adjoining the acreage I'm giving you," he said. "You'll have five thousand for your own. I must say, I'm gratified. The Tucker fortune is solid, and that's more than one can say for some of the other planters around here. When I think of the men I knew during the war, started out with great fortunes, and most of them bankrupt now—" He shook his head. "Your future is provided for, Nancy. Handsomely. You'll have more to leave your children than I've got, by a pretty penny. This marriage is the best thing that could have happened. For all of us!"

Nancy was silent, struggling to overcome a sense of depression. Her father nudged her mother.

"When are you and Roger setting the wedding date, Nancy? Have you talked about it?"

"Oh, yes, we've talked about it."

"Did you make any decision?"

"It will be the first day of spring. March twenty-first."

"Six months is a long time," her father grumbled. "What if he should change his mind and cry off?"

Nancy smiled a little. "Roger won't change his mind."

Her mother smiled approvingly. "We'll begin collecting the linens and curtains and blankets as soon as we get back to town," she said. "There is a little French dressmaker in Annapolis who would be very good for your wedding gown. And you must talk to Miss Abigail Harper about gloves—six months will be just about enough time for everything to be ready. And we must send out the engagement announcements as soon as we return. . . ."

When Nancy climbed into the traveling coach with her parents and Grandmother Carey and knew that she would not see Roger for another week, until the races began in Annapolis, she had a sense of relief that was almost buoyant. She turned her mind from that at once. She dared not dwell on her feelings about the engagement.

Chapter 4

"*I* TELL YOU!" Jonathan Carey roared, pounding the mahogany table with his fist until it shook. "We're all going to be ruined at the rate these confounded Republicans are carrying on! They're going to bring this country to its knees!"

He sank down in his chair, breathing heavily, his face crimson, his wig askew, and glared around the table at his family.

"Now, dear, don't upset yourself so!" Lucy Carey got up hastily and moved around the table to pat her irate husband on the shoulder and lean her cheek against his. He shook his head like an angry lion.

"Someone's got to get upset!" he cried. "Look at that paper! Read it! Nobody's got the right to print filth like that about the President of the United States!" He was shouting again, and his wife soothed him patiently.

"I know, my dear. But come into the library and let me get your pipe and a little brandy. You can't help the country or the assembly either, if you work yourself into a stroke!"

Grumbling loudly, Mr. Carey glared at Tom and Nancy and stumped out of the room behind his wife.

"Well!" Nancy breathed when her parents had closed the door of the library behind them. "What brought that on?"

"That horrid Republican paper, of course!" Grand-

34

mother Carey's black eyes were snapping. "Criticizing the hardworking administration the way it does in every issue! It's enough to throw any good Federalist into a seizure. When I recall the things they said about our saintly Mr. Washington! I'm going up to my room and lie down. I'm getting upset myself, and at my age it does me no good."

She rose, plump and dignified and outraged, and left the dining room. The offending paper was scattered over the floor where Mr. Carey had flung it in his explosion of rage.

"How did that paper come to the house?" Nancy asked Tom.

"I subscribed to it," he said. She stared at him, shocked. "I knew Nick Dana at the university, and he must be working with his father on this paper. They're putting out a good journal, and I want to support them."

He sounded somewhat defensive. With another anxious glance at him, Nancy picked up the scattered paper and began reading it aloud.

"CITIZENS AWAKE! This man Adams, by violence and folly, has brought our country to the very brink of ruin. Your trade is languishing, your coin is being shipped abroad, British goods are ruining your own manufactures. And more and higher taxes are being laid upon you to support this folly.

"Now Mr. George Tucker asks you to send him back to the Congress a second time: a Federalist who has upheld the administration in this insane determination to ruin this country. He will perpetuate the criminal folly of the Adams administration.

"Rise up while you are still free to cast your ballot! Show the tyrant Adams and his royalist government that you are still a free people! Reject this Federalist congressman, and choose the Republican who can serve the Constitution and the liberty of a free people!"

There was quite a bit more about the dreadful danger of electing George Tucker to office, and Nancy found herself as angry at this attack on Roger's father as Jonathan Carey himself. Now that she was going to become part of the Tucker family, the attack seemed aimed at her personally.

"Tom! Surely you can't agree with this attack on Mr. Tucker!" she cried. Tom grinned at her teasingly, and tears of rage came to her eyes. She mopped them away, blinking fast.

"The Tuckers will be my family one day," she said. "How can you sit there and laugh at such a vicious attack on old friends?"

Tom leaned back, tilting his chair on the back legs, with his hands thrust into the waistband of his pantaloons.

"The Tuckers may be your family one day," he agreed, "but that doesn't make them my family. I've never thought old George was a very good congressman."

She gasped with the shock of such irreverence for a congressman, and blazed at him, "But you know I'm going to marry Roger! How can you take sides against him like this? He's going to be appointed to the diplomatic staff in London if his father returns to the Congress!"

"Nancy," her brother said kindly, "pray collect yourself and do not talk such nonsense. Whether you marry Roger or not, his father has been a lazy and negligent congressman. And Roger would be a very indifferent diplomat. If that's the only reason you're marrying him, perhaps you should reconsider!"

She gasped again. "That's not the only reason. But Tom! If you could just persuade the *Centinel* not to print such horrid things about Mr. Tucker, there would be no problem at all."

"If you want to persuade Mr. Dana to be nice to Mr. Tucker, you'll have to do it yourself. That's an errand I'll not run for you."

36

She lifted her head with a teasing smile. "I might just do that!"

He looked alarmed. "If you insist on being the strong-minded female Mother worries about, you can go right ahead! But as a man, I think it would be most unwomanly!"

She had not actually thought of doing such a thing. But at Tom's words her mind began suggesting all kinds of teasing challenges. She could be persuasive when she tried to be. She was an aristocrat, a planter's daughter. Surely the publisher of that mean little sheet must be impressed if she came to talk to him. She might even persuade him to write such good stories about George Tucker that Roger's future in the diplomatic world would be enhanced. All this she would accomplish in secrecy and enjoy the secret satisfactions of power. If worst came to worst and persuasion failed, she could threaten arrest for publishing sedition.

Nancy sat there, the sun on her back, her chin on her hand, smiling to herself. Tom watched her uneasily.

"Nancy, you've got some mischief in mind," he said sharply. "Now forget about trying to persuade the *Centinel* publisher about anything! You'll only make things worse."

"Oh, I don't know about that!" she said airily. "That's not at all what I had in mind."

The clock was striking, and Tom sprang up. "It's high time I was back at Judge Chase's chambers," he said. "Now, Nancy! Do not do anything foolish, I beg of you!"

"I don't do foolish things, Tom," she told him with wide, hurt eyes.

Now he was really concerned. He hesitated at the door. "I wish I could believe that! Nancy, if you'll forget about this *Centinel* article, I'll say something to Nick Dana myself."

"But, Tom! I wouldn't want you to do anything foolish, either!"

He threw up his hands. "I've no more time for this nonsense, Nancy. Now, for goodness' sake, don't get Father upset again."

"I'll be spending most of the day hemming my linens," she said.

He left, obviously worried. Nancy picked up the *Centinel* and read over again the story that had angered her, pursing her lips thoughtfully as she went over it. The sun slanted through the small panes of the long window and lay upon the figured rug with a warm light. Nancy paced the sunny room, thinking about the *Centinel*.

Then she ran up to her room to change to street dress that would impress Mr. Dana. She chose a crisp little walking dress in flowered chintz and a pink bonnet with a perky brown feather standing up in front, and slipped on a spencer—a short little jacket in moss green velvet, buttoned up under her chin. She picked up a pink parasol and glanced at herself in the mirror. She looked both elegant and mature, and she was sure that what she wished to say would be heard with respect and admiration. Folding the offending newspaper small, she tucked it into her reticule and set forth.

The wind tossed and scattered the sunlit clouds across a brilliant sky, and in the sunlight the colors and scents of the Annapolis fall blew across her face. She turned into Maryland Avenue and gasped at the crimson oak against the rosy brick of the Hammond House, across the street from Mary Lloyd's house. It had turned color while she had been away last week. The clipped boxwood borders smelled tangy in the late afternoon sun as she made her way around State Circle into Francis Street and thence to Main Street.

The door of the printing shop of the *Annapolis Centinel* stood open under the hanging sign with its painted sentinel. Nancy stood in the sunlit street a moment, looking into the dark and grubby little shop. One man was working there alone, standing before the type case, filling a composing stick. He was so intent on his work, and his fingers moved so quickly over the type case, that she was impressed in spite of herself with his skill and swiftness. The smell of printer's ink was strong and ugly. Nancy wrinkled her nose in distaste. The man turned to slide the type onto the galley tray and saw Nancy standing in the door.

"How do you do?" He came to the door, wiping his fingers on his ink-smudged apron. "Did you have something you wished printed, Miss—?"

He was tall and dark and blue-eyed and young, and Nancy stared at him, thrown off stride. "But I thought— Where is Mr. Dana?"

"I'm Nicholas Dana. My father's ill today, and I'm setting up the next issue of the paper myself. Will you come in and sit down?"

He moved back from the door and pulled out a chair from behind the press, wiping it carefully with a clean rag. Nancy sat down on the edge of the hard chair, clutching her reticule in both hands, her feet firmly on the floor. Nicholas Dana stood beside the compositor's table, one arm resting upon the lower case, and looked down at her. She was momentarily tongue-tied.

"I could probably take care of any order you wished to place, Miss—"

"Carey," she told him crisply. She decided to stand up.

"Could you be Tom Carey's sister?" He smiled at her like an old friend.

She ignored his question. "Mr. Dana, my business with you concerns that dreadful story you published in today's paper about Mr. George Tucker's campaign."

"Indeed?" He raised one eyebrow questioningly. "What was wrong with it?"

"It was a lie from start to finish!" Her anger rose hotly as she thought of it. "Why—lies like that could prevent his election! How could you print such a thing?"

"Now come, Miss Carey. That was no lie." He smiled as if he were humoring her, and suddenly she was too angry to be persuasive.

She lifted her chin. "Can't you tell the difference between lies and truth, Mr. Dana?"

He dropped his elbow from the type case and straightened up, angry in turn. "If you were a man, I'd call you out for a question like that, Miss Carey! But perhaps you misunderstood something. Can you explain to me exactly what was untrue in the story?"

She pulled the paper out of her reticule, tearing it as she unfolded it with shaking hands. "Here it is." She read aloud. " 'This man Adams, by violence and folly, has brought our country to the very brink of ruin. . . .' " Hearing her own voice saying those words, she was struck suddenly with the uneasy question, How do I know that's not true? Unwillingly, she could remember her own father making similar criticisms of the President. She stole a glance at her listener and saw him attending gravely with no hint of a smile. She skipped the rest of the paragraph about Adams.

"This is the part that's untrue." She looked up confidently. "You said Mr. Tucker 'will perpetuate the criminal folly of the Adams administration. . . .' " Her voice trailed away. She felt suddenly, foolishly, that the words that had seemed so rabid when she read them at home did not sound entirely unreasonable when she read them aloud in the office of the *Centinel*. The suspicion attacked her again —what if the paper was right after all? How could she know?

"Well, isn't Mr. Tucker running as a Federalist?" Dana inquired.

40

"Of course he's a Federalist! What has that got to say to anything?"

"And you are engaged to his son, so naturally you have an interest in Mr. Tucker's election." He spoke as casually as if her being engaged to Roger Tucker made no difference to him. But Nancy found her cheeks flaming again.

"Mr. Dana, there's no reason to bring my personal affairs into this discussion. What I want you to do is write an article that will undo any damage to Mr. Tucker's campaign for Congress and put it in the very next paper."

He stared as if he could not believe his ears, and his mouth twitched into a smile in spite of himself.

"Miss Carey, I'm afraid you don't understand the meaning of a free press."

"Of course I do!" she cried impatiently. "But I don't understand the reason for a press to move into Annapolis to attack honest men like Mr. Tucker."

"We're not attacking Mr. Tucker personally. All we said was that this district ought to elect a Republican instead of a Federalist."

"Well?" She challenged him triumphantly. He shook his head sadly and began again. "Look, Miss Carey. We happen to be Republicans. We say what we believe. Is this against the law?"

She gnawed on her lip, trying to think of an answer.

"Look—" he said again, searching around in a pile of papers on a bench against the back wall. "Here's today's issue of the *Maryland Gazette,* the Federalist paper. Did you read it today?"

She shook her head. "This is what it said." He glanced at her to see if she was listening, as he read aloud.

"These Republican anarchists who oppose the administration of the American Government are traitors and should be hung by the neck for treason. It is patriotism

41

to write in favor of our Government. It is sedition to write against the Government. This French faction wishes to drag our country into the same flaming destruction visited upon France by its revolutionists. Federalists, arise! Put down these malefactors and evil-doers!"

"Well?" she questioned him impatiently, when he had finished reading. "They're absolutely right!"

"Miss Carey, wouldn't you say that article was just about as strong as the one in the *Centinel*?"

"That's a matter of opinion, Mr. Dana. The *Gazette* is talking about the danger these Republicans threaten for the country, and of course they should be put down!"

He stared at her as if he really cared about what she thought.

"The point is, Miss Carey, if we have free speech in this country, if we have a free press, then we Republicans have the clear right to speak and publish our opinions, whether we agree with Federalists or oppose them."

She had not heard that argument before, and while it seemed highly dangerous, she could not answer it quickly. She frowned in puzzled thought.

"Miss Carey, about Mr. Tucker—he really was not a very good congressman in the past two years."

"But I don't know how you can say things like that about someone who is serving the people!"

"The business of a journalist is to tell the people whether they are well served, Miss Carey. Mr. Tucker hardly attended any meetings of the Congress in its last session. He has thrown a couple of editors in jail for writing criticisms of the administration." He smiled at her engagingly. "We're against that!"

She found herself floundering among many new ideas. It was a helpless, horrid feeling. She hated this ink-smudged man for making her feel that way. Roger never forced her to answer hard questions or to think about Republicans.

"Miss Carey," Mr. Dana said comfortingly, "tomorrow the *Gazette* will answer our article just the way you'd like it answered. Mr. Tucker will not be undefended."

"But you'll just write something worse the next time!"

"I'm sure it will be worse if possible." He grinned at her.

Nancy flounced into the street and marched away, seething. She seemed to smell the printer's ink a block away, and she looked at her hands, wondering if she had carried smudges of it with her.

Chapter 5

O F ALL THINGS, Nancy declared to herself as she turned in at her own door, she would not say one word about this unsatisfactory interview to Tom. He had been absolutely right when he told her not to talk to the Danas. But he was never going to know it from her.

She sat down at once to read both the *Maryland Gazette* and the *Annapolis Centinel*. Each contradicted every claim of the other. Each prophesied death and destruction if the other party should win election to office. Between the two papers, all candidates for office would bring upon the country starvation, taxes, invasion, monarchy, and the destruction of freedom. Nancy found herself more confused than before.

But the thing that unnerved her was the way Nicholas Dana's face kept appearing in her thoughts, the way she could hear his voice saying teasingly, expectantly, "Well—?"

She vowed to herself that she had never seen a man she disliked more. And yet for the next three days she found reasons to pass the printing office. Dreading beyond anything to glimpse that hateful man, she slowed her steps as if she were caught in a web of bewitchment.

If she laid eyes on him again, she told herself, she would threaten to denounce him to the federal courts and have him thrown in jail for sedition. Amazing that she had not thought of it when she was talking to him before. Then one day she saw him, and every hostile thought left her mind.

He was pulling papers from the drying line, folding and stacking them. Nancy's knees began to tremble in spite of herself. Her throat was dry, and she knew if she had to speak to him she would find no words at all. Setting her head high, she tried to get past the shop without being noticed. Successfully by, she suffered a sad disappointment that she had indeed not been noticed.

In spite of her disappointment, she kept walking toward Miss Abigail Harper's house at the bottom of Main Street, only a short block beyond the print shop. It was a small brick house with a neat white door and an iron-railed flight of four steps leading up from the sidewalk. A pinched little place, Nancy thought.

She skipped up the steps and lifted the heavy brass knocker.

"How nice to see you, my dear." Miss Abigail opened the door. "And how pretty you look this morning. Come right back here. Your mother's gloves are ready."

Nancy followed the little glove maker through the tiny hallway into the room at the back of the house, overlooking a walled garden. She stood by the sunny window, gazing at a bright bush against a whitewashed brick wall, while Miss Abigail found the finished gloves and laid them out on the table for Nancy to examine.

Miss Abigail Harper had grown up in this house with her father and sister and two brothers. She had been twenty when her fiancé was killed in the Revolutionary War, and she had never had another sweetheart. Her brothers had gone west after the war to find land for themselves. Her younger sister had married a man who took her to Philadelphia to live. When Miss Abigail was thirty, her father died, leaving her the house and a small quantity of worthless Continental money. So much Nancy had always known about Miss Abigail. She was a gentlewoman whose family had not left her enough to live on.

She moved away from the window and bent over the gloves.

"They're lovely, Miss Abigail. Mother says your gloves are much the finest in town."

Miss Abigail looked pleased as she rummaged around to find a piece of paper to wrap them in. She must be about the same age as my mother, Nancy thought, watching her, a frightening example of the dire fate that befell a woman who did not marry and had no money.

But Miss Abigail did not look unhappy. Cheery and brisk, she went to the door with Nancy and looked at the billowing white clouds in the brilliant sky and the golden maple at the bottom of the street. "What a pretty day!" she cried, as if it was a tonic to her.

So far as Nancy could see, the need for a woman to work was a fate worse than death. The French émigrées who had fled the revolution to come to America—they now conducted schools for the daughters of the planters, taught music and French, made elegant gowns. They had been gentlewomen, too. Nancy shuddered at the pictures her imagination called up.

When she returned home, Roger was there waiting to talk with her about the Lloyds' party on Friday night and the Jockey Club races during the following week. He had brought house plans to show her, and he pointed out the changes since she had last seen them and the designs for carving his wood-carver had sketched. She approved the changes and the sketches. The house was becoming more real to her now, and she was truly interested in details Roger showed her.

He began rolling up the plans and said, "I'll see you at

the Lloyds' party then, tomorrow night. I asked them to include Mr. Blaney in our invitation, and they were most gracious about it."

"Mr. Blaney?"

"A very fine person," Roger said. "He is showing an interest in Molly, and I daresay it may come to something."

"How nice." It seemed a weak response, Nancy was dazed at the news. It must be only two weeks since Mr. Blaney had first met Molly at the Assembly ball. Shaking her head, she went upstairs to look over her wardrobe and decide what to wear to Mary Lloyd's party the next night.

The Lloyd family was one of the oldest and most distinguished in Annapolis, and Mary was Nancy's closest friend. She was a pretty girl with golden hair and an air of aloofness with most people. But she had always been close to Nancy, and the two girls constantly talked and giggled about romance and sweethearts and marriage.

Mary was only sixteen, and Francis Scott Key had been courting her since she was thirteen and he was a student at St. John's College. Nancy had watched Mary tease and rebuff Frank Key all those years, laughing at him, showing a tantalizing interest in his best friend, Daniel Murry. And yet for some reason, Frank had never been discouraged.

The Lloyds had returned to town for the season the first weekend in October, and they always gave a ball to open the festivities of the racing season. Now, on the second Friday in October, the Careys arrived among the early guests, and the Tuckers joined them soon afterward. Mr. Blaney came with the Tuckers. Nancy felt a disagreeable recoil when she met the appraising look in his eyes and the meaning in his smile. Roger might approve of him, Molly might be in love with him—Nancy found Mr. Blaney detestable.

47

"Is Tom here tonight?" Kitty had slipped around to ask Nancy.

"He came with us—" Nancy looked around the room. "Perhaps he has already found a game in the cardroom."

Kitty was openly discontented, and Nancy wondered how the girl could allow herself to show her preferences so strongly. It was shockingly bad etiquette.

Mary Lloyd, as pretty and composed as ever, greeted her guests with her mother. Mrs. Lloyd said to Nancy, "We are so happy to know of your engagement." She patted her arm affectionately and visited with the two mothers for a few minutes.

The fiddles were tuning, the dancing was about to begin, and Roger led Nancy out to the first set. Mr. Blaney and Molly followed them, and Mary Lloyd and Frank Key joined their set. The music struck up, and Mary and Frank opened the dance.

They kept glancing at each other with private understanding, as they paraded between the other couples, separated and took hands with other partners, and then joined together to parade back again. Watching them, Nancy knew, suddenly, that Mary cared more about Frank than she had ever admitted. The thought attacked her—how strange and lovely it must be to feel about someone the way Mary must feel about Frank!

When the dance ended, Nancy fanned herself and turned to cross the floor with Roger. "Tell me more about Mr. Blaney, Roger," she murmured. "I haven't seen him since that dance in September."

"He is Joshua Giddings Blaney, IV," Roger said impressively. It was evident that he enjoyed pronouncing such a distinguished name. "From New York, up the Hudson. Fine old family, ruined in the war. They were Loyalists, of course, and lost everything. He'll rebuild their fortunes, though. Especially if he marries a good fortune."

"I'm sure he should have no trouble doing that!" Nancy suppressed a smile and spoke as seriously as Roger himself.

Everyone in Annapolis knew that Molly Tucker would have a goodly fortune when her marriage contract was signed. And there was no question that she was happy with Mr. Blaney. His attentions tonight were marked, and her personality was transformed.

"Did you say he's studying with Judge Chase?" Nancy asked. "You know Tom is reading law with him this year. Frank Key studied with him too."

"Oh, Key!" Roger glanced around to be sure he was not overheard. "I cannot understand the Lloyds' accepting his attentions to Mary as they seem to. A Republican! I have no patience with the breed, Nancy, and I must say there are a lot of them here tonight."

"You must admit they are as gentlemanly as any of the other men," Nancy teased, glancing coquettishly at Roger over the edge of her fan. Suddenly, beyond him, she saw Nicholas Dana standing in the doorway from the hall.

He was looking over the crowd, as if he was searching for someone. He raised his chin and smiled. Nancy was wildly curious to know at whom he smiled like that. She stared at him with the strange sense of knowing him well and yet of never having seen him before. His evening dress was as handsome as any man's there—a well-cut tailcoat in dark broadcloth, with fawn-colored breeches, silk stockings, a froth of linen at his throat. She had never imagined him a gentleman when she had met him in his shop, yet now it seemed the natural role for Nicholas Dana. He turned and disappeared in the direction of the garden.

Nancy fanned herself, trying to catch her breath. "Roger, shall we go outside? It's so hot in here I feel faint."

He turned at once to offer his arm, and she steered him toward the hall that led to the open terrace. Nick was standing there. As she approached, he turned to join Tom

Carey. Had he not seen her? Or did he not know her? She felt a shock of disappointment, even as she realized it was a good thing that he had not spoken to her.

"Roger!" Someone beckoned him to join a group of men talking about horses. "I have great news! My gray filly ran like another Selim this afternoon! She'll be ready for the Jockey Club race after all!"

Roger fell at once into conversation about horses and racing, forgetting Nancy entirely. She stood near him, glancing at Tom's group some ten feet away and trying to hear what was being said there.

"Nancy?" Tom looked across the terrace and held out his hand. "I want you to meet my good friend Nick Dana."

She moved across to join her brother and looked up at Nick Dana, smiling. "How nice to meet you, Mr. Dana," she said primly.

"I thought I should know you, Miss Carey." He smiled down at her with a mischievous glint. "Your brother is a good friend of mine."

"So I understand."

"May I get you a glass of punch, Miss Carey?"

"I should like that very much, Mr. Dana."

"Would you care to accompany me?"

He made a way for her across the terrace and inside to the punch table, where he fetched her a glass of ratafia.

"My brother doesn't know I met you once before," she said.

He met her glance with complete understanding. "I know," he replied. Somehow she knew he would not betray her.

"The last time I saw you"—he handed her the glass—"you were furiously angry. I was sorry about that."

"Sorry? I thought you were highly amused, sir."

"Did I give you that impression?" He glanced at her,

50

eyebrows raised, and she took a sip of ratafia to quiet her nerves. "Well, perhaps I was for a moment only. When you were gone, I was sorry."

She looked up and found his eyes were bluer than she had remembered. She looked down hastily, as he went on, "I thought if we had talked a little longer, I could have persuaded you to my way of thinking."

"The Republican way? I hardly think so, sir!" Her eyes sparkled with indignation. "The Republicans are in love with France after that dreadful revolution there, and all those sad émigrées—and now Napoleon! How can you!"

"But do you forget that France helped us when we needed her years ago?"

"Napoleon is not the Frenchman who helped us fight our Revolution!"

He was regarding her seriously, as if they were crossing swords instead of words, and turned his questions from political to personal ones. "How does it happen that your brother should turn Republican in such a Federalist family? Does it make trouble?"

"I'm sure our father is not happy about it." She looked thoughtful. "What he hates most about the Republicans is their attacking men who served the country well, like George Washington."

He was suddenly serious. "Miss Carey, you're absolutely right about the name-calling and venom in today's papers. I'd like you to know—" He looked away, unexpectedly self-conscious, but he looked into her eyes again. "I'd want you of all people to know that I have a different conviction about journalism. When I have a paper of my own, I don't intend to write that way."

She managed with an effort to glance aside before dropping her eyes, intrigued in spite of herself with what he was saying. "Oh, do you plan to have your own journal sometime?"

"That is why I apprenticed myself to my father after college, Miss Carey. When I have learned all he can teach me, I shall find a way to set up my own paper." In a low voice he asked, "Is that gentleman over there looking for you?"

She glanced in the direction he indicated and met Mr. Blaney's observant gaze.

"I should be returning to my mother," she said regretfully. "My next partner must be looking for me. But it is not the gentleman you noticed."

Nick Dana turned at once, as if closing a door he had inadvertently opened.

"I have kept you too long, Miss Carey. But may I say that it has been truly interesting to talk to a girl who cares about politics?"

He offered his arm, and she tucked her hand into it.

"Even the wrong kind of politics?" She smiled up at him.

"When I was in Philadelphia the girls thought of nothing but dress, parties, and gossip. I'd heard that the women of Annapolis knew more about politics than those in any other part of the country, and I believe it now."

She looked down, blushing with pleasure.

"May I see you again?" he asked, as they entered the drawing room where her mother sat with Mrs. Tucker.

"Why, of course!" she smiled up coquettishly. "You're a friend of my brother. We're neighbors in town. Undoubtedly I shall see you again."

She knew that was not what he meant. But it would be dangerous to encourage him further.

He bowed to Mrs. Carey and Mrs. Tucker, and Nancy introduced him.

"Mr. Dana is a good friend of Tom's," she said, unaware that her face betrayed her lively interest in him.

Lucy Carey smiled politely. Mrs. Tucker said, "Mr. Dana—of the *Centinel*?" Her tone was ice-hard, and Nancy wanted to sink out of sight. But Nick, smiling with proper flattery at both of them, said, "That is my father, Mrs. Tucker."

"Oh!" She was thawed in spite of herself. "You must tell your father that Mr. Tucker resents very much the attack on his candidacy, Mr. Dana. My son has spoken of taking steps about it."

"You may be assured that I'll do what I can," Nick said, with a proper blend of apology and assurance.

Nancy's next partner claimed her. Nick excused himself and disappeared. When Nancy glanced back from the dance floor, he was standing alone, watching her from the door. As the dance began, she tripped over the first figure.

Chapter 6

NANCY LAY AWAKE a long time after the party, watching the moon sail low through the trees outside her window and thinking of the evening just past. Nick kept invading her thoughts, and determinedly she turned them in other directions. Restless, she flounced over in bed and thought about Tom.

He had danced with a dozen pretty girls tonight. Was he thinking about one of them seriously? He must think about an heiress. Was Nick thinking about an heiress, to get that paper he spoke of having someday? She flounced back again. Money made everything so difficult. She remembered Miss Abigail Harper, and when she finally fell asleep, she dreamed about making gloves the rest of her life.

With the first rays of the morning sun and a gasp of relief, Nancy woke to recall Roger and the money that was no problem. It was a pretty, sunny day, and she must pay a party call on Mary Lloyd.

Out on the brick sidewalk she raised her parasol to keep the sun from her face and moved up King George Street, turning into Maryland Avenue. The handsome State House stood upon an elevation in the center of the circle dominating the city. Looking down Maryland Avenue, she saw its slender dome gleaming in the sun against the deep-blue October sky.

A salt breeze from the bay brushed her face, caught her with salt-scented and spicy drifts. Her steps slowed at the sight of the golden leaves of the elms and the scarlet of the oak trees. Dried and brilliant leaves drifted down and crunched underfoot against the bricks. The black-eyed Susans were still saucy. Mauve and golden asters fringed the gardens. Tiny yellow chips showered down from the locust trees like confetti. Nancy turned into the walk up to the Lloyd house, feeling that last night had been a passing dream.

Mary looked as if she had been dreaming about last night too. But for her it had all been real. Nancy set down her teacup and said, "Frank seemed more devoted than ever last night, Mary. The way you treat him, I'm amazed he comes back to you!"

"But he's so *funny!*" Mary giggled. "The poems he writes me! Let me read you the one he sent last week."

She pulled from the bodice of her dress the folded slip of paper, its edges already worn. Nancy listened to three verses about how Frank was thinking of his love during the nights when he looked up from his lawbooks to see a full moon, and how he wondered if she was looking at that same moon.

"I think that's very romantic," Nancy said approvingly. "I wish someone would write things like that about me."

Such poetry was quite beyond any effort of Roger's imagination, and she sighed. Mary tucked the poem into her bodice again, smiling with a secret satisfaction that tantalized Nancy.

"Frankie is really very romantic," she said complacently. "But he does make me angry! Always calling me Polly, when I've told him and *told* him I hate that common name!" The smile that twitched at the corners of her mouth belied her words.

"I think you're madly in love with him," Nancy told her. "Why don't you tell the poor fellow you'll marry him, and let him get his mind on his lawbooks?"

"But I'm only sixteen!" Mary protested. "I could never decide anything like that yet! My mother would never hear of it. And besides, Daniel Murry asked me to wait and give him a chance."

She stared out of the window with a dreamy expression. Nancy stirred restlessly. The dreaminess looked artful, and Nancy was convinced that Mary had already made up her mind. Sixteen was none too young. Look at Peggy Mason. . . .

"Tell me about Roger," Mary turned to Nancy. "Have you set your wedding date yet?"

"Next March," Nancy said. She should be bubbling with romantic anticipation. But she was not eager to talk about Roger with Mary—not after the revelations of Frank's romantic courtship, not when Frank wrote such lovely poems to his sweetheart, not when Mary had that rapt, faraway look of love.

Nancy tried to be gay and teasing. "He's building a new house at Green Hill for his bride." She looked at her hands, her cheeks growing hot, and she laughed. "I just thought of that old story about Matthias Hammond—how he built that lovely home for his bride and she ran away with someone else before it was finished."

She looked out the window toward the Hammond House across the street. There were many who said it was the most beautiful house in Annapolis. It would be gratifying to have a house people spoke of like that.

"But I'm sure this bride will live in Roger's house," Mary said. "Since he's a good Federalist"—she stirred restlessly —"there'd be no argument in your family, and I can tell you that would be a pleasure!"

"Frank is Republican, isn't he?" Nancy quickened at the scent of minor scandal.

Mary lifted her head defiantly. "I can't see why it should matter at all. Frank is very courteous and well-bred, not coarse and ill-kempt like some of them." She frowned as she recalled the most recent romantic scandal. "Sometimes I do wonder what it must be like to marry someone who thinks so differently. Like Peggy Mason! She told me once her parents refused Benjamin Brown the house. But I never dreamed she'd run away with him! How could she do such a thing?"

"And to the frontier besides!" Nancy agreed. "Such a different way of life!" She thought for a moment of the security of her own choice. "I could never marry a Republican!" she proclaimed. "My father flies into a red rage at the very thought of them." She caught Mary's eye and giggled. "My father tries not to notice that Tom turned Republican! But it's hard on him."

"I know," Mary said with a sigh. "My brother Edward likes Frank. My mother says, 'Let's wait and see.' " She giggled again, as if pleasing her mother was purely accidental. "If I decided to marry Frank Key, I wouldn't think twice about his politics. Not even if my family objected—"

Nancy stared at her. Mary had betrayed more than she realized.

"What's Frank doing since he finished his law work here?" she asked.

Mary plucked at the lemon-colored muslin of her gown, studying it with more care than it deserved.

"He's practicing law in Frederick. It's terribly far away, but he comes to Annapolis every couple of weeks." She was smiling to herself with some secret amusement, and she added with a sideways glance, "But then there's always Daniel Murry too," as if she were reminding herself.

Nancy laughed and made ready to leave. "I promised Mother I'd make three calls this morning, and here I've spent almost all the time with you. I must leave now. Tell Frank I wish him well."

She wondered as she paid the other brief calls why she was discontented when she left Mary Lloyd. Dawdling over dinner with her family later, Nancy kept her mind firmly fixed upon all the certain advantages that would follow her marriage with Roger. She loved her home—the sun falling upon the shining silver of the coffee service, the gleam of the damask cloth, the fragrance of the garden tended with many loving hands through decades of bloom, the assurance that these things would never disappear, no matter what her father feared about bankruptcy. She let her thoughts drift among the choices she would make for her own home, the wallpapers, china patterns, velvets and chintzes—already six months seemed a short time to prepare.

She leaned her chin on her hands and let her thoughts go back to the party again. Again she saw Nick standing there in evening dress. A wave of melancholy invaded her spirit, despite the sun's striking cheerful glints from the polished silver.

Lucy Carey left the table, remarking that she must tell Clio how to tear the linen napkins from the bolt, for hemming. Jonathan Carey announced that he was returning to the State House to work for a couple of hours. And Tom said, "I'm going to walk around town on this fine day. Want to go along, Nancy?"

She ran to her room, melancholy forgotten, changed to a peach-colored muslin dress, tied on a bonnet with an upstanding brim lined with white pleats, and ran down to join her brother. He sauntered slowly enough for her to walk easily beside him. He looked thoughtful as he pulled off a fragrant twig of juniper to sniff. Nancy was thinking again about Roger, and her mind skipped a couple of steps.

"Tom, what happened to Father's money?"

He shrugged. "Lots of things. The land at Fortune is worn out, so there is less tobacco every year. And Father put all the money he could lay hands on into western lands, thousands of acres on the frontier. But the western lands aren't selling as expected, so that money is tied up for no one knows how long. And he borrowed money to buy land in the Federal City some years ago—"

"But the Federal City is a wilderness! It won't be built up for years yet!"

"Exactly! So that money is tied up too. He's carrying a load of debt, and hardly any money coming in." Tom furrowed his brow. "Who's to tell how to come out of this tangle? Father only followed the lead of some of the best financial minds in the country. Already some of the other developers in the Federal City have gone into bankruptcy. Everyone is trying to make money fast these days, and everything is a gamble."

"Tom!" Nancy was struck by his melancholy tone. "You didn't speculate in anything, did you?"

"Well, yes, I did." He looked self-conscious. "But only a thousand dollars. Sam Smith needed some money to set up his newspaper last year, and I bought an interest in that. I've got a lot of confidence in Sam Smith!"

Nancy was struck with the coincidence that he was taking about a journalist founding a paper, just as Nick had spoken last night of founding a paper of his own. Money again, she thought with foreboding.

"Sam Smith is a very sound journalist," Tom was saying. "I liked the paper he was putting out, and I went to call on him. That's why I backed him. Taking a chance on a sound man isn't as much of a speculation as western lands, the way I see it."

Taking a chance on a sound man. Nancy's thoughts leaped ahead of his words. She might be taking a chance on Roger, she thought, wondering if she was making jokes with herself. She did not care to share that joke with Tom. They were turning into Francis Street, and she pulled her brother over to the milliner's window, where a fetching bonnet in black velvet was adorned with pink lining and a feathery ostrich plume. "Look at that bonnet, Tom! Isn't it darling? It probably came from England. But it costs fifteen dollars!"

"I can't buy it for you today." Tom pulled her away from the window. "I'm saving my money just now. And you have a bonnet."

She laughed. "You can see that I must marry a man with a fortune," she said. "How could I ever dress properly if I were the wife of a poor man?"

He dragged her past the black velvet bonnet as if he were late for something important, and she squeezed his arm encouragingly.

"Perhaps when you're a lawyer you can rescue the whole family," she told him. "Mary Lloyd says Frank says there're millions of dollars for lawyers in this town. Especially with the Government moving to the Federal City by next fall." Then, idly, "Is there a living in newspapers? I mean, do you think Sam Smith is going to get along all right?"

"You mean, will I get my money back? There will always be plenty of readers for a good publisher like Smith."

They were in front of the *Centinel* office, and Nancy wrinkled her nose at the black and oily smell of printer's ink. She wondered if a printer smelled of ink when he came home at night.

60

"Nick?" Tom stepped inside the door. Nick squinted against the light and broke into a wide grin.

"Tom! Good to see you here. And Miss Carey!"

He wiped his hands hastily on the damp, ink-stained cloth nearby and held out his hand to Tom, smiling at Nancy. In his working clothes, sleeves rolled above his elbows, leather apron covering him, ink smudges on his forearms and one cheek, he seemed to have bluer eyes than ever.

But this grimy working printer was not the man she had found so appealing at the dance. She stared beyond him to the printing press with a sense of being deceived.

Nick turned toward the men working at the drying lines. "Father, I want to present my friends."

A small-built man shuffled forward. He was as skinny as a wire, with a bony face permanently creased into angry lines. His mouth clamped downward in a hard semicircle, disapproving of most of the world. He nodded somberly at his visitors.

"Carey, eh? Assemblyman's family?"

"Sir, it's a pleasure to meet you." Tom reached out his hand. "Yes, my father's been in the Assembly some years now."

"Hah! Guess he'd be none too pleased to have his family knowing Republicans," Dana commented.

Nancy disliked Andrew Dana intensely. She nodded to him politely, with nothing to say to him, and pulled at Tom's sleeve in a signal to take her away from this horrid hole.

"Time to get to work, Nick!" Andrew Dana snapped. He turned his back and shuffled away to pull more papers from the drying line.

"Good to see you again, Tom," Nick said briskly. "I'll hope to see you some evening, when we can talk."

61

"If they don't keep me too close to the legal grindstone," Tom said. "I've got a real interest in publishing. Maybe I can find a way to combine it with law someday."

"We could use a lawyer," Nick said, only half joking.

"And the country could use more good journalists," Tom said.

Nick replied, "We need moderates, like Sam Smith."

The flash of recognition blazed between the two.

"I saw Smith before I left Philadelphia," Tom said. "He told me that Tom Jefferson has asked him to set up an administration journal in the Federal City this fall."

"If he comes to the Federal City, I'll ride over there just to shake his hand!" Nick said, his eyes lighted with excitement.

From the back of the shop Andrew Dana barked, "Nick!"

He turned with a half smile of farewell for Tom and a last quick glance at Nancy. She dropped her eyes and followed her brother into the street in a dark and thoughtful silence.

Nick in his ink-stained working clothes was a different man in a different world from the gentleman of last night. This was all so strange it was frightening.

Chapter 7

THE RACING SEASON began on Tuesday that year, October fourteenth, and the weather was the loveliest of the year—sunny, with a fresh salt wind blowing from the bay. Leaves skipped frivolously through the air. The town was filled with the scents and sounds and colors of gaiety. Seemingly everyone in town and from miles around took holidays from work to watch the races at the circular track north of Church Circle.

Law students took days off from studies. The clergy stood at the track cheering favorite horses. Fishmongers, dock workers and college students were there. Black slaves of every family were following the races in their finest garb. The children had a holiday from school. Shopkeepers greeted their customers at the track. It was a week everyone celebrated together.

The Careys had friends with horses entered in at least six of the races. Jonathan Carey took hours away from the State House to watch the races he was interested in. The Tuckers, surrounded by all their household and accompanied by Mr. Blaney, were there to watch Roger's Red Maple, who was supposed to have the best chance of winning the Jockey Club purse that week. Roger was riding the horse himself.

Nancy stood beside Tom, watching the track where the horses were parading to the post, when she saw a wizened little figure who looked familiar. She squinted, trying to recall where she had seen him before. He looked disgruntled, and that alone set him apart from the gay and laughing crowd. He was staring at George Tucker with dislike and muttering to the man next to him, who nodded at whatever he was saying. Suddenly Nancy recognized him—Andrew Dana. Seeing him reminded her of her visit to the shop last Saturday and the disillusion she had felt, meeting Nick in working garb. Dana's sour face cast a shadow over the day. Resolutely she turned her attention back to the horses. Yet Dana's presence brought to mind now Nick's attention at Mary's party. The two pictures of Nick mixed oddly in her mind. Somehow the gentleman always came clear.

"Nancy! We were looking for you!"

Kitty Tucker's high-pitched voice sounded behind her. Nancy turned. Kitty smiled happily up at Tom.

"We thought you must be here to see Roger's horse win this heat!" she cried. "Let me stand with you! This is a much better spot than I had before!"

She squeezed between Tom and Nancy, glancing at Nancy as if she were an intruder, and announced cheerfully, "You must be very excited to have Roger running a horse this year!"

Kitty was prettier than ever. And more foolish, Nancy thought gloomily. She wondered if Tom found Kitty attractive. He was staring at the track, leaning his head toward Kitty enough to hear what she was saying, neither ignoring nor encouraging her.

The flag dropped.

The horses came out of the starting line, and the crowd was suddenly intent upon the race, calling to their favorites, screaming as the last horse pulled ahead to run second. Then it was over. Red Maple had won that heat.

64

Kitty clung to Tom, protesting. "I swear, I am absolutely faint with excitement! I couldn't support another race like that one!"

At that Tom caught Nancy's glance with a wry wink, as he said to Kitty, "Shall I take you back to your family? Do you wish to return home?"

"Oh, no!" She revived immediately. "I wouldn't miss any of this for the entire world!" Hopefully she added, "Shall we see you at the theater tonight?"

She would, of course. Everyone in their circle was going to the theater that night, to some party or another every night of the week. At the theater the Tuckers and Careys had adjoining boxes. Roger invited Nancy to sit with the Tuckers, so Kitty was invited to sit with the Careys. Nancy was not sure how that happened, but she suspected the two mothers had arranged it. Lucy Carey openly betrayed her hope that Tom might find an attachment for Kitty.

Nancy was fairly sure there was no possible attachment there. She wished she could be as sure in her own case—Mr. Blaney seemed more interested than he should be, although it was hard to explain what proved it. But there was that leer in his glance when he greeted her, a certain lingering over her hand, a sense of his watching her too much, meeting her eyes too often. . . .

She was thinking about that when Red Maple won his second heat on Wednesday afternoon. While both families were standing together at the rail cheering the horses on, Mr. Blaney in some manner managed to insert himself between Nancy and Molly. And while he whispered in Molly's ear and told her to watch the second horse in the race, his elbow was nudging Nancy's arm. Once he glanced at her over his shoulder as if to say "Excuse me," but afterward the nudging was closer than ever.

A horrid man, Nancy thought with intense distaste. If she remarked about his manners, he would tell her with florid apologies that he was quite unaware of offending. If she spoke to Roger—but she could not say anything to Roger about Mr. Blaney, when the whole Tucker family was so hopeful about his marrying Molly.

The heat was over. Nancy turned to Tom, ignoring the pressure of Mr. Blaney's arm on hers.

"That was the only race I cared about today," she said in a low voice. "I think I'll go home and get out of the sun. I feel the headache coming on."

"I have a wager on the next race," Tom said, his eyes on the track. "If you can wait through that race, I'll walk home with you."

"No need for that. I'll just go on now."

She slipped away from the rail and through the crowd, wishing only to be far away from Mr. Blaney. Roger was still with his horse, and she did not care to see him either, just now.

"Miss Carey!" She stopped at the call and turned to see Nicholas Dana striding toward her.

"I saw you leaving and hoped I might talk with you. Must you go so soon?"

"I had a touch of the sun, and I thought I'd find some shade until it passed." He was looking gentlemanly today, dressed in fine clothes for the races, and his look of concern for her was comforting. She smiled at him, and, looking into his eyes, she did indeed feel giddy. She glanced toward the rail. Everyone was watching the horses prepare for the next race, but she did not want Mr. Blaney to observe her talking with Nicholas Dana.

"Perhaps we should get away before we're noticed," she said, flushed with embarrassment. She had not intended such an open invitation.

Nick Dana said only, "Let me take you to a shady spot. You shouldn't be alone if you feel some giddiness. I'm surprised your brother allowed you to leave alone."

"He had a wager on the next race. I couldn't bear to take him away. I told him only that I had a headache coming on."

"I'd like to get out of the sun myself," he said, falling casually into step with her. "Church Circle should be quite shaded by this time of day."

He offered his arm, and she took it, staring at the brick walkway as they moved along, trying to sort out her thoughts. He had a magnetic attraction. But where could such an attraction lead? Only to trouble for everyone—herself, her father, the Tuckers, Nick himself. It was foolish to have allowed him to accompany her like this, to have allowed herself to flirt with disaster so thoughtlessly.

She looked up at him primly and said, "Mr. Dana, I think perhaps I should go straight home. I wouldn't want my family to worry about me."

He was smiling at her with wicked persuasion. "But, Miss Carey, your family is at the track. No one is going to be concerned about you for another hour."

"I know, but—"

"But you think it's dangerous to be friendly with a journeyman printer," he told her. "Is that what you mean? I'm surprised at such snobbery!"

Her face flamed with embarrassment. "But it's not like that!" she cried. "Mr. Dana, you do indeed mistake me! I had no such thought—"

"Do I?" he challenged her teasingly. With the slightest pressure, which indeed Nancy did not even notice, he was conducting her through the gate into Church Circle and around toward the back of the church. "Suppose you tell me how I mistake you? I'm very curious."

67

She stopped in the shade of a great chestnut tree, provoked and distressed, and he pulled her gently across the grass toward the cool stone wall of the church, in deep shade.

"Why don't we sit here while you explain this problem?" he said, gesturing toward the cool and inviting spot.

She laughed and sat down, leaning against the wall. He sat beside her, pulled a sprig of wild mint, and chewed it contemplatively.

"Is it because you're engaged to be married that you feel you shouldn't even talk with anyone else?" he inquired solemnly. "Or perhaps you consider it dangerous to have speech with a journalist? Or are you frightened of Roger's overwhelming jealousy? Or are you afraid of me?"

She was smiling at the mockery of his tone, so his last question caught her unaware. Her heart seemed to stop.

"Well?" He questioned her silence. "There must be some reason. Can you tell me forthrightly that you do not wish to know me?"

She must pull herself together.

"None of those reasons, Mr. Dana," she said coolly. "My reason is my own alone, not to be given out. Suppose you tell me why you insisted that we should sit down here and talk."

He shrugged. "I find you interesting to talk to, that's all."

She felt oddly let down. "Did you have something special you wanted to say today?"

He glanced at her. "I can think of a thousand things I'd like to say, and all of them would be inappropriate," he remarked to the sky.

She felt it better not to ask any further questions.

"How do you feel about Mr. Tucker's campaign now?" he asked.

She stiffened. "Of course I want him to win! How could I have changed my mind about that?"

"And would you hold it against me forever if he loses?"

"But he shouldn't have to lose! Must you attack him all the time?"

"I'm afraid we must. That is something I wanted to talk about. The *Centinel* will carry another attack on Mr. Tucker before the election next Tuesday and I wanted you to know in advance."

"But why?" She sat up straight and angry. "Why could you not change your attitude just this one time? You know how much it means to me."

He was studying her with a thoughtful expression. "Miss Carey, would you truly have me change my principles for a whim?"

"Whim!" She was outraged. "Why should you say that? Are you talking about my changing?"

He grinned at her wickedly. "I wasn't asking you to change your principles, Miss Carey. That was your idea. But I wouldn't hold it against you if you did. A man should be steadfast, but that's different."

"And why not a girl?"

"I'd expect to bring her around to my way of thinking, if I have any skill in argument," he said, his eyes mischievous again.

She carefully looked away. "Sir, do you think a woman's principles are less fixed than a man's?"

"Not necessarily." He tossed away the sprig of mint and found a fresh one. "But she may have less reason for her stand than I do."

She tossed her head. "Now, sir, will you try to explain why my principles have less reason than your own?"

"Because you take them from your father, or from Roger, or," he grinned at her challengingly, "perhaps Mr. Blaney?"

She flushed at the recollection of Mr. Blaney's impertinences, and yet it was comforting to know that Nick had observed them.

"Perhaps I should examine them more closely," she said.

"That's what I wish you would do. Because a dedicated Federalist could not possibly marry a Republican. Could she?"

She was silent, feeling a trap yawning.

His hand fell upon hers. She felt a small flame run through her, and she knew it ran between them. With an effort she pulled her hand away.

The church bell sounded three strokes. Nancy sprang to her feet. "I must go home quickly! How long have we been here? The races are over, they'll wonder—"

He was on his feet at once. "Sometime will you meet me again?" he asked her. "We never seem to finish a conversation, and I still have a thousand things I'd like to say to you—"

She looked at him, then quickly looked away. "Another time, perhaps—"

She was running, before someone should notice that she was missing.

Chapter 8

SHE COULD RUN AWAY from Nicholas Dana, but as the days went slowly by, she found that she could not put him out of her mind. The attraction she felt for him frightened her. She could understand clearly now how someone could be very foolish indeed, under the spell of such an attraction, and regret it forevermore. A girl who made such a mistake would never have a chance to leave it behind—she would live with it the rest of her life. She must be reasonable! She must not allow herself to play with danger.

So Nancy kept reasoning with herself. She recalled all the advantages of her marriage with Roger Tucker. She assured herself from the example of many people she knew that one found love in marriage even when one went into that state without it. She reminded herself of Peggy Mason, whose mad example seemed terrifying.

So the week continued, with parties every night, dinners and balls and festivities, and Nancy's emotions confused her. She saw Nick Dana again at the racetrack on Friday, and he smiled at her from a distance. She smothered an impulse to respond and clung to Roger, at her side, with a very real sense of safety.

Red Maple won the Jockey Club purse, the most distinguished prize of the week, and the two families celebrated that triumph with a party at the Tuckers' on

Saturday night. Roger talked of nothing but Red Maple, his bloodlines, his promise, his record, and how Roger could build an entire stable of racehorses with his winner.

Then race week was past, and the talk turned to the coming election on Tuesday, October 21. Tucker, in spite of the attacks of the Republican press, was confident that he would be reelected to Congress.

"Nancy," he said Saturday night, "by next spring you may be spending your honeymoon in London! No question, I can get Roger on the diplomatic staff there. How would you like to be presented to the queen in May?"

"I'd love to be internationally famous," she laughed at him. "Mr. Tucker, do you really think that will happen?"

"No trouble at all," he assured her. "The President has always been a good friend of mine."

"Could you get the appointment this fall?"

He lifted his eyebrows. "No doubt I could. But you don't want your sweetheart leaving you before Christmas, do you? Or would you like to get married before Christmas? I've been asking Roger why he's willing to wait till spring."

"Oh, we couldn't possibly be ready before spring," Nancy said hastily.

"Well, with the election coming up, nothing much matters until the new President is in office."

The talk about politics went on. The gathering was unanimous in feeling that the election of any but a Federalist President would be disastrous for the entire country. But such a disaster was impossible.

The next morning Nancy sat beside her mother and brother for the morning service at St. Anne's, wearing a new fall bonnet in green velvet and trying to be very devout, while her mind kept wandering away from the ser-

72

vice. Dr. Higginbotham was preaching a political sermon, warning his congregation in fiery threats about the election.

"In this time of tribulation," he declaimed in sonorous tones, "when the people of this nation are preparing again to choose their President, duty requires me to speak out against the man who is now our Vice-President, and who will certainly try to seize the power of the Presidency in this election." He paused and glared at his listeners.

"This atheist will deny the comforts of religion to the people who came to this land to find them! The country will rise against him! An insulted heaven will take just vengeance!"

Nancy had been listening to threats of heavenly vengeance for so long that she had almost ceased to hear them. But today she found herself wondering how Dr. Higginbotham's direful warnings could be untrue when spoken from the pulpit, and what Nick would say if he heard them.

The rector ended his sermon with an appeal to God to compel his people to elect their own saintly Mr. Tucker to the Congress, and Nancy wondered if God could prevail against the Republicans. That idea was not only frivolous, but almost atheistic in itself, so she read the order of service in the Prayer Book devoutly, hoping she had not drawn wrath down upon herself with such irreligious thoughts.

When they emerged into the Circle after service, the Careys joined the Tuckers for Sunday dinner. All through the dinner the conversation went on about the vile tendencies of Jefferson and all Republicans and the gloomy outlook for the country if those troublemaking Republicans could not be suppressed in some way.

"I don't know what to make of all the young fellows upholding such radical principles," said George Tucker heavily. "We can be thankful that Roger doesn't hold with that nonsense."

Nancy glanced at Tom. He was holding his peace with some effort. His mouth was tightened into a hard line as he toyed with his drinking glass attentively. Kitty was smiling at him with jesting sympathy, but he never noticed.

When the long, dull dinner was over at last, the young people escaped to the garden, where Tom talked with Roger about racing. Kitty's eyes never left Tom, and after some minutes she jumped up, crying, "Tom, you must see our new sundial. I'm quite impatient to show it to you!"

He strolled away with Kitty toward the box-edged walk that led to the newly set sundial. Nancy watched them go. Kitty made no secret of her attachment for Tom, and there was something irritating about her persistence.

"Is Kitty interested in Tom?" she asked Roger.

He laughed. "Kitty wouldn't look at Tom unless he gave up some of his Republican ideas."

She wondered if he knew his sister as well as he thought he did.

"Do you think political principles are so important in a marriage?"

He stared at her as if she was out of her mind. "For a girl to go against her family, to forget the principles she was raised in," he demanded, "wouldn't that be important to you?"

"I don't know," she said, thinking of Tom. And of Nick.

The afternoon dragged slowly past. It seemed hours before she could go home with her family. Roger bade her a most affectionate farewell. He was going to Green Hill after voting on Tuesday to supervise the building of his house, but he promised to return to town within a week or so.

Walking home with her mother, Nancy wondered why

she was so low and bored. As soon as she reached home, she picked up the towel she was working and tried to concentrate on her fine hemstitching. But she threw down her sewing and sat before the fire, staring into the flames and trying to escape the distracting thoughts.

"Miss Nancy?" Samson stood at the door. "A messenger brung a letter for you."

"Thank you, Samson."

She looked at the envelope, not recognizing the writing, and ripped it open.

My dear Miss Carey:

I have thought of our short visit last Wednesday every moment of the past three days, and I long to see you again. I meant it truly when I said I had much to say to you. Can we meet tomorrow morning at ten, at the Liberty tree on the St. John's campus?

Yours always
Nicholas Dana

Nancy read the note over and over, gnawing upon her lip until it was sore. The tone of the letter—she should take affront at his assumption that she would meet him whenever he named a place and time! Yet—her heart seemed to be falling breathlessly—how could she say no?

"The messenger say can he take back an answer," Samson said.

"Well, perhaps—" Nancy was irresolute. When she had read that he wanted to see her again, she had felt as if sunlight fell upon her, and all despondency disappeared. But she knew she should not see him. She had known on Wednesday that this was a dangerous course.

But if she never saw Nick again, could she forget him? Would she really be better off? Of course she would. And if she meant never to see him again, surely she should see him once, to tell him so. She must explain how this attraction that drew them together must be ended, once and for all.

"I'll give you a note for him, Samson."

She almost ran to the desk to pen a note saying she would meet Nick at ten in the morning. As Samson departed for the back of the house, where the messenger was waiting in the kitchen, Lucy Carey came in, looking very sober.

"What is this about a letter, Nancy? I found, sitting in the kitchen, a boy, who said he had brought one for you."

Confounded, Nancy stared at her mother, trying to think of some explanation that might allay her mother's suspicions and watchfulness.

"It was just a note from Mary Lloyd, asking if I could bring her a needlework pattern tomorrow morning," she lied. "I don't know why you must know about every letter I get!"

Instantly she knew that was a mistake. Lucy Carey sat down, her back very straight, and motioned to Nancy to stand before her. The girl felt like a culprit standing there, head hanging so that she could look at her mother.

"Nancy," Mrs. Carey said very gravely, "there is no reason to be excited about a letter from Mary Lloyd."

"But there is no reason to have to explain it," Nancy insisted. "Can I not have a letter come to me without having to read it aloud on demand?"

"Let me see the letter," her mother said sternly.

"Mother, you have no right—This is my private affair—"

"Nancy, while you are in this house you are under my orders. What is so special about this letter that you don't want me to see it?"

Nancy set her mouth tightly and said nothing. Her

76

mother rose, looking both angry and hurt. "Is—Mary writing secrets that you cannot reveal?" It was evident that she did not believe the letter came from Mary, but was reluctant to disbelieve her daughter openly.

Nancy grasped at the suggestion. "She asked me to tell no one what she wrote—"

"Very well," Mrs. Carey said coldly. "But Samson will deliver all letters to me from now on, and I myself will give yours to you, or determine if you should have them."

She swept out of the room, her back stiff, and Nancy sank down on the sofa trembling with anger and fear. She read the letter again, tore it into tiny pieces, and went slowly over to toss them into the fire.

So the danger had widened. She dared not think what her parents might do if they found that Nicholas Dana was writing to her—even more, that he had asked her for a secret meeting.

But she was determined more than ever to keep that engagement with him.

Monday was another golden day. Nancy walked around the campus of St. John's, by the great tulip poplar, watching for Nick. The students had been moving across the campus when she arrived, but they were now in class, and she was alone. It had been at least fifteen minutes since the church bell had sounded ten o'clock. For those fifteen minutes she had been planning how she could say to Nick, "This must be our last meeting."

Suddenly she saw him, almost running, waving when he saw her there. She stood still, watching him approach, and for some reason all her prepared speech faded entirely from her mind.

"I'm truly sorry to keep you waiting, Miss Carey! Just as I was leaving, my father arrived and had to be served."

He was evidently disturbed, and unexpectedly she wanted to reassure him. She smiled at him radiantly.

They moved behind the great trunk of the tree and sat down, leaning against it. "I couldn't leave until he was satisfied that I was doing an important errand, collecting news," he grinned at her like a conspirator. "I must attend at least part of the Assembly session and carry some report back with me."

She leaned her head against the tree and closed her mouth with a sigh, looking away toward a scarlet maple that flamed against the sky. She wanted to scold him for being late and to recite the firm little decision she had been rehearsing while she waited for him. At the same time she must hold herself in check, not to slip close, lean against him—

"Enough of my troubles," he said. "I only want you to understand that I would never keep you waiting one moment if it were in my power to wait for you. That's how it is for a journeyman working for his father. Perhaps one day when I work for myself I can manage better."

She smiled at him again. "I was angry for a few minutes. But it's not important now." She glanced at him teasingly. "You said in your note, Mr. Dana, that you had much to say to me."

He laughed. "And so I have. You never did answer my question last Wednesday."

"What question do you mean?"

"Could a dedicated Federalist marry a Republican?"

She glanced at him, frowning in thought, recognizing the hazards of the question, and yet wanting to discuss it.

"I don't suppose it's entirely impossible," she said slowly. "But I do think it must be very difficult."

"How difficult? Please explain why you think so."

78

"Well—look at Peggy Mason! That sad story must prove something!"

"What about Peggy Mason?" he demanded. "What proves anything except that she was very much in love with Benjamin Brown?"

"But to run off to the frontier, to live in poverty like that—how can that poor girl ever be happy?"

He sat up straight, as if he had some ideas of his own about Peggy Mason and Benjamin Brown. "How do you know she's not happy with the man she loves, no matter where she lives?"

"But no one has heard from her since she ran away! Her poor mother is distracted!"

"Perhaps I know more about the story than her mother does."

"Do you really? What happened?"

"Benjamin Brown was a good friend of mine. He talked with me about his plans." Dana turned to Nancy. "You must understand he was a fine man and a fine artisan—a blacksmith who did beautiful ironwork. He'll have more work to do where he went than he ever had here—pots, pans, andirons, hinges, fences—he'll be wealthy someday."

Nancy was incredulous, but she had to know more.

"But where did they go? What happened after they left here?"

"They were going to be married in Alexandria in a church, the same night they left Annapolis, and spend the night in a comfortable little inn there. Ben had made very careful plans. They were joining a wagon train the next morning, leaving for the Ohio country, and he expected to be living in Marietta. That is a well-built little town within a stockade, on the river—quite safe from Indians and lots of people for neighbors. Certainly, it isn't as if they were alone somewhere in a forest!" Nick spoke as if all the

79

clamor about the elopement to the frontier was quite hysterical.

"But his father could tell Mrs. Mason nothing of all this!" Nancy cried.

Dana grinned at her. "I don't imagine Ben told his father all he told me," he said casually.

"But why didn't you tell Mrs. Mason? You must have heard how she grieves for Peggy!"

Dana glanced at her and shrugged. "Mrs. Mason has never recognized me in her life. Probably she disapproves my politics so much she wouldn't let me speak to her if I wanted to."

"Did Peggy know he was taking her to the Ohio country?"

"Of course she did!" Dana glanced at Nancy as if he wondered whether she would do as well. "She thought it would be a great adventure!"

It was evident that he approved of Peggy's sense of adventure. Nancy contemplated that idea. For a moment the challenge of settling new country touched her with a quick and unexpected exhilaration. She drew back from it.

"But why?" she questioned, half to herself. "Why would he want to go away from parents and friends, everyone Peggy knows—so terribly far?"

"Perhaps he thought it would be easier that way!"

Nick sounded as if he too would like to go out to the frontier and see the new world there. Nancy felt an unwarranted chill. She sat silent a long time. The unknown world his words brought alive seemed so dangerous a risk that she shivered even to think about it.

"And now," he was getting to his feet, "I must go on and get my report from the State House. We always seem to leave our conversations unfinished. Will you meet me again one day?"

His question caught Nancy unprepared after all, and she nodded in spite of herself. All the things she had planned to say were still unsaid, and now it was too late to discuss all the reasons. He held out his hand to help her up, and they walked down to the gate.

"I'll be away from town for ten days," he said. "But I'll look forward to the next time." He held out his hand in farewell, and she laid her hand in his. Unexpectedly he raised it to his lips. "Till we meet again," he said, turning and striding away.

She stood there, watching him go. As she came to know Nick Dana better, she was becoming more confused. He acted as if he were strongly attracted to her, and yet he was independent of her wishes. He cared more about his principles than about pleasing her. He knew she was engaged to Roger Tucker, yet he acted as if it didn't matter. He left her uncertain—he had run off to the State House as if he forgot her quickly.

And yet—he had kissed her hand.

Chapter 9

I
T WAS OCTOBER 30, and ten days since Nancy had
seen Nick. You would think, she reflected as she worked
on a needlepoint fire screen, that he might at least have
sent a message through Tom, to let her know he had not
forgotten their meeting. You would think, she told herself
sternly, that she herself would have forgotten this infatua-
tion in ten empty days. Why, then, was she melancholy
with the conviction that there was nothing to look forward
to? Roger had sent her a letter about his horses at Green
Hill. Still, she was bored.

She glanced out of the window at the western sky. It was
just after dinner, and sunset came earlier each day now.
But there was still an hour of daylight, and it was a delicious time, with belated warmth and a nostalgic memory
of summer hanging in the air.

She threw down her needlework and stood up.

"Where are you going, Nancy?" her mother asked. She
had been questioning Nancy's every move these past ten
days, and the girl was growing impatient under such
surveillance.

"I'm restless, Mother. I'm going to take a walk."

"Where are you going?"

"I'm almost out of wool for my screen, Mother. I must
get more if I want to keep working."

"Very well," her mother conceded. "But don't be late,

Nancy. It's not at all suitable to be alone in the streets after dusk."

"Mother, it won't be dusk for an hour yet. I'll be back long before that!"

Nancy tried to move casually, as if there was no hurry, but the moment she was out of sight of her house, she found herself half running. She had no plans, she kept telling herself. But she sped around State Circle and into Main Street, driven to haste.

On Main Street she compelled herself to slow down and look into shopwindows, trying to calm herself. She was being very foolish. She was looking for trouble. . . . But I'm so bored, she thought, swept up in a tide she refused to name.

She stopped before the apothecary's window and tried to think what she could buy there. She could think of nothing, and she moved on to the mercer's, where she bought some wool thread for her needlework in great haste. From there she could see that the street was empty near the *Centinel* office, and she must walk that way to see Miss Abigail Harper. She had taken this walk half a dozen times in the past ten days and never seen Nick Dana.

This time, she was just passing the door of the printing shop when Nick emerged as if he had been looking for her.

"Miss Carey! I have been thinking of you while I was away—can we meet again soon?"

She forgot her boredom. She forgot ten empty days. All she knew was the happiness of seeing Nick smiling at her again.

"I think I could meet you," she said. "Just once more."

He cocked an eyebrow. "Only once?"

"I shouldn't be meeting you at all," she told him, feeling virtuous.

"But perhaps one more time, just to explain it clearly?"

83

he suggested with a twinkle. She laughed in spite of herself. "Tomorrow? At our tree? At eleven?"

"I'll be there," she assured him. "And now I must hurry. I promised not to be out long."

He nodded casually and went into the shop. She hurried back the way she had come, and her heart was singing. She would see Nick again tomorrow—one last time.

She was waiting under the Liberty tree at eleven the next morning, and again he was late. Was she to spend her time waiting like this every time she agreed to meet him? She paced with quickening temper, telling herself it would indeed be a good thing to cut short this secret friendship. This was the very last time.

But when she saw him coming all her anger faded, and it was an effort to let him know she was annoyed. She said, "I wondered what was keeping you this time!" trying to be severe. But she spoiled the whole effect with a trembling smile.

"It was the paper, of course." He spoke as if she would understand, of course, that what the paper demanded it must have. "A ridiculous thing, at that! The drying line fell down, of all foolish mishaps! I had to pick up all the sheets and fasten the line so it would hold. I was beside myself, but everyone else was busy, and it had to be done at once."

She heard him with a strange sense of separation. The paper seemed always to stand between them. She could not believe that just because Nick was an artisan, his work must get his first attention. Roger might forget her for his horses. But somehow horses were different. Or perhaps her feeling for Roger was different.

She stood very still, looking away across the campus. It was a beautiful day for the end of October, with the sun warm upon the fading lawns, a soft breeze stirring off the

Chesapeake. She wanted—she could not say what she wanted, and that was the most unsatisfactory feeling of all.

Nick took her hand and raised it to his lips. "Shall we walk in the sun while we talk?" He offered her his arm, and they strolled toward the creek that ran along the north side of the campus. "I wanted to see you," Nick said. "I thought of you all the time I was away. I was riding around the state collecting the election returns, and it took the better part of nine days."

Election returns. She had forgotten all about them.

"What happened in the election?" she asked.

"George Tucker was defeated for Congress."

"But what will that do to Roger's future?" she exclaimed. That Mr. Tucker had been defeated was a real shock. All his friends had been so sure he would win.

"What has his father's election to do with Roger's future?" Nick demanded sardonically.

"Why—Roger was going into the diplomatic corps!" Nancy exclaimed.

"I don't think his father's election would have provided Roger with any more sense than he has right now," Nick said. "And that's not much. Is it, Nancy?"

In spite of herself, she giggled. At that, Nick lifted her hand to his lips again.

"That's what I love you for," he said. "You see things the way I do—the only girl I ever knew who laughed at the right time!"

They had reached a lonely wooded section of the campus on the bank of the college creek. Nancy stared at the shining water beyond the trees, his casual words ringing in her ears: *That's what I love you for.*

She looked up at him, wanting him to say it again, not wanting him to say it again, not knowing what she wanted. Nick, holding both her hands, looked down at her questioning gaze, and she half whispered, "Nick—what did you say?"

He seized her in his arms, his mouth was on hers, demanding, possessing, loving, until all her resistance was drained away, and she was reaching for him, answering with her own lips. Stunned, she clung to him, blind with wonder at the revelation gripping her.

Slowly he pulled away, searching her eyes with hungry questions and holding her shoulders as if he would never let her go. With dazed recognition, she thought, So that is what it's like to be in love! And I never knew!

"I said I loved you, Nancy. I've been wanting to say it ever since the first day I saw you."

Her knees were trembling. She let herself sink down against a chestnut tree, supporting herself with her hands firmly placed against the ground. Nick sat down beside her.

"I didn't know," she said aloud.

He picked up a scarlet leaf and began shredding it carefully along the veins, watching the bright bits fall to the ground.

"You loved me when I kissed you," he told her.

"Yes," she nodded, still dazed in the thrall of that long moment. "I didn't know it would be like that."

He took her hand and held it firmly. "Nancy, are you in love with Roger Tucker?"

She met his eyes in a quick glance, feeling as if he had uncovered a humiliating secret, and shook her head.

"I never thought you were," he said.

"But now, what can I do?" she begged.

He sobered suddenly and held her very close, his blue eyes looking into hers with a promise and a question.

"Nancy, all we can do now is to wait for each other." He spoke painfully. "Can you do that for me?"

She nodded, and he kissed her again.

When she had separated from Nick, only after he had walked her back to the campus gate and told her she must get home before her dinner hour, Nancy was singing inside. Her happiness glowed in her cheeks and eyes. Unaware of her radiance, she ran lightly through the house and up to her bedroom, wanting to be alone with her dreams. Clio looked at her searchingly.

"Miss Nancy, you done look as if you found gold somewheres."

"Oh, Clio!" she burst out. "I did indeed find gold today!"

"Miss Nancy, you all right?" Clio sounded scandalized. Suddenly Nancy knew she must be more cautious.

"I'm fine," she said, feeling as if she had fallen from a cloud and struck the ground sharply. "It was such a gorgeous day, Clio. We won't have many more of them."

"Your mother was asking and asking what kept you so long," Clio told her. "You sure you're all right? Ain't you got a fever?"

"But I told Mother I had to make some calls!" Nancy cried. "I wasn't gone so long, was I?"

"Your mother said you left before eleven, and it's going on three right this minute."

"Oh, of course. But some of the calls took longer than I planned." Nancy began loosening the laces in her slippers. "I'll change to my new blue muslin, Clio. Are there guests for dinner today?"

"Just the family." Clio sounded depressed. Nancy lifted her head. "Is anything wrong?"

"Mr. Carey, he don't like Mr. Tom's newspaper."

"Oh, I'm sure that isn't important."

"Samson told me Mr. Tom don't like to be crossed."

There was more here than simple disagreement, Nancy thought, as she slipped her arms into the long puffed sleeves of the fresh gown and stood for Clio to fasten up the tiny buttons in the back.

"But the election is over—what difference does politics make now?" she asked, impatiently.

"I wouldn't know about that, Miss Nancy."

Nancy ran downstairs, hoping she had not kept her family waiting, hoping there would not be probing questions. She smiled when she thought of Clio's remark about Mr. Tom—she didn't like to be crossed, either.

Tom and his father were standing before the long window in the sitting room overlooking the garden. Nancy slipped in quietly and sat down on the couch to begin working on her screen again, hoping that when they noticed her they would think she had been there a long time.

Her father was jabbing his finger at a newspaper and shouting at Tom. "And now you tell me you backed this Republican sheet with your own money! I cannot believe it!"

"Father," Tom said patiently. "I have never concealed my Republican sympathies. I do not feel Republican principles are treasonous. And I'm only trying to explain to you that this paper is vastly better than the *Centinel*. Here is one good journalist writing a Republican paper."

Jonathan Carey was puffing with anger, and his face was beet-red. "I say the Republicans are traitors! I won't have Republican sentiments spoken in my hearing. And if you want to live in this house, you will not insult my intelligence and my convictions with your Republican arguments!" He hurled the paper toward the fireplace, and Tom caught it in midair.

"In that case, I'll take my leave now, sir."

Tom bowed to his father and stalked upstairs, carrying the paper with him. Nancy slipped after him and followed him up to his room, standing by while he called for Samson and began pulling clothes out of the wardrobe. She picked up the paper.

"What paper is this, Tom? The *National Intelligencer*—from Washington?"

"That's the first issue of Samuel Smith's new journal—Friday, October 31. He sent me a copy because I'm one of his backers. It's a very well written paper, and I cannot understand Father's stiff-necked obstinacy. He refuses even to read one copy."

"Are you going before dinner?"

"I hardly feel welcome at my father's table today," he said grimly. "I'll be at Williamson's Hotel until I find a boardinghouse, and then I'll let you know where to reach me. I can assure you it galls me as much to live in a Federalist house as it bothers Father to have me here!"

He followed Samson downstairs with his boxes and portmanteaus. A few minutes later Nancy heard hoofbeats clattering out of the stable yard. She had wanted to talk with Tom about Nick Dana, and now when would she have a chance?

Very soberly she went downstairs again for dinner. This quarrel rent more than father and son. Nancy quailed inside when she thought what her father might say or do if he thought she was in love with another Republican journalist.

Chapter 10

NO WORD came from Tom on Saturday or Sunday. No word came from Nick. Nancy spent hours over her sewing thinking about him, wishing to see him, and wondering—after that blazing moment on Friday, wouldn't he at least send some word to her? Yet she had told him that would be hazardous. If only Tom were home she could have talked to him. As it was, all her newfound love was bottled up in isolation, without a word to prove it true.

By Monday afternoon disappointment was turning into anger. Did Nick Dana think he could make love to her and then let her await his pleasure until he found the time to think of her again?

Late that afternoon, as they were sitting at the tea table, Clio brought in a letter for Miss Nancy. She reached for it eagerly, too eagerly. Her mother said, "I'll take it, Clio!" She opened it, glanced at the signature, and handed it to Nancy with a smile.

The letter was from Roger. "I hope to return to town in another week," he wrote. "The house goes well, and I shall not be needed here for a few days. I long to tell you all about it."

Nancy had an impulse to tear the note into bits, but she felt her mother's gaze upon her. "What does Roger say?" Lucy Carey asked.

Nancy managed a smile. "He's coming back to town in another week or so."

"How lovely! I shall be happy to see him," her mother said. "I miss him myself. So cheerful, so attentive—" She recited her feeling for Roger as if she was instructing her daughter, and Nancy compelled herself to put on a sunny face. Her mother must not suspect more than she already did. But Nancy's spirits were more cast down than before. She escaped from the tea table and her mother's observant eye as soon as she could. When she found Clio cleaning her room, she closed her door to talk to her.

"Clio," she began. "You're my friend, aren't you?"

"Of course I am, Miss Nancy."

"If a note comes for me, try not to let my mother know. Would you do that for me?"

"But Mrs. Carey say all mail goes to her, Miss Nancy!"

"Clio—if she doesn't know about it, can't you just see that I get it myself?"

"I could try—maybe." Clio looked doubtful.

The next morning another note arrived for Nancy while she was at the breakfast table, this time from Tom. Her mother read it first, frowning at the message.

Nancy:

I shall be staying with Mrs. Polly Franklin on St. John's Street, should you wish to be in touch with me.

I rode to the Federal City last Saturday with Nicholas Dana to visit my friend Samuel Harrison Smith, and have subscribed to his very good journal.

Everything fell into place again. Tom had not forgotten her. And he had taken Nick Dana to Washington with him. She wondered if Nick might have said anything to her brother of his love for her. And if so, how must Tom take such news, when she was engaged to the man approved by her family? She began turning over in her mind ways to see Tom, smiling to herself. It was amazing that her mood could change so swiftly at the sight of Nick's name in Tom's note.

Late that day a note came from Nick at long last. Clio, looking very uneasy, gave it to Nancy when her mother was out of the room. Clio knew it was not from Mr. Roger and with her instinct for undercurrents in her family, she knew that something was afoot. Nancy caught her expression, but she was too much absorbed in her note to pay attention to Clio's feelings. Nor did she realize how her face lighted and softened as she read.

My very dear:

It has been so long since I have seen you, a century to me. But you must know I've thought of you every hour since last Friday. Never forget, my darling, that I'll love you till I die.

My Aunt Abigail Harper has said we can meet at her house, if you can see me there. Can you come on Friday at eleven? I have much good news to tell you.

Ever your devoted
Nick

Nancy read the note over and over, biting her lip and trying to control the elation that rushed through her veins at his declaration. Of course she would meet him. And how wonderful that Miss Abigail was his aunt!

She dared not send him a note. Anyone in the house who carried a note for Miss Nancy to the shop of the *Centinel* would wonder why she was sending it, might very well mention it to her mother or father. She gnawed on one fingernail. Clio already suspected something. Samson, who was courting Clio, confided every thought to her, and Clio must do the same.

It was raining too hard to walk out. Nancy wanted beyond anything to talk to Tom, to ask him to carry a message for her. This continuing need to hide her love, to let no one suspect, depressed her spirits until she was fretful. The secrecy seemed to blow into blazing hunger the flame that had kindled last Friday. She must see Tom. She must talk to someone.

By the time the sun came out the middle of the next day, Nancy declared she must take a short walk to recover her spirits, and Lucy Carey exclaimed, "By all means, Nancy! You have been quite impossible lately! If a walk will brighten you up, please be gone! But take Clio with you. I do not like this walking alone so much."

They set out at once, and Nancy found Tom's boarding-house on St. John's Street, which ran alongside the campus of the college, only a few blocks from home. It was a low, wide brick house, with a gambrel roof and dormer windows overlooking a little covered porch three steps up from the walkway—the kind of house built by some respectable tradesman.

Nancy lifted the polished knocker and struck the plate three times. Hurried steps sounded inside, and the white door was flung open.

"Mrs. Franklin? I'm Mr. Carey's sister. May I see him, please?"

Mrs. Polly Franklin was a rosy, plump dame of middle height, with a cheerful expression and a shrewd glance. She had been left widowed and penniless some ten years before and since then had run a well-regarded boarding-house in Annapolis.

"Miss Carey!" She greeted Nancy with a bobbing curtsy. "Your brother has just gone to his rooms. Come right in, Miss."

"Come, Clio." Nancy stepped into the hall. "May Clio sit by your kitchen fire while I'm talking with my brother?"

"Certainly." Mrs. Franklin led her a few steps down the hall and knocked on a closed door. Glancing around curiously, Nancy saw that a cheerful little parlor opened across from Tom's door. Woodwork, brass work, floors—all polished and shining.

"Mr. Carey? Your sister wishes to see you," Mrs. Franklin called, and Tom's door opened.

"Tom! I miss you at home! I just had to talk with you." Nancy stepped inside and said, "Clio is waiting in the kitchen by the fire. Would Samson like to visit with her?"

Grinning widely, Samson departed for the kitchen. Tom closed the door again and showed Nancy a small rocking chair by the fire. She sat down, reaching out cold hands to the blaze. Tom sat in a wing chair facing her.

"I'm glad to see you, Nancy. But what brings you here?"

"I have to tell you something." She kept watching the leaping flames with a mesmerized stare. It was very hard to bring the words out. She started again. "Tom, tell me about your trip to see Samuel Smith."

He talked about the trip with great enthusiasm. "Nick was very much pleased to meet Mr. Smith. They feel alike about what they wish to do with their journals. While Nick works for his father, he can hardly do other than his father demands. But someday—" He seemed to be weighing his words. "Someday I think Nick may rank with Smith as a journalist."

Nancy had been holding her breath, unconsciously, and now she let it out in a long, happy sigh.

"Nancy, what's troubling you? Did you come here for a special reason?"

"Tom," she half whispered, "you asked me once if I was in love with Roger. I didn't know then what love was like—"

He was watching her intently. "And now you think you

94

do?" He cocked one eyebrow skeptically. "Perhaps you'd better tell me the whole story, Nancy. It wouldn't be easy to cry off the Tucker alliance!"

"I know. And it won't be easy to go through with it, either."

"Who's the man?"

"Nick Dana."

There was a long silence. Then Tom got out of his chair and began striding back and forth. "How has this happened? Have you been seeing Dana?"

She nodded. "I met him at the Lloyds' party, you know. And somehow it just—happened. Now he's asked me to meet him at Miss Abigail Harper's house, and I dare not send a note to let him know—" She looked up at her brother, and some of the frustration poured out. "It's so horrid! To have to be secret—and yet—"

"If Father suspected, he would surely have a fit of apoplexy."

"And I cannot imagine what would happen to me," she said, wincing.

He paced some steps in deep thought.

"Do you know what you're doing, Nancy?" he demanded sternly. "Are you sure what you're about? I'm very fond of Nick. Whatever happens, I don't want you to toy with his feelings and then reject him. If you're going to marry Roger Tucker, leave Nick alone!" Then, "Nick knows about Roger, of course?"

"He knew about Roger the first time we met. It had been announced. But he always acted as if he didn't really believe it." She smiled at the memory. "And now I cannot marry Roger, when I feel this way about Nick. Tom, what am I going to do?"

"You must be very sure indeed, Nancy," Tom said soberly. "You can't conceal an affair like this for long. Someone will suspect. Someone will gossip. And how can Nick marry you? He has no income but wages from his father—a journeyman's wages are a pittance!"

She rung her hands in desperation. "'But I keep thinking of all those things, Tom. I can't imagine what will happen. But I know I must see him. I thought in the beginning that marrying Roger was the only thing I could do, and now—I don't even care about Carey's Fortune!" She looked up with a wavering smile. "I keep thinking about Peggy Mason. I'd even go to the frontier with Nick, if he asked me to." She shivered. "The whole thing is so terrifying. And yet—there's nothing else for me at all."

Tom shook his head, recognizing all the difficulties. "I'd better talk to Nick myself," he said.

Nancy was staring into the fire again. "The last thing I ever thought would happen to me was marrying a printer!"

"Pray don't talk as if Nick were a peddler!" Tom said impatiently. "He's a well-educated man with a high purpose and a lot of ability. The only problem here is that he has no fortune but what he can earn with his pen. Still, that's not impossible. When I saw the Smiths last week I learned that they had married just before they came to the Federal City, with no fortune on either side. They're living very frugally in small rooms, waiting for a small house to be finished. And they're the happiest couple I've ever seen."

"But Nick's working for his father. How could we possibly manage, here in Annapolis?"

Indeed, the prospect seemed intolerable—to come down from the high social position she had always enjoyed and be the wife of a journeyman printer, living with his family in a tiny house on Main Street. She shook her head again. It was impossible.

"The Smiths waited three years before they could marry," Tom said.

"But how could I cry off my engagement with Roger—and live at home three years, waiting to marry Nick Dana?" Nancy demanded.

He shook his head again. "I'll take your note to Nick. Perhaps, if the Republicans win this election, the future will be brighter for a Republican printer."

When she set out with Clio to make her way home again, Nancy was very little encouraged. Things looked even darker now that she and Tom had discussed all the difficulties.

She only knew that she would see Nick again on Friday, and she clung to that thought like a lifeline.

On Friday morning it was raining again. The golden leaves were drenched in the mud, the asters hung bedraggled, and the walkways were filled with puddles. Her mother protested any idea that she should walk out in the rain. But Nancy, driven to desperation by her knowledge that Nick would be waiting, made a great fuss about walking, not driving. When she finally left the house, she knew that she had aroused her mother's suspicions to a dangerous pitch.

The water splashing over her boots as she walked around the Circle and down to Main Street was one more penalty of concealment. By the time she reached Miss Abigail's house, she was very unhappy.

The little house was forlorn today, with the flowers beaten into the mud under leaden skies. Miss Abigail welcomed Nancy brightly, hung up her wet mantle by the fire, and fetched her hot tea and shortbread. She smiled at Nancy in happy conspiracy. But far from responding, the girl saw the dreariness of Miss Abigail's life with fresh melancholy. She sipped her tea and heard the clock strike quarter past the hour.

Miss Abigail glanced at the little clock on the mantel shelf. "Nick said he'd be here at eleven," she remarked with a maternal smile. "I've never known that boy to be on time in his life. Something always goes amiss with the paper at the last minute."

"That must be very aggravating, isn't it, Miss Abigail?"

"Oh, I never mind when I know the reason. He's so wrapped up in that paper that it comes before everything. I like to see a man take to his work like that. It's a good sign."

"I suppose so."

Miss Abigail looked at Nancy keenly. "It's hard, when you're not used to waiting," she observed. "Nick tells me he'll have his own paper sometime. He's going to make a name for himself. I never saw a man with such energy. And with the education he's had too—not too many journalists like that today."

Contrarily Nancy wondered how long she could put up with being kept waiting because of a newspaper. A chime struck half after eleven.

She glanced at the clock. "I really don't know how long I can wait for him," she said, sounding a little haughty.

Miss Abigail was flustered and unhappy. "I can't imagine what's keeping him this time. He's never been so late before when he's had an appointment."

Irrationally, Nancy was suddenly convinced that Nick had met other girls at Miss Abigail's. The lowering anger that had been smoldering all day boiled up. She stood and looked about her for her mantle.

"I'm really sorry," she said frostily. "I think I'm not going to wait any longer, Miss Abigail. Perhaps it was all a mistake anyway."

"Oh, Miss Nancy! Don't feel that way—!"

Wringing her hands, Miss Abigail looked out her window up the street. The rain was falling harder than ever. Nancy wrapped her damp cloak around her, tied on her bonnet, and marched to the door.

"It wasn't your fault, Miss Abigail," she tried to reassure the desolate little glove maker. "I appreciate your letting me come here. But I'll have to think about things. I just don't know—"

She hurried down the steps and splashed into a puddle of water. She was so unhappy, so uncomfortable, and so angry that tears rolled down her cheeks as she made her way through the rain in the opposite direction, so she would be sure not to meet Nick.

By the time she had reached her home and taken off her sodden clothes, she had made up her mind. This whole affair with Nick was clearly impossible.

She thought again about the spring wedding that would be the talk of the town, the beautiful house overlooking the river, the stable of handsome horses and carriages, a houseful of children to divert her when Roger was tiresome—She had been a fool to think she could substitute love without money for that sure future.

But she broke down again and cried as if her heart would break.

Chapter 11

AN HOUR after she reached home, a messenger brought Nick's note for Nancy, and Clio delivered it to her, looking very curious, the more so since her mistress had been in a fit of the dismals since she had come back from walking in the rain. Nancy tucked the note into her dress, as if she were quite indifferent about it.

She shook her head sadly but firmly. Love was never going to be enough to carry her through the dreary time of secrecy and waiting. Love was never going to feed them, if she married Nick. It was a hopeless dream. She must put such romantic ideas out of her mind, out of her plans, out of her life.

Then she escaped to a private corner to open his note. When she read "Nancy, my darling," she broke down and wept again.

He was distracted, he wrote, that he had been prevented from meeting her on time. One of the pressmen had crushed his hand, and Nick had had to bind it up and then take his place in getting out the paper. He wrote as if he knew she would understand the necessity for getting the paper out on time.

And so she did, Nancy thought, irritation welling up again. There would always be a paper that had to be got out. She crushed the note in her hand and let her anger comfort her. She sent no answer.

She filled the next week with sewing, with calling upon her friends and visiting her mother's friends. The days dragged interminably. She tried to keep her anger warm, and in spite of herself she moped. She tried to persuade herself that she looked forward to Roger's arrival—he was late too. But there was so much to discuss about the furniture for the house, paper for the walls, plans for the garden. Nancy kept trying to make those plans and choices, and wondered why it could not really seem to matter.

She read the latest election results in the *Maryland Gazette*, finding it a dull paper indeed. Finally she stopped following the long-delayed returns. The Presidential election no longer mattered in her life. There would be no more uncertainty about anything. She could enjoy the traditional world where she had been so content until she had met Nick Dana only last month. He had upset her life for a few weeks. Now that was behind her, and she could feel sure again of where she was going.

Why, then, was she crying again?

During the month of November, Mary Lloyd was entertaining a house guest, Betsy Patterson from Baltimore, a lively, sparkling belle of fifteen, who had attended the Assembly dance as a guest of the Lloyds. She had found half a dozen beaux happy to call upon her, beg for her dances, and invite her and her hostess to theater parties.

Nancy had seen Betsy at a couple of those parties, and she did not like the girl much. But now Nancy needed diversion. Betsy talked of the kind of world Nancy knew, with exciting and amusing dreams of her own. Nancy enjoyed the morning calls at the Lloyds, listening to Betsy rattle on about her own plans for marriage. They diverted Nancy and at the same time supported her own reasoning.

"I decided long ago I was going to marry someone romantic and famous," she announced, sparkling at her audience over her coffee cup one morning. "Right now, the most famous man in the world is Napoleon Bonaparte! *Quel homme!*" She rolled her eyes ecstatically. "Would it not be the most romantic thing in the world to marry someone like that?"

"But how does one let General Bonaparte know?" Nancy asked with a straight face. She was feeling pretty good today, thanks to Betsy's nonsense.

"How does one inform the stars about one's wishes?" Betsy asked, jestingly. "I say, all one has to do is to decide her own fate, and she can bring it about. I have decided. Of course, at fifteen the stars have several years to do their work! Would it not be the most romantic thing in the world, to marry a man like that?"

Bonaparte—France—Republicans loved France, and Nancy had once loved a Republican. In a compulsion to top Betsy's dream, Nancy cried, "But you must be a Republican, Betsy, to wish to become French!"

"Me, a Republican!" Betsy tossed her head. "Never in this world! I will be queen someday!"

Her audience laughed with her, but Nancy felt a sudden longing for a world where there would be no queens, no aristocrats.

"I think it could be even more exciting to open a new world than to reign in the old one!" she announced. "Can you imagine the adventure it must be to go to the frontier?"

"Why, Nancy Carey!" Betsy cried. "What must your fiancé say to that? Does he expect to take you to the frontier? Have you told him about your ambition?"

Suddenly cautious, Nancy smiled as if she had been jesting so wildly that Betsy was foolish to ask about it. "Not my fiancé," she said. "We'll go instead to the court of

London. I'll meet the queen of England before you meet Napoleon."

She was weary of the conversation, tired of Betsy Patterson, uneasy about this ridiculous conversation. She rose to make her farewells.

"I look to see both you and Roger at my party for Betsy on the nineteenth of November," Mary reminded Nancy as she went with her to the door.

Nancy walked home thinking of her remark about the frontier. She must have been mad to have said such a thing. But still—Betsy Patterson must also be mad to have a dream of Bonaparte. And yet the girl sounded as if she really meant what she jested about.

Betsy had spoken truly, Nancy reminded herself, when she said one could determine one's own course. Nancy clung to that idea. Her circle of friends here in Annapolis, the social gaieties she was enjoying so feverishly—these were the people she was truly at ease with, even while she was bored with them. This was the life to which she belonged, even though she had turned her back on it momentarily.

Her decision not to let her life be changed from its normal course was wise and sure. She would be famous with Roger when he went into the diplomatic corps. She would go to the court of England. She would make him important. And she would never regret a moment of it. How could one regret fame and fortune? Even Mary Lloyd, crossing her family in keeping Frank Key at her side, looked to his becoming rich and famous someday.

Nancy had forgotten that Frank Key was a Republican and that she would see many of his friends at Mary's party. When she entered the house on Roger's arm, the first person she saw in the hall, standing with Mary and Frank, was Nick Dana. He looked as aristocratic as he always did at a party, and she trembled with the unexpected shock. He met her eyes coolly and then looked away as if he did not know her. That stiffened her resolution. Angrily she vowed to herself that she would show that Nick Dana.

Roger muttered, as they went on into the drawing room, "I don't know why the Lloyds always have that rabble-rousing Republican editor every time we go to one of their parties. He has done me more damage than any man in town, and he's going to pay for it—"

Nancy was hardly listening to Roger. She was occupied with recovering her poise. For the next hour she hung on Roger, letting everyone see that she was madly in love with him, laughing so gaily, dancing so languishingly, and refusing everyone but Roger, so that all eyes were following Nancy Carey. She was behaving like such a romp that Tom scowled a brotherly warning. She ignored him. But the effort she was making with such feverish gaiety was exhausting. At last Roger seated her with her mother and excused himself to claim a dance with the guest of honor.

Nancy watched them indifferently. Betsy was flirting with Roger as she did with every man who crossed her path, and Nancy cared nothing at all. Then she stiffened, and her eyes narrowed as she watched them.

Betsy was chattering rapidly, batting her eyes, teasing Roger about something, and Roger's face was darkening into a sullen scowl. Suddenly her distrust of Betsy struck Nancy with a quivering tension. What could that girl be saying to Roger? Once he looked across the floor at Nancy with a dark glare. She fanned herself rapidly and smiled brightly in return.

When Roger returned to Nancy, he was still angry. She decided to ignore it.

"What is this nonsense you've been telling Betsy Patterson about wanting to go out to the frontier?" he demanded, as he led her out to their next dance.

"Oh, Roger!" She could have killed Betsy Patterson for repeating her foolish remark of days back. "We were just talking wild dreams. Did she tell you she wants to marry Napoleon Bonaparte?"

"That makes more sense than the frontier," he grumbled. "She said she thought you really meant it!"

Nancy held her head high. "I think the girl is a trouble-maker," she pronounced. "I should think you'd have more sense than to listen to her, just because she flirts with you like a courtesan!"

She tightened, as she saw Betsy Patterson dancing with Nick. He was flirting with her outrageously, bending to her, kissing her hand. How could he! How dared he! Nancy was burning with rage, and she could not take her eyes from them. And Betsy was sparkling in her most challenging mood.

The girl was impossible. She went much too far, Nancy told herself. She looked for Mary, wondering how her hostess must feel about the wild conduct of her visitor. But Mary was gazing into Frank's eyes, noticing nothing else. Tom was noticing nothing unusual either. He was watching Betsy with amusement.

Nancy wondered what was wrong with everyone. This party was growing far too wild and free. It was a shocking display of bad manners and bad taste. She must be the only one in the room who disapproved of what was going on, who was not enjoying herself. Suddenly the dance was over, and Betsy was leading Nick straight toward Nancy.

She turned her head sharply to visit with the lady next to her. But she could not keep her eyes from straying to Nick and that girl. He was looking straight at Nancy with an expression she could not read. Was he hurt? Did he hate

105

her? Was he proud to be with Betsy Patterson of Baltimore and wanted Nancy to see it? She lifted her chin disdainfully and refused to know him. They walked on toward the door and disappeared. Nancy was so agitated she was afraid she was going to swoon. It took her a long time to compose herself.

When Roger came to take her out for supper, she saw Nick again with Betsy, listening to her with fascinated attention, responding with evident approval. Roger saw her gaze fixed on them, and he was scowling and sulky. As they sat down with their filled plates, he said, "I don't know why that Republican must be in my way every time I turn around. After what he did to my father, I consider him my worst enemy. The man is dangerous!"

Nancy found herself bitterly amused when she remembered how she had first met Nick, marching into the *Centinel* office to protest his attacks on Roger's father. She was in no mood to defend him now. Thinking of him and Betsy Patterson, she choked with anger. But she was tired of listening to Roger carry on about his grievance, and she tried to turn the subject.

"I don't know what difference it makes now, with the election over. There is no way to stop a paper from printing what it thinks."

"Oh, yes, there is!" he said grimly. "I can't call out an oaf like a Republican printer! But I can horsewhip him, and I'll do it in his own shop! It'll be a long day before he prints another story about the Tuckers!"

"The election was weeks ago," Nancy said again. Her head was spinning dizzily at the idea of Roger thrashing Nick. She closed her eyes and breathed deeply, determined not to swoon.

"I've been planning this past fortnight to do something," Roger went on. "It wasn't convenient to come into town

106

earlier, and I could see no reason why I should put myself out for a scoundrel like that. But now that I'm here for the next week, I can take care of this question of honor."

She held her hand to her forehead. "Roger, could you get me a glass of water?"

She watched him cross the floor, striding angrily through the guests without speaking, while one after another turned and watched openmouthed as he approached the supper table. Nick and Betsy Patterson were at the table again. Alarmed, Nancy leaned forward to watch Roger, sick with fear after his threats.

Betsy spoke to Roger coquettishly and turned to bring Nick into the conversation. Roger's head snapped up, and Nancy could hear him. He shouted an ugly name at Nick and threatened to take a whip to him the next time he saw him.

Nick's head was high. His eyes were hard. Suddenly his hand came up and cracked across Roger's face with the sound of a shot.

Betsy gasped and covered her mouth with both hands. Nancy sprang up to make her way to the men. But all the other guests moved in the same direction, and she could not get through. She heard angry voices, a babble of orders, a voice crying out, "Separate them, somebody! Don't let them come to blows! Somebody stop them!"

Then Roger was coming toward her, his face white and furious.

"Roger, what did you say to Nick?" she cried. "What happened?"

He snapped, "I don't know how you can be well enough acquainted to address him so familiarly!" He bowed. "With your permission I must leave at once. An urgent message reached me at the table."

He turned on his heel and left. Nancy watched him,

stunned. The guests drifted back to their seats, but she saw Nick and Tom leaving too. Nancy made her way back to her chair with the chaperons and found her knees trembling so that she could hardly sink gracefully into her seat. On one side an elderly friend of her mother's was saying, "In my day we believed that manners were important. These young people today are positively shocking in their disregard for civilities. I cannot imagine what the world is coming to—"

A few chairs away Betsy was using her fan to suggest privacy. Glancing over it to assess her audience, she said quite clearly, "That Mr. Dana — the one who prints the Republican paper, you know? He is a fascinating young man! Strange to think he's a journalist! He seems almost like a gentleman!"

Someone asked in breathless suspense, "Betsy! What happened? You were right there!"

"Oh, la! Mr. Tucker was most disagreeable, and Mr. Dana chastised him with great style!"

"But wouldn't an insult like that provoke a challenge?"

Betsy stared with round eyes. "I didn't hear anything more. It was too shocking! But most exciting!"

Nancy stirred uneasily, wishing to hear more about Nick and yet not wishing to. She saw some of the guests leaving and wished she could go home. She was humiliated that her fiancé had made such a scene. Yet, to be quite honest, it had made so much conversation that you might think the guests had enjoyed it all greatly.

She watched for her mother, who had sat down to cards with some friends. The evening seemed to drag on forever, and Nancy was frantic to get home. At last her mother came to say that it was time to leave. They found their hostess, made their farewells, and departed.

Lucy Carey had heard nothing of the quarrel, and

Nancy said nothing about it. Her mother chattered happily about the gossip she had heard at the card table. Mrs. Mason had finally received a letter from Peggy, who was living in Marietta, Ohio! Could one believe such a thing? Peggy said they lived in a comfortable house and had found many friends. Mrs. Mason did not believe a word of it. She thought Peggy was trying to save her mother worry. And everyone said that young Edward Lloyd, who was the head of the family, liked that strange Mr. Key who had been courting Mary all these years. And he was a *Republican!* Lucy Carey could not *imagine* how a girl of a good Federal family could marry a Republican. When you considered Peggy Mason, and now, perhaps, Mary Lloyd, it was frightening—it truly was.

Nancy listened in silence, holding her head as if it pained her. Inside their own door, she kissed her mother good night and ran upstairs. She was going to cry again any minute, and if she did, she would really have the headache.

Clio was waiting for her, and she burst out the moment Nancy entered her room, "Oh, Miss Nancy! I got real bad news tonight. Samson told me, and I got to tell you."

"Samson told you?" Nancy asked sharply, out of her own fears. "How did he happen to come here from Mr. Tom's place tonight? When did he come?"

Clio deftly unlooped thirty tiny buttons down the back of the lime-green silken dress. "I does think maybe Samson wanted you to know," she said, broodingly. She slipped the dress off her mistress and hung it away in the wardrobe.

"But what is it, Clio?" Nancy demanded. It must be something about Tom. She began to tighten all over.

"Miss Nancy, Samson told me Mr. Tom is going out to fight a duel in the morning early."

Nancy was rigid. "Tom! A duel? But why?"

109

"Samson, he don't know. He just say Mr. Tom want his horse ready to ride at six. He going to a duel with a friend. Miss Nancy, Samson don't like duels!"

Nancy sat down at the dressing table, ghostly pale. Clio began loosening her hair and brushing it out.

"Clio, didn't you find out any more than that? Where is it going to be? Did Samson tell you that?"

"He riding out the Post Road up to Baltimore somewhere—"

Yes, there was a dueling ground out on that road. Nancy had heard rumors about it. Dueling was against the law, and men who insisted on defending their honor in that manner slipped away secretly to meet on hidden grounds. Tom going out to duel—

Nancy recalled the angry scene at the party, Nick's hard slap across Roger's face. Of course that would force a challenge. She buried her face in her hands and tried to think.

"Is you all right, Miss Nancy?"

She lifted her face. "I'm all right, Clio. That's all you found out?"

"Samson, he come here about one o'clock. He say Mr. Tom was in bed then. He just slipped away to tell me because he worry—"

Nancy nodded. She fell still again, clutching her fists at her sides. She had not spoken to Nick tonight. She was never going to speak to him again. But the thought of his being killed in a duel opened such a void that she swayed where she sat.

She stared, chalk-white, at the loving black face in the mirror. "Clio, isn't there any way to stop this thing?"

"Samson want to stop it. But Mr. Tom say he go alone. He tell Samson if he talk about it, Mr. Tom sell him first thing in the morning."

"Clio—" Nancy leaned her head on her hand. "I don't

know what to think. I'll try to figure something out. You can leave me now. And have a good sleep." She tried to smile.

Clio looked unhappy. Somehow she expected her young mistress to know the answers to troubles like this.

"I hope you sleeps well, Miss Nancy." The door closed behind her, and Nancy was alone with panic.

Chapter 12

NANCY SAT at the dressing table a long time, until the trembling terror subsided and she could think again. Nick had forced that challenge, but who could blame him, with Roger talking about horsewhipping and such nonsense. Duels. She tried to recall what she knew about them. Principals—that would be Roger and Nick. Seconds— Tom would be Nick's second, of course. How would they fight? To her knowledge, no one had fought with swords at least since the war. It must be dueling pistols. She began to shake again. Roger had been dismissed from college because of a duel, though Tom said the man he had hit lived. Had Nick ever fired a pistol? Would he know how to face someone who had dueled before?

She began to shake again. If one man was killed in a duel, the other was guilty of murder. She had heard once, years ago, of a friend of her father's who had killed his man in a duel. He had fled to the frontier, whence he could never return without standing trial.

No one could win in a duel. If Nick killed his man, he would have to flee the law. If Roger killed—Whatever happened, Nancy's future was lost. How insane this was!

The clock was striking, and she heard it numbly. In three hours the men would be riding out the Baltimore Post Road to a dueling ground. She could not sleep this night, with such a fate hanging over her. Must not the outcome involve Tom also, for seconding one of them? What then would become of his law career?

Without warning the thought struck her—If Nick had to escape to the frontier because of this duel . . .

She got up restlessly and paced the floor, watching the full moon shining low outside her window. The frontier might not be so bad, if she joined Peggy Mason, found friends there. . . .

The clock struck four. Nancy knew what she was going to do.

She began to dress very quietly. It took longer to get into her riding habit without Clio's help, but she managed it. As she did so, she thought with a kind of exhilaration that she could manage to get along without Clio, without any help, if she had to.

She sat down again by the window and watched the sky for the first showing of dawn.

The clock struck five. It was pitch dark, and she must saddle her own horse. None of the stableboys must know she was riding out at such an hour. And she must find her own way out to the Post Road. She shivered at the thought of riding alone in the blackness. It took all her courage to make her way down the back stairs in the darkened house, to unbolt the back door, and to find her way into the black stables. She groped around, found the lantern hanging inside Marigold's stall, and got it lighted. Other horses were stamping and snuffling. She must hurry, before some of the stableboys came to see what was disturbing them at this hour of the night.

By the time she had saddled the filly, the sky in the east was lightening with the glow before dawn. She opened the gate and walked the horse quietly out of the yard into the cobbled street to the nearest mounting block. The sun would be up shortly. It was going to be a beautiful, clear, sharp morning. And that was too bad. If it were foggy and damp, the pistols might not fire.

She walked Marigold gently through the street and halted suddenly as she heard the town crier calling, "Six o'clock and all is well. It will be a fine day!" Nancy stood there waiting until the crier should have gone some blocks farther, and she could hear the sounds of the city awakening to the new day. A creaking farmer's cart crossed the street ahead of her, on its way to the market. Somewhere down by the port, she could hear an oyster vendor already calling his wares, blocks away. It was funny how sounds traveled in the dark. The sound of a creaking winch on a ship at dock carried clearly to where Nancy sat. Sea gulls were crying as they sailed over the city and back to the ships in port.

Her horse would not be heard now, amidst the awakening noises in every street. Nancy rode forward gently until she reached the Post Road and left the city behind her. She took Marigold into a gallop, moving off the road to the grassy border, where the noise of the hooves would not be heard. When she rounded a curve a few miles out of town, she saw two riders a quarter mile ahead of her, trotting their horses. As she watched, they turned off the road into a lane on the right.

The sun was up now, and Nancy was riding almost directly into it. Beside her the forest was dark and fragrant with the damp, frosty night. She moved along slowly, watching for the place where the horsemen had turned off. At last she saw a footpath leading from the road into the woods, marked with fresh hoofprints. She followed it, twisting between trees and undergrowth for a quarter of a mile or so.

There, some two hundred feet away, was a grassy clearing, with horses tethered on one side and four figures moving about. Nancy slipped from the filly, fastened her where she stood in the trees, and began to move cautiously and soundlessly toward the clearing.

She could see the men clearly now. Nick Dana stood at the far side facing her. Roger, with his back to her, was pacing restlessly. Tom was conferring midway between the two principals. When the other second turned, to show Roger that loaded pistols were in order, she recognized Mr. Blaney. Tom was performing the same service for Nick. Each second spoke to his principal about the rules. She could hear Blaney quite clearly, from where she huddled behind a thick pine tree, only thirty feet away from Roger.

The principals took their positions ten paces apart. Nancy shuddered at such close range. Beyond Roger, she could see Nick's face, composed, hard, and arrogant. She had never known he could look like that. He looked heroic to her. It all moved faster than she expected. The seconds withdrew to the sidelines. Roger and Nick raised their pistols, sighting along the barrels.

She ran out into the clearing just as Tom cried, "Fire!"

"Don't!" she screamed. "Stop! Stop!"

Two shots sounded, and she saw Nick spin and fall. Roger whipped around and faced Nancy, his face pale, his eyes glaring.

"What in the name of heaven are you doing here? You might have been killed!" To Tom, already kneeling beside Nick, he cried harshly, "Get your sister out of here, Tom! This is an appalling disaster!"

"You've killed Nick!" she screamed at him. "You murderer!"

Escaping his effort to stop her, she rushed past to bend over Nick. Tom was padding the wound and stanching the blood. Nick's eyes were open, and he was white with pain. "Caught me in the shoulder," he said to Tom.

"Lie still while I get this bandage in place." Tom was feeling around the shoulder with expert fingers, and Nick said faintly, "I don't think anything is broken—" He set his mouth tight and closed his eyes while Tom worked with the bandage.

"That bullet will have to come out," Tom said. "We must find a surgeon when we go back. Can you ride that far?"

"I think so," Nick muttered. "Is Nancy all right?"

For the first time Tom turned and looked at his sister, with a scorching glance. "No one must know about this morning," he warned her.

She ignored him and knelt beside Nick. "You're alive, Nick! I was so frightened for you!" She added, "How could you be so foolish?"

Nick glanced at Tom with an expression that said, "Don't expect a woman to understand." He looked at Nancy, smiled, and closed his eyes. She held his wrist firmly. The pulse was strong. She kept on holding it, while she accused Tom. "How could you let this happen? Nick might have been killed!"

"You might have been killed yourself, Nancy! Running out on a dueling field! Are you out of your mind? How did you find us?"

As if she didn't hear him, she turned back to Nick. He opened his eyes again. "Threw off my shot," he said, speaking more strongly. "I couldn't take a chance of hitting her—" He smiled at Nancy almost jestingly. "Maybe you saved me from murdering Tucker. I was ready to."

Roger was standing beside Nick now, puzzled and angry.

"You're going to be all right?" he leaned over to ask. He glared at Nancy. "I swear I don't know what you're doing out here! How did you find out?"

Nancy stood up. "Never mind how I found out! I didn't want either one of you having to run from the law. This is a stupid business, dueling! Someone ought to stop it!"

116

Mr. Blaney spoke to her for the first time. "This kind of interference is most unsuitable, Miss Carey," he pronounced, both scolding and pompous. "Highly improper." He looked at Tom as if he expected him to take some immediate disciplinary action.

"Mr. Blaney, I shall take care of my sister myself," Tom said in freezing tones. "And now if you'll escort your principal back to town, I'll look after mine."

Blaney bowed in stiff annoyance and turned to Roger.

"I must say something to Miss Carey before I leave," Roger Tucker told him. "Nancy, if you'll walk over here with me, I'd like to talk to you alone."

He was furiously angry, she knew from the controlled, icy tone. She wanted to spill out the whole story, to tell Roger she was going to break her engagement, to tell the world she was going to marry Nick. Luckily Roger did not give her a chance to speak for several minutes.

"I must say, Nancy, I'm astounded that you should be so foolish, so thoughtless, so entirely improper as to do a thing like this! I must believe you came on my account, although even so, I disapprove beyond words! But your concern with that printer! It's beyond anything! You forget yourself, my girl! As your fiancé I am bound to tell you that this is intolerable! Now what can you say for yourself?"

He had quite a few more things to say before he let her answer. She stopped listening and began to think about Nick. Roger's knowledge of her interest in Nick was dangerous. Nick was the one who was vulnerable. Roger could bring money and power against him. She must persuade Roger for the moment, at least, that he had nothing to worry about.

Suddenly she realized that he had stopped talking and was glaring at her impatiently, waiting for her to say something. She reached out one hand placatingly and touched his sleeve. Angry as she was, she must persuade him.

"But, Roger, I told you." She let her voice quiver a little. "If you had killed Mr. Dana, you would have had to flee the town. I was so worried! It would have spoiled all our wedding plans. I could not sleep last night knowing you were taking such a chance. I had to come out and try to—" Her tongue balked at the words, and with an effort she made herself say them, "Try to save you from the awful consequences. You know duels are against the law! How could you put yourself in such a dreadful position?"

He stared at her suspiciously and thawed a little. "But, Nancy, you don't understand matters of honor. This man had insulted my father continually. When I charged him with it last night, he offered me an intolerable insult. There could be no other action. It was a matter of honor."

"But, Roger—" To her own dismay, tears began falling. Fortunately Roger now assumed they were on his account. He put one arm about her shoulders and tried to comfort her.

"But still," he reminded her, "it's galling to have you concerned about my enemy. Because Dana is my sworn enemy, Nancy. He must be yours too! I shan't call him out again—hitting him today has avenged the insult. But if he crosses me again, I swear I'll put him out of the way! And I want you to regard him as I do—an enemy the more deadly because he has a printing press to publish his vile charges."

She was choking with the effort to hold back all the things she wanted to say defending Nick. She said, "He's a good friend of Tom's, Roger. I couldn't have believed he was an enemy of yours."

"Blaney has pointed out many times the affronts, the insults, the lies he has spread about the Tuckers," Roger cried angrily. "I'm sorry to say it, Nancy, but his being a

118

friend of Tom's is not reason enough for your defending the scoundrel. I knew Tom had come home from college with Republican sympathies. But to associate with a vile printer like Dana is too much!"

He was not yet prepared to forgive her enough for a caress, and she was grateful for that. She looked back at the group on the ground. Nick was sitting up now, while Tom was clearing any bits of litter.

"Roger, Tom will take me home. And perhaps you and Mr. Blaney should ride back by a different road, to avoid suspicion if the patrol should meet any of us."

He bowed to her. "I'm glad your brother can take care of you," he said stiffly, still disapproving of Tom. "This entire event has been a serious shock to me, Nancy. I shall want to see you very soon and talk it over further."

They walked slowly back toward the others. Nick got to his feet as Roger approached, eyes intent upon both Roger and Nancy.

Roger said, "Good morning, Mr. Dana. I'm happy that the conclusion of this meeting has been satisfactory."

Nick bowed to him, without saying anything, and Blaney shook hands with Tom. Then Roger and Blaney crossed the clearing, untied their horses, mounted, and rode away.

Nancy stood there waiting for Nick to speak to her, wondering if he too was angry about her part in this day's business. A woman's interrupting a duel was unforgivable. If anyone learned of this day's happening, the men would be figures of fun.

Of course! That was what worried Roger more than anything else. Nancy's lips twitched at the thought, and when she glanced at Nick his lips were twitching too, as if he read her mind.

"You'll ride back to town with us," Tom said brusquely.

"And remember—say nothing about this to *anyone*, Nancy. Even with this outcome, Nick could be in trouble!"

"I wasn't planning to mention it," she said loftily.

"How are we going to explain your arm in a sling?" Tom asked Nick.

"We'll say I was practicing jumping on a strange horse," Nick invented. "Broke my arm when I was thrown. I know a doctor who's a good friend. I'll go to my aunt's house and send for him there."

They rode back very quietly. Nancy was more shaken now by her own temerity than by Roger's anger. And Nick had not said anything to her directly. Not even a smile. She wondered if he still cared.

They turned into the street where Miss Abigail lived, and Nancy felt tears forming at the memory of her last visit there.

"I'll take the horse around to the stable," Nick said. "I'm all right now."

"I'll be back after I take Nancy home." Tom turned toward Francis Street.

Could he send her away like that without a word? Nancy wondered. Her head dropping and tears falling, she followed Tom slowly for some fifty paces. She looked back one last time. Nick still sat there on his horse, watching her go with a look that hurt, like mourning.

She wheeled and rode back. "Nick! I've missed you so much!" She reached out her hand to grasp his. He smiled at last.

"Did you mean that, Nancy?" He held her hand close, kissed it, and said, "Best run now, before anyone sees you here!"

She smiled radiantly and turned to follow her brother home.

Chapter *13*

NANCY SLIPPED into the house unnoticed by anyone except a stableboy, who saw her ride into the yard, and Ophelia, who was throwing out some slops as she came in. Both looked questioning. But Nancy told them she had been out for an early ride with Mr. Tom and went inside without further conversation. When she had changed her clothes and assured Clio that there was nothing to worry about, nothing at all, she went down to breakfast to face her mother's questions.

Her father had already departed for the State House. Her mother wondered why she should have been riding so early, on a chill November day after a late party. But Nancy had been planning her answer.

"Tom said last night that he wished to talk to me privately," she explained. "Early morning was the only time he was free of his law studies. Is there anything wrong with riding with my brother?"

"But I don't see why he could not have come here to talk to you!" her mother objected.

Nancy shrugged. "As long as he wished to ride, I thought it would be pleasant."

Her mother looked unconvinced. But she went back to the list of things she must do that day without fail. And Nancy went back to her dreams.

An hour later Tom came home.

"I was thinking about Ophelia's hot bread," he told his mother, after an affectionate greeting. "I just thought I'd stop for breakfast here before going on to Judge Chase's chambers."

"Oh, it's so good to have you home!" Lucy Carey cried. "How we miss you! Get your breakfast and tell me how the law work is going."

Tom went to the sideboard filled with breakfast dishes and dropped a twist of paper in Nancy's lap as he passed her. When he sat down, looking pleased with the plate before him, he said, "I think I'm doing well enough, Mother. Judge Chase seems pleased with my work so far."

"I wish you were living at home," Lucy Carey said wistfully. "I wish you could get on better with your father."

He shook his head. "It's easier to study where I'm living," he said. "No strain about politics."

His mother sighed. "I must say I cannot see the reason for all this bitterness. I'll be glad when the returns are in!"

"Even if a Republican wins?" Tom teased her.

"Just to get it over!" she repeated.

Tom finished his breakfast and departed, whistling the "Marseillaise." His mother winced. "That horrid song! I cannot see why the Republicans must be so in love with France, when the revolutionaries there are doing such dreadful things."

When she began checking her list again, Nancy opened her note and read it discreetly in her lap. Nick had written, "I shall be staying with Miss Abigail most of today. If you can come here, I have much to tell you. I've missed you so much, my darling."

She looked out of the window as she stirred her coffee, and her hand shook so that she spilled it over the edge of the cup.

"Lovely day," she said.

122

"Isn't it nice for November, now that the sun is up?"

"I'm going to walk out this morning. Is there anything you'd like me to do for you while I'm out?"

Her mother looked up from the list and regarded Nancy thoughtfully. Nancy could almost see her thoughts: Can I let her go out alone? Can I insist that Clio go every time she leaves the house? What can happen in the next couple of hours?

"You might stop at Mr. Stevens' apothecary shop and ask him for some more of my little silver pills." She rose from the table and went out to the cupboard to find the bottle. Returning, she said, "Let him fill it for me, Nancy. And while you're in that street, ask Mr. Wilby for a pound of your father's tobacco."

"I must stop at Mary Lloyd's and pay my party call this morning, too."

Her mother was looking thoughtful again. "I should think you would be home within the hour," she said.

"An hour!" Nancy cried. "But I wish to visit with Mary longer than that!"

"And I wish to know just how you're spending your time," her mother told her.

"An hour and a half," Nancy bargained. "Mr. Wilby is very slow."

She flew upstairs to find her most becoming bonnet, her prettiest street gown, to fuss with her hair, and to add some color to her cheeks. An hour and a half—so short a time.

When she set out upon King George Street, she had to hold herself down to keep from running. All the way to Francis Street she was trying to decide whether to do her mother's errands on the way to Miss Abigail's or after she started home again. But she could not wait an extra moment to see Nick, so she went directly to Miss Abigail's little house.

123

"My dear, I'm so glad to see you!" Miss Abigail was twinkling with pleasure when she found Nancy at her door. She took the girl back to the little sitting room overlooking the garden, where Nick was waiting, pale and tired, with one arm in a sling. With a bright smile, Miss Abigail told them she must be in her shop at the front of the house, closed the door, and left them alone.

"Nick!" Nancy flew across the floor. "How is your shoulder? Is it terribly painful?"

"If a duel was the only way to get you to talk to me, it was worth it," he said, wincing a little as he straightened up in the chair.

"Oh, Nick, I've been so unhappy!" She sat down on the hassock before him, suddenly shy and uncertain as she had not been before. She looked into his eyes and then looked down, her heart pounding so hard that she had no breath to speak.

"I was so angry with Roger," she managed.

He smiled at her with that jesting expression she was never quite sure how to take. "I was pretty angry with Roger myself," he said. "If you hadn't come running out on that field, I would certainly have killed him!"

"Nick!" she breathed, aghast. "You wouldn't! You would have been marked for a murderer! How could you be so foolish?"

"Perhaps because I wanted to prove that when I'm insulted I can shoot as fast and as straight as a gentleman!" he said. "And I could—Luckily I saw you a second before you called out, and fired into the air."

She reached for his free hand and clung to it with the sense of having escaped mortal danger.

"Nick, you're the only one who hasn't scolded me about being there. Roger was furious with me. Tom was very angry—"

"I knew you'd hear about it from them. Why should I be repetitious?"

"That's what I like about you," she said. "You know how I feel—better than anyone else I ever knew."

"Like?" he asked with that quizzical smile again. "Is that the best you can give me?"

She blushed scarlet and looked away. "That's the best—for now."

"If I weren't handicapped, I could show you," he said.

"Nick!" she said severely. "I came here because you had something of great importance to tell me."

"So I have," he remembered. "But it's only important if you love me." He was looking into her eyes, and she could not look away.

"Well—" she wavered. "Perhaps you'd better tell me then."

He laughed aloud. "Nancy, are you going to make this hard for me?"

She smiled mischievously. "You were making it pretty hard for me, you know—never meeting me that day. I was most upset, and I'm afraid I upset Miss Abigail too."

"But, darling, if you marry a newspaperman, you must be ready to think of the newspaper before anything!"

She bit her lip, wondering if he was teasing again, wondering if she should tell him she loved him, wondering how they could marry, wondering about that newspaper itself. The flood of problems silenced her.

"Now hear my news," he said. "I went to Washington with Tom to meet his friend Samuel Smith. Do you remember when I told you he was my idea of what a journalist should be?"

She remembered. That was the weekend that Smith's paper had come to the house and caused the quarrel between Tom and his father.

"I remember, Nick. Did you like him when you met him?"

"Very much. He's a fine person and will be a great journalist. Now—I heard from him last week. He wants an assistant in his work in the Federal City, and he has invited me to come and talk with him about that job!"

Nancy sat up, her eyes glowing. "Nick! What a wonderful opportunity for you! To live in Washington!"

"I have written him that I'd ride out there the first week in December. My shoulder should have mended well enough by then. He is entirely confident that Mr. Jefferson will be elected to the Presidency. When that happens, Mr. Smith will be publishing the official paper of the new administration. In that event, my salary will be enough for us to marry on! Darling, will you marry me?" He smiled a wry smile. "I cannot ask your father for your hand! But I asked Tom if I might ask him for your hand, and he gave his consent. He will help us to arrange it. So, can you tell me now how you feel, Nancy?"

She reached for his hand again. "Nick, I think I've loved you since that first day I saw you. I'll marry you as soon as you can make it possible!"

He held her close with his good arm, kissing her again and again, until she pulled away gasping, "Nick! You shouldn't jerk your other arm that way!"

He looked at the sling in surprise. "I think it must be good for my shoulder," he said with a smile. "It hasn't hurt since I began telling you my good news."

She sat down again, holding his free hand in both of hers.

"Now tell me more about it. How soon can you come back from the Federal City?"

"I should think within a few days, from that first visit. As soon as I return, we can talk about our plans."

126

"They must be entirely secret," Nancy said. "If my father even suspected I was in love with a Republican, he would lock me up until I came to my senses. And more than likely he would marry me off to Roger the day after he heard about the danger! So—" she looked unhappy. "I must let the engagement stand, let Roger suspect nothing—" She shook her head vehemently. "I hate to do it like this, Nick! I wish we didn't have to deceive people. Mary and Frank can be quite open about their attachment. Why do my parents have to be like this?"

"I wish there was another way," he said soberly. "Perhaps if the election returns are in by the end of the year—and South Carolina will send in returns late in December, the last of all—perhaps we can be free to marry before the new year."

"I'd like to push my wedding day up to January first!" she said in wistful anticipation. "All it takes is a little fortitude."

She rose from the hassock, hearing the clock strike twelve. She had been there longer than she had planned. She must do her errands and be home soon. "The only thing that worries me is keeping it secret, Nick. If it gets out, we'll be prevented!"

"I know." He reached for her, as she stood beside him. "Nancy, my darling! This is going to work out the way we want it to. I shouldn't send you notes at home—I know that's dangerous. But can you meet me here again, three days from now?"

"I'll be here," she promised. "But three days seem so long!"

When she closed Miss Abigail's door behind her and started up Main Street, her happiness was mixed with foreboding. She wanted with all her heart to marry Nick. Perhaps because she wanted it so much, she was oppressed

127

with uncertainties. All it took was a little fortitude, she reminded herself—courage and patience. She wondered why those ordinary virtues seemed so excessively hard.

She stopped at the apothecary shop and asked for her mother's pills.

"My supplier in New York says Jefferson is going to win," Mr. Stevens told her gloomily. "I suppose we'll all have to learn to live under a Republican government."

"I suppose so." Nancy tried to hide her satisfaction at his words. Three doors up the street, Mr. Wilby, the tobacconist, said, "I hear we're going to win for sure. It's about time we got rid of the Federalists and their taxes!"

"Do you really think so?"

"Oh, we won't know for weeks yet." Mr. Wilby was measuring and mixing the tobaccos of her father's blend. "But it looks promising."

She carried her packages up to Maryland Avenue and paid her party call on Mary Lloyd. Mary was dying to know what had been going on between Nick and Roger Tucker, after the quarrel had erupted at her party, but Nancy swore that she knew nothing about it. She had been angry with Roger for quarreling at a party, she told Mary, but he had refused to tell her anything about it. He had said only that it was a man's affair. So she supposed it had been settled. She wished someone could tell her about it.

"Frank said there was some talk of a duel," Mary told her with round eyes. "That's so dangerous! I mean, the law charges both men, and my brother says a friend of his had to flee the country because of an ill-considered duel!"

"I'll ask Roger if he comes to call," Nancy said. "But men won't talk about duels."

"But I have great news!" Mary said, bubbling with excitement. "Edward says I can announce my engagement right after the first of the year! Isn't that wonderful!"

"Oh, Mary, I'm so happy for you! I envy you—"

She stopped before she gave herself away, and Mary was so much engrossed in her own news that she didn't hear Nancy's last exclamation.

She did indeed envy Mary Lloyd, more than she could say, Nancy reflected on her way home from the Lloyd house. What happiness there must be in a love that was open and approved by both families!

Chapter 14

TWO WEEKS LATER Nick was gone, to work with Samuel Harrison Smith on his *National Intelligencer*. Nancy had met him three times in those two weeks, and he had promised to send letters at least twice a week to the post office, where Nancy could pick them up privately. With Nick gone, she had the horrid feeling that the town was deserted. All she seemed to hear were the Federalist hopes about the election returns from South Carolina. Reports from other states gave the Federalists a very good chance of winning.

"After all," Jonathan Carey said almost every day, as if saying were believing, "that's a Federalist state down there. They can't help but throw their votes to Pinckney— he's their hero. That would elect him instead of Adams, and we'd have a good Federalist administration."

On December 14 the *Maryland Gazette* reported that South Carolina had elected the entire slate of Republican electors. That meant that Jefferson and Burr were elected to office. Jonathan Carey stormed around the house in the blackest temper Nancy had ever seen.

She herself was so filled with incredulous delight that she was hard put to conceal it. She dressed to walk out in the snow to the post office and slipped out of a side door, so her father would not ask her where she was going.

Surely, Nick would have written about this great news.

As she plodded and slipped on the snowy walks, she recalled his farewell promise: *When this election is decided, I will come for you that same day—*

What day would the election be so decided? she wondered.

His letter was short, but his delight shone in every line:

> We learned here on December 12 that South Carolina has elected Republican electors. You can imagine what unconfined rejoicing took place here at the Smiths. We all went over to Jefferson's boardinghouse to congratulate the new President, and I was proud indeed to be presented to him by my good friend Mr. Smith.
>
> This report is, of course, an early one, and as yet unconfirmed. However, it comes from Mr. Jefferson himself, who received the news from a Republican editor in Columbia, South Carolina, so there can be no question that it is true.

He had already told the Smiths of his plan to return to Annapolis for Nancy, and he promised to write within a day or so to tell her further details.

> They wish me to bring you directly to them. Mrs. Smith will have the marriage performed in her home. She is rejoicing with me at this happy turn in the political events that control our plans.

Six inches of slushy snow lay upon the walkways of Annapolis, but Nancy walked the streets for an hour to compose herself before she went home, so that she would not betray unseemly joy.

Even so, when she came to the dinner table that afternoon, her mother said, "You look so happy today, Nancy. What has happened?"

She dropped her eyes and said, "Nothing special. I just seem to feel good today."

131

Her father looked up, knife and fork in hand, and grumbled, "Don't tell me you're rejoicing over this blasted report of a Republican victory!"

She was so startled that she stammered, "Why, Father—what Republican report?"

He eyed her suspiciously. "Now don't tell me, my girl, that you don't read the *Gazette* the first thing every morning. I've been noticing you take more interest in politics than you ever did before. What's behind it?"

She shook her head in panic, finding no words to answer him, and he pursued his questioning.

"Funny thing too. That Republican friend of Tom's—young Dana, was it?—he seems to have left town."

"Has he?" she murmured, very busy picking bones out of the fish on her plate.

"Humph!" her father snorted, as if he suspected that something was going on that he ought to know about. "Have you heard from Roger lately?"

"He writes every week."

"How's that house coming? When I was young we didn't wait to build a house before we married the girl we wanted. I'd like to see that wedding come off sooner." He turned to his wife. "Lucy, why don't we try to have that wedding during the Christmas holidays? I'm all out of patience with this delaying things. These young people have been engaged long enough. What are they waiting for?"

Nancy, feeling the color drain from her cheeks, sat very quiet, hoping he would not notice her distress.

"I'm going to take it up with George Tucker myself," he announced. "This kind of delay is dangerous. I'd like to see Nancy tied up with a good Federalist before she gets any of these mad Republican ideas."

Fortitude, Nancy thought to herself, holding desperately

onto her quivering nerves. Don't say anything. Don't let him suspect anything more—

"Lucy, we'll spend the Christmas holidays at Carey's Fortune. Invite the Tuckers to stay with us the fortnight. That ought to help things along a bit."

"Why, Jonathan, that would be delightful!" Lucy chirped, as if nothing could please her more.

"The way things are going today, there's too much uncertainty in the air to take any chances," Jonathan Carey pronounced.

"Now, Jonathan, get hold of yourself," Grandmother Carey said tartly. "Things are no more uncertain today than when you ran away with Lucy! Nancy wants to live in a house of her own when she weds, and who's to blame her for that? I wouldn't want to live with the Tuckers myself!"

His mother's sharp words seemed to hang in the air, and the dinner ended in silence. Nancy escaped to her room as soon as she could, to compose her nerves. She would not go to Carey's Fortune for the holidays, she vowed to herself. She could not spend two weeks in Roger's company.

What if Nick came to fetch her, and she was not here? She wrote a long letter to him. By the time she had finished it and hidden it securely until she could carry it to the post office, she felt calm again.

A few days later the weather was worse, and she stayed by the fire hemming curtains. If the snow fell heavily enough, perhaps it would not be possible to go to Carey's Fortune.

She clung to that hope when it was still snowing the next morning. The *Maryland Gazette* lay on the breakfast table at her father's elbow, and he was too genial. It was December twentieth, and he had spoken of leaving on the twenty-second.

133

Suspicious, Nancy filled her plate and tried to read the paper upside down, not daring to pick it up while he sat there watching her. But even upside down she could read the headline: "JEFFERSON TIED WITH BURR."

"What does the paper say today, Father?" she asked, trying to sound indifferent.

"Why, it seems Jefferson has not won after all!" he announced. "With Burr and Jefferson tied, the election will go to the House of Representatives, and the Federalists hold control there. Of these two Republicans, Burr will work with the Federalists. Nothing to worry about after all."

Nothing to worry about! Nancy's heart dropped like a stone. Her father ate heartily and left the table with the cheerful announcement that he was on his way to the State House, and he hoped that when the Federalists were back in office Tom would give up his ridiculous ideas and come home to stay.

Nancy waited until the door closed behind him before she dared to pick up the paper. She read the article three times before she could believe it. Something had gone wrong in the South Carolina election after all, and it had resulted in a tie between Thomas Jefferson and Aaron Burr. Suddenly she was too tired to walk out, too tired to do anything but return to her room, lie down, and get accustomed to the collapse of all her plans.

She lay there a long time, fighting the hopelessness that had made her break with Nick before. She wondered if this kind of uncertainty and defeat was going to be her lot for the rest of her life. It would be four more years before the Republicans would have another chance to elect a President. How could she pass four more years?

But Samuel Smith had hired Nick. Why should it matter who was President? Her hopes revived again. By the late afternoon she made herself walk down to the post office to collect Nick's letter; he had sent it with a copy of the *National Intelligencer,* marking articles for her attention. She opened the letter to read it in the post office:

The news today of a tied vote between Mr. Jefferson and Mr. Burr is a sad disappointment to all of us who hoped for Mr. Jefferson's election. This means the vote must go to the House of Representatives and may not be decided before the end of February. The most alarming hazard for us is that the Federalists hold control in the House.

She stopped reading to blow her nose and wipe her eyes. The postmaster was regarding her curiously, but she ignored him.

This is a disastrous development for our plans to marry. My employment cannot be secure unless Jefferson takes office. The Smiths are much worried too. Mr. Smith assures Mrs. Smith that he can support her without such an administration. But privately he has warned me that he may not be able to keep me in his employ if the temper to support a Republican paper should change.

I had hoped that by this very date I could be on my way to bring you back here with me. This miserable election result has changed those plans. Tied to the government now, as I am with Mr. Smith, I can make no plans of my own while everything here is so uncertain. I can only tell you I love you more than ever and miss you sadly.

Always yours,
Nick

She clutched the letter in an angry fist, crumpling it tight and stuffing it into her muff, as she trudged through the snow toward home. How could she possibly wait until the end of February? And yet, how could she not wait? Taut with strain, she sloshed along. How could she tell her family she would not marry Roger Tucker? How could she live at home if she did? And where else could she go?

The dark skies opened, and wet snow began falling heavily again. Nancy was shivering with cold now, and she hurried through the dreary gloom, feeling her spirits sag lower and lower with the sinking light.

By the time she reached home she was chilled to the bone. She crawled up to her bedroom, shaking and feverish, and asked Clio to get her hot bricks and a tray of hot tea. As she sank into the soft, comforting warmth, she wondered how she could ever do without Clio. While she waited for the hot tea, Nancy opened the *National Intelligencer* and read it carefully.

She found herself surprised at the style of writing, the logical and dispassionate arguments for a Republican administration, the editorial point of view. The difference between this Republican paper and Andrew Dana's *Centinel* was marked. For the first time she understood how important it was for Nick to be working with an editor like Samuel Harrison Smith. She could understand too why Tom had backed Mr. Smith with a thousand dollars of his own money.

The hot tea came up from the kitchen, and Nancy grew drowsy with comfort. She was just dropping off to sleep, when she came to with a start, thinking about the *National Intelligencer*. Her parents must not know she had this paper. They would ask too many questions. She managed to stay awake until Clio took the tray away. Then she crawled out of bed to conceal the paper carefully in the bottom of her desk drawer. She was so weak and shaky by now that she could barely get back in bed.

Nancy was ill for several days. The doctor came to see her, pronounced that it was an influenza she had picked up from getting chilled and wet in the snow, and left medicines for her to take. She was alternately hot and cold and aching all over, while Clio changed hot bricks and tried to keep cold cloths on her head.

She worried about Nick's letters and about his not hearing from her. When she had been sick for three days, Tom came to see her, and she asked Clio to leave them alone. Tom promised to pick up letters and papers and bring them to her twice a week. She managed to scribble a short note to let Nick know she was thinking of him, and Tom took it with him.

After that the illness provided some advantages. Her father treated her with great consideration and said nothing at all about Republicans. Roger wrote about how the house was progressing, hoped she was feeling better, and did not offer to visit until she was well again. Her father decided that between Nancy's illness and the election confusion, they would not think of going out to Carey's Fortune after all.

In any case, the Tuckers were spending the Christmas season in town. They brought great news with them. Mr. Blaney had proposed to Molly, and they wished to announce the engagement immediately.

Nancy was out of bed and downstairs for the first time when Mrs. Tucker came to visit with the news.

"He wants the wedding on February twenty-first," she told Lucy Carey gleefully. "Less than eight weeks! Just fancy! I wish Roger and Nancy would be married as soon. Roger *will* insist on waiting for that house to be finished. Oh, but it's going to be so lovely!"

It was not clear whether she was talking about Molly's wedding or Roger's house. But Nancy tried to listen enthusiastically. With Molly's wedding date set for eight weeks hence, the Tuckers would be too busy planning for that to notice her. Roger himself talked endlessly about Blaney's plans for Molly.

"Joshua says he wishes to practice law in Annapolis," he said with great satisfaction. "He finds it quite the pleasantest town he's ever known. My father is giving Molly the ground adjoining our property at Green Hill, where they will build a house close to ours! Is that not delightful? And he is buying them a house in Annapolis where Buckland is reputed to have done the woodwork."

Nancy had stopped listening. With Nick, there would be for her no question of fine furniture or carved trim, no talk of a large house. She could remember when she had thought that would be a strange and intolerable way to live. Now she wanted only to make a home with Nick, however it might be.

Roger was looking at her with a strange expression. She realized, with a small gasp, that he had said something she should have answered. She began to cough to cover up her inattention, and sputtered between paroxysms, "Let me lie down somewhere, Roger. I'll get over this in a moment."

He was alarmed, believing the spasm due to her recent illness, and led her gently to the sofa in the morning room. He ran to call Clio to come quickly and see to her mistress. Minutes later Nancy deemed it safe to let the cough subside and be well again.

"Roger," she said apologetically, "you had just said something when I had that seizure. Tell me again, what did you ask?"

He was so relieved that she was recovered, that he thought nothing of her inattention.

"I said the house is going to be finished by the end of February, and we can be married some weeks earlier than we planned." He was watching her hopefully. "I'd like us to be married the end of February, Nancy. I'm quite impatient now—" He smiled at her with such confidence that she closed her eyes, unable to face him.

"But I couldn't get ready so soon!" she protested.

"Nonsense! Molly is getting ready on much shorter notice. I'll speak to your mother myself."

She closed her eyes again and turned her head away. He stood beside her looking very stern.

"Nancy, you make me wonder what reason must be behind this nonsense! After three months, surely the wedding can be advanced a few weeks without throwing all plans into turmoil! Or do you wish to cry off?"

At that she opened her eyes and forced a weak smile.

"Roger, it must be weakness from being ill." She sounded pathetic. "I'm too tired to talk about the wedding. Two months will be enough to prepare. . . ."

The effort to deceive him really did exhaust her, and she closed her eyes again. He was so thoughtful about asking no further questions and leaving her to rest quietly, that when he was gone she felt quite guilty about her deceit.

Chapter 15

AS THE SLOW DAYS of January crawled past, Nancy
could make less and less meaning out of the uncertainty of the tied election and Nick's position. Often
enough she wondered how she could have chosen a man
in such unpredictable circumstances.

Reports persisted from week to week about the situation.
Eight states could be counted for Jefferson. They were
standing firm. Six states were as firmly standing for Aaron
Burr. Two were divided and tied. It took the votes of nine
states to elect the President.

The Maryland delegation was divided four and four.
Rumors flew constantly about the pressures on the delegation to make them agree on one man or the other. Nancy's
spirits soared and dropped as the rumors contradicted each
other.

One day early in February she walked past the *Centinel*
office just to look at the place that meant Nick. His father
was looking out of the door, dour as usual. Nancy smiled
and stopped, and he opened the door reluctantly.

"Good day, Mr. Dana. What do you hear from Nick
these days?"

"Sends his paper regular," Dana said gloomily. "Never
writes a line. Said once the paper tells what he's doing."

"What do you think of the *National Intelligencer,* Mr.
Dana?"

"Oh, it'll do all right, I guess. If Jefferson gets in, that is."
He was pessimistic. "Can't tell about none of these things.
I guess if Jefferson loses, Nick can come back home and
work on the *Centinel*. If it's good enough for me, it ought
to be good enough for him!"

That idea left Nancy cast down, and she walked on to
visit with Miss Abigail. She could not imagine being married
to Nick, if he worked in that grubby little shop right
here in town.

Miss Abigail twittered with pleasure at her visit.

"Oh, my dear! I'm so happy about Nick! I know he loves
working with Mr. Smith. He sends me a copy of the paper
every day, so I won't have to wait to read the paper he
sends his father!"

She thrust the paper at Nancy as soon as she had seated
the girl by the fire, pulling an ottoman forward for her to
put her feet on.

"You read what it says here about the election, while I
make the tea."

She trotted out toward the kitchen, as Nancy rubbed her
cold hands together before the fire. The cheerful warmth
stole through her, and she looked around the little room,
noticing cheerful notes she had never seen before—a
crayon portrait of a younger Nick hanging over the little
harpsichord, the soft colors in the rug upon the floor, the
bright brass fire tools sparkling in the sunlight that fell
through the window.

Miss Abigail brought in a tea tray and set it on a table
beside Nancy.

"This is a darling house," Nancy said, wondering why it
had never struck her that way before.

Miss Abigail nodded, pleased. "It's a cheerful place. And
now it holds all my memories. My father kept it tight and
mended. I must say it's comforting to look out my window

with the fire at my back and watch the snow blowing down the street." She glanced at Nancy a little shyly. "I always like to see the big houses. But I must say I'd never feel cozy in them, as I do in this one. And the way the sun comes in across the garden in the mornings—well, I've never wanted anything better."

Nancy sipped the strong black tea, well laced with milk and sugar, and thought about keeping a "cozy" house for Nick.

"Did you read the paper?" Miss Abigail asked. "Did you see this story here?"

"I forgot all about the paper because the house was so interesting," Nancy said. "What does the *Intelligencer* say about the election?"

"The Congressmen meet on Wednesday to take the vote," Miss Abigail said. "That's just a week away—February eleventh. It's hard now to imagine that all this uncertainty will be over by then."

"Will they elect the President that same day?" Nancy asked, incredulous that the day was so near, after so long a wait.

Miss Abigail nodded solemnly. "They begin balloting at noon, and they will continue until a President is chosen. Andrew is making arrangements to bring out the *Centinel* just as soon as the news arrives—a special edition." She smiled mischievously. "I don't know what the *Maryland Gazette* plans to do, but Andrew is determined to beat them with the news! Nick has promised to send the word the instant it's known in the House."

"Let me see that story again, please."

Nancy picked up the paper and read it attentively. The paper, published the day before, reported that members of Congress were arriving that day for this special occasion and jamming all the boardinghouses in the Federal City.

The *Intelligencer* would report all events in this election as rapidly as they occurred.

Nancy rose. "Miss Abigail, thank you for the tea and the paper. I'll call on you again. This election means so much to me." She held out her hand, and the little glove maker held it tight. "I don't see how I can stand the next few days!"

"They'll be hard on me too," Miss Abigail assured her. "You come and sit by my fire any time you like, Miss Nancy. It will be a comfort to have you here."

Nancy walked up Main Street, tense and anxious. Only one more week to keep her family from suspecting her love, to be ready for—what? One more week to live through, still, when each day seemed so much of a strain she was not sure how she could face the next.

Wednesday the eleventh of February arrived, after seven days that had dragged more slowly than any Nancy could ever remember. All day she was restless and uneasy, sewing on her sheets to calm herself, then flinging them down and pacing the floor. How soon might she hear the results? By five o'clock she knew it would not be until Thursday. At ten o'clock she heard the crier: "Ten o'clock and rain tonight. No election yet!"

No one had suggested that when the Congress convened it might not elect one of the two men that same day. Nancy felt herself in empty space with nothing to cling to. If they could not settle this question on Wednesday, how many days would it take? Her wedding was set now for two weeks from Saturday. What if no election had been determined by then?

Thursday, in spite of a chill wind driving a cold rain, she slipped out of the house about four o'clock. There had been no news cried in the streets since the night before, and the *Maryland Gazette* that morning had reported that the

House had taken several votes, with no change in the results: eight states for Jefferson, six for Burr, two tied, with no vote. Only one more state's vote was needed for Jefferson to win the election.

At the *Centinel* office Andrew Dana was busily drying papers and folding others from the drying lines.

"What news do you hear of the election, Mr. Dana?"

He looked up. "Oh, howdy, Miss Carey. No election yet. They're still voting." He seemed more cheerful today, strangely enough.

"Still voting! I hoped it was over!" It was a devastating letdown. "What happened?"

He shrugged. "Who knows? They took twenty-seven ballots from noon yesterday up to eight o'clock this morning, and not one vote was changed from the first ballot!" He grinned at her slyly. "I'll tell you this, Miss Carey—everyone for Burr was talking how the break would come on the second ballot, how he'd get the Maryland vote for sure after that. Well, I'm telling you, they took twenty-seven ballots, and nothing happened. I think Jefferson's going to make it now."

"Do you really think so?" she cried, radiant. "Oh, Mr. Dana, do you really think Jefferson may win?"

He looked at her curiously, his beady little black eyes smiling in spite of his down-turned trap of a mouth. "You want Jefferson to win, Miss Carey? A good Federalist like you?"

She laughed aloud, "Yes, I want Jefferson to win, Mr. Dana!"

He stared at her again, as if he was measuring her. "Well, good enough. You come back tomorrow, and maybe there'll be some real news. Nick sent me a note about this thing." Inwardly, she tightened at the sound of Nick's name. "He's arranged for a messenger to start out with the results every noon, within the hour. So I'll have the latest tally by three thirty, four, or so each day."

Aglow in spite of the ugly day, she splashed through the streets, glazed now with freezing rain. Come back tomorrow, Mr. Dana had said. That would mean Nick would come to her soon—perhaps tomorrow?

At tea a couple of hours later, her father said he had heard in the Assembly that the Maryland delegation was bound to go for Burr any minute now.

"Stands to reason," he said confidently. "They've given Jefferson his chance. All they had to do was to weigh how much the people really wanted him. Now they can switch their votes, and tomorrow it'll be Burr."

The light faded from Nancy's face, and she was uneasy and tense again. Her thoughts leaped to her wedding date. Two weeks from Saturday. She had been so sure the election would be over before then. But if Burr won—?

"What are you shaking your head about?" her father demanded. "You mean you don't want Burr to win?"

She looked up, startled, afraid he was reading her mind.

"But, Father, you said yourself that Mr. Hamilton came out for Jefferson!" she reminded him.

"Pshah!" her father cried scowling, "Hamilton can say what he likes, it's a bad choice between two bad candidates. I'd take the Federalist-leaning one over the Republican, no matter what Hamilton says! And that'll be Burr. You'll see."

Nancy said no more, drinking her tea and trying to show bland indifference. She was not sure she succeeded, but her father stopped badgering her.

She slipped out of the house the next afternoon and found the messenger from Washington sitting in the *Centinel* office with a hot drink while he rested up for the return ride.

"What was the last count?" she asked breathlessly.

Andrew Dana ignored her, glowering over his press. The messenger looked at her, enjoying an audience for the message he had carried.

"That's a near thing going on in the Congress, there," he told her with solemn excitement. "Mr. Nicholson's been sick in his bed for two days now, but he won't go home. He's carried into the chamber to keep voting for Jefferson every day. No change yesterday. No change today. They've put over the next ballots to Saturday."

No change. Another day to live through. Nancy made her way home again, thinking fearfully about wedding plans, about Nick working at his father's press right here in town, about Peggy Mason Brown, happily far away on the frontier. As she came into the house and slipped upstairs unnoticed, the town crier was ringing his bell through the street, calling in a mournful voice, "Twenty-nine ballots and still no election. Five o'clock and all is well!"

It was impossible that all her happiness should hang upon a vote for the President of the United States! But there was no other way to see it. Nancy was uneasy enough to feel ill, unable to eat supper, unable to sleep. When her mother questioned her about it, she blamed it on her earlier illness and the bad weather. Lucy Carey looked at her with skeptical eyes and told her she must stay in bed until she felt better. In no circumstance must she leave the house in this weather.

It was easier to stay in bed Saturday and Sunday than to persuade her mother there was nothing wrong. The crier called late Saturday afternoon, "Three more ballots and still no election!"

On Monday the vote was still deadlocked. Nancy got up and sat by the fire, waiting for news. At dinner her father reported, "This is an ugly situation. Mobs are beginning to

146

collect in the streets over this election." He shook his head. "Might have to call out the guard, if things don't quiet down. Virginia has already called out the militia to keep order."

By the time the crier called on Monday night, "The election is still deadlocked. We have no President yet!" Nancy could not conceal her anxiety. She went early to bed, hoping she could sleep till the whole thing was over.

Tuesday morning her mother looked at her across the breakfast table and said, "Nancy, you are behaving very strangely, my dear! Tell me what's wrong. I know you're unhappy about something, and it cannot be this election! That is beyond reason. What troubles you?"

Nancy shook her head and struggled to think of a plausible excuse. Eyes cast down to avoid betrayal, she muttered, "I don't know, Mother. It just seems important to me—and I cannot understand Father's devotion to Aaron Burr—"

"It's all out of reason to be so concerned about this vote," Lucy Carey told her daughter sternly. "There must be something behind it! Your wedding is less than two weeks away, and all you can think of is a Presidential election! I vow, I never heard of anything so strange! Is there someone —but how *could* it matter so much?"

She looked at her daughter expectantly, and Nancy burst into tears.

"Well!" Her mother rose, looking at her with deep suspicion. "I'm forced to think that there is something very serious behind this, perhaps something dangerous. I must talk with your father. Maybe if you were farther from it, you would find it less important."

She left the room, and Nancy paced back and forth, wringing her hands and trying to reason with herself. Now that her mother's suspicions were aroused, she was in real danger of being removed from Annapolis—probably, as her father had threatened at Christmas, to Carey's Fortune, where Nick would never find her, where she could not escape.

Head throbbing, she slipped upstairs to her room to think what to do next. Clio was mending one of her dresses. She looked at Nancy with concern.

"Miss Nancy, you looks real haggard," she said. "Does you feel poorly?"

"I've got a raging headache, Clio. If I just lie quietly, I'll feel better." She dropped on her bed.

"I'll go down to the kitchen and get some vinegar water," Clio said, dropping the mending. "That'll help your head."

Nancy lay with her eyes shut, stiffened against the bed, questions and answers running through her aching head. If she could go and talk to Tom, he might be able to help her. If she could run away—Would they find her at Tom's? if she ran away to the Federal City? to Mrs. Smith? to Nick?

But that she could not do. A stringent pride balked at going to Nick like that. He must come for her. And if he could not marry her, if he had no work with Mr. Smith— The headache throbbed more acutely. She moaned.

Her mother came in with Clio, looking more stern than sypathetic.

"Clio said you were sick with the headache," she said, standing by the bed and looking down at Nancy. The girl stared at her mother and flung her arm across her eyes to shut out the light and the uncompromising authority that saw through her every effort to hide.

"Your father thinks you will be better off at Carey's Fortune now until the wedding," Lucy Carey told her daughter. "I'm sure you are only suffering the wedding fears that come sometimes without warning."

148

She sat down and held Nancy's hand, trying to be understanding while she compelled obedience. "My dear, we are only concerned for your happiness. Roger is like a son to us. We know you'll be happy with him. So you should put your fears aside. Everything is ready for the wedding—there is not a thing to worry about. I'm sure you're missing Roger when he's so far away. If you're staying at Carey's Fortune, he'll be with you every day, and you'll feel much better. Won't you, dear?"

The question sounded like a threat, and Nancy turned her head aside with a moan. "I couldn't make the trip today, Mother," she said, "I feel ill."

Her mother laid a cool hand on her forehead. "You may have a touch of the fever," she conceded. "But you can travel tomorrow, I'm sure." To Clio she said, "Take good care of her, Clio. She'll feel better after a good night's sleep. And pack her clothes to take to Carey's Fortune. You'll go with her. Don't you think it will be a pleasant change?"

"Yes, ma'am."

Mrs. Carey left the room, with an uneasy suspense hanging in the air, and Nancy uncovered her eyes. A thought struck her in this dire moment like an inspiration.

"Pack all my bridal clothes, Clio. And all the linens—I'll want them out there, before the wedding." She covered her eyes again as if she felt faint.

"You going to be the prettiest bride anyone ever see!" Clio told her, relieved that her mistress was not objecting to Mrs. Carey's orders.

For a moment Nancy's mood was high too.

The church bells sounded two o'clock, and she closed her eyes again, thinking intensely. Clio picked up Nancy's clothes, packed the portmanteaus, examined dresses for mending, and finally left the room with a half-dozen gar-

149

ments over her arm to work with them in the wash room.

Nancy sat up. Miraculously her headache had disappeared, although it had been genuinely severe when her mother was with her. She was not sure how she could manage it. But she was not going to Carey's Fortune.

Chapter 16

SHE PUT ON her furred pelisse for warmth and over it her warmest coat. As she was tying a beaver bonnet over her ears, steps sounded on the stairs. Hastily she took off the outdoor garments and hung them out of sight. She was lying down on her bed again when her mother opened her door.

"I'm going to rest until dinner," Nancy told her mother. "My head is better now. But I'm very tired."

"That would be a good thing," her mother said approvingly. "I'm looking forward now to a nice quiet time at Fortune, before the wedding. A rest will be good for all of us." She patted Nancy's cheek. "Your father will be late at the State House today," she said. "We shan't have dinner till five or so. Would you like Clio to bring up some tea now?"

"I'd rather sleep," Nancy said. Her mother went out, closing the door behind her.

The girl lay still some minutes. Then she sprang up, put on her wraps again, her goloshoes, her beaver bonnet and muff. She opened the door silently. The hall was empty. She stole to the back stairs that led down to the back hall, from which she could reach the small door to the garden. The stairs creaked under her feet. She stopped, listening for answering steps. No one had heard her, and she reached the small passage unseen. Behind the kitchen door she

151

heard her mother telling Clio that Miss Nancy wanted to sleep until dinner and should not be disturbed. Nancy slipped silently down the hall and out the side door.

She sped around the wall, out of sight of the house, to the gate. Safely outside, she leaned against the wall to catch her breath. She would not be missed until dinner time. She must make the most of that time. And if this should be the day when Jefferson was elected, or not elected—At the thought her heart pounded so fast that she gasped for breath.

She made her way through the wet snow to the *Centinel* office by other streets than she usually took. The streets seemed unusually full of people milling around, but she slipped through the crowd and into the printing shop. Andrew Dana was bustling around, preparing the paper to receive the news that might come any moment. He had run off two pages with news of Annapolis people and advertisements. To keep her mind off the dragging minutes, Nancy huddled in a chair out of the way and read one of the galley sheets she had found on the floor near her.

A roaring sound distracted her, and she looked up.

"You waiting for something, Miss Carey?" Andrew Dana glanced across from his work.

"I'm waiting for the late news, Mr. Dana. But what's that noise outside?"

He looked out indifferently. "They's a lot of other people out there waiting for news too," he told her. "They were here yesterday and again this morning, and now they're back again. Some of them might be pretty angry if Mr. Jefferson isn't elected today."

He turned back to filling a composing tray. Nancy got up restlessly and looked through the glass pane in the door at the crowd gathering. It was still growing and people were arguing noisily now about the chance of an election today.

Dana cocked his head for the sound of hoofbeats. "No knowing how long it'll be. But I'm telling you, Miss Nancy, there's going to be rioting in the streets if those men in Washington can't elect a President pretty soon."

He locked the tray of type into place, seized the inking ball, rubbed it over the type face, and pulled off a galley. The ink smelled black and strong. It said "Nick!" to Nancy so clearly that she was wrenched with a pang of loneliness. Mr. Dana read his galley, nodding with satisfaction, dropped it, and began running off the pages of newsprint.

Nancy picked up the galley and read it. Dana had reviewed the progress of the voting during the past week. He told the story of the heroic Mr. Nicholson of Maryland, who lay on his cot with a high fever, insisting he would stay through every ballot. It was a good story, and Nancy recalled Nick's excitement about getting the news. At last she really understood how important it was that the news should get out as soon as possible.

Look how patient she had been, sitting here in this grimy shop, just waiting to get the first word. She was going to be the kind of wife who understood a newspaper husband, who would encourage him, work with him, sit up waiting for him to come home from a late press run at night. . . .

She heard a familiar voice outside, and she froze. Her father was just outside the door, talking to the crowd of men, trying to find out what was going on.

"I must go, Mr. Dana." She stood up and edged around out of sight of the door. "Could I slip out a back door so I wouldn't have to go through that crowd? They sound frightening!"

He looked out at the crowd. "Best you should get away," he agreed. "If the news don't please them when it comes, no telling what they might do to a Federalist!"

He led her around the press to the back of the little shop.

"Watch your skirts, Miss Nancy. Don't let them get smeared on the press there—" He opened a door for her that led into a tiny back yard. "There's a gate in the far corner, whence you can get out between the houses. Best go behind them up the block, beyond the crowd."

She thanked him and plowed through the snow to the gate he had pointed out. It opened into a narrow lane running along the walls of the other buildings. She made her way as quickly as she could toward State Circle, where she turned left to reach Main Street. Somewhere she heard hoofbeats, an unmistakable sound of urgency, muffled by the snow. The courier? Her heart began again that hard heavy pounding of expectancy.

As she reached Main Street, the horseman rode toward her from Church Street. She stood where she could wave at him and ask him what news he carried. It would truly be exciting to hear it even before Dana or the crowd heard it! Suddenly as he approached, she saw that the horseman was Nick himself.

Nancy stepped off the walkway into the street, thrusting back her bonnet so that he could see her clearly.

"Nick!" she cried.

The bay horse skidded as Nick reined him in, and Nick looked into her eyes with glowing excitement.

"Nancy!" he shouted. "*Jefferson won!* I've got to get the news to the *Centinel* at once before the *Gazette* gets it!"

Before she could open her mouth, he was off again.

She stood there and stared after him. The news was good. It was wonderful! And he had not even dismounted. She wanted to cry. Anger choked her. Was this all she had waited for, these long hard weeks and days?

She whipped around, blinking angry tears from her eyes, setting her head high, and walked proudly up Main Street. She asked herself, why should she not go out to Carey's

Fortune tomorrow morning after all? But she could not bear to go home now, not when she wanted to fling herself upon her bed and weep forever.

Turning into St. John's Street, she found herself in front of Tom's boardinghouse. She thumped the shining brass knocker upon its plate and waited, shivering with cold and with shock. At least Tom could tell her what to do.

Mrs. Franklin opened the door. "Is my brother here?" Nancy felt as if she could not wait two minutes longer to fling herself upon Tom and tell him of her heartbreak.

"Why, it's Miss Carey, ain't it? And out in the snow like this. Come in, miss. You're shivering with cold. Sit down on the settle by the fire here, while I take that wet coat."

Nancy followed her numbly, reaching out for the blazing little coal fire in the sitting room. Mrs. Franklin disappeared with her wet coat and bonnet, and Nancy looked about the plain little room with its painted, uncarpeted floor and starched, immaculate curtains. The inner shutters were drawn against the cold wind outside, and there was a warm quilt on the settle beside Nancy. She drew it around her shoulders, still quivering.

"A little hot tea will warm you up just fine." Mrs. Franklin bustled into the sitting room again, bearing a tea tray heaped with scones and raisin muffins. "Now, you were asking for your brother." She handed Nancy a steaming cup of tea with milk and sugar. "He's not here this minute, and I'm sure I wouldn't know where he went, except maybe to learn the news about the election."

Nancy looked at her warily. "Could I wait for him here? I want to see him as soon as possible."

"Of course you can!" Mrs. Franklin poked up the fire. "Let me check his room and see if the fire is going and the place is warm. Maybe you'd like to stay there."

She was gone again, and Nancy ate two of the raisin

155

muffins and three buttered scones, in spite of her conviction that she could not touch a mouthful of food. Between the tea and the delicious breads, she was beginning to feel stronger. The shivering had stopped, and a faint cheer was beginning to break through the gloom. She stared into the fire over her teacup and found she was thinking coherently again.

Surely Mrs. Franklin must be wondering how Mr. Carey's sister happened to arrive at this time of day, on foot in such ugly weather. She might even ask Nancy if her parents knew where she was.

She scowled at the thought. But however she might dislike being questioned by the likes of Mrs. Franklin, she must make some answer that would be persuasive, or Tom's landlady was more than likely to send word to her father.

Outside in the deepening dusk she could hear the crier calling, "Mr. Jefferson is the President of the United States! Five o'clock and all is well!" and again, "Five o'clock, and we have a new President! Mr. Jefferson was elected today!"

That brought her sharply back to her reason for sitting here in this little boardinghouse. Nick had come himself from Washington and had not even cared to dismount when he saw her standing there in the street.

She drew her brows together again and stared fixedly at the breathing coals before her. How could she have jeopardized her whole future for a man who cared so little? She knew what she must do.

Feeling more decisive since she had had tea and contemplation by the fire, she rose and looked around for her goloshoes and outer wraps. Mrs. Franklin must have taken them to the kitchen to dry, for they were nowhere in sight.

Down the little hall, she could hear sounds of Mrs.

Franklin stirring about in the kitchen, whipping something in a copper bowl, slamming an iron skillet upon a wooden tabletop with a heavy clunk. Nancy turned toward the kitchen to ask for her wraps and leave word that she could not wait for Tom after all. She was going back home.

The only thing that mattered now was to get away from all thoughts of Nick Dana, to put him out of her life. And where better than at Carey's Fortune? It was the only place where she had no association with Nick. Once there, she would never have to think about him again, nor about all the problems that went with his kind of life. Somehow that decision raised tears again.

The inviting fragrance of chicken and spices drifted into the hall as she opened the kitchen door. Mrs. Franklin was beating up some corn bread to cook in the skillet for supper. She smiled at Nancy. Behind her the wide kitchen hearth was warm and welcoming, with a spindle-backed rocker sitting beside it, a small oven standing before the andirons, a grate over the red coals for a skillet.

"Come right in, my dear. It's likely warmer here than in the sitting room. Are you feeling some better now? I daresay Mr. Carey will be home any minute. He's always here for supper at six. I've got a nice chicken pie here—your brother always says it's his favorite meal. I figure it'll make a celebration supper, what with Jefferson getting elected today, and your being here to eat with him."

"Thank you very much, Mrs. Franklin. But I think perhaps I'd better go home now."

"Oh, come now, Miss Carey. It'll soon be dark out. I wouldn't think of letting you go home alone on foot and all. You want me to send my little Johnny with a note to your people to send a carriage for you?"

Nancy's decision was draining away. Perhaps after all it would be better to talk to Tom. If he was coming any minute now, she could wait and let him take her home. The smell of the chicken pie was indeed tempting.

"Well, if you're sure Tom will be here for dinner—"

"I'm as sure of that as the sun will rise tomorrow. Any time he wasn't going to be here, he's sent me a note. And he knows the hour we eat in this house."

Nancy sat down in the spindle-backed rocker and felt the waves of warmth flow around her. Somewhere in the house a small striking clock rang out six hasty strokes. She wondered what her parents were doing. They must have missed her by now. They would be looking for her. Suddenly she did not want them to find her after all. Not until she had had time to talk to Tom.

A pounding on the kitchen door brought her to her feet in a tense impulse to escape.

"That'll be the *Centinel*," Mrs. Franklin said, showing no surprise at Nancy's sudden motion. "Do you just open the door for the boy, Miss Nancy? I can't let go of this dough this minute."

Nancy went to the door uneasily. But it was a small boy whom she did not know, thrusting a folded paper into her hands and crying cheerfully, "Election news! Mr. Jefferson is the new President!"

"Give him a cookie for good news on a cold night," Mrs. Franklin cried, nodding toward a cookie jar.

The boy scampered off, his mouth crammed with ginger cookie, to deliver his armful of papers.

The familiar smell of printer's ink hit Nancy suddenly. She sank down in the rocking chair again, struggling to keep from bursting into tears.

"Will you read me the news while I put this into the oven?" Mrs. Franklin asked, as if she did not notice the girl's distress.

Nancy stared at the headline through brimming tears

158

and gulped. She wondered which paper had won the contest to bring out the news first. Next she thought, Now that the paper is out, Nick will come—But he wouldn't know where she was. She put her head down and began to cry again.

Mrs. Franklin glanced over her shoulder and decided not to notice that her guest was distraught. She rolled out the piecrust, fitted it onto the dish of chicken and vegetables, slipped it into the oven, and began to clear up the table, with her back to Nancy.

The knocker on the front door shouted through the hall. Nancy jumped, mopped her eyes, and tried to compose herself. "Please!" she cried. "Don't tell anyone I'm here, Mrs. Franklin! Let me wait for Tom."

She looked around the kitchen for a place to hide. Her coat and goloshoes hung by the hearth. She snatched the coat and threw it around her, tucking the goloshoes out of sight in a nearby cupboard.

"Miss Nancy's folks are all upset," she heard clearly. That was Samson, coming down the hall with Mrs. Franklin. Nancy opened the first door she saw and found herself in a pantry off the kitchen. Closing the door silently, she huddled herself together in her coat, trying to keep from shivering and to hear what was going on outside.

"But, Samson, where is Mr. Carey?" Mrs. Franklin was asking as they came into the kitchen. "I've been waiting for him all this time for dinner."

"He told me to get back here, tell you he can't eat here tonight," Samson said. "He's having dinner with a friend because of election."

Nancy's heart sank. How long could she wait in this house without being discovered? Evidently Mrs. Franklin had not told Samson she was here. Hope revived again.

"Why would Miss Nancy run away from home?" Mrs.

159

Franklin's voice sounded strained, as if she wondered where Nancy might be.

"I ask Clio," Samson said. "She say she have no idea. But she say too Miss Nancy ain't much interested in getting married to Mr. Tucker in two weeks."

Nancy was torn between outrage at the idea of her affairs being discussed between Clio and Samson and then between Samson and Mrs. Franklin, and her curiosity about Samson's own feelings. If she could trust him not to betray her, even to Clio—

"She say Miss Nancy don't talk much. But Clio can tell she ain't happy. She tole me that likely Miss Nancy would go to Mr. Tom."

"I see," Mrs. Franklin said. "If she comes here, I can take care of her all right. Would Clio tell anyone else Miss Nancy might be here?"

Samson chuckled, a soft, comforting sound of sympathy that Nancy found more reassuring than any other tone she had heard that day.

"Clio just tell me things like that," he said. "For the others she just as worried as they is, and know as less—"

Mrs. Franklin bustled about the kitchen. It sounded as if she was laying out supper for Samson. Nancy wished she dared to join him. She was hungry again, and the chill in the tiny storeroom penetrated her very bones.

Mrs. Franklin said, "When does Mr. Tom expect to come back, Samson? I think he should come early tonight. There's important business afoot—"

"He worried about Miss Nancy too," Samson said, through a mouthful of chicken pie. "And so is Mr. Dana."

Nancy leaned closer to the door to hear every syllable.

"Oh, so he's spending the evening with Mr. Dana!" Mrs. Franklin sounded approving. "I'm going to send a note to Mr. Tom, Samson. Can you give it to him within the hour?"

"Yes, ma'am, I can do just that."

It seemed to Nancy as if that entire hour had passed before she heard Samson leaving the kitchen, and Mrs. Franklin's voice bidding him to hurry, not to get lost, not to let Mr. Tom wait too long. When the kitchen was quiet again, Nancy opened the door an inch to look out and flew back to the hearth to warm herself.

Chapter 17

"AND NOW, MISS, I think you'd better tell me why you were hiding just now." Mrs. Franklin spoke as if she had waited too long already to find out Nancy's reasons for waiting in her house.

Nancy stared into the fire. "I'm sorry, Mrs. Franklin. I'd rather not talk about it. I'll just wait for Tom, if you don't mind."

The clock struck seven. Mrs. Franklin filled a dish with chicken pie and slapped it on the trestle table. "You'd better eat some while you're here," she said. "Maybe you don't like to talk about family troubles, but I can't have a runaway daughter of one of our best families sitting in my kitchen while her parents are worrying out of their minds about her whereabouts. If someone else comes over from King George Street, I'll have to tell them you're here."

Nancy fell upon the chicken pie ravenously. It was as delicious as anything Ophelia had ever cooked.

Mrs. Franklin finished picking up the kitchen and sat down opposite Nancy with her own bowl of chicken pie. "Now you can tell me why I shouldn't send word to your folks," she told the girl. "There must be more reason for running away than I've heard yet. And you to be married within two weeks!"

Nancy looked at her empty dish, then over her shoulder at the fire in the hearth, then at Mrs. Franklin.

"I came here to see my brother, Mrs. Franklin, and if

you're going to send word about my being here, I'll leave and go somewhere else."

She rose and began to put her coat on again.

"Well!" Mrs. Franklin was outraged. "It's on your own head, then, Miss Carey. I'm sure I wouldn't know where else you could go tonight. And the snow blowing harder than ever!"

"If you'll excuse me," Nancy said, "I'll go and sit in Tom's room, Mrs. Franklin."

She swept out of the kitchen and into the little hall leading to the front of the house, where Tom's rooms were opposite the sitting room. The fire was burning low. One oil lamp lighted the gloom. She closed the door behind her, turned the bolt, dropped into the wing chair before the fire, and composed herself to wait. All night, if need be. If Mrs. Franklin tried to open the door, she'd have to break it down.

Nancy could see the snow blowing outside the windows and feel the cold east wind around the edges of the sash. She stared out at St. John's Street, fearing with each moment that her father's coach would come rolling up to the door.

The muffled sounds of hoofbeats and carriage wheels sounded down the street. She shrank away from the window into a dim corner, fearing that the light of the lamp could betray her presence. The carriage stopped before the house and hasty footsteps pounded up to the door.

Someone must be coming for her. She sat down before the fire again, holding her arms tightly folded against her and waiting.

The knocker sounded. Mrs. Franklin's shoes rattled across the polished floor. The click of the opening door was clear and ominous.

"Good evening, Mrs. Franklin." Tom's voice was friendly

and hurried. "I was sorry not to be here for dinner tonight. I had to celebrate this election with an old friend of mine!"

Nancy jumped from her chair and unbolted the door. Without opening it, she waited again.

"I'm sure glad to see you, Mr. Tom!" Mrs. Franklin sounded vastly relieved. "Your sister has been waiting for you, and she'll not say why she's not at home. She came in the snow, soaking wet and chilled to the bone, the poor child. I hope she'll not catch her death from this weather!"

"Where is she now?"

"She wanted to sit in your rooms, so I daresay she's there now."

The latch lifted, the door opened, and Tom strode in. Nancy flew to him. "Oh, Tom! I thought you were never coming!"

"I brought my friend with me, Nancy."

Behind Tom stood Nick Dana, and behind Nick, Nancy could see Mrs. Franklin standing in the doorway, goggling with intense curiosity.

"Thank you for looking after my sister, Mrs. Franklin." Tom turned to his landlady. "I'm sure she only wanted to talk to me about this election, since she would get no sympathy at home. I'll take care of her now."

He closed the door gently and bolted it in Mrs. Franklin's disappointed face. Nancy stood there, staring at Nick, frozen into stillness.

He came over to her and took her hand. "Nancy, my darling! I sent a note to you, and it never reached you."

"I went home," Tom told her, "as soon as the crier called the news, hoping perhaps Father and I might be friends again, now that the election was settled."

"Was he still angry about your Republicanism?"

"Nick's note had arrived, and Mother knew of its coming

and made Clio give it to her. So between your being missing and the note from Nick, they were all in an uproar. They wanted me to find you and bring you home at once."

"Are they looking for me? What can I do now?"

"I told them I'd call at the Lloyds and Miss Abigail's, without letting any scandal arise. They won't send out any other searchers until they hear from me—"

"What did the note say?" Nancy cried. "Oh, Tom! They were taking me to Carey's Fortune tomorrow morning to stay there until—" she gulped, "until the wedding day. I couldn't go back home."

Nick was holding her close. "The note said, would you go to the Federal City with me tomorrow?" He smiled wryly. "I knew no other way to reach you. And now your parents know what's afoot—"

She clung to him, all hurt forgotten. "Oh, Nick! When you rode right past me this afternoon, I didn't know what to think! I believed you didn't care after all!"

"Of all the idiotic notions!" Tom exploded. "Did you know nothing about the great contest between the *Centinel* and the *Gazette* to print this news first? Tom Green was racing Nick on another route! The *Centinel* got the news first by fifteen minutes. But if Nick had stopped to chat with you, he would have lost that race!"

Nancy stared from one to the other. It could not have mattered less to her which paper got the news first. And she knew that neither Tom nor Nick could have any understanding of the way she felt.

She tried to laugh, a choking effort that came out halfway between a giggle and a sob, and buried her face on Nick's chest.

Then she remembered the note and looked up, terrified. "But what about that note? Will they suspect you of helping? Will they send someone here?"

"They're much alarmed, Nancy. I must go back and reassure them tonight. The best thing will be for you to go with Nick tonight, and let me take a note of farewell home for you."

"Tonight?" She looked up, glowing. "Tom, you're going to let me elope with Nick?"

"There's no one I'd rather see you marry."

"I told the Smiths when I left them today that I was going to bring you back to the Federal City when I returned," Nick told her. "Mrs. Smith bade me—ordered me —to bring you straight to her. We can get a license tomorrow and be married in her home. The coach out there is hired to take us to Washington, as soon as you will leave with me."

She clasped her hands, distracted. "But—my clothes! Tom, how can I go away without clothes or linens?"

"Clio had packed your portmanteaus with all your clothes and linens, and Samson had already stowed them in the carriage for Carey's Fortune tomorrow. Nick and I managed to transfer everything to this coach before we came here."

She looked from her brother to Nick. "Of course I'll go with you tonight, darling! I could not believe it would ever happen!"

He swept her into his arms and kissed her longingly.

"Shouldn't Tom go with us? To stand up with me?"

Tom shook his head. "Mr. and Mrs. Smith will be your wedding party, and you could not wish for better. I'll go home to soothe our parents."

She was dazed with happiness, and Nick kissed her again.

"And now I think you two should be on your way," Tom said warningly. "There's nothing to wait for—" The clock chimed nine. "You should be in the Federal City soon after midnight."

166

"The whole town will be celebrating the election." Nick said. "The Smiths will be waiting for us."

Tom ran out to the kitchen to collect Nancy's coat and goloshoes.

"Mrs. Franklin is very romantic," he said, handing the wraps to Nancy. "I told her we were going to take you away now, and she says, 'I hope your sister will be very happy, Mr. Tom!'"

Nancy was scribbling a note for her brother to take to her parents. Then she ran down the hall to bid farewell to Mrs. Franklin, who was sitting by her warm hearth, knitting and rocking.

"You don't need to worry about me anymore," Nancy said, beaming. "My brother is taking care of everything."

"And I'll wager that nice-looking Mr. Dana is taking care of a few things himself," Mrs. Franklin said, with a sly little grin.

Nancy laughed aloud and ran back to Tom's room, where she wrapped up in her warm coat and boots, picked up her reticule, and tucked her hands into her muff. I'm all ready, Tom."

Suddenly she was shy about asking Nick if he was ready. But he linked Nancy's arm firmly in his own and pulled her toward the window to look out. "The snow is clearing," he showed her. "There will be a bright moon before long. It must be a good omen, Nancy, my love."

Tom was opening the door to the hall, ushering them out of the house to the coach standing at the curb, its driver patiently huddled under wraps and blankets for the long ride to Washington. Nancy glanced at the luggage carriers. They did indeed hold her portmanteaus. It was satisfying that all those linens she had spent months hemming were going with her for Nick's home. The horses snuffled and stamped in the cold, and she feared again that some alarm might be raised.

Tom opened the carriage door. Nick helped her up the step and followed her into the carriage. Tom poked his head in and reached in to shake hands with Nick.

"Take care of her, Nick!" he said with a wide grin. "Happy days to both of you!"

He shut the door and stood back while the coachman slapped the reins. The horses began moving up St. John's Street, to turn around Church Circle into West Street, the road to Washington.

Nancy looked back through the window to see Tom one more time, but the night was too dark, and he was gone. She sank back in Nick's arms, excited beyond measure, and frightened. She was carrying all the rest of her life in her hands, in this dark carriage rattling through black streets toward a city she had never seen.

Nick felt her shaking, and he held her close.

"It's going to be a great adventure, Nancy. All of it. All of our lives."

Better the unknown with Nick, she thought, than the well-known life with Roger she had run away from. She thought of Peggy Mason again. Now she knew how Peggy had felt.

She laughed aloud, and Nick kissed her. "Why so gay, sweetheart?"

"I was thinking," she told him demurely, "that I wouldn't object to riding all the way to Marietta in the Ohio country with you, Nick!"

"Not tonight," he told her. "But who knows how far we'll go one day?"

A Note from the Author

Annapolis today is still a colonial town with the old brick paving, most of the original street names, and many fine old houses. Most of the houses before the Revolutionary War were built by William Buckland, and of these the "Hammond House" is today considered the handsomest example. Buckland did the finely carved woodwork, and the building of the house took so long that Matthias' affianced bride eloped with another before it was finished.

The town is still the state capital, and the Maryland Assembly meets today in the old State House, built in 1779, where the Continental Congress accepted Washington's resignation from the army.

Mary Lloyd's family were old-time residents of Annapolis. She married Francis Scott Key in 1802, after a courtship that began when she was thirteen and he was a young student at St. John's College. He became a highly successful lawyer in Washington, D.C., and is most famous for writing "The Star-spangled Banner" in 1812.

Betsy Patterson's story has been told many times—she married Jérôme Bonaparte, the brother of Napoleon Bonaparte. The marriage ended in tragedy, when Napoleon refused to recognize her as part of his family.

Samuel Harrison Smith was a Republican journalist in Philadelphia when Thomas Jefferson invited him to establish a paper in Washington to speak for his expected administration. This offer enabled Samuel Smith to marry Margaret Bayard, of the Federalist Bayards, after an engagement prolonged until he could support her. Margaret Bayard Smith kept a journal of their life in Washington that is now an important record of the life of that day.

Biography of Anne Emery

Anne Emery was born Anne Eleanor McGuigan in Fargo, North Dakota. She has lived in Evanston, Illinois, since she was nine years old and there attended Evanston Township High School and took a B.A. degree at Northwestern University.

Following her graduation, her father, a professor of pharmacology and therapeutics at the University of Illinois, took the family abroad for a year, where they visited his birthplace in northern Ireland and toured the British Isles, France, Switzerland, and Italy. She spent nine months studying at the University of Grenoble in France.

On her return, Anne McGuigan taught in the Evanston schools, four years in the seventh and eighth grades, at Haven Intermediate School, and, after her marriage in 1933 to John D. Emery, six more years in the fourth and fifth grades at Orrington School.

Then she retired from teaching to keep house and take care of her family. There are five Emery children: Mary, Kate, Joan, Robert, and Martha.

ELIZABETHAN COMMENTARY

ELIZABETHAN
COMMENTARY

By
HILAIRE BELLOC

HASKELL HOUSE PUBLISHERS Lᴛᴅ.
Publishers of Scarce Scholarly Books
NEW YORK, N. Y. 10012
1967

First Published 1942

HASKELL HOUSE PUBLISHERS Ltd.
Publishers of Scarce Scholarly Books
280 LAFAYETTE STREET
NEW YORK. N. Y. 10012

Library of Congress Catalog Card Number: 67-31526

Haskell House Catalogue Item # 707

Copyright 1942

Printed in the United States of America

CONTENTS

GENERATION

A HUMAN BEING is compact of a material body and, animating that body, some vital principle which many still call its " soul."

This inhabiting " soul " not only animates the body with life but thinks, feels and reasons. The one reacts continually on the other and the resultant of these motions is the personality of the individual.

In studying such personality (or character) we must begin with the body because it is the more ascertainable : a man may dispute the reality of a soul animating the body, but no one can be so sceptical as to deny the reality of the body ; moreover it may be debated how far conscious or unconscious mood can affect the body, but there can be no doubt of the truth that bodily conditions do affect thought and mood. There is no doubt (for instance) that the bodily condition called " sleep " lessens or deflects our moods.

It is well, therefore, in studying a Personality, to consider the body first. What was Elizabeth Tudor physically when she entered upon active life, in the first stage of maturity and onwards ?

There are two things certainly known on this, first that she was sexually abnormal, second that we have today no sufficient full and definite evidence upon the *exact* physical conditions of her abnormality. Clearly she would never bear children ; but that might be a temporary accident or a natural sterility. In her case we can judge her oddness only by certain accompaniments thereto. Other causes of these effects remain unknown. They have remained so far, and will probably always remain, one of the best kept secrets in history. We can consult—and conjecture from— heredity. But of direct evidence upon more than one particular malformation none has been preserved.

She was born in the night of the 6th to 7th of September, 1533. Her father was undoubtedly the diseased, violent and unstable Henry Tudor, Henry VIII. Her mother was (even more undoubtedly) Anne Bullen, a well-born woman about the court who had captured Henry and got him away from the admirable—but now outworn wife of his youth, Katharine, daughter of the great Royal House of Aragon. Upon the little girl's health or ailments in the first dozen years of her life we have little. She was presumably, therefore, until puberty, much the same in constitution as other children of her age. But with her fourteenth year fell an accident which was to have a permanent effect upon her temperament and to deflect the whole of her life. She was mixed up in a precocious and low intrigue with her base uncle, her father's brother-in-law,* Thomas Seymour.

Who he was, what power he had to pursue his unpleasant courses with his niece, we shall see when we come to speak of their relationships. The important points in connection with this despicable affair are two : one certain, the other debatable. *First*, the intrigue was probably never consummated. What Victorian ladies called " the worst " never seems to have happened. We know pretty certainly that such was almost certainly impossible in any case ; but the essential thing to note is that it did not, so far as we know, take place. Elizabeth's claim to be technically *intacta* (which she advertised so loudly all her life thenceforth) was verbally true.

So much is reasonable history. But the second point is far more important to a judgment of her inward nature. Was the responsibility in this matter hers or his ? Did Seymour or Elizabeth begin the intrigue ?

On the whole we must conclude that the responsibility lay more with Seymour than with his much-too-precocious

---

* Brother-in-law by yet *another* marriage. Henry never wearied of experiments. He was what is called today " temperamental."

niece, but that he would not have approached her had he not found in her dispositions agreeable to his plans. The story in its broadest outline is simple enough.

The huge and hopelessly diseased body of Henry Tudor, Elizabeth's father, breathed its last breath in the night between the 27th and 28th of January, 1547. Even as he died he whispered, " All is lost."

He was in such a condition that his corrupted carcase burst before burial. In his last three-and-a-half years he had had for a half wife, half nurse, one Catherine Parr, a woman of good birth, no longer young, twice widowed and somewhat contemptuous of the age-long universal, yet still national, religion to which Henry himself was so deeply attached. Henry had no doubt on the main test doctrines —particularly on the Sacrament of the Altar. He was even passionately attached to them : insisting on them. All he repudiated (for the sake of Anne Bullen) was the Supremacy of the Roman See. But that Supremacy was (and remains) the test of Unity. When Henry Tudor pulled out that rivet for a caprice, the machine of unity broke down, as it was bound to do. Catherine Parr knew nothing of deep discussions. She was attracted by what was fashionable ; and what was fashionable, at that moment, was speculative Renaissance ideas, whence later sprang the full Reformation and the disruption of Europe. Catherine Parr even found it amusing to tease and exasperate Henry on the new gospellers. Indeed, her disputes with him on this matter at one moment imperilled her life. It would have been very complete if he had put her to death as he had put to death two other former wives who had found the temptation to make a fool of him irresistible.

Hardly was Henry dead when this woman Parr married as a *third* husband a former paramour of hers—and he was that very uncle of Elizabeth's, Thomas Seymour, whose adventures we shall later have to follow !

Thomas Seymour was of good birth also, and probably

approaching the age of forty—thirty-eight or thirty-nine years old, certainly at least thirty-seven—when Henry VIII (who had married Seymour's sister Jane as his third Queen) died. On the death of his brother-in-law, King Henry, Edward Seymour, the elder brother of Thomas, had so successfully benefited and cozened his fellows in the Government that he had made himself the active head of the state, whilst his sickly little nephew Edward VI, a child, was nominally King. Thomas Seymour did not aspire to oust his brother; he was content with the second place and the great income which he—the younger (second) son of a Somerset squire—now enjoyed. He was Admiral of England, a post which he had given himself and which was full of immense and continual perquisites and patronage. Yet his brother feared him as a rival in the wild confusion of the time, and watched him jealously. That brother had good cause to be jealous, for Thomas had already considered his chances with the young Princess Elizabeth, the precocious heiress to the throne. Though the husband of the Queen Dowager, he had in some confused way considered the getting hold of his young niece by marriage—the next heiress to the throne after her elder sister Mary.

It is hardly tenable that he contemplated an ultimate marriage with that young girl Elizabeth Tudor. He was later accused of poisoning Catherine Parr, but the accusation was unsupported by any evidence save the obvious convenience to him of getting rid of her. A man does not marry a Queen Dowager with the immediate intention of murdering her. It is most probable that his erotic and violent temperament was attracted to Elizabeth's person. And here we return to the original doubt : whose was the initiative in this early affair between young Elizabeth and Thomas Seymour ?

On the face of it, when a man in the late thirties compromises a very young girl, not only the blame will fall on him but the presumption must be that from him came the origin of the whole scandal. Moreover, Thomas Seymour was an utterly unscrupulous fellow, capable of anything in the way of base intrigue. It was further vastly to his advantage to establish a close bond between himself and an eventual heiress to the throne. Young Edward's was clearly a poor life and anything might happen. We may take it, then, that Thomas Seymour was the maker of the situation.

On the other hand, that situation could never have arisen between him and a girl of more reputable manners. Elizabeth Tudor was exceedingly approachable even at so early an age and we must remember her environment. She had been living from childhood in a pigsty of a court surrounded by every sort of turpitude, lewdness and quarrel. The woman, Catherine Parr, responsible for her education, made assignations with a former lover, letting him in herself secretly by the back door and letting him out before it was light of a winter morning, and this woman Catherine Parr, widow of Henry VIII, the girl's father, who was doing all this, who was the person deputed to keep the girl under her eye, was carrying on so very soon after Henry's death that contemporaries feared lest, if there were a child born of such clandestine union, royal blood would be claimed for it and the paternity ascribed to Henry himself, the King just dead.

Elizabeth received letters in which her lover poked fun with the utmost licence of speech at such physical attractions (rather of form than of feature) which she offered, and received from Thomas the doubtful compliment of jocular assault in connection with these charms.

A modern study of the girl's character has called these goings on "romps." It is certainly one name for them! But romps carried to such lengths would have appalled any decent household in England. Elizabeth admitted Thomas to her bedroom ; and even the Queen Dowager, Thomas's wife, who certainly cannot be called squeamish, was made ill by the evidences of his cynical appetite. There was one notable occasion when she surprised him in the act of cuddling the Princess privately within her own house. The neglected wife was furious. She " wanted to bite him " (she said) for such viciousness. He would certainly have bitten back ; for he was not to be bullied.

In the midst of all this, Catherine Parr died in childbirth. It was the 7th of September, 1548, and the problem of Elizabeth's relations with Thomas Seymour suddenly became extremely grave. He was now free to marry and obviously would aim at marrying Elizabeth the Princess, his niece. The thing only needed a dispensation and Cranmer was there to provide it, since the authority of the Roman See in such matters had been abolished in England. Even had that authority still stood, dispensations were not difficult to come by, granted sufficient funds.

Edward, the elder Seymour, who had made himself ruler of England, was now more terrified than ever that his brother Thomas would supplant him. Edward Seymour had been away in Scotland on a military expedition when Thomas made his Parr marriage and the peril of her being followed by the Princess Elizabeth had appeared. Edward Seymour had won his battle against the Scotch on the 10th of September, 1547. Within a very few days he must have had news from the South. He came pelting back, covering the 400 miles in well under three weeks. Later, Thomas began intriguing with the young child who was momentarily King, Edward VI ; and now—with the turn of the year 1549—there was acute danger of Thomas Seymour replacing his brother. That brother had him arrested. Specifically charged with plotting to marry the girl Elizabeth with whom he had tampered, " one of his Majesty's sisters, second in heir after his Majesty," with succession possible to her.

The Royal Council—that is the acting Government— and in particular, Edward Seymour its chief, drew up a bill of Attainder against Brother Thomas. (Under Attainder any man could be put to death without a trial) and so was Thomas Seymour beheaded on the 20th of March, 1549, regretted by none—save Elizabeth Tudor.

He had been her first lover—if lover be not too fine a term for such a lecher. She was awfully affected by his violent death coming upon so intense an experience as hers and remaining as a memory so bitter. There followed an illness of a grave sort as might have been expected. Not only was the man who had entered her life violently killed by the axe of the executioner, but his shocking public death had come horribly upon her own public disgrace. The whole story of his attack—and her acquiescence—was now public talk. She was put to open shame. It had been said (falsely) that she was with child. She was at pains to deny the accusation—in detail. The thing had been so widely noised abroad that she asked for an official refutation of it to be sent out everywhere (just before Thomas Seymour was beheaded).

The responsible woman in all this was Elizabeth's governess, the woman Ashley. It is upon her evidence and that of others, most reluctantly dragged out of them, that we know the details and when the Ashley and other confessions (including her own) were read out to her she was much abashed and half breathless—but she carried on and held fast. Those who admire tenacity more than integrity will admire her tenacity.

The Ashley woman was dismissed. Lady Tyrwhit was put in her place as governess, Elizabeth in disgrace and apart under the Royal roof of Hatfield ; and so the first of her affairs ended : in her sixteenth year.

* * * * *

The scandal and shame prostrated Elizabeth. She fell very ill. The illness recurred on and off for three years— 1548 to 1552.

Before we examine it we must deal with this strange woman's descent and inheritance, which is some considerable supplement to our evidence on her physical condition during these first years of womanhood. Let us then consider Elizabeth Tudor's physical descent.

II

THE TUDORS

PHYSICAL descent and inheritance are, in one way, more easily traced in the case of royalties than in any other. The unions of the parents are planned and are advertised widely. Not only the parents, but the grandparents and great-grandparents are fully known (as a rule) and their antecedents and special personal traits are fully recorded. We have not only written matter—often in profusion—but portraits and busts. If lineage were all the formation of Princes and Princesses they should be more thoroughly known in history than any other humans.

Now lineage is not all—far from it ! Even where we are quite sure of the generations without having to allow for chance admixture from random amours, we have to allow for what the breeders of animals call " sports " and " throwbacks." The product of a union between A and B may be surprisingly unlike either parent whether from some freak or accident (a " sport ") or may suddenly, unexpectedly, reproduce the nature of some more or less remote progenitor (a " throwback "). Still more confusing is the incalculable element of personality affecting progeny through the combined action of three forces : of the will, of memory, and environment.

The nineteenth century was wedded firmly to calculable causes and liked to have them material—so as to feel them exempt from the disturbance of organic complexity. It loved to deceive itself by simplification and to deal with the mysterious tangle of Life, as though it were a single mechanical process. Today we are rightly contemptuous of that short cut, we are awake to mixed processes in the case of living beings and especially of humans. Still the determinations of physical characters by generation is our main standby in judging cause and effect in human descent,

9

so we must give it the first place in judging the origin of a man or woman.

Elizabeth Tudor's father was certainly Henry Tudor, Henry VIII, who begat her in his forty-second year, late in 1532. Her mother was, as certainly, Anne Bullen, a Howard on the mother's side.

Anne Bullen's father came of prosperous London merchants, whose wealth permitted them to marry into the great families, and Anne's mother was the daughter of the Duke of Norfolk. It was this connection that counted most in her descent : we must always think of Anne as a Howard rather than as a Bullen in the estimation of her contemporaries.

This Anne Bullen, Elizabeth's mother, was a woman of *probably* nineteen when she came back to England from the French court where she had been brought up. She *may* have been much younger and have come over just before she was of marriageable age. But all that followed makes the earlier date for her birth (1502) the more probable. We may fairly conjecture, then, that she was already well mature, as age counted in those days, and too long unmarried at the essential date, 18th of May, 1525.

Henry VIII was captured by Anne. He was attracted to her physical type. He had at one moment taken her elder sister for a mistress (and married her off to another after he had lost interest in her company). He would have done the same by Anne. But Anne was a determined schemer : she refused him satisfaction and he naturally grew the more inflamed by her resistance, as she had calculated he should. He became completely infatuated. She kept him " on a string " (as the phrase goes) for years. Her price was that he should get rid of Katharine of Aragon, his true and faithful wife. Anne was determined to be Queen.

Katharine had now (1525) long ceased to bear children. What is more important her husband, Henry the King, was by this time already rotten with syphilis. He had caught it (we know not precisely when or how) years before. As a result, the children of his unfortunate first wife, Katharine, daughter of Ferdinand, King of Aragon, and Isabella, Queen of Castille (the King and Queen of the new united Spain), were either stillborn or died in babyhood, one after the other. By 1525 only one survived—to inherit wretched health all her life.

This one surviving child was the Princess Mary, a little girl not ten years old in this critical year 1525 when her father, King Henry, began his affair with Anne Bullen—or rather when Anne Bullen began *her* affair with *him*. Mary Tudor, therefore, was adolescent and most sensitive to all formative influences just in the years of her father's original main catastrophe, his capture by the woman who was to be the mother of Elizabeth.

The year when Mary Tudor passed from eleven to twelve years old was that in which her father first openly spoke of divorcing her mother. Anne Bullen pursued her campaign for making sure of the King during six long years. In 1525 Henry VIII was entering a phase of life which was, for those of his epoch and station, middle age. He was thirty-four. He had, of course, full licence such as the Princes of the Renaissance suffered or enjoyed and one consequence of such licence was the horrible venereal malady which devastated not only his own life but those of his children. Henry's physical disaster was a general accident befalling many princes in the early sixteenth century. The disease was then new and as ill-understood as it was, in these its early stages, virulent. No precautions were taken against it. It was nursed carelessly or not at all and the King of England was its chief victim.

By the time Anne felt herself secure enough to gratify her lover, Mary was a woman of seventeen. She was eighteen when the local and irregular Declaration of Nullity between her father and mother was pronounced by Cranmer (who came to Henry through the Bullen connection).

B

Cranmer had not, by the fixed ideas of the time, any right to give a decision against Henry's legitimate marriage with Katharine of Aragon. Such a decision would lie within the papal court. No one believed that Henry and Katharine had ceased to be man and wife merely because a weak cleric, who was notoriously a creature of the King's mistress, had said so. Through all those fearful months during which Mary Tudor was bullied and harried into repudiating her loyalty to that Catholic Unity of which her lineage was so proud, all Mary Tudor's agony was passed—in the first years of her womanhood !

Meanwhile her little half-sister Elizabeth grew up as a child in that moral chaos. Little Elizabeth had heard—without understanding it (when she was not yet three years old)—of her mother's violent death. Seeing immediately after, and only half understanding, stepmothers whom, in her seclusion she hardly knew, Elizabeth was a young companion in adolescence to the last of her father's wives —Catherine Parr—who maintained a most ineffective guardianship over her until her critical thirteenth year when her father died. That guardianship abruptly ended in the Seymour scandal.

From her father, Henry, Elizabeth Tudor seems to have inherited certain characteristics apart from the awful legacy of this loathsome disease. She suffered continually, like Henry, from a running ulcer in the leg. It was odourless and therefore the less repulsive, but it lowered her self-esteem. From her father, Henry VIII, Elizabeth inherited her capricious and violent angers, especially aroused in brief passionate protests against restraint, her singular incapacity for affection, and her taste for erudition (in which she excelled him). From her mother (of whom we know little) Elizabeth at least got her capacity for intrigue—not amorous intrigue, I mean, but peering into one character after another and playing on each in turn. What she did *not* get from her mother (that we know of) was her instinctive dependence upon guidance, the choice of it, and her certitude in that choice.

Henry VIII, her father, had always been ruled by some firmer and more balanced character than his own. At first, and for the few good years he enjoyed, he had been guided by his admirable wife, Katharine of Aragon, a Fleming in all her main physical strain, a true daughter of the Burgundian heritage. Then came the mastery of Wolsey over Henry, next the contemptuous despotism over him of Anne Bullen. Towards the end of Henry's life the Seymours did what they willed with the invalid.

Henry, then, was always ruled : but Elizabeth was *not* ruled. She accepted and used any condition necessary to the retention of that without which she would have been at once doomed—to wit, the crown which had so tortuously reached her.

She suffered from the Tudor physical heritage—and here let that physical heritage be examined.

The origin of the Tudors is comic and instructive.

Owen Tydder (Anglicised to " Tudor ") had been an upper servant who flourished (" flourished " is the right word, for he did indeed flourish !) during the sad decline of the great Plantagenet line. These high lords, the Plantagenets (" The men of the Broom Plant " which they stuck in their helmets as a sign in battle to show who they were), had been the ancient Lords of Anjou in the old days when that province of the French monarchy had been a virtually independent realm like Normandy. When William the Conqueror's line died out, in an heiress, Matilda (less than a century after Hastings), this Matilda married, being then a widow of the Emperor (barely sixty years after the Norman conquest), Geoffrey the Lord of Anjou. *Their* son, *her* son, inherited from her the crown of her grandfather, William the Conqueror, King of England, hence it is that the Plantagenets are the great family of our monarchy throughout the high creative Middle Ages. Matilda married

Anjou in 1128. This son of Matilda's, Henry, was, through his mother, by descent from the Conqueror, King of England. He inherited in the full tide of youth, at the age of twenty-three, not only all the Norman lordship (Normandy and Maine) but all Anjou and Poitou, etc., as well. He married the last heiress of Aquitaine and so held half of what now is France south of the Loire.

The Plantagenet name and the glory of it shine over the French and English Middle Ages from the high Middle Ages at the beginnings of the great reigns, till the approach of the great change at the end of them. All those three hundred years, from the twelfth century to the fifteenth, the governing, directing will, from the Grampians to the Pyrenees, was French-speaking Plantagenet. The Plantagenets fixed the development of chivalry (and its bastard offshoot, heraldry) for all these centuries.

So far so good. But how came the thin trickle of Plantagenet blood and glory into the Tudor (or rather " Tydder ") stream ?

It came thus : Owen Tudor, a steward or bailiff of the Bishop of Bangor, had the good luck, as a wandering soldier of fortune, to attract a very loose woman, not quite the mistress of herself (though willing to be the mistress of others), Katharine, the widow of Henry V of England.

This Katharine was a Valois, the sister of that gravely deficient, indeed mad, King of France, Charles V. Henry V had married this Katharine of Valois in order to claim the French throne. The true King of France, Charles VII, was her son by her first husband, the former King of France, but to secure her position as Queen of France and England, this impossible woman said that her son by her first husband was a bastard, and that her husband, the recently dead King of France, the insane Charles VI, had not been the young man's true father. This impossible Katharine of France, widow of Henry V, the Plantagenet victor of Agincourt, being left a widow on the death of that narrow-faced soldierly man, took to herself a lover. This lover was the robust gallant Owen Tudor—the son of the Welsh bailiff—a soldier of fortune. But though he was an adventurer he had the Welsh sense of lineage and preserved the memory of his own family.

There is no proof that the very loose widow of the French King and of Henry V was ever married to Owen Tudor, the bailiff. But they certainly had two sons, Edmund and Jaspar by name, who were playmates with and companions to Henry VI, that amiable half-wit child of Katharine by her marriage with the Plantagenet Henry V. The boys grew up together and this companionship made the fortune of the more robust little half-brother Henry VI, the last Lancastrian Plantagenet. There was no doubt which of the lads would dominate the other, seeing of what blood each was on the father's side ; Edmund Tudor, in spite of the bad blood inherited from his Valois mother, was the master. He forged ahead. His queer parentage notwithstanding, he established himself ; and his playmate and half-brother, Henry VI, made him Earl of Richmond.

All these last years of the Plantagenets were a hopeless tangle of battles in which Edmund Tudor, Owen's son, was killed, but remember that he had already got plenty of money from his hit-or-miss ancestry, and it is wealth, not lineage, that advances a man. This Edmund Tudor had been accepted as a sort of half-royalty, and himself married the last Plantagenet heiress—a true Plantagenet though of bastard descent—Margaret by name. The decaying blood of the great Plantagenet line did not spare her. She was a dwarf—perhaps from too early child-bearing. But anyhow, there she was, a Plantagenet and she had a son by Edmund Tudor.

This grandson of the original adventurer, Owen Tudor, was soon established in great wealth. Men of that kind always make hay while the sun shines and go furiously to work at that task. It was easily and rapidly accomplished, for he had under his power the woman whose revenues were those of a French Queen Dowager and an English Queen Dowager combined. Edmund Tydder could also boast that through his mother—whether married or not—he had the blood of the high French Royal Line, the Capetian, who were the model for monarchy to all Europe.

Edmund Tudor's son, Henry Tudor, inheriting from his father the Earldom of Richmond, was the one male upon whom centred every hope of restoring a united English monarchy after all these murderous exploits between warring factions. He, the young Earl of Richmond, the son of the Plantagenet dwarf woman, was himself poor in physique with rotten teeth and a bad skin. But he had a strong will. He determined to fight a last battle for his claim to the English crown. He came over from France to Wales with an army of French soldiers and recruited a mass of Welshmen after landing. The Stanleys, with an English faction, also joined him. The last Plantagenet, Richard III, met the invaders on Bosworth Field in 1485, was defeated and killed.

This oddly bred Tudor batch lasted just over one hundred years—from 1485 to 1603—Henry of Richmond himself (Henry VII), his son Henry VIII, and his three grand-children : Edward, Mary, Elizabeth, in their order of reaching the throne. When Elizabeth Tudor died in 1603, the male line of the upper servant, steward and adventurer, Owen " Tydder," died out, but not without leaving a title to the most intensely revolutionary epoch in the English story—the Tudor epoch. For it was with the Tudors on the throne—ruling a now absolute monarchy—that England lost her ancestral religion and thereby became a new thing altogether. Later in the reign of the last Tudor, Elizabeth, what is, after religion, the most important factor in every society, its literary expression, produced a high and prodigious record. A new spring and new glories of

English literature arose, stamped at its first mature growth with the name of William Shakespeare.

When the first Tudor—Owen—was being so astonishingly raised by Henry V's widow from the obscurity of a domestic dependent to being the secret paramour of a Queen Dowager, what we call today " The English Language " was being formed and had been already used, even in the higher part of society, for a lifetime. This new " English " had arisen through the action of The Black Death (which broke up the old form of education among the wealthy governing class in the middle of the fourteenth century, 1348–50). That class, until the Black Death falling in 1350–60, had been French-thinking and French-speaking ; but by the earthquake of the great plague all the civilisation of that governing class had been turned topsy-turvy. The learned higher classes, who were the main directors of such education, became more and more a mixture. Less and less of them spoke or thought in French. More and more of them spoke in loose dialects of what used to be called the " Anglo-Saxon " sort : Midland, Northern, etc.

The process of amalgamation took about a century. Chaucer's verse and prose stand as the principal early monument of the new tongue. His work belongs to the last thirty years of the fourteenth century, and certainly ends with 1400. Contemporary with that transition are the Wycliffite translations of the Scriptures from Latin into English. The other great contemporary figure, William of Wykeham, the founder of New College and of Winchester, thought and talked in French. But the new, more or less *standard*, English language descended from either influence and the material base of it, clipped Anglo-Saxon and French combined, became universal. Outside the court, at least, this new tongue which today we call " English " had become the common medium of the governing class. Well before the first Tudor King at

Bosworth in 1485 had seized the crown, what we call today " English " had become the only universal medium of those who directed and formed the nation. The men of the century before the English Reformation, which means 1350 to 1450—both those who opposed that religious revolution and those who fostered it, were alike of English speech.

When we say, as we can truly say, that what we call today *England* springs from the English Reformation, we can establish more securely the truth of that formula from the fact that English speech and English literature, though their first formation is prior to the religious revolution, come into full existence almost contemporaneously with Protestant England.

WARPED CHILDHOOD

IN the making of a human character we begin with the physical causes (because they come first in order of time and of calculability). There are two further influences which are of the highest importance (1) the action of the child's mind and will during what may be called " The Formative Years " and (2) surrounding circumstance. The formative years of character lie between the beginnings of clear observation to well beyond puberty. After this they gradually merge, sooner or later, according to the precocity or tardy development of the case, into matured form.

These " Formative Years " may be put, in the case of Elizabeth Tudor, in one brief flash, from just after the death of her father, when she was four months into her fourteenth year—to the execution of her would be seducer, Thomas Seymour in the moment when a political intrigue thrust her forward as the figurehead of a faction. The moment was the 17th of March, 1551, when Elizabeth was 17½ years old —a full grown woman. Some might stretch her formative period to the death of her brother, in 1553, but this would be to prolong the period unduly, for Elizabeth Tudor matured very early, she was fixed and hardly changed after that eighteenth year. However, little happened during the seclusion of her later teens to mould her character or to change it one way or the other. Elizabeth's affair with her uncle which did more to " form " her than any subsequent event, was over for good when that worthy was put to death by his own amiable brother on the 20th of March, 1549, and doubly concluded when that brother, who had made himself King for the moment, i.e. Protector as Duke of Somerset, was put to death in his turn by another of the gang—Dudley, who had made himself supreme and called himself Leicester. Then until her brother Edward's death two years later, Elizabeth is out of the picture.

The time in which little Elizabeth began to remark the world and to produce her own reactions upon that experience, may be said to date from the first stories she heard of her mother's tragedy, and therefore of her own tragic inheritance.

Anne Bullen, Elizabeth's mother, got into her tangle of suspected incest and the rest within a few months of her triumph in capturing Henry the King and ousting her benefactress and Queen, Katharine of Aragon.

When Anne's child was born, the King suffered a first shock. He had taken it for granted that the child would be a son. He had no rational ground for this, but that was Henry all over; a man of sudden violent passion, eager expectation and sharp disappointment which he couldn't endure, for he was a man hopelessly unstable. A son to prolong his ill-rooted dynasty was essential to him. Therefore he took such good luck for granted.

Another point which must never be forgotten about Henry is this : that all those who came into close contact with him—and particularly the women—took advantage of his instability. They might dread his inherited external powers, for a King's word was life in the England of that day : but that most subtle internal power which is exercised over the violent by the more restrained he could not escape. He knew it was being exercised. He felt it especially in the contempt he suffered from his women—and the knowledge of that contempt exasperated him.

Little Elizabeth was much too young to witness these scenes of wounded vanity, but the consequences of them lasted on into the years when she could notice things about her. She was a toddler of less than three when her father cut off her mother's head. But all England—and the court—talked about the enormous news, and no one talks more of such things than the servants of a household. By the time Elizabeth could think or feel at all she thought and felt in a surrounding air of bloodshed coupled with tragedy and despotic restriction. The allowance made for the Princesses was insufficient : neither of them was officially recognised as a Princess at all. Both were orphans. Henry's only legitimate daughter —Princess Mary—was officially bastardised because, in order to marry Anne Bullen, after she had lassooed him, the King had to annul his marriage with his real wife, Katharine of Aragon. That kind of thing was common enough in the dying Middle Ages. Marriage was indissoluble of course. Divorce in our sense of the term was unknown and was still inconceivable. But *annulment* was, with the really important, a matter of three conditions only : wealth, influence and consent. If you had wealth you could fee the service of ecclesiastical lawyers who fattened on the ill deeds of others, if you had influence and place your plea for annulment of marriage on this or that cause would be favourably heard, but the most potent of the three factors was then—as now with modern divorce—*consent*.

If a man and his wife who were in high position desired to have their marriage declared null and void, the first thing was to discover " an impediment " : i.e. some condition which would make the marriage null and void from the start. Now an impediment of *some* kind could always be discovered as a matter of course. There had been built up in the scheme of morals at the end of the Middle Ages a vast mass of " impediments " which rendered a marriage null and void *ab initio*. Thus cousinship even as remote as the third degree, was an impediment ; so was a previous contract ; or again (most fruitful of pleas) " lack of freedom of contract." The expense of steering a nullity case through the ecclesiastical courts was high—very high ; and such expense formed an effective barrier against the universal spread of a plague which had it become common would have threatened the very institution of marriage on which the family (and therefore the State) was built. Annulment of a marriage was therefore rare, but people above a certain degree of income and influence could always get their annulment of a marriage which both parties desired to end. Above a certain high level of income no marriage *need* stand—if both parties to it agreed to admit defects in the original contract.

Now most marriages which it was proposed to dissolve could certainly hope for such consent to annulment from the party concerned. They could be bribed into it or blackmailed or threatened into admitting annulment in the rare cases of not wanting a price or a motive for giving way.

Well, Katharine of Aragon had determined *not* to give way. She was the great daughter of what was, at the time, by far the highest family in Christendom. She had been a devoted and faithful wife for twenty years. At the moment of Anne Bullen's success Katharine's time for childbearing was past. It had been past for years already. All the more was Katharine's sense of justice outraged by Henry's extravagant caprice and folly. She was the more determined not to release her husband because he had been led into this attack upon her by an intriguing woman of her own court. Remember that she knew Henry as no one else knew him—and that her affection for him had not died though all the rest of his intimates were now disgusted with him.

This, Katharine's inflexible dignity, had been the obstacle that could not be overcome during all the years when Anne Bullen was leading Henry by the nose.

But by 1540 Katharine of Aragon, Henry's legitimate wife, was dead ; and shortly after Anne Bullen, Henry's sham wife, the mother of the tiny child Elizabeth Tudor, was dead also : killed by her husband in his fury against what he had been told of her infidelity and incest. Little Elizabeth was six years old and already had some childish graces about her when Catherine Howard, her cousin, became the new and fifth wife of Henry. That new step-mother was kind to the child for a moment : but little Elizabeth and her much older half-sister Mary were now in a sort of exile from their father. She did not even sufficiently see her brother, the little boy who was four years younger than herself, and whom (perhaps) in her way she loved a little.

Another influence formed Elizabeth in childhood, and continued all through her early life till she was twenty at least, and even beyond that : this was the intense scholarship of her rank and day ; a deep and accurate knowledge of the classical languages, Greek and Latin.

Elizabeth's student training had been very thorough, and after her disgrace following on Henry's death in early 1547, she had ample leisure for wide and regular reading until her scholarship grew firm indeed. That classical scholarship was Elizabeth's most permanent acquisition and she became at the same time, in her teens, familiar with the principal court languages of her day : notably French, the language in which her mother Anne Bullen had been brought up. Elizabeth was thus strongly instructed, and those chosen to teach her leaned, like so many leading scholars of the day towards the Reformers—but of that later. When Henry, Elizabeth's father died, she faced life alone save for the lady who managed her household, and managed her—and her household—ill.

So things went with Elizabeth, through a difficult child-hood, insufficiently companioned, insufficiently befriended, till she heard on that late January night of 1547 that her father was dead. In his will he had reinstated his two daughters Mary and Elizabeth—Royal authority it was, not the formality of Parliamentary registration that really counted in that day and decided the inheritance of the Crown. In his will Henry had not only recognised the royal rank of his two daughters, but also the order of their succession to the throne. After his little son, Edward,

Mary should succeed if Edward had no heir. If Mary had no heir, then, at her death, Elizabeth. He provided ample incomes and an ample dowry for each of these daughters— subject to their subservience to their brother and the Council.

So went he to his reward, dying on the 28th of January, 1547 ; and Elizabeth was entering her fourteenth year.

IV

THE EARLY CRISIS

WHEN Elizabeth Tudor was in her fifteenth year there took place an episode which profoundly affected the whole of her life. This was the affair with her worthless uncle, Thomas Seymour ; and it is essential to fix as far as possible the date of the business. We know that as early as February, 1547, only some few days after the death of Elizabeth's father, King Henry, it had occurred to Thomas Seymour that he might with luck obtain Elizabeth as bride. She was marriageable according to the ideas and social customs of those days, for she was certainly nubile in the legal sense of that word. She already had a separate establishment of her own with not less than 120 retainers of one kind or another under her roof—servants and the rest. . But being still so young there was set over her a woman whom we may call her governess in the less restricted sense of the word, that is, a married lady who should be responsible for the conduct of the girl and for the direction of her life and companionships. Such a woman had been for some time chosen, when Elizabeth was still younger, in the person of Catherine Ashley, who had reached the post through the influence of the Bullen family, with which her husband was connected. It is important to remember that connection because, though Elizabeth was remarked never to mention her mother's name, there is no doubt that her affections or at any rate her instinct made her cling to that mother's blood. That mother, Anne Bullen, had long disappeared at the moment when Elizabeth was entering womanhood, having been put to death, as were so many, by the unstable and passionate Henry.

Now when King Henry died he left behind him a widow

—that last of his six wives, of whom I have said that she was a sort of nurse for his premature and bloated old age. This widow was, of course, Catherine Parr. The elder Seymour, Edward, having made himself Protector of the kingdom and intrigued for himself a power equal for the moment to that of a king, the younger Seymour, Thomas, equally ambitious, not so fortunate, proposed some corresponding advantage for himself. Catherine Parr was already thirty-five years of age ; she had already been twice a widow before she caught Henry, having been wed at fifteen to Lord Borough and upon his death two years later, or shortly after that date, to the elderly Lord Latimer. It was shortly after Latimer's death that Henry married her, on the 12th of July, 1543, as his last and sixth wife.* Catherine Parr was naturally eager enough to marry after the constraint of those difficult last years as a sort of nurse to the King. She seems to have kept her marriage secret and the husband ready to hand was the late King's brother-in-law, Thomas Seymour. Edward Seymour, now the Protector with the title of Somerset, opposed the marriage after it had taken place without the knowledge of the Council ; but Thomas Seymour had his way, for he had worked upon poor little Edward, the nominal king, and Edward had actually pressed his step-mother to accept the suitor. That suitor had already got for himself the title of Lord Admiral. It meant something very different from what we mean by the word "Admiral" nowadays. It meant an office the holder of which had all manner of lucrative rights connected with the sea, though to hold that office one needed no knowledge of seafaring whatever, nor any practice of it. In England, as in France and elsewhere, this title of Admiral was sought for its revenue. For instance, amongst other lucrative items and probably the chief of them, the Admiral of the Day had the right to

---

* It is possible that the marriage took place somewhat earlier, even perhaps as early as May, 1543.

wreckage.* Now Thomas Seymour, thus married to Catherine Parr, was brought into immediate contact with Elizabeth Tudor, for that young woman had been put under the roof of Catherine Parr, as we have seen ; and Thomas Seymour, being what he was, at once attempted an intrigue with Elizabeth : his new wife caught him with Elizabeth in his arms. Here we have an initial date for the very important business that followed. The ensuing angry quarrel between Catherine Parr and Thomas Seymour belongs to Whit-week, 1548, in which year Whit Sunday fell on the 20th of May.

Meanwhile, Mrs. Ashley, probably bribed, was preparing to help forward the affair between Elizabeth and her uncle. What that man wanted was obviously not an immediate marriage, because that was impossible while Catherine Parr was still alive ; but a relationship such that he could later use it if an opportunity offered for marrying the Princess. It is not easy to unravel the confused motives of men like Thomas Seymour—vanity played a large part in him, ambition a part almost equally large and avarice certainly a large part again. He was keen on discovering the exact income which Elizabeth enjoyed and of which he might later be the master ; for Catherine Parr died in her belated childbearing and Thomas Seymour was free to marry. After the date of that death he began intriguing with Thomas Parry, who managed the financial affairs of Elizabeth. Edward Seymour had added to all the other revenues which the Lord Admiral had swept into his grasp something like £20,000 a year extra in modern money, but he had gone too far and he had become dangerous to everyone well before the death of his wife. Catherine Parr died on the 7th of September, 1548, Elizabeth being then just on fifteen. The Council took its precautions and almost with the opening of the next year, on the 16th of January, 1549, the

---

* What the post meant is best seen in the case of Richelieu, who made himself Admiral of France with the same perquisites in the following century.

elder brother, Edward, had the younger brother, Thomas, arrested. His trial for high treason and, therefore, his death were prepared. At the same time Mrs. Ashley and Parry, the steward, who managed the affairs of the Princess, were thrust into the same prison and Elizabeth herself was kept virtually a prisoner at Hatfield, with Robert Tyrwhit, as agent for the Council, to overlook all she did and to obtain all he could out of her by way of confession and admission.

And here appears for the first time in Elizabeth's life, and in most striking fashion, a talent or quality which she retained throughout the whole of her life. It was not so much a talent for dissimulation, although there was plenty of that, as a talent for conducting a retreat. The young thing by her wantonness had put herself into very grave peril indeed. He who had been working to capture her, Thomas Seymour, was marked down for death and Elizabeth's own fate seemed to point down the same road.

There followed that duel between the young woman and those who were watching her every step and eager for her every admission : a battle whence she emerged ultimately victorious. But she only obtained that success at the price of her reputation and the last shreds of decency. The drama is played out during the first month of the next year ; that is, immediately after the extravagances of the Seymour business.

What that business was we know in some at least of its details from the interrogation of Mrs. Ashley ; for her replies have remained.

THE INTERLUDE

WHEN these days were accomplished—these brief but tempestuous days—there followed a long and, to a close observer of English history, a strange interlude. It is the interlude between that business which, as I have said, stamped and determined the whole of Elizabeth's life, through the impress it made upon her inmost being during the essential and formative years, and the moment nearly ten years later when she was free, as crowned and accepted Queen, to act at large : not indeed upon the State, which she never wholly conducted, but upon the public and, in some degree, upon foreign relations—particularly with the then highly separate Scotch Monarchy.

Her journey through real life opened, as do so many sea voyages, with a very sharp tossing in the passage out of harbour, followed by an appreciable interval of comparative calm, followed again by violent emotion and distress ; to be succeeded in its turn by another lull. All her earlier womanhood was woven on this uncertain, irregular and occasionally violent pattern, yet throughout it all there was no real change in her after the early passage through the furnace which annealed her. Just as we cannot understand Elizabeth without appreciating to the full the intensity and consequent result on her character of the first brief Seymour episode, so we cannot understand her unless we also consider this second episode which I have called the Interlude.

The violent turmoil of the Thomas Seymour affair came to an end abruptly when her guilty governess, the Ashley woman, and her husband, who was almost certainly her accomplice, were dismissed by the Council ; or perhaps a better terminal date is the 16th of January, 1549, when the Admiral (as his title was) suffered sudden arrest on the charge of high treason ; or one might even say that a more complete and satisfying date was the 7th of the following February when Tyrwhit writes to the Council admitting that he could not drag any substantial evidence from the young woman, who was thenceforward (though not yet under lock and key) a prisoner. For the very last possible date no one can fix a day later than the 20th of March, when Thomas Seymour's head fell on the scaffold. This last is also a memorable date in the inner story of Elizabeth : the story of her soul. They came at once to tell her the news, in the hope that, shaken by it, she would say something new. But apparently all they got from her was that famous, quiet remark : " There has died a man with plenty of wit and little judgment."

Yet certain it is that the image of this man remained the dominant and permanent furniture of her mind. The ghastly, bleeding head of Thomas Seymour was always before her.

*　　*　　*　　*　　*

The unfortunate decaying body of poor young Edward ceased to live on the 6th of July, 1553, not before having attempted the transfer of the Crown from the House of Tudor to that of Grey, though one can hardly say that the initiative was his ; he was little more than a child and almost within the arms of death. Mary, his elder sister, had been given the throne by acclamation. She was the next in natural succession to her little brother, and at the moment idolised by the people of London, as indeed by the whole kingdom, except what was still a very small Calvinist minority, who had behind them, however, the organisation and obvious strong motives of those who had everywhere come into possession of the Abbey lands : that is, one might almost say, not only all the landed gentry of England, but hosts of their hangers-on and beneficiaries and purchasers at second, third or fourth hand, of the looted ecclesiastical endowments.

After the dangerous insurrection which had this very large vested interest behind it, and after Mary's disappointment in the expectation of a child and heir, that queen died on the 17th of November, 1558, as we have seen. And immediately after the perilous passage described in the preceding pages, Elizabeth was Queen. The interval, therefore, lasted nine years and ten months; or, if we reckon from the death of Thomas Seymour, nine years and eight months. We have seen how packed with incident was that brief time; but for the understanding of Elizabeth Tudor and of her inner story, the mark of that interlude was absence of action, restraint and a permanent practice of silence. Under the pressure of that self-imposed discipline, the new character of Elizabeth appears. She emerged from it a woman still young, though not very young by the standards of those days. There was no bloom of youth left upon her. Illness and unceasing anxiety had seen to her losing all that; and we can safely neglect all panegyric in that direction, even the observation of foreign envoys; for each panegyrist had an axe to grind. But she still had her hair, including her eyebrows, and she had already an aquiline profile, not yet very pronounced, which added strength to her countenance. Her glance was not without vivacity, still livelier the sharpness of her voice, when it was not lessened by her very numerous and often dangerously prolonged spells of illness.

So stood she at the entry of her reign.

Let us now follow the various incidents of what I have called " The Interlude " and see how they illustrate and also how they fashion the woman who was to be so famous.

*   *   *   *   *

The vicissitudes of that determinant moment, the ten years and less of Elizabeth's passage into early womanhood, are generally marked in our official histories by meaningless terms; and labels are attached to them without the reader of popular history being told what underlies the labels nor why the craft called England, just after it had been launched, swung thus violently from side to side.

We read that after Henry VIII's death, when his son, a little boy of ten, had been put upon the throne in Westminster Abbey (with his little legs dangling from the high seat thereof), a strong " Protestant " movement swept through England. It would really have been astonishing had that happened—but, of course, it did not happen. The nine or ten thousand rural communities, the few score of market-towns, the handful of larger boroughs which made up the English homesteads of that day—roughly a million— went on as they had always gone on ; and there was no reason why they should do otherwise. The intellectuals, especially the academic people whom the Renaissance had strongly affected, were contemptuous of the fatigued and false old habits of thought, especially of the legends and popular superstitions. Everybody who had paid dues to ecclesiastical landlords was glad with one-half of his mind that most of those landlords had been got rid of, but was still actively annoyed at having to pay the same dues to the new and mostly upstart men who had replaced them.

But when it came to the Mass, the core of the whole business ; to the sacramental system of which the Mass was the essential example ; to the general habit of mind which men had inherited from their immemorial ancestry, the momentum of that habit of mind would carry everything before it—or would have done so save for one overwhelming consideration—the rich had suddenly been made much richer by coming into a mass of new property which the Crown had filched from the Church and had rapidly dissipated among the squires and newer owners. One cannot insist upon this truth too much in the history of England. One cannot repeat it too often. This was the turning point ; this was the essential watershed in the whole business. The monasteries had decayed ; they had decayed obviously and physically. About half the old number of religious were enjoying the same rents as had been enjoyed by their so much more numerous predecessors. The widespread tangle of ecclesiastical endowment had been subject to pillage, which had already gone far and might go on piecemeal indefinitely. The moral vitality of that religious system whereby England had lived for centuries (though for the last three generations less and less profoundly) was sapped. The natural greed of the lesser local magnates to batten on the more and more defenceless body of clerical benefices had gathered great driving power : it had been nourished by initial success. *But there was no active and sufficient moral motive for any doctrinal change ;* such was not wanted by the mass of the people ; there was no reason why it should be wanted. They lolloped along as they had always lolloped along. They went to the parish church— and they were probably a fluctuating number, for the custom of subsidiary Masses had long been established and there had come as yet no effort to compel attendance—and heard as their ancestors had heard for centuries what a modern English poet has, not too politely, called, " the blessed muttering of the Mass."

The one active force at work and at work inevitably (when you consider the mind of man and its attitude towards money) was the colossal economic revolution. If one puts it by saying, as we have seen on a former page, the transference of one-fifth (it was probably more like one-third) of religious endowment to lay hands, one does not express the significance. Think what it meant in every parish of that agricultural England. This field, those fishing rights, the timber rights in that copse, the rents from those water meadows—by parcels all over the parish— were no longer paid to certain corporations, which had disappeared, but to new men or to older men with quite new wealth. Think what it would mean today in modern

England if by some revolution one-third of the stocks and
shares, of debentures, of government scrip, of pensions,
were suddenly to be transferred—with a promise of further
loot. That is what had happened and that is what lay behind
what our official history calls a swing to the right or to the
left—or what not. Further, that earthquake had not
dissipated the power of the rich ; it had enormously and
in a few years increased such power. For those who were
now enjoying the old rents and rights were not the community (of course), still less the average popular family.
They were the already enriched or the new rich ; what was
becoming a special class within the nation. Those who
represented the interests of that class (whereof the Cecils,
though they had not directly taken part in the loot, were
later the most prominent ; and whereof on Henry VIII's
death, the Seymours were the most outstanding, restricted
and prominent type) were inevitably the agitators in every
movement making for the religious revolution ; and still
more inevitably the captains and leaders of the march
towards a total change. Thus it was that the Seymour
brothers, the only *men* with a Royal connection about them,
the uncles of the little boy nominally enthroned, went bald-
headed for every innovation, however scandalous and
however insincere. The populace who were unorganised
and, therefore, almost powerless, did indeed arise. The
yokels, coming into their parish churches for the Sunday
Mass and hearing to their astonishment sundry vernacular
prayers in the place of it, were naturally angry enough.
They rose all over the place sporadically. Their clumsy
unconnected crowds were massacred and down they went.
The vested interests of the newly enriched gentry were
for the moment unchallenged ; and in that day when the
kingly office outweighed all others, the capture of the little
boy on the throne decided for the moment the religion of
England or rather the destruction of the religion of England.
But the thing was too enormous and too rapidly unnatural

to last ; for all the crushing economic power which lay behind it and the awful name of the Crown.

When little Edward died with his fingers rotting off at the joints and his whole unfortunate young body ruined through the inheritance of his father's corrupted blood, his elder sister Mary appeared, not only as a natural heiress to the throne but as the only certain legitimate claimant thereto : a real Tudor. But she was personally devoted to the ancient traditional religion of the English, and, on that account, all the new fortunes were ranged against her. They received heavy support from the Queen's decision to marry the heir to that widespread Spanish Monarchy which overshadowed all Europe and against which of Royal powers the French Crown alone stood in opposition. It is not true that the Queen's decision to marry Philip ruined her in public esteem because Philip was a foreigner ; though she would have been more solidly established had she married one of her English subjects, of whom Courtney, being of direct Royal descent, was the most obvious candidate. He was personally quite unfit and was impossible. But it is true that every drop in the cup (and the Spanish marriage was more than a drop, it was a dollop) brought it nearer to the brim and to overflowing.

The rebellion of a Kentish squire, leading great numbers of Kentish men who had, of course, the strong interests of the new fortunes behind them, was the mark of that revolutionary movement. The rebellion failed, though it nearly took London. It principally failed through the personal courage of Mary Tudor herself. She refused to fly or to yield ; and the Tudor challenge won.

There followed that chapter in the story of England which is the most generally emphasised and in the nature of things exaggerated ; but which is also in the nature of things very vivid, and also in the nature of things has permanently impressed the English mind after that mind had been captured much later by the new religion. For what followed was the famous Marian persecution of heresy. Drastic action by government was certainly necessary ; for the chief organised power of wealth was at issue with the government itself and would now support rebellion in any form, unless rebellion were finally crushed.

But what form should that action take ? I repeat and emphasise it again, for it is the key to our understanding of the whole position. The threat of social anarchy had two heads : a religious head and a political or social head. These two heads were not separate ; they grew from one intertwined common neck. The one head was political the other not exactly doctrinal, but at any rate anti-doctrinal, and both were making for the break-up of society as it then existed. The tendency to anarchy, which circumstance had thus rendered very real and exceedingly and immediately dangerous, might have been met on the doctrinal or on the political ground. Queen Mary's Council, the central organ of government, might have decided to prosecute individual rebels for treason or for heresy. Today the word treason still has a meaning because it is opposed to what men still worship : the nation. But the word heresy has none, because it is opposed to something the importance of which most men fail to understand : to wit, unity of religious doctrine as a necessary principle of a united state. For nowadays we all take it for granted that unity of devotion to the nation is essential but that unity of religious doctrine is unessential.

The Emperor, whose son Mary had married, advised that the repression of the anarchic movement should be made through the prosecution of treason. Rebellion was to be treated as treason. He advised *against* the policy of prosecuting the rebels for heresy. It was one of the wisest pieces of advice ever given by one government to another. It was rejected. The first prosecution and execution for heresy, in the movement that follows, was that of Hooper, the Bishop of Gloucester, an intense religious revolutionary, who had given it as his opinion that all Catholic priests should be drowned. The Council had decided to take this course at the parting of the roads. The influence of the Queen's husband was also on the other side. Philip's own confessor urged that opposite course. Unfortunately, the Council was strongly nationalist and this advice, with its savour of Spanish interference, determined them to prosecute the rebels for heresy. Hooper the Bishop had been burnt on the 9th of February, 1555 (Rogers, a devoted gospeller had already suffered). It is the burning of Hooper that really opens the story and that story goes on for much more than three years. It does not end till the death of the Queen in mid-November of 1558. By that time, nearly three hundred had suffered, much the greater part of them for heresy and all of them under the imputation thereof.

It is an old story, and hardly worth going over again at this time of day, that burning was the habitual punishment not only for rebellion against the general sanctities of one's fellow citizens, but for other crimes. Nothing can prevent its appearing to the modern mind as an atrocity. The mild and cultivated Evelyn, passing through Smithfield during his walks abroad, much more than a century later than this, casually noticed a woman being burnt at the stake for poisoning her husband and paid no more attention to it than we should pay to a man being taken off in the " black maria " to prison. It seemed to him quite normal. What the men and women of the time felt about the burnings, was not the cruelty of the procedure but the cause of it. Heresy was hated, just as treason was hated, by the mass of the people. But it was less and less vehemently hated because a central social certitude upon doctrine was wavering. We are seeing its last disappearance today, with what consequences we cannot foretell : but they will certainly be formidable.

It is a general rule in history that implacable official action against a minority, especially an unpopular minority, is successful in stamping out whatever innovation that minority has supported. Probably had Mary lived the policy of persecution would have succeeded. She did not live. Her expectation of a child was disappointed, though at one moment it had seemed well-founded. She had come to an age when further child-bearing was improbable. She died.

Meanwhile, Elizabeth, her half-sister, younger by seventeen and a half years, had gone successfully through one narrow strait after another, borne along the torrent of her early life, and had gone through each without shipwreck.

She had survived because she was the figurehead and symbol of the new preponderant financial power, created by the confiscation of the Abbey lands. Such a position was quite against her nature and contemptuously, against her somewhat indifferent will, she had lived and grown up since the death of her father Henry, from childhood to womanhood through a dozen most dangerous years, and had survived them because behind her was the vested interest of those who had acquired the Abbey lands ; for those vested interests Elizabeth stood. She was not their champion, she did not sympathise with them particularly ; the mass of stuff that has been written on that side from the moment of her accession to the present day, is historically false. If anything, she was irritated at having to play an ambiguous part, for it was not natural that the head of an ancient Christian kingdom should appear even as a figurehead for religious rebellion. But circumstance was too strong for her and the major force at work was the determination of the wealthier classes throughout the country to keep their rapidly acquired recent spoil.

The pace at which the change had gone ministered greatly to its success. The preliminary attack upon ecclesiastical property had been tentatively launched almost coincidently with Elizabeth's birth ; the major attack, ruining in rapid succession one great monastic house after another, had opened like an explosion while she was still a baby and the

whole thing was over before she was seven years old.
There followed the " mopping up," which always concludes
a victory of any kind. Minor endowments such as chantries
were captured and added to the store of the despoilers, but
the great monasteries, and with them the whole monastic
system of the English, had come to an end when Harold's
great foundation, Waltham Abbey, fell in mid-August, 1540.
Elizabeth reached her seventh birthday in the following
month. No attempt to destroy the ancient liturgy, which
all Englishmen took for granted was made, or could be
made with success while Henry VIII lived, but at his death
it was attempted violently and a new liturgy in English was
imposed. This astonishing innovation, thrusting a startling
change upon all national life and custom, had a difficult
struggle to survive during Elizabeth's teens.

When her brother was dying, the return of the old
national religion to the parish churches with the next reign
seemed only natural. It happened when Elizabeth was
twenty. It lasted till Mary's death and Elizabeth's accession
when she was twenty-five. A space of years not
much longer than the interval between our two great
modern European wars had seen the whole structure of
English religion centred in the Mass ruined, then precariously built up again, then ruined once more. At such
a rate did the thing proceed. In 1533 an England without
the great monasteries would have seemed impossible. Yet
there it was, apparent before men's eyes in the high summer
of 1540.

In 1540 an England without the Mass would have seemed
fantastic. Yet there it was present to all eyes before 1553.
Such earthquakes, society had never known before and was
never to know again. It is worthy of long historic medita-
tion that the overthrow, something which had seemed
eternal, could be witnessed in much less than half a generation ; and greed was the driving force : such is the invincible
attraction of wealth over the minds of men.

VI

ERUDITION

SO far, in considering the character of Elizabeth Tudor I have been mainly concerned with matters negative and detrimental, her irreligion, her absurd vanity, the escapade of her youth. Even that strong element of caution which marked the years before her accession may be counted against her on the moral side, for her motives were bad motives, understandable and excusable enough, but still base. She was fighting for her life, no doubt, and if any one of us were in her position he would probably have done what she did, even to the degree of playacting which made her put on the make-belief of puritanism, in spite of her contempt for all that emotional side of religion. She did indeed use good judgment in taking advice from those who knew best and particularly in carrying on the tradition of William Cecil. She would have been a fool had she done otherwise, and no one ever has or could accuse Elizabeth Tudor of being a fool. She had found ready to her hand one of the best political brains in history and she took every advantage of that good fortune. But there is no virtue in mere judgment. Indeed there is no virtue without sacrifice, and of desire for sacrifice Elizabeth never showed a trace.

But though there is nothing to admire morally there is something to admire in the way of tenacity, though that tenacity was not used in the service of the good. But there was as a counterweight to her evil qualities something which is not connected with right and wrong but something of very high value in one who is called upon to govern : I mean Erudition : classical learning and a knowledge of contemporary literature as well.

She was fortunate in the moment of her eclipse, for those nine years between the extravagances of her very early youth and her maturity, during her half-brother's reign and that of her elder half-sister Mary, may be called the peak of development in the English language. English had not indeed reached its fullness by the middle of the sixteenth century : but it was on the eve of reaching its fullness. The height of development in the English language, the moment of its formative period is undoubtedly the end of the sixteenth and the beginning of the seventeenth centuries. We use for the great moment the formula " Elizabethan " ; the use of that word has a political and a religious root, for that use is prompted by the instinct for making the most of everything in England opposed to the Catholic Church. No one will deny that the chief moment of the English language was that which produced the plays and sonnets attributed to William Shakespeare of Stratford-on-Avon, and all will equally admit as a matter of course that this famous interlude followed on a certain short but intense period of preparation for its advent. Marlowe is great enough, Heaven knows, and Marlowe was born after Elizabeth came to the throne. His *Tamburlaine* may have been written just before the Armada but did not appear until 1590 ; indeed, it has been well said that what we call the " Elizabethan " period and influence in the literature of this country should more properly be called " Jacobean." Both *Julius Cæsar* and *Hamlet* belong to the last moment of Elizabeth's life, but *King Lear* and all that followed it, including *The Tempest*, belong to the reign of James I. And William Shakespeare if he were the author of such things (as tradition and common sense compel us to believe),* did not die till the spring of 1616, when Elizabeth Tudor had been dead thirteen years.

---

* This judgment seems to me both accurate and sound. A very great poet may write a mass of inferior stuff and even be indifferent to his immediate fame, so that his reputation grows slowly and does not become the toppling thing it deserves to be till long after his death, but those people still alive who know what great verse is will agree with me I think that it is not usually produced by a committee or in partnership. However, we must remember that some few of the most famous half-lines were conjectures and emendations and that others were not printed until after William Shakespeare's death.

It is possible to suggest without blasphemy that the reputation crowning this great body of writing is uneven. It looks as though the man who wrote the plays, or most of the plays, was not avid for contemporary praise, though certainly the man who wrote the sonnets knew well that he had done immortal stuff. But to return to Elizabeth.

The range of her known erudition is remarkable rather than extraordinary. She was on a level with the young women of her rank and time. She had so completely mastered under able and continuous tuition the modern languages of her contemporaries that she could speak in them with perfect ease. She could speak with equal ease in Greek, and that indeed is something to be proud of. I know no one of whom the same could be said today, if only because no two scholars seem to be agreed upon how that classical tongue should be pronounced ; and apparently the greater the scholar the greater the violence with which he disputes the matter with his equals.

Undoubtedly the touchstone of this contemporary erudition in Elizabeth Tudor was her complete absorption of French. It is here that we must remark the nearest thing to love she ever knew : her attraction towards Anjou. Her eyes were always dry save when Anjou took his leave ; and when he had gone away she avoided the places where they had met because the memory was more than she could stand.

There could be no bond save language. The Valois were pipsqueaks ; they were not at all the kind of men who appeal to ladies of Elizabeth's temperament, yet her feeling was so violent that it is probable (though not certain) she would have gone to the experiment of a nominal marriage with him in order to have him always about her.

When a woman, even a distorted woman, is strongly moved by affection, she will run a risk for the sake of companionship. There is something of the comic and the tragic again in the fact that the warped, discredited, unhealthy, Tudor blood found this attraction in the decaying blood of the Valois.

Yet so it was. If at the end of her long and unhappy life this woman could look back with some real regret to any separation it must have been to her separation from Anjou.

It is rare indeed that even a gleam of real affection is found in a character of this sort, but I do think she had felt it in the matter of Anjou. She never felt it again unless one may speak of such a thing in connection with the fatuous, half incestuous, maternal arrangements with the unfortunate Essex.

In connection with Elizabeth Tudor's really remarkable erudition—remarkable even in comparison with the erudition of her contemporaries and equals—one must pause to consider Ascham. Of Ascham it must be said—as it must be said of everyone at that moment—that he must be taken with a grain of salt. If your affection is with the Reformers you will make a great deal too much of him, but if the Reformation with its destruction of a united Christendom revolts you, you may treat him too lightly.

Of the latter error there is less danger for the modern English reader who has heard nothing but the other side.

The truth is simply this, the Reformers and all their crowd came in on the top of a wave, and that wave was combing, curling and frothing still even as late as the days when Elizabeth was learning her classics under Ascham.

We may discount of course his extravagant language to the learned German Sturm, who was known as Sturmius. To read this worthy one might imagine that Elizabeth Tudor was a sort of miracle ; not only a miracle of learning in those early years but a miracle of memory and application. She certainly was not that, but she did read continuously and consecutively ; she read Cicero in the afternoon and even Tertullian in the morning ; rhetoric is easier to read than philosophy. Nor, I think, did philosophy hold any great attraction for Elizabeth Tudor; the moderns who prefer what they call " action " to thought, will commend her for a neglect of philosophy, which was best shown in her neglect for religion. I am not learned enough to say whether she dabbled in Hebrew but it was quite the fashion to do so among the smart young women of the day. Fashion governs mankind (and even womankind) more than does any other passion, and the fashion in those days ran among the younger females of the rich to learning of this sort. Well, they might have spent their time worse. Such employment did give Elizabeth Tudor a sort of solidity in the foundation of her character which is not to be despised.

Meanwhile she was rightly advised—principally by William Cecil I think—to study and understand the interests of the New Millionaires. They would certainly be, short of a revolution, the masters of the England to come. The whole mass of the landed families were moving like a herd of cattle towards the Great Change.

There is any amount of misunderstanding about this. People write and talk about " Catholic " and " Protestant " in that mid-sixteenth century England as though the two words stood for two contrasted religious temperaments as they do today. They stood, of course, for nothing of the kind. " Protestant " stood in the main for those who would accept pretty well any new arrangement of religious doctrine, *so long as it did not upset the fundamental economic revolution, which had put the squires, large and small, in the possession of the Abbey lands.* The poor instinctively felt, and had it brought home to them by something sharper than mere instinct—by daily experience—that the enormous transfer of perhaps a third, certainly more than a fifth, of England from the old communal landlords to the new looters would be their ruin. But in any social revolution the wealthier class, if it is united, can hardly fail to win.

No one could lead a party, in the England of the said sixteenth century, for the restoration of the old religious endowment to their former masters. There could not even be a serious talk of such a thing, after the failure of the rebellion in the North.

But apart from the obvious economic motive (and it was overwhelming) there was that overmastering tide in human affairs which I have already spoken of as " fashion." Those of my own generation can remember a day when a certain drab and silly form of godlessness which called itself by the absurd name of " ignorance "—" Agnosticism "—was all the rage. It was as much as a man's intellectual life was worth to admit under the later Victorians his doubts upon this ephemeral but then universal creed.

There were indeed a number of more intelligent men, but they hardly counted against the main flood of materialist dogma which advanced under cover of pretending that it had no creed ; though indeed it had a creed which in its time was almost omnipotent. Men of my age can remember an England in which no one would have dared to defend the doctrine of miracle, except as an eccentricity.

Now let us turn to another point. Why was the reforming movement and its contempt of the old religion, its universal popularity among the cultured of the day associated everywhere with the new study of Greek ? There is no doubt that the torrent of change rushed foaming forward on a wave of Greek learning, Greek texts, the Greek language. That was the mark of this resurrection of antiquity from the dead. Though the change came somewhat late to England, as all things come to England from Europe with a certain time lag, it was in full activity when the instruction of Elizabeth was at work.

It is a commonplace to ascribc this flood of new Greek (which swept over cultivated Christendom in the sixteenth century as German stuff swept over it in the mid-nineteenth century), to the fall of Constantinople in 1453. We are told that this disaster, the breakdown of the bastion of Christendom, flooded the west with Greek manuscripts. That is true enough, but as usual the victorious cause is exaggerated.

The new spate of Greek, the new flood, had deeper springs than that, and the main spring thereof was a violent reaction from fatigue with the ancient Latinity. Such is the nature of us Europeans ; we suffer or enjoy a sudden enthusiasm for new things.

On the tide of the great change came the making of English prose. We mourn today at the grave of that great creation. But there remained something of English prose, not only to within living memory, but even on into the middle of the nineteenth century. I myself who am in the middle of writing this page met in my youth not a few elderly men who could still practise the art. English prose sprang not suddenly, indeed, but within a lifetime into vigorous activity, before the religious revolution ; and the new phase played no small part in bringing this country, though it was a province of universal Christendom, on to the side of disruption.

Let it be remembered that heresy is fruitful while the drive of it lasts.

The novelty of experiment, the appetite for new things, that element of vision which is always present in revolution, animates the ferment. There follows, as a sequel, the disease called pedantry, when learning has fallen into self-worship. But while the movement is going it does bear fruit indeed.

What is the making of good English prose ? Whence the decline of its glory today ? That decline has been rapid. The catastrophe has passed before our very eyes, but if I am called on to answer the question " whence came the catastrophe," I must answer, " I do not know."

That glorious structure of the human spirit, English prose, was not a function of rhetoric, as too many people on the example of the Authorised Version of the Old Testament have supposed. The greatest master of English prose was free from enthusiasm, and his name was Jonathan Swift.

I say again, I cannot say, nor can any man, how and why this great thing died. Some blame the newspapers. They had better look into their own hearts. Thomas Huxley was one of the last exponents of this solid achievement.

I fancy that there lay behind the florescence of English prose a combination of power and learning. The learned princes of the Renaissance, the patrons—in a sense the creators—of its art were responsible here also in England for the Great Moment. But English prose is but one province, and a belated one, of the sudden conquest achieved over the human mind by the culture of the sixteenth century.

We were, in this country of England, not wholly well served in the matter of the Renaissance. The full stream of it was soon deflected by a strange religious enthusiasm such as led one of the greatest of the English reformers to translate the word Ecclesia by " Congregation," which has deceived even the elect.*

Well, we might waste even more space than I have already wasted in discussing the modern degeneration of English prose. The disaster may be put down to print even, I suppose, more than to every other cause, but I would like to pay an honourable tribute to Empire and things of that sort while I am about it. Nor let us forget the effect of physical science, study of which seems to breed bad English

* There is another dreadful example. On the only recorded occasion when Our Lord obeyed a mortal and followed the injunctions of His Mother. He said to her, when she asked Him most admirably to provide wine, " Lady, it is not Our concern," nor was it, for Our Lord on this occasion was not host but guest, and we all of us know how awkward it is to suggest to a host that a little more wine would do no harm. His recorded reply runs, " Lady, it is not Our concern," which was true enough, but the anti-catholic feeling of the moment has left that reply in another form. " Woman, what is that to you or to me ? " See how important is exact translation.

automatically. A friend of mine who is a Fellow of his
College, and yet a great scholar, told me once in a long
walk through the northern red-brick suburbs of Oxford,
that he for his part put down the disaster to the growing
ignorance of French. He said to me, " Among my
colleagues today I find hardly anyone who can even do the
ordinary ' parlez-vous '."

So let me conclude this lament for better times with a
quotation from a language which is also disappearing from
the common talk of cultivated men.

O curas hominum quantum est in rebus inane.

On the other hand, more and more of us now possess a
familiar acquaintance with the glorious German tongue in
which it is possible to converse with animals.

I have wandered far indeed from my main theme, the
nature of Elizabeth Tudor, which I had intended to illustrate by her remarkable erudition. But I return to it before
I conclude this section. Her diligence during those years
of her later teens and early womanhood steeped her in such
erudition. One can fairly say that it was one of the three
or four main elements in the structure of her character. I
wish that I had heard her speaking Greek to know how she
pronounced it and also what selection she made of the tags
upon which she relied !

Her French conversation with Anjou I can imagine well
enough, for the language has not so greatly changed ; and
her Italian also. But the guess at what her Greek may have
been fascinates me.

And by the way, what was her Latin ? It is conjectured
but not certainly known (I have heard it debated by men
who have gone thoroughly into the business, which is
more than I am capable of doing) whether there were not
a revolution during Elizabeth's reign in the English
pronunciation of Latin. I have heard it said that the
unbroken tradition of Roman Latin was deliberately and
consciously abandoned for the insular vowel sounds which

have succeeded it, and which reigned supreme until quite recent times.

Nowadays, of course, this English-Latin is, like everything else, in chaos. But how interesting it would be to know in her very accent and intonation the sound of Elizabeth Tudor crying out when she heard of her accession to the throne, " Domino factum est istud et est mirabile in oculis nostris " it was her comment upon that event which she had taken for granted and was preparing for in full confidence with the aid and support of William Cecil and, still more of the King of Spain : her accession.

THE CROWN

THE reader of this study on Elizabeth Tudor will observe, I think, the recurrence of a note which is no longer heard in modern England. The note of Monarchy : personal government : active authority exercised by an individual and the concentration of executive power in that form.

The whole story of Elizabeth's personal policy through those obscure days when she was thrust aside by the capricious changing decisions of her father, through those middle years when she was in retirement and when her character was so strongly modified and deepened by adversity, on to the last mature years of her young womanhood, expecting the succession—all her policy, I say, during those eleven years which made her what she was, turned upon her rapt and intense attention to her prospects of succeeding to the throne.

All those who watched her intrigues and her reactions, down to her very features, during that scarcely interrupted silence, were concerned with this one business : " Shall we see this girl when she comes to womanhood occupying the throne ? " That is what gives all its meaning to the ardent effort of the still small, but intense and well supported anti-Catholic clique of politicians and enthusiasts to claim her as their leader. That is what gives all its value to the direction into which she and those who guided her— especially Cecil—deflected the story of England.

We shall examine upon another page her strong and persistent individual methods, and the course of her tortuous approach to the throne. But first of all we must understand what the throne, the crown, monarchy, meant to the men of that day. It is a matter very difficult for the modern English reader to grasp. We have had less experience of Monarchy than any other European nation. What was in those days its nature and effect? Why was kingship still supreme when Elizabeth came to the throne?

To begin with let us fix this essential truth. Monarchy is the normal, permanent form of human government. Democracy, the attempted control of the country by the country itself, is obviously impossible save in small societies. When you are dealing with larger units there is no possible effective machinery for putting the governed into command of those who govern them, still less of subjecting those who govern to the mere opinion or mood of the governed. There is, indeed, a check or limit to Monarchy, which is the friction between the individual will of the monarch and the vague diffused general will of the people. That vague diffused general will must always have the last word and must be, in proportion as it is clear and continuous, the atmosphere of the State. Monarchy would not work, for instance, where the monarch was of a religion and morals hostile to his or her subjects. It would break down quite quickly were it to attempt novelties shocking to the public habit of mind. But normally the executive must and will be centralised ; the helm must normally remain in the grasp of one hand.

There is indeed a powerful form of government alternative to Monarchy, which may generally be called Aristocracy, though that term is ambiguous. This alternative to Monarchy is government by an accepted and revered oligarchy. We call it in England today, " class government "—whenever we talk accurately about the affairs of the modern English state. But whatever name we give it, this system of class government always remains an exceptional thing peculiar to some one state and contrasting with the general habit of Monarchy in other nations around.

Monarchy requires special conditions, permitting it to arise and to continue alive. Those conditions have generally been found in rich commercial states where wealth was more or less worshipped and where such worship lent moral authority to the wealthier classes. Moreover, that system of government alternative to Monarchy, which we call loosely, aristocracy or class government, can hardly flourish save where the community is protected from external pressure. Where there is continual threat or actual presence of invasion Monarchy is invariably established in the long run because " war creates the king." Men cannot endure the strain of arms unless they are bound together ; and they are most naturally bound together by the visible and tangible presence of a monarch, actively commanding.

Now in the mid-sixteenth century in England, Monarchy was taken for granted. It was, as a fact, on the eve of losing its power and of being supplanted by the oligarchy of class government, which, not long after the last of the Tudors, undermined and finally overset the throne. But of this coming change, the Englishman of 1560 and 1600 had no vision at all. That Englishman was fully governed by personal authority and accepted such authority as a matter of course.

The authority of the monarch was strengthened by all manner of adjuncts, chief of which were certain religious sanctions, the monarch was for centuries anointed as well as crowned. It was the French monarchy which had set the example in this, for the French monarchy was the central political institution of Christendom from the early Middle Ages onward for hundreds of years.

The Royal Office, here in England and elsewhere, was sacramental. That is, it functioned through a close union between material and spiritual things, so that the material things were more than symbols and acquired a life and strength of their own. The monarch was crowned with a real crown at his or her Coronation, and a real sceptre ; and was approached with religious awe and every form of obedient ceremonial up to and beyond limits which were fantastic : for instance, in serving the simplest meal, those who bore the plate of meat to the table of the monarch behaved like men serving an altar. When Elizabeth Tudor would eat a bit of mutton, the servitor who had to present it genuflected three times under the influence of the Royal Presence. It is to be remarked that all these forms were at their height just at this moment : the active life of Elizabeth, when Monarchy was approaching its end in England.

So absolute was the position of the monarch that he or she could even determine the succession. That was particularly true of England where the succession had been so violently disturbed by perpetual usurpation and the warring of rebellious factions.

There was present in these last days of true personal monarchy, in the final lifetime before it crashed, a certain factor of decline more potent in its effect even than the action of time and fatigue. This factor was the change in the value of money ; in the purchasing power of the precious metals. The change was apparent, of course, in the corresponding rapid change of prices ; the special value of the precious metals, gold and silver (and particularly silver) was violently affected by the discovery of America. A new flood of currency began to swamp Europe within less than a lifetime of the astonishing Spanish adventures in Central and Southern America. The simplest way to put it is this. Before the death of Henry VIII, that is, before the middle of the sixteenth century, a given weight of the precious metals would buy twenty-five times as much goods as the same weight would buy today. Before the men who had seen the beginning of the change as boys reached the limits of old age, the multiple had already fallen from twenty-five to twelve and less than twelve. It continued to fall to *six*, to *five*, to *four*, and at last, before the ultimate breakdown of the throne under the last Stuarts, to three.*

Why was this cataclysmic fall in prices of effect in reducing the power of the English Monarchy ? After all, foreign monarchies, and particularly the French, weathered the storm though they were suffering from the same economic phenomenon. In France, as in England, the housewife of the later sixteenth century found herself paying more and more for the provision of the household in Paris as in London, until by the turn of the sixteenth century all the old incomes had lost their meaning.

The reason that the revolution in prices affected the English Monarchy so violently was that the *real* power of the monarch was slipping in England all the time. In France it was maintained and increased. The French government, like the English and every other government of the time, had to pay out more and more for labour and materials, decade after decade, as prices steadily rose. But in England the main fiscal institutions of the country were in the hands of the wealthier classes : a condition which is generally called " freedom." In France they were more and more at the arbitrary disposition of the King.

The Crown of England was thus progressively impoverished ; it could undertake nothing of consequence. This had the advantage of keeping the country out of any considerable aggressive warfare, the most expensive political luxury of those days ; it had the disadvantage of ruining the secular power. Monarchy went begging.

---

* Such was the process which may be roughly affirmed of the change in the value of currency and the corresponding rise in prices between the death of Henry and the flight of James II. The whole calculation is very confused and difficult because an essential or necessity of life at one date may have ceased to be such a lifetime later. New habits arise, new inventions and a number of services ; and their diversity may expand indefinitely. But, roughly speaking, the rate of this compelling change was what is here given. An English pound a little before the death of Henry VIII had fallen to half its purchasing value in the midst of his daughter's reign, and to a quarter of it when the next dynasty appeared.

During the reign of Elizabeth herself, it lived as best it could but only with the inconvenience of extreme parsimony. After her time it had to throw itself more and more upon the expedient of voluntary grants from its subjects. These grew much later into a whole system of taxation which came at last to be taken for granted, first as a main, and later as a very considerable, source of revenue. But at the beginning there was no such thing as taxation in our sense. There were the customary dues, payable specially by those who held land, but those dues became less and less, progressively, as the value of money declined. The crisis came, as everybody knows, with the advent of the Stuarts and especially with the determination or necessity of the English government to create a powerful fleet.

That fleet was, of course, begun and increased by the Stuarts. It was under them and especially from Charles I's early years and onwards that English sea-power appeared in Europe. Religious feeling has persuaded men to say that English sea-power arose under Elizabeth ; that is quite false. What arose somewhat tardily and only sporadically in the course of Elizabeth's reign was private adventure by sea, especially adventure conducted by pirates and buccaneers. But what also did really arise in Elizabeth's reign was the growth of mercantile adventure, which was necessarily maritime. The personal revenues of the Queen herself were engaged in such speculation, so were the private revenues of her rich subjects. The profits were all the larger because the enterprises with which they were connected were politically risky as well as physically unsafe and uncertain. Englishmen had the advantage of coming late into this field. The trade and the discovery of Spaniards and Portuguese had shown the way and the latter especially established themselves in Asia. When I say that the late coming of England into this activity was an advantage, the statement may sound paradoxical. Yet that advantage was very real. A later generation of Englishmen garnered the experience of soldiers from the Continent of Europe, not only of the Portuguese and the Spaniards, but to some degree of the French and much more of the Dutch. The development of trade by those whom we now call the Dutch, that is by the maritime provinces of the Spanish Empire, and particularly by the merchants of the Northern Netherlands from the ancient establishment of Antwerp to the prodigious development of Amsterdam, was to mark all the next lifetime. It was upon the Dutch model that the English undertook their new commercial oceanic adventures. It was upon the Dutch model that they formed their new groups of merchant adventurers and upon the Dutch model that they developed what was later to become the main pillar of English prosperity : banking. It was natural that those who handled the balances of trade, and especially those who acquired those balances by their control of transport, should initiate the system of banking, which system essentially consists in the use, not only of other men's money concentrated in particular centres, but what was more important, of promises to pay more than the money in hand. For a prosperous banking system connotes the use as actual currency of promises to pay rather than of existing cash. When men discover that a paper promise to pay is honoured, they will in due course exchange such promises for goods far in excess of the actual amount of metal money available at any moment for the redeeming of those promises.*

If all the promises to pay were presented at the same time, they could not be met. It is this which makes what is called a run on the banks so dangerous and this which led later on to exceptional legislation whereby the Government protected those who had promised to pay from having to meet their obligations. But of all this, Elizabethan England knew little. The business of banking came later in the story

---

* Paper promises to pay—credit notes—already stood a lifetime ago in England for *ten* times the cash available for redeeming such promises.

of the country. What did grow very rapidly after the end of Elizabeth's reign and prodigiously during the next life-time, was the direct exchange of goods through the growth of the ports, whereof London was by far the chief. The mere physical growth of London, the expansion of the area over which the capital spread, was proof from the end of the sixteenth century onwards, of the growth of English commercial power.

But it is time to cut short the discussion of a process which was as yet only in the germ during Elizabeth's active life-time and, indeed, had not taken on its full shape even at the date of her death. Only let us never forget that those essentially formative years in English history—the years 1560 to 1600—were not only the seed-plot of modern England ; that is, Protestant England : the England which came to its greatest relative power in the Napoleonic Wars and to its greatest actual wealth and strength in the nine-teenth century ; the England which Elizabeth Tudor had seen growing under her eyes, but not under her guidance and still less under her influence. She would not have wished it to be what it was. She would have been appalled, I think, if she had seen what it was to be. Nor would it ever have occurred to her that an England which had ceased to be a full Monarchy could be an England at all.

It is true of Elizabeth Tudor as of all of us ; that she was in the main a passenger through life and a spectator of the scenes through which life carried her : not a maker thereof.

While the Crown was thus losing revenue and becoming poorer and poorer in comparison with the big new fortunes which were to destroy Monarchy at last (though the rich had as yet no consciousness of their future success and would have angrily denied any such intention) the moral power of the Crown was falling at the same time.

We associate moral power with money power so closely in these our times that we almost take for granted that the decline of the English Crown was due to the decline of that

Crown's revenue. But the identification of the one decline
with the other is not shallow but unhistorical. At the very
moment when the English Monarchy was declining to its
ultimate ruin, the institution of Monarchy elsewhere was
rising to heights it had never known before. In almost
every country except England Monarchy in the seventeenth
century won its battle against plutocracy, and the
consequences of that victory remain to our own day as
do the consequences of the opposite in this country : for
here, in England, the rich conquered the King. The
consequences of plutocracy's victory over Monarchy in the
English seventeenth century made of England thenceforward
an oligarchy. An oligarchy England has since remained ;
and it looks very much as though the habit of oligarchy
has become so native to the English mind that it will never
disappear from the English polity. It is possible that the
ideal of " the gentleman," which is still of such moment
in our affairs, will decline or be transformed, but it is hardly
conceivable that Englishmen, unless their nature changes
more than seems possible today, shall become egalitarian
or shall admire the kind of government called democracy.
Everything in England is hierarchic ; not only is society
divided into strata—often most elaborately so divided—but
Englishmen are not at their ease when the distinctions of
class are violated. Nothing is more foreign to them than
those foreign communities (largely colonial) where human
equality is really taken for granted and is acted upon.
Most foreigners whose observations on England are worth
following, have noted the strength which this instinct for
oligarchy gives to the English nation. It provides that
nation with *cadres* : that is, it provides commanders in a
fairly ordered sequence of superior and inferior, who shall
conduct the commonwealth as an army is conducted by its
commissioned officers and its non-commissioned officers.

There is, of course, another side to the matter ; the grave
disadvantages of oligarchy as well as advantages. But most

of those disadvantages are merely moral and, therefore, appear somewhat insignificant to the men of our time. It is a disadvantage that citizens should feel inferior to their fellows, because such inferiority wounds human dignity. It is especially a disadvantage that their sense of inferiority should be connected with inferior wealth : for wealth and virtue are not connected : if anything Wealth and Virtue are rather antagonistic than linked in a common nature.

There is even a disadvantage attaching to class government (whether we call it aristocracy or oligarchy or what not) which is little suspected by those who enjoy the advantages of the same. This rarely appreciated disadvantage has nothing to do with the moral degradation of man by his denial of human quality. It is more direct, simple and material. The worst political disadvantage proceeds from the absence of a strongly organised, highly cultivated middle class. From such a middle class all the strongest direction of society has in the highest moments of history been naturally drawn. When such a class is dissolved nothing can take its place. Such a class gives us the men of science, the engineers, most of the poets, nearly all the philosophers. In a sense you may say that you are withdrawing the soul of a society when you bring its cultivated middle class into contempt and loss of power.

During the transition period when England was not organised as an oligarchy under a governing class and yet was failing to retain the full power of Monarchy, the country went politically through a phase of danger and confusion, the chief mark of which was the Civil War or Great Rebellion. The decline of Monarchy, which was so marked a feature of the late sixteenth and mid-seventeenth centuries and of which the symbolic centre was the killing of Charles I, seemed to the more thoughtful men of the time an irremediable tragedy. The idea that anything else could take the place of kingship did not occur to them. The mere revolutionaries who rose against the Crown did so under

E

no aristocratic theory of government ; the theory of government arose after them, in spite of them, and without any conscious plan.

The main political point of the time was, then, the strange extinction of kingship, though men still continued to think the name of kingship indispensable to the strength of the community. This must be accounted for. How are we to account for the increasing breakdown of the Crown's moral power between the accession of Elizabeth and the Civil Wars, or rather between the accession of Elizabeth and that so-called " Restoration " which came a hundred years later and so far from " restoring " the King made him a powerless puppet in the hands of the money-power ?

The causes were various and they combine in a strange fashion. The combination has no clear common cause running through it, and if we set out separately the main causes we are surprised to find how adventitious the whole arrangement seems. One might almost call the combination of causes which destroyed kingship in England a caprice of fate, were it not that our modern minds hesitate to regard destiny as capricious. We go rather to the other extreme and think of all that takes place on the stage of this world as something determined.

But whether we are right or wrong in this attitude we must recognise that the various causes which brought down the English Monarchy were disassociated and very separate.

To begin with the most obvious. You have a succession of monarchs ill-suited to play the part of monarch at all. Just when king-worship had reached its height and when the foundation of a durable system was most needed you get the illegitimate, usurping Tudor dynasty, with its first founder, Henry VII, not even daring to proclaim his titles to kingship, his son, Henry VIII, so terrified of every rival that he puts them to death right and left. Then you have a succession of two women, Mary Tudor and her half-sister Elizabeth Tudor, the first possessing all the strength of virtue and a clear moral course, the second possessing, as these pages are written to show, a certain random tenacity, combined with her caprice. But neither of these women were other than women and neither of them presided over a monarchy with that simplicity and firmness which could have been furnished by men of a suitable kind. These two women followed on the reign of a child, for their half-brother, Edward VI, was only fifteen when he died and had been a hopeless invalid, suffering from a complete breakdown of the body, at the end of his brief boyhood. At Elizabeth's death no one could tell you who should rightly be monarch in England. The succession was jobbed by one statesman to the advantage of an unpopular Scottish foreigner whom Englishmen did not respect. By the time he died the English Crown had thus been of an uncertain personal value for the whole of a very long lifetime. There was no one left alive on James I's death who could remember Henry VIII, save perhaps a score or two of very old men who had heard in their early childhood that the king of the time was called by that title.

During much of this period the monarch could not even compel obedience. Elizabeth was openly disobeyed in spite of her paroxysms of anger at the humiliation inflicted upon her. Her successor was not indeed disobeyed, but was compelled, as his reign proceeded, to envisage dependence upon the gifts provided by the House of Commons. He ridiculed the pretensions of the Parliamentarians but he had to accept these pretensions and his acceptance made it inevitable that under his son the House of Commons should supplant the throne itself.

Then there was the permanent division throughout the State in the most foundational matter of all, which is the religion of its citizens. Such division was not peculiar to England : it was a feature of the time nearly everywhere. In France it had led, as might be expected from the French temperament, to civil war. In England civil war was prevented, but that social ill-ease, which comes from a divided philosophy, was apparent. Society had to depend for its guidance upon a religious minority and, before that, society had to depend for its moral unity upon a reign of terror—for the axe and the gallows of Elizabeth's day were the instruments of the terror ; and the perpetual use of the rack, though not proceeding from the desire to terrify, left a lively memory of terror which colours all that time.

One way and another, with the catastrophic decline of the Crown's revenues, with lack of continuity in the royal personages, with the topsy-turvy of violent religious change, with the absence of any great and heartening event, whether of military glory or of more peaceful conquest ; what with the bad title of the Tudors to begin with and the foreign character of the Stuarts to go on with, it is strange that the Crown should have survived such a lifetime rather than that it should have broken down. We must remember that the myths and legends on which our own generation has been nourished had no reality for contemporaries. To them the whole chain of these disconnected episodes was catastrophic and utterly uncertain. We only begin to get a settled government again with the appearance of modern class rule at the Restoration in the beginning of Charles II's reign, by which time the reality of Monarchy had disappeared from England. By 1660 English Monarchy as an institution was dead, ready to be replaced by the wellknit rule of the rich, the stability of which rule none could then guess.

VIII

THE ENGLISH REFORMATION

THE English Reformation is obviously of the first importance to an understanding of English history and, therefore, of England : for all that we call England today arose from it and was made by it. But this great Revolution was more important than anything merely regional or national ; it determined the whole story of our civilisation thereafter. For England was the only ancient wellrooted and fully developed province of our common civilisation which broke away finally from that civilisation between the middle of the sixteenth century and the middle of the seventeenth. Lesser units or fragments of Christendom were lost to the unity of Christendom, to the common faith whereby Christendom had been formed and by the relics of which it still precariously survives. A local government would declare its revolt from the old order : it might be a single lordship or an isolated mountain valley which acted thus. It might be a whole province ; more often it was a section of a province ; a whole fragment of the population thereof which broke away, or a whole social class or part of a social class. Thus, in some places, the quarrel which divided Christendom would be enthusiastically taken up by an urban population or by smaller squires of the countryside in opposition to the general lordship of the whole. In the first vigour of the movement its effect was that of an explosion shattering the general structure of society. But this pristine energy was of its nature ephemeral and was confused with many another interest, economic or what not ; the tendency to reunite was strong and would have triumphed everywhere had it not been for the powerful exception of England.

What then was the English Reformation ? What was

the driving force behind it ? What confirmed it and gave it endurance ?

The Reformation as a whole was not a new religion, for it had no unity of structure or purpose ; but in England it had one strong foundation which determined all its fortunes, and that foundation has been described in the simple form of two words : the " Abbey Lands." Such was the title given by contemporaries to what was altogether the most important feature of the great change.

There were any number of other factors at work. There was the new sectional feeling which we call today " growth of nationalism," but which appeared to the people of the time as loyalty to local dynasties or local forms of government ; what men called " the Prince," the desire of a European group for unity under its " Prince." The mastering claims of loyalty to such a " Prince " had much to do with the affair. It was a feeling the intensity of which had been growing three lifetimes before the Reformation broke out. Thus, among the French the following of national kings determined the issue. Had the French Monarchy gone anti-Catholic the nation would have followed. There was the universal ferment of new geographical discovery ; the territorial expansion of the mediæval world at its close which was so strong as to burst the boundaries containing that world. There was the growth of a new scholarship, learned men not only steeping themselves in the classics but becoming enthusiastic for the perfection and beauty of thought expressed in Latin and in Greek : a passion for the ordered beauty of pagan antiquity. There was obscurely present but ubiquitous that permanent feature in European society which may · be called " the scepticism of the peasant " ; the hereditary dwellers of Christian lands had combined a strong veneration for local deities and saints with a corrosive doubt as to whether such beings or qualities really existed : an itch for ridiculing as imaginary those very objects which with another part of the mind, were venerated. There was the more superficial but much clearer effect of what we call today " rationalism "—a desire to make any affirmation conform to external experience and reason.

There were all these things at work together, but here in England one event more than any other—overwhelmingly more than any other—decided the issue and had canalised the tumultuous flood of change into a fixed channel. That event was the sudden rapid and complete confiscation of monastic property. The thing came in one crashing blow, prepared, it is true, by preliminary experiment, but when it fell falling like a thunderbolt. The enormous revenues of the greater and lesser convents and monasteries were seized by the Crown.

Had the Monarchy kept the loot acquired in so rapid and prodigious an act it would have become at one stroke by far the strongest executive in Europe. Small though England was in comparison with her principal rival, the French Monarchy, the strength given by the centralisation of economic power would have made up for numbers and the English Crown would have been the greatest of political forces. Unfortunately for that Crown it had proved impossible for the government of Henry VIII to keep its booty. The looting of that booty was only feasible with the aid of the greater and lesser lords of land, from the chief nobles down to the simple village squires. At first it looked as though the Crown might still have kept the greater part of its new wealth, but in the short seven years between the fall of the last great monastic establishment, Harold's foundation of Waltham Abbey, and the death of Henry, the Abbey Lands passed from hand to hand by grant and purchase until they were dispersed among a large body of new owners whom it would be impossible to displace. From that moment, the early days of 1547 onwards, rules by far the most permanently powerful of human motives—greed of wealth, firmly anchored in the English polity.

From that moment every policy was judged among the beneficiaries of this economic revolution by its effect one way or the other upon the future ownership of the Abbey Lands.

No exact estimate can be made of the total Abbey rents bore to the rentals of England as a whole, but it was certainly more than a fifth of that total and perhaps more than a third of it. So fantastic a resettlement of income among the only class that counted had never been known before and has never been known since ; and the fruit of it was not only a new social structure, but the destruction of what had been for time beyond memory the religion of Englishmen.

Obviously, such a collapse could not have fallen upon the religious structure of the country had not that structure been already heavily weakened here as in every other province of Christendom. The mere number of monks and nuns had already shrunk to about half its old total before the attack was made. But even that diminution in numbers was nothing compared to the diminution of respect and affection felt for the organised religious bodies. This loss of special prestige varied very much from place to place. It was less in the north of England than in the south, partly because the north was more independent of the central government, but more because the influence of commerce and travel was less. It was more widespread and more taken for granted in the one big town, London, than in lesser places ; and London was the largest single social force in the kingdom by far. It varied also with the presence of foreigners come from overseas and especially from the Germanies ; but it was everywhere a strong force, and throughout the nation as a whole a determining one. Men had come to think of monks and the monastic institution not exactly as an anachronism but as something not fully in tune with the general life and becoming rapidly less consonant with it.

The situation could have been restored by reform of abuses, but the vested interests were, as usual, too strong for the effort at reform. It was growing to be a commonplace among the learned that the monks stood for ignorance and for the resistance to the growth of classical learning : and, as classical learning was the intellectual idol of the time, this reputation of the monks for being its enemy progressively weakened them.

Conversely, there was no effective defence. Not only was there no effective reform of abuses—such as the great mass of legend passing for true history, and false relics and even in places false miracles—but there was no sufficient argument, no sufficient appeal to the reason and to common sense in support of the traditional thing. It came at last but it came too late so far as this country was concerned. Of the moral corruption, that is of the vicious habits cropping up here and there in the isolated lives of the religious, too much has been made. That was inevitable when the other side had won its battle, for celibacy is a natural target of attack for the natural man. It has been truly said that if even a tenth of the enormities ascribed to the monks by their official accusers were true it would be enough to establish an appalling picture of monasticism in its decline. But there is no reason to believe that any such proportion of truth existed in the flood of official persecution. Had there been so much truth in the accusations, they would certainly have been heard before ; they would not have been suddenly produced. Had there been so much truth in the accusations the persecutors would have been numerous and in a large proportion reputable and free, instead of being very few, wholly servile and of base character. Most convincing of all is the plain fact that men drawn from the dissolved communities were thought as a matter of course worthy of other endowments when such were available and were, as a matter of course, presented with office. The myth of an impossible turpitude during the decay of mediæval monasticism in England must be treated as all sensible men treat stories that arise against anything that is vulnerable because it is failing or too obviously open to assault, like the equally decayed and impoverished local nobility of France before the Revolution or, for that matter, the accusations that are beginning to be heard against wealthy men today during the modern break-down of the capitalist organisation.

But what is true, significant and illuminating of all that time is the as yet unchecked, unretarded and rapid decline of those religious establishments which had been, till after the Black Death, two hundred years before, the vigorous homes and propagators of our culture everywhere.

Granted then that the decay of mediæval monasticism made attack on the huge landed wealth of the English regular clergy (monks and nuns) not only possible but easy, we have next to ask what it was which introduced a real change of religion. Let it first be clearly understood (against the mass of our official history) that there was no general demand for such a change. It is not true that the English people as a whole were eager to be rid of their ancient social habit in the matter of worship. The clergy were not corrupt, indeed the Church was less unpopular here than in most provinces of Europe. The monastic estates were not identified with the cause of religion. There had been here, as everywhere at the end of the Middle Ages, an uneasy discontent with fossilised religion and with forms from which the vital spirit was ebbing. But England was a country (in those days) of villages, and the inherited habits of worship bound up with all the life of the people, were taken for granted. What new force was there to support or rather to reinforce, to mix with and strengthen the assault on what had already become a somewhat lethargic and half-hearted defence of custom in these affairs ?

When new-fangled people went about with enthusiasm for a Change, who would back them up and why ? Whence should come the necessary allies of Change ? It came, as do nearly all great social affairs, from the influence of one man and, as do most such revolutions, from the influence of a book.

The man was a northern Frenchman called Jean Cauvin. His name was also spelt with an " l " (for which the vowel " u " was elided). In Latin, the universal language of thought and discussion at the time, he was known as Johannes Calvinus, or rather as " Calvinus," short and simple. And his book was " The Institute." He proposed (perhaps without knowing it) a new religion, he being then a young man of the University of Paris, writing about ten years after the initial confused revolt of those who surrounded Martin Luther in the Germanies—a man powerfully backed by secular rulers, also German, who were already mainly free from the discipline of the Emperor and active as petty sovereigns. This man, Calvin, to give him his commonest name, had a very definite doctrine to propose. His book is dull and for modern readers difficult to read (I have read it, though with what difficulty, God knows). Its success powerfully illustrates the strong intelligence of the time, for lacking intelligence no man would be troubled to follow its somewhat pedantic argument.

That argument is this : That there is only one Will in the Universe. Calvin's message was not only the universality and the omnipotence, but still more what St. Thomas and his predecessors have called the " simplicity " of God. That profound and capital mystery which the superficial Gibbon has called in English " an abyss," the mystery by which we must reconcile Free Will and the Divine Purpose, was with Calvin dissipated into something very like nothingness. He left the Divine Will—the universal Will of God—working, as it were, absolutely, and the Free Will of Man wholly relative thereto.

Those who are so ignorant or so muddle-headed as to

imagine that doctrine is not of ultimate consequence in human affairs, will do well to note the scope of the movement that followed. It covered the whole of European life ; it nearly wrecked our civilisation. Calvin's phrase " the immutable decrees of God " rose as a sort of hard rock against which Europe struck and almost made shipwreck. Such a doctrine ultimately bred an appetite for material wealth as the only available good ; it bred also paradoxically and conversely in opposition to itself, as doctrines do, a countervailing hatred of the best that wealth can bring, which is grace and beauty, the arts and a certain lesser fulfilment of mankind.

Men must worship something, if only for this reason— that unless there is an object of worship for which men will sacrifice themselves nothing profound or permanent can be done. Aquinas said it, himself not the first (but as it was true before him, so it remains true after him) : " If men abandon the worship of God, they will fall to the worship of wealth."

Today men have in the main abandoned (for the moment at least) the worship of God ; they have substituted an idol which is the image of themselves and which may be called the nation or the community. That worship has had a long career already and is beginning to fail, though men still accept extreme suffering in its service. When here in England, by the seizure of the Abbey lands, religious sanction was shaken to its foundations, the more acceptable religion began to appear. A worship of the Prince and, therefore, ultimately of the nation or community had already come into being, but it had not yet acquired full substance and vitality. . When the new and intense interest of greed, provoked by the necessity of keeping the Abbey lands, arose, the new worship of nationhood gradually took the place of other sanctities. The process took three lifetimes but it matured, and it enjoyed at last unquestioned success. Treason to the Prince became less and less, treason to the country more and more until at last it was the only treason accepted as an unforgivable crime.

At the inception of the English Reformation in its active phase, that is with the advent of Elizabeth to the throne, a new sort of worship, which made the nation supreme, took root. It grew to maturity, it produced the English aristocratic State ; it reached its climax in our own time. Such a form of polity is the strongest that can be imagined. When it is conducted by a small highly organised wealthy class, it is called (in the modern use of the term) " democracy," and still enjoys an undisputed authority among us today.

So much for the next factor in the English Reformation : Nationalism, following upon the impulse of Calvin. But let it be remembered that Calvinism was never here in England, as it was in the Lowlands of Scotland, identified with a national movement. Calvinism was mixed into the religion of the English as a powerful ingredient. It never dominated that religion, wherein the nation remained supreme. It gave England the whole Puritan movement which is still the most powerful ethical force among the English, but it did not narrow the latitude of English humour (the most English of English things), nor the passionate sense of beauty (in verse especially), nor that creative doubt which continues to inhabit the English mind.

This new and confused conception of religion, based rather upon national feeling than upon doctrine, was generally accepted after the exhaustion of conflicting policies which had filled the first years of Elizabeth. The sudden swoop of the Crown upon monastic wealth was not so much as launched until she was three years old ; the great spoil was not completed until she was seven years old, and she was entering her fourteenth year when her father died and the opportunity for complete loot appeared.

When I say " complete loot " let it be remembered that there was a large margin of property still in the hands of ecclesiastical or quasi-ecclesiastical corporations still to be looted and wealth transferred to the pockets of the governing rich who had found the earlier spoliation so unexpectedly successful. There were hospitals for the relief of the poor, there were the chantries, which meant both the elaborate altars at which masses were said for the repose of the souls of the benefactors, and also the endowments for those masses. All these went after Henry's death, when his brothers-in-law, the Seymours and their gang were free to pillage at will.

The Colleges of Oxford and Cambridge were also marked down for destruction for the benefit of the robbers. What saved them we know not, but apparently it was the hesitation of grasping so enormous a haul while the Crown was still in minority. There was no doubt that Henry himself would have taken for granted the opportunity of thus destroying the Universities or at any rate dividing their income among his supporters. But, lacking the direct authority of the king, the Seymours and their hangers-on drew back and the Universities were saved. Nor were the scholastic endowments wholly lost. Many of the schools founded in better times were still continued though their revenue was cut down. These often appear as new foundations and the credit of their establishment goes to the little boy who nominally reigned under his uncles with the title of Edward the Sixth. Before that unhappy child's body had rotted to its horrible death the platter was eaten clean ; even the bishoprics and deaneries had been sliced, part of their endowments here, part of their endowments there, passing to laymen. One bishopric was kept empty during the whole of Elizabeth's reign in order that its income could be diverted to the Queen—that is to the Courtiers. The work was so thoroughly done that for a whole lifetime later its results were almost entirely accepted as unchangeable. I say " almost entirely " because there was some attempt at protest by Charles I in the matter of a fragment of the Scottish

Church endowments ; that protest, mild as it was, began the ruin of the Crown. The destruction of the Royal power in England can be traced step by step from this first timid effort of Charles to recover some small portion of what had been snatched away from the Monarchy by the new governing class.

There is a last consideration in connection with the religious revolution in England. Just as it was doctrinally imperfect and vague, having but one fixed principle behind it—the loot of religious endowment—so it was slow to the extreme in developing and was never completed.

Why should this have been ? Every move towards definition, beyond the general principle that England should be finally separated from the general unity of the Christian West, was halted. Certain doctrinal formulæ were attempted, as in the Thirty-Nine Articles and, nearly a century later, in the revised pronouncements made at the beginning of Charles II's reign. But they were never actively enforced.

In the beginning of the Revolution it was not even thought advisable to press too harshly upon those who retained in varying degree their affection for the traditions in which they had been born, and for the Mass, which was the test and centre of those traditions. Men would take Communion after the model of the new Church which had been set up, or under the old Catholic forms almost indifferently. The whole thing was a policy of weaning and of gradual extirpation, against which there was less and less reaction as time went on. The main body of those who adhered—most of them without enthusiasm—to what had been from their origins the religion of their fathers, admitted their traditions, and were reckoned in conversation and correspondence as adherents of the general Church. But the term was a loose one and would certainly in time dissolve.

There was indeed one rather sharp rally supported and

propagated by the heroism of missionary priests, mainly
Jesuits, determined upon recovering England. That effort
led to intense, but not widespread persecution of particular
victims. But there was no great effort to impose new
ritual, still less new doctrine, by force. It has been truly
said a hundred times that the English people were robbed
of their religion, but they were robbed by stealth and not
by violence. Lastly we must remember, if we are to
understand the English Reformation, that it had not in its
beginning been regarded as final—it had been but a compromise capable of revision even so that compromise might
be revised with the coming of a new reign—though, of
course, it would be necessary to secure those who had
benefited financially by the general confiscation of Church
goods. On this the wealthy classes upon whom the government depended were immovable even at the beginning.
When Mary attempted a return to the Roman communion,
the wealthier classes, acting through their organ the House
of Commons, had stipulated that in any case their newly
acquired wealth from the ecclesiastical revenues should
be maintained. Those ecclesiastics who thought that
anything else could be possible quite misunderstood the
temper of the landed gentry. That temper took the
Abbey lands seriously ; the Abbey lands were the one
article of religion firmly anchored in their souls. This
is the central historical pivot of the whole affair and the
effects of that original point of departure are vigorously
alive to this day.

Next to Elizabeth herself the principal political character
for examination in her time is that of William Cecil, for
it was he who was chief agent of the reign, especially in
its earlier part. Great as was his genius it is not difficult
to see him exactly as he was because his character was
essentially simple. He directed all his considerable energy
and still more considerable perspicacity and power of
judgment to the single purpose of benefiting himself. Men

of this kind are always more easily understood than men
of divers objects and appetites.   They pass through life
free from any tragedies of their own making ; they do
well such work as falls to them to do and they do it especially
well when it fits in wholly with their advantage, particularly
with their material advantage.   They suffer less than other
men from the vagaries of appetite ; and as a rule do not
suffer at all from the vagaries of affection or any other
spiritual motive force.   They must of course, be served,
as even genius must be served, by circumstance.   If
William Cecil had not found circumstance around him
favourable to the career on which he had been launched
by fate or providence, he would not have achieved so
much—though he would have achieved much in any case.
As things were he was the principal, though of course not
the only architect of that new thing arising in his time
which today we call England.   This it is which makes
William Cecil a figure of such very great stature in the
story of his country.   Not that he actually created, through
efforts of the imagination, the institutions properly connected with his name.   He had not that creative power
which has been found in many other statesmen of less
influence upon the story of their nation.   There was
nothing in him of what we call today " the artist."   The
two pillars of his character and achievement were those
which you find supporting many another successful public
life : industry and judgment.   But though he had these
two in common with all such men he enjoyed them in a
special degree.   He was not chosen by Elizabeth of
course.   She found him there ready to hand with his
advice and already matured knowledge of men and of the
world.   Cecil was without enthusiasm, as such men always
are ; yet he could see in exact proportion the part which
enthusiasm plays in human affairs.   The most revealing
point about him in that moment of violent dispute and
conflicting loyalties is one little picture which I beg the

F

reader to bear well in mind, putting upon it as strong a light as he can. You must see William Cecil in the days when Mary Tudor was Queen, walking about with a specially large pair of rosary beads well displayed upon his somewhat meagre person. He was even less susceptible to religious emotion than was the Tudor woman whom he rather guided than served—or rather, guided in great part, though not wholly. He could not foresee, any more than could any other man, what would happen to that strong Protestant flood which in his youth was already lapping at the shores of England. What he did understand even more thoroughly perhaps than anyone else (though it was understood thoroughly enough by the great bulk of the comfortable classes who determined the character of their country and its government) was that a dividing line had been drawn across the story of the country by the seizure and later the dispersion of the Abbey lands. He did not know that the attempt at the Catholic reaction would fail ; no one could know *that*, because it failed from accidents not subject to human control. It failed in particular from the comparatively early death of Queen Mary, one of the least healthy of the unhealthy Tudor brood. It is conceivable that had Mary lived, especially had she lived to be the mother of a son, the Catholic liturgy and social habit would have survived as a man survives who has been maimed and crippled by the loss of limbs. It is possible that such a future would have seen England again repeopled with monastic institutions and that the distinctively anti-Catholic spirit of the seventeenth century in this country would not have had an opportunity to develop. In that case William Cecil would have lived on as a useful and laborious public servant, set various tasks by the husband and wife who would have been his sovereigns. It is possible that among those tasks would have been foreign embassies, which he was very well fitted to present and conduct in every quality but one, which was presence. He gravely lacked presence,

so that one man would compare him to a weasel, another to
a rat, another to a fox. But no one would have compared
him to a sheep or to an ass. As things were, or rather as
things turned out, William Cecil needed not to oppose, nor
even to intrigue too much. The English Reformation had
put a tide under him whereon he could float up to the full
success of his remarkable career. For someone was needed
to hold the main stewardship of English policy during the
transition out of which England arose ; and William Cecil
was exactly suited to play that part. Only one thing could
have interrupted his steady ascent to greater and greater
wealth and to wider and wider political power. That
would have been the death of Elizabeth, which more than
once in the course of his public service threatened to snap
that service in two. Had Elizabeth died after any one of
her recurrent illnesses, he would have had to fly had flight
been possible, and the whole history of the country would
have been changed, perhaps upon the whole reversed. But
Elizabeth survived and, with her survival, survived also the
work of William Cecil.

The danger of writing on any great historical figure,
especially if it be remarkable for personal talents, as was
William Cecil, is a danger of dramatisation, of making out
the subject in hand to be more than he was and to have done
more than he did. The old tag that no man is a hero to
his valet may well be supplemented by a new tag : every
man is a hero, or at the worst an heroic villain, to his
historian.

William Cecil made many mistakes ; mistakes more
numerous than those of his modern remarkable descendant,
the Victorian Lord Salisbury (one of the very few Parliamentarians to approach greatness). He overdid the
Protestant play-acting and thereby made himself something
of a butt for Elizabeth. For she had so much of the true
woman in her that she loved to annoy whatever was nearest
at hand. He pressed, often out of season, for that which he

ultimately secured, as much as, or more than, did any other agent : the killing of Mary Stuart. He had very good reason to press for it, for until Mary Stuart was out of the way he himself could not be perfectly safe. He sometimes—though very rarely—misunderstood the nature of some servant or colleague. When he did so, it was commonly through that chief defect of very able men : the inability to allow for sincerity in others. Walsingham, for instance, really did detest the ancient religion of his fathers. Such an emotion was too foreign to William Cecil for him to understand it at all thoroughly.

Oddly enough he somewhat misunderstood Elizabeth herself, though she was there right at his elbow all through his life for him to study at leisure. He never really grasped her devotion to the majesty of kingship. Probably or certainly it was not possible for William Cecil to understand devotion of any kind. But he used, continually, well and in detail, this natural respect which his strange royal mistress felt for that institution of monarchy without which she herself would have counted little. One of the oddest and strongest components in William Cecil's make-up was his talent for successfully taking risks. Never was there a man less of a gambler or less of a truster to chance. Yet on more than one occasion, notably in that move which I will discuss later on, the retention of the Spanish ships at the risk of war, he did gamble and he won. No man can tell today whether he was justified in taking the hazard. At any rate, the event justified it.

Indeed, perhaps the most conspicuous adjunct to the long story of William Cecil is his evenness. The gigantic sums of money which he acquired were not acquired at one bound as were the fortunes of most adventurers in those days. One may even say that the family grew slowly. William's own father had been an important civil servant before the Reformation and had enjoyed, probably through the same qualities as his more illustrious son, the high favour of the

Crown. William Cecil had entered public life almost in a modern fashion ; that is, through the University. He was (like the gentleman in the boat that drifted ashore) a Cambridge man.* It is true that the more comfortable classes had not yet captured the Universities, but they had already begun to do so. Furthermore, William Cecil entered his career modernly in other ways, for after something of a *mésalliance* into something not unlike a public-house when he was barely of age, he had the good fortune to lose his wife within three years and his second marriage was more than suitable. By it he entered the family of Cooke and thence enjoyed from his twenty-fourth year onwards the lucrative protection of the Seymours. When Seymour fell he did not jump quite in time, but he was always ready to abandon the fallen and he climbed up again quickly. He was active in government ; just after his thirtieth year, during the minority of little Edward and so on till nearly his seventieth year (he did not die till he was just on sixty-eight) he remained on the crest of the wave. All the active lifetime of a man he remained, in spite of occasional peril, fully established, and during all the latter part of it increasingly rich.

For so great a man few of his judgments have been preserved for us. The most famous, the most characteristic and certainly among the truest, was the pregnant remark : " Nobility is but wealth grown old." That truth is pretty obvious in the nature of things and it was especially obvious in Cecil's time, when families newly wealthy were cropping up like mushrooms all over the field (but they were mush-

---

* It has little to do with history, but for the benefit of posterity and to cast a light on the society of our own time, let me recall here the story of the Cambridge man. A venerable vicar, incumbent of a parish in Cornwall and an Oxford man, was famous in spite of his years for his remaining athletic abilities. One day they ran to tell him that a boat without oars, holding the body of some poor fellow who had died of exposure, was drifting into the local cove beneath the cliffs. The excellent divine clambered down the rocks until he could distinguish the features of the unfortunate castaway. Gazing upon them he was heard to murmur, " a Cambridge man."

rooms most of which turned into sturdy trees, for they formed the oldest and most revered stratum in the peerage of England).*

It is well to remember that wealth so old as to run back into the Dark Ages, or even as far as the twelfth century, has an aroma of its own. Lineage so protracted is far commoner on the Continent of Europe and especially in France than here in England. For indeed, Englishmen care on the whole less for lineage than do most other people, though we hear a lot of it in novels. Some say that the blessed dead pride themselves upon their achievements during this earthly life, and even, more probably, the less blessed dead may obtain some mixed satisfaction of this kind. If that be so, the spirit of the great Lord Burghley carries with it much matter for conversation with its peers in whatever sphere it now inhabits.

When we have appreciated when and what William Cecil was : the master spirit of that perilous time (when what we call England was astir and about to be born but not yet born) we must pass on to judge his true relation to Elizabeth Tudor, whom he guided, counselled and in part politically formed.

Technically he was her adviser in chief, her great minister, her official director as it were, without whom her years of reign, her epoch, could not have been and, therefore, without whom this same " England " could not have arisen. But what was his real place in relation with hers ?

The natural error of the last generation, seeing the way in which Victorian England had lived under the superstition of a phantasm called " the unwritten Constitution," was to think of Cecil as someone whom the Queen had called and chosen to take her place, as it were, and to do the real work of governing. The Victorian illusion was

---

* Families of direct male descent which can trace their wealth, that is, their importance, to the Reformation, are not numerous. Those who can trace it further back than one or two lifetimes are but a handful.

not so desperately wide of the mark as to think the mid-
sixteenth century identical in spirit with itself. It knew
very well that there were real, active and very strong
forces in the throne. Nevertheless, it was difficult indeed
for the men who wrote history here during the last generation (especially when those men were writing towards the
end of a whole lifetime during which active monarchy had
apparently disappeared), to understand the sort of parity
there was between Cecil and his sovereign. It is not true
that she appointed him ; rather did she inherit him. He
was the only possible man to be put at the helm ; he had
already behind him a long experience of administration ;
he had been a part of government for years and he was much
her senior. Each had been born in September, but his
September birth had preceded hers by thirteen years. He
had been her adviser and supporter behind the scenes during
the last years of her excellent, noble and unhappy sister.
One might almost say that Elizabeth owed her throne to
him, though she would not have obtained it unless she had
also owed it to the good offices of her brother-in-law, the
King of Spain. She had entered her twenty-fifth year by
three months when Cecil thus aided her in her determination
to be Queen. He was at that same moment entering his
thirty-eighth year and to be thirty-eight was to be, not
venerable but almost middle-aged in those days. We must
beware then of the slight but perceptible error in focus made
by the generation immediately before our own when, in
supporting and maturing the Elizabethan legend, they made
of Cecil something like a Victorian Prime Minister. In a
sense he had more power than any Victorian Prime Minister,
but that power was co-ordinate with another power which
our time has amost forgotten. That power was *Monarchy*,
which we have already discussed on a former page. We
must always look at history through the eyes of contemporaries and, in the eyes of contemporaries, Cecil was
still a subordinate while Elizabeth was, at least potentially,

the master. He so thought of the relationship and *she* so thought of it—and the man in the street so thought of it.

But in practice things did not stand thus. Each of the two, Elizabeth Tudor and William Cecil, was necessary to the other and this was especially obvious to each in the earlier years of their partnership : the first ten to eleven critical years during which her unstable throne was gradually confirmed. Of course, as time went on the relationship was strengthened by custom until it seemed impossible to imagine its ending. The thing was bound to become more and more permanent, granted that Elizabeth survive.

There are two main things to be grasped by those who would understand what that partnership was. These two main things are : first, that each of them, William Cecil and Elizabeth, was fighting for his and her life. The second is that for a long time he did not know her carefully guarded secret. He did not know that she was physically abnormal and he *thought for years that it was possible she should marry and bear children.* Let us consider the two points in their order. Each I say, Elizabeth and William Cecil, was fighting for his and her life, though with different weapons and in differing degrees of peril. Their objects in survival were not identical ; nor, though each was in peril, were their perils identical. To take only one aspect of the contrast between their two positions : the ultimate success of the English Reformation was absolutely vital to Cecil ; he had staked everything on that. It was not vital to Elizabeth who might (though more and more doubtfully as time went on) have compromised with the general Catholic tradition of the general, less wealthy, mass of her subjects.

Cecil's policy and personality were necessarily unpopular. His policy because it was that of a minority which, though intense and active, was out of sympathy with the general though ill-defined Catholic social conditions which made up the stuff of English life for years to come. His personality was unpopular, especially with his immediate colleagues, simply because he was what he was ; an unpleasant, pinched, scheming little man, the less genial because he had genius. Certainly no one really respected William Cecil, though all feared his power ; still more certainly no human being loved him.

Now for the second point. Without at this moment or in this place pretending even to a general statement on that matter, it is enough for us to know that Elizabeth could not possibly have had an heir, and that she herself, perhaps alone in all Europe, was *fully* cognisant of that capital truth. Her knowledge of it accounts not only for the absence of children and for the ultimate refusal to accept marriage—though she came very near to that abortive experiment during her fit of affection for the French Prince. It accounts also in measure, I think, for her very uneven moods, her fits of passionate anger and her sullen regrets. At any rate, whatever the connection between this permanent misfortune and her personal character as time developed it, the main fact is certain. Elizabeth Tudor was barren.

IX

TORTURE

THE reign of Elizabeth was in this country (speaking of England in particular, apart from Scotland) the heyday of judicial torture, and those who write about Elizabethan England, omitting or under-emphasising this capital feature, torture, therein, give a totally false view of their subject. It is a subject so repulsive to a healthy mind that it is naturally understressed : but when you are dealing with the special problems or special character of a particular place or time historically, it is of the first importance to get the proportions right. Truth lies in proportion, and to pretend a true judgment upon that prolonged moment in our history, which opens in 1559 and ends with the outbreak of the Civil War—a very long lifetime—without bringing into high relief the permanent presence of torture as an instrument of government, and its especial practice here in England, is to get the whole thing out of perspective. You might as well write of legal procedure under Queen Victoria without stressing the growth and character of cross-examination and its special effect on State trials and official prosecutions, as deal with the England of the later sixteenth and early seventeenth century without heavily emphasising the constant presence of torture as an instrument of government. It colours the whole time and is the special mark of that time.

It is the more necessary to emphasise this feature because our popular and official histories do the opposite. They produce a false effect, not indeed by leaving out all mention of what was the salient characteristic in that generation, but, as usual, by neglecting degree.

Further, the truth about torture is warped by a perpetual repetition of the thoroughly irrelevant point that the use of torture was unknown to the common law of England,

84

even at the moment when the national life was specially
distinguished by the presence of this feature. It is necessary
to emphasise it, repulsive though the subject is, for yet
another reason, which is that our comprehension of the
matter is arrived at with the greatest difficulty. We have
so lost familiarity with torture in judicial procedure and
as an instrument of government that it is difficult indeed
for the modern man to realise either the scale of it or its
ubiquity, or even its purpose and nature ; but history is
essentially the telling of a true story about the past, and if
the story leaves its readers with an insufficient impression
of the part played by torture in Elizabethan times and the
earlier Stuart times immediately succeeding them, it
propagates untruth. It does that which it is the whole
business of an historian to avoid doing. Let us begin by
appreciating the purpose of torture and why we find it
taken for granted through all the Courts of Justice in
Christendom, but particularly in our own : only when we
have estimated this point can we proceed to the next important matter, which is the conditions under which torture
was used. All consideration of its justice or injustice,
value or lack of value, should come later.

The first thing to seize then is this : that torture came
into play everywhere with the object of obtaining evidence.
It was not a penal infliction, even though cruel and vindictive men and women might delight in the opportunity
for its exercise, and, even though it was abused for the sake
of terrorising or for any other irrelevant purpose. Its true
function, which was kept in view from the beginning of
the period to the close of it, was exactly what the function
of cross-examination is today, the establishment of certain
evidence. The simplest example and the clearest is that of
a man who refuses to divulge the names of accomplices or
suspected accomplices. A crime has been committed ; it
could hardly have been successfully committed by one man
alone ; it is of the highest moment to the authorities that

they should obtain an accurate knowledge of those who are opposed to them. Since it is dangerous to be in opposition to the authorities, those names and characters will always be concealed as far as possible ; and torture was employed in order to obtain information upon not only the personalities involved in some effort hostile to authority, but also upon the details of that effort. Torture was expected to reveal, and nearly always did reveal, a certain number of circumstances hitherto unknown to the authorities and only presented to their knowledge through the application of this duress.

An attempt is made to destroy some public man or place necessary to his action. It is made, let us say, by the use of explosives. The authorities seek to know who are their enemies at work and also the respective importance of these among themselves. Working on some first cue, which betrays the presence of at least one culprit (for instance, a man caught in the act of handling the explosives), the effort to increase the scope of government action takes the form of enquiring who, beside this single victim, can be certainly discovered ; and the first step towards this extension of information is establishing the connection between the known culprit and his unknown aiders and abettors. Since, by the nature of the case, the witness would be reluctant to testify, recourse is had to torturing him. It is bad judgment to decry the value of the method because evidence so obtained may be false and will nearly always be somewhat wild as well. The point is that one piece of evidence corroborates another and that by torture you are extending the circle of what is known in the matter. The use of torture has been abandoned in modern times, not because it was found uncertain and futile, but because it was increasingly repugnant to the moral sense of modern times.

So much for the *raison d'être* of torture. The cause of its use and the defence thereof by nearly all those who were principally concerned, was the discovery of actors and motives, especially in conspiracies. There was a subsidiary but very important object borne in mind by those who used torture for the discovery of truth : and this subsidiary but very important object was the obtaining of an avowal from the author of some act hostile to authority.

This is a matter which has been ill-represented and is still imperfectly grasped by the modern reader of history, for whom not only the procedure of another period but the moral motives at work are unfamiliar. We have in modern times forgotten or abandoned the conception that there could be no complete evidence against a man unless it were provided by himself. Today, the most solemn denial pursued up to the last extremity and continued to the very presence of death has left little effect on public and private opinion. The causes of this change may be debated, but that it has taken place there is no doubt at all. Judges and other authorities are today usually at pains to explain, when no confession of guilt has taken place but on the contrary vehement assertion of innocence, that these must weigh nothing compared with the chain of evidence presented.

I have said that the causes of the change between the older time, when a confession of guilt was thought of the first importance, and our modern indifference to the same, was still debatable, but I would suggest that the very wide extension of the methods by which evidence can be found, the vast growth of modern physical science, and the corresponding growth of the rapidity of communication and the universality of information has a great deal to do with it. When such a voice as that of the modern press has repeated the same affirmation in the same terms at the same time to millions of people, it acquires an authority of indefinitely greater weight than isolated statement. An expert appears in Court and gives his reasons, based on scientific knowledge, for concluding that, let us say, a stain was originally caused by human blood. Such weight has physical science today that the expert's opinion will decide the event; and we have all of us a sufficient working knowledge of the vocabulary of at least elementary physical science that we are the better prepared to trust the expert in it when he gives evidence. So much for the object of torture or of any other method of ascertaining true evidence. Now let us consider the method of application.

It has been remarked by all those who approach the use of official torture in the past that it was surrounded by all manner of safeguards and restrictions. Why was this? Why was a thing, of its nature extravagant and extreme, so limited by rules?

It was limited in this fashion precisely because without limitation it would have run wild. It was to prevent the use of torture as a mere satisfaction of cruelty or a mere satisfaction of hate that the elaborate code in connection with it arose.

Now we know the *Purpose* of that outburst of torture which will always be associated with the reign of Queen Elizabeth in England. Its purpose was to discover and expose secret plotting against public authority. But what was the *Occasion* of it? Why did this particular moment in English history so vividly exercise the use of torture? Why can no one with a real knowledge of the English past recall the Elizabethan period and its immediate sequel without associating it with the perpetual presence of this, to us abominable but to contemporaries commonplace, adjunct of political life? Torture did not hold that position in the preceding lifetime, although in the preceding lifetime torture as an occasional method had been taken for granted. Torture is not the outstanding accompaniment of public life between the beginning of the English Reformation and the advent of Elizabeth : nor does it fill the whole scene until the later years of the reign and the beginnings of what followed. What is even more extraordinary is that the use of torture (that exceedingly vivid and highly particular episode in our history) declines rapidly enough at the end of that long lifetime and then disappears altogether.

Well, it is never possible to follow exactly, nor even in sufficiently general lines, the causes of a fashion in political action ; but I think we can find an answer to this monstrous question. Why did men accept this sudden and intense use of a most inhuman thing ? Why did it achieve so peculiar an intensity in England, a country where the temper of men is, as a rule, amenable and averse to extremes ?

The explanation would seem to be that this was the one moment in English history when there was acute danger of ruin from conspiracy to a major interest in those who governed : in what we call today, " the governing class."

A social system which was not in the traditions of the nation had been quite suddenly imposed by revolution. That revolution had been driven by the extravagant cupidity of a comparatively small body of wealthy men. This new orgy of Elizabethan torture had not behind it any considerable popular backing, neither did it arouse against it any considerable popular opposition. A very large proportion of wealth had been suddenly transferred to new hands. The loot had not been a loot undertaken by the poor against the rich ; it had been loot of one old-established but weakened set of beneficiaries (the ecclesiastics and especially the monastic ecclesiastics) at the hands of another set—a lay set : and that other lay set was not a well-defined band of robbers ; it was made up of a mixture of groups : feudal lords already possessing plenty of revenue—from one-manor men to the greatest lords dominating half a shire—new men who had come in as speculators on the dissolution of the monasteries or rather on the later sale of the monastic lands by the Crown, and below these a sort of general riff-raff of hungry adventurers, many of them on quite a small scale. Thus, one of the most marked characteristics of the great turn-over was the change in what had been customary tenure into competitive tenure, so that quite small farmers, who had held their land by habitual inherited quit-payments, found themselves more and more regarded as permanent owners. Conversely, there had begun to flow an opposing current which swelled greatly in the next lifetime. The capture of the small customary tenant by the large local landed Lord who was aided in his rape by a powerful ally : the lawyer interpreting ancient phases in more modern terms : the lawyer calling a man who had been a feudal superior an absolute possessor.

Meanwhile there had been growing rapidly throughout Christendom, and had become especially strong in England, the conception of absolute monarchy (in plainer words, of despotism) as a simple and satisfactory solution of political difficulties. It was a change of fashion more superficial but even more abrupt than that which had created the revolution in rights over land. Men became ready, almost overnight one might say, to accept the will of the monarch for unquestioned law.

There again it is very difficult indeed to trace a chain of cause and effect. Some have put down that violent, sudden, moral revolution in political thought, which had so specially strong though brief effect here in England, to the breakdown of the older aristocracy, through civil war among the nobles at the end of the Middle Ages. Others have put down the change to a sort of political disease caught from the Continent in a moment when throughout Christendom king-worship had captured the popular soul. Others tell us that the cause lay in the growth of the urban and mercantile middle class, which demanded above all things security and was indifferent to tradition feudal or other.

But whatever the cause, the *thing* was most certainly there. Absolute government in the starkest shape had appeared in the centre of English institutions and was there to remain, apparently invincible, until the unsuspected but inevitable rise of plutocracy undermined it and pulled it down in a very few years—less than the lifetime of a man.

When we consider all these factors of political confusion boiling together in a sort of cauldron, the flame beneath which was the violent conflicting religious emotions of the Reformation, it is no wonder that the time was a tangle of ceaseless plot and counter-plot and that those in possession, trembling for the continuance of their new good fortune, should turn savage in their determination to maintain that good fortune. It is no wonder that with so many forms of wealth grown unstable and such a huge gamble going on, men should intrigue perpetually for the chance of snatching some fragment of the swag. It is, therefore, no wonder that they should instinctively take up any weapon which might guarantee them some kind of future stability. For stability is commonly maintained among men by an established, sanctified moral system, but such a system had dissolved in the turmoil of the Reformation.

Well then, torture, a social habit, a thing taken for granted and even gloried in during the spacious times of the great Elizabeth, dwindled and died out within a lifetime. Less than forty years after her death, the use of torture in England had ceased. Her contemporaries and subjects would have been very much astonished to hear that such a revolution could be possible. But so it was. It died out in rather more than half a lifetime after its moment of glory which should ever be associated with the Elizabethan name. It died out here in England earlier than it did elsewhere, although in England it had flourished with a peculiar vigour and seemed at one moment ineradicable—a very part of our life and habit. Now why did it die out?

The best answer here, as in nearly every other case of the sort is, " Because the social mind had changed," and to get at the hidden sources of change in the social mind is difficult indeed. It is within living memory, for instance, that he or she who was humorously called " the guilty

G

party " in a divorce was banned from the society of his or her equals among the wealthy. Today, divorce and its consequences are taken for granted. The baiting of the bear, and even of the more dangerous bull, was a genial sport in the eyes of our immediate ancestors. It would provoke violent and universal protest today.

But though the proper and sufficient answer to the question, " Why did torture die out? " is that the social mind has changed, it is impossible to write history without beginning from causes of some kind : even the most sudden. Of one answer to the question, we may be almost certain that it is false : the use of torture did not die out because it had proved futile. Many well-rooted habits of coercion die out because they prove futile, as, for instance, our ancient but now abandoned habit of punishing share-shufflers who rob people of their savings, or again, our ancient, but now abandoned, habit of imprisoning men who publish obscenities. But the ancient and established habit of torture in our English Courts of Justice did not perish after this fashion.

It certainly did not perish through half a dozen academic pronouncements that the use of torture formed no part of the common law of England. No one ever thought or said it did. Such protests had no effect whatever on the fate of this well-rooted institution.

We must seek as best we can elsewhere the causes which led to the decline and final disappearance of what had been the prime lawyer's habit.

I will not pretend to any final decision in the matter because I do not think a final decision can be arrived at. Cause and effect in vague but profound emotional changes of this kind escape our analysis. But I will suggest that one cause was the rise to power of the rich and the corresponding decline of Monarchy.

Under Monarchy the central government is sacred. What it does cannot be questioned without sacrilege. But once

let a rival power come in, such as, for instance, the rapidly
increasing power of the rich during the seventeenth century
with the growth of " enlightenment " and liberal ideas, and
to torture a witness in order to get the truth out of him
would have involved, as it had involved in the past, the
occasional gross interference with the comfort of men
enjoying a certain minor social position.   We all know how
in our own time the worst sufferings following on a breach
of the law are, if not remitted, at any rate softened for law-
breakers of the wealthier sort.   Now I take it that not only in
England but in most countries of Western Christendom, the
occasional example of men, not indeed prominent through
great wealth but at any rate of a minor social position,
began to shock those who had come to believe that drastic
suffering should apply only to the dregs of society.

At any rate, this main revolution of the last few lifetimes,
the increasing social privilege of wealth, has something to
do with the change.

Another cause of the change, which I think had a great
effect in England especially and was one of the causes that
torture was abandoned earlier in England than elsewhere,
was the connection of the use of torture with the ecclesiastical courts.   The average uneducated man of the present
day associates the word " torture " as at one with the word
" inquisition."   It is not his fault ; he knows no better.
The association is illuminating.   Just at the moment when
free affirmation upon all and every doctrine however
repugnant to the ancient traditional morals was growing to
be universal, the use of torture for the discovery of secret
heretical teaching was lingering into an odious old age.
Men here grew ashamed of torture as being something
foreign ; and that was enough to damn it in our system
of judicial procedure.

Let us consider the last question in connection with this
amiable subject.   I must apologise for returning to it, but
there is no understanding the Elizabethan period without

knowing also why torture played the part it did ; and to understand this we have also to answer the question, Why did torture disappear ?

Now in dealing with that question we have at once suggested to us another subsidiary question, which is not usually brought forward.

Will the use of torture revive ?

No man can foretell the future ; but if we are balancing chances, the chances would seem to be that sooner or later, and sooner rather than later, torture will reappear among judicial methods and take its place once more amid the paraphernalia of the lawyers. That such a suggestion sounds at the moment wild and absurd is of no weight against it. There is not any major development in history which would not have appeared wild and absurd to the people of an older generation. What we have to consider is the possibility of torture returning and its probability. It is not against the nature of things that it should return, rather the other way.

We have today only a relic of torture remaining and that in a highly diluted form. We have now moral torture. We allow the most offensive insult and browbeating under the cover of judicial procedure and, what is morally worse, under the cover of pretending that such things are necessary to free advocacy, and under the still worse moral principle that advocacy is a necessary adjunct to the discovery of truth. Well, if we allow moral torture, as we most un-doubtedly do and have increasingly done during the last two generations of judicial procedure (though carefully keeping the judge in the background and leaving the instigation of torture to the advocates), there is no rational or moral plea against the gradual restoration of physical torture. It now lies in the background of much police examination, though it has not yet come into the forefront thereof. For instance, a man suspected by the police may be threatened with consequences which would end in his imprisonment, not without being previously knocked about. Among those consequences might be, if he were goaded and badgered enough, a prison flogging which is certainly torture, but torture without the excuse of a search after truth : something merely vindictive or merely retaliatory or merely punitive or merely repressive.

How the beginnings of revived torture would appear, it is not difficult to conjecture. They would appear as exceptional police coercion under the veil of that secrecy which covers everything done by the highly organised modern police in every modern state. Seeing that all such things are today secret, the seed thus sown would grow in a fruitful soil.

All this is mere speculation for we know nothing of what is to come. It may be that the society immediately succeeding our own time will be as chivalric and generous as it will be brave, and as merciful as it will be just. If you can believe that you can believe anything ; but the affirmation is not open to positive disproof. It may be that cruelty—that vice which we have so happily diminished, alone of all the vices, while cultivating all the others—may die out altogether among us.

We shall see ; at least the very young among us will live to know within perhaps a long lifetime whether cruelty in connection with the discovery of evidence has returned or not. By all the precedents of action and reaction in the past it is due to return and perhaps fairly soon.

X

TOLERATION

IN connection with all this it is well worth while to consider the meaning and value of a doctrine which descends from that time and has still great vitality among ourselves. This doctrine may be called in popular parlance " the virtue of religious toleration " : the doctrine that permits differences of philosophy, however acute, however violent, co-existent in the same political community is, in some way, a political virtue : the doctrine that political action against the propagation of some philosophy different from the official philosophy of the state—not only the toleration of it, but the propagation of it, is a statesman's duty.

On the face of it, by mere definition, it seems the doctrine is nonsense ; and throughout the ages humanity has in practice decided against it. If you differ too much from the general standard of your fellow citizens in the judgment of ultimate theological values (which means, in practice, your judgment of right and wrong) they will have nothing more to do with you, and, what is more trying, get rid of you. After all, the attitude of men towards the universe, their conclusion as to the relations between themselves and the Creator (and therefore between themselves and the created world, including their own fellow beings) *must* be the deciding thing.

If any proof were needed of this obvious truth it would be furnished by the violent hostility of the English tolerant world towards the Catholic Church and all its work and fruits. When men´ excuse—though it is no thing for excuse—this natural hostility they usually explain it rather lamely by citing the intolerance of the Church itself ; and they are fond of emphasising the evils done by Catholic governments to those who rejected the religion of the philosophy of those governments. The whole thing has

96

been put into one phrase by a French commentator on the
past, himself full of a specially violent French opposition
to Catholicism : " We do not persecute you, but we will
oppose by violence your pretension to persecute others."
Now that explanation will not wash. All it means is " We
only persecute you when you propose to enforce official
doctrine against the conscience of free men." But this
excuse or explanation has no legal value.

You must first decide what it is that you regard as
morally essential to right living among citizens, and when
you have decided that you must inevitably act against
whatever force militates against such right living.

Usually the difficulty is evaded by taking it for granted
that all are agreed upon certain major propositions about
right living. If this were so there would be no problem
at all : there would be no discussion, still less any danger
of what is called " religious persecution." But as a fact
men are not so agreed upon accepted general principles in
philosophy and conduct. If they were history would be very
different ; but history sufficiently proves that men will
suffer torture rather than abandon convictions upon
ultimate truth in practice and morals, and will die in agony
for the right, not only to hold such convictions, but to
propagate them. The thing is inevitable and we must
accept it.

Amiable intellectuals of the universities are never tired
of presenting an imaginary golden age in which all men
did, in effect, accept a common philosophy, but they will
find no such golden age actually existent in the past.
Blaspheme the Gods and you will be cruelly attacked by
those who defend the Gods.

The real distinction between those who know what they
are talking about and those who do not know is that those
who know what they are talking about define their terms,
proclaim their creed and insist upon its application. Those
who do not know what they are talking about take their

creed for granted and they vaguely, rather stupidly imagine that everybody else is at heart of the same mood. You cannot have a better example of this than Cromwell's quite sincere and astonishing attitude towards the Catholic Church in Ireland. He solved the matter quite simply by saying that he drew the line at idolatry. He would allow all manner of freedom of services and whatnot, but not the freedom to worship the Real Presence of the Saviour in the Sacrament of the Altar, and the sublime sacrifice of the Mass.

Now, the men who conducted the transition of English political life under Elizabeth Tudor, and especially during her last years, were under no illusion about all this. They saw quite clearly that the return of the old religion meant the loss of their new incomes, and the loss of their new incomes was more than they could bear. Who shall blame them? We should have felt just the same. In fact we do feel just the same today. There was a touching scene in the court of a London magistrate some years ago when sundry culprits who had been guilty of preaching communist doctrines were offered their own choice between abandoning such propaganda and imprisonment. They decided, if I remember rightly, for the less pleasant alternative. All men brought up in the old liberal tradition applauded this decision. Saying (in accordance with their inheritance and tradition) " Citizens should be free to make any expression of opinion " : to this admirable statement they would add, " so long as it does not lead to acts." But the trouble is that opinion always does lead to acts. When you take an extreme example in order to prove the truth of this to your reluctant, muddle-headed fellow citizens they protest that the example being extreme is absurd. But the contrary is true. The whole value of the example lies in the fact that it *is* extreme. If you doubt it try to found a sect which advocates cannibalism, and you will soon find very active opposition to a propagation of

your ideas. In vain would you plead that you only proposed to eat the dead bodies of those who already died
natural deaths. A universal religious horror would seize
upon those who witnessed such monstrous acts. It would
be no good to meet them by saying that the principles of
religious toleration would guarantee your freedom to act.
It will guarantee no such thing. It will guarantee nothing.
You would not be safe.

Now our fathers were in much the same mood in the
matter of insult to the Sacrament of the Altar, which was
to them sacred. Some very brave, exceptional men
publicly jeered at it, and suffered the consequences of
their disrespect.

You may discover exactly the same thing today in the
matter of our modern religion of patriotism. It is true that
this religion is now beginning to be shaken, but it is still
predominant and the sentiment supporting it is still intense.
A man who should openly and contemptuously speak against
the interests of the nation, especially in time of war, and
support the interests of the enemy, would be an object, not
only of hatred, but of direct action, which would be called,
if you like, " persecution." He would at any rate have
discovered the limits of " Freedom of Thought."

All that happened in seventeenth century England after
the end of Elizabeth Tudor's reign was this : that a Catholic
minority was allowed rather precariously to survive. It
was a very large minority at first. It only slowly dwindled.
It was stamped and hallmarked as being something hostile
to the community. This was not due to the action of the
community which had, in fact, very little to do with the
matter. It was due to the action of government through
the direct personal moneyed interests of the classes who controlled the community. It may be debated whether these
classes would have prevailed against the strong popular inheritance of Catholicism. The Faith had been opposed
mainly to the leaders of that society, the principal lords of

agricultural land : that is the village squires and their superior rich colleagues, the big landed aristocracy. But there was another element in the affair, the Townees.

It has been said with a good deal of exaggeration that the Reformation succeeded in England because it was supported by London, and failed in France because it was opposed by Paris. I repeat, that judgment is exaggerated and even enormously exaggerated. But there is an element of truth in it. The population of large towns, and particularly of the capital (which commonly holds the executive government as a hostage or, if it does not hold such government as a hostage, can exile it from its natural centre and keep it in dread of losing power by such exile), is necessarily a dominant factor and may be a decisive one. It was always easy to raise in London, before the process of the Reformation was complete, a considerable and violent mob in support of the new doctrines and in attack upon the old doctrines whereof the Mass was the symbol. You could not raise such a mob before the end of Elizabeth's reign, but the opportunities for raising it had already appeared and well within a lifetime it was a common saying that the London mob could be roused against Papistry. The converse is true, and emphatically true, of the Paris populace, and the great historical symbol of its attitude was the Massacre of St. Bartholomew.

The Massacre of St. Bartholomew exactly coincided with the main turnover of government in England. The whole movement was contemporary with the establishment of William Cecil and the new religious compromise or settlement upon which he and his were determined. It may be debated to exhaustion what were the numerical and moral factors on either side which decided the issue. Certainly our modern habit of counting heads and deciding by what are called " majorities " had not much to do with it, save that the persons of an active and admitted majority on either side in a vast popular quarrel does certainly have its weight ; but intensity of conviction, acceptance of sacrifice, continuity in direction, each played their part in the result.

The Massacre of St. Bartholomew dates, as its title indicates, from the 24th of August and the year was 1572. The English religious revolution, having captured the national government more than ten years earlier (for the turning point was the confirmation of William Cecil as Secretary of State finally and permanently at the end of 1558), was by that time well in the saddle.

It may further be debated how much individuals had to do with the success or failure of the movement in the two western monarchies, but undoubtedly the decisive factor in either case was the revolution in economic power. In France where the monastic institution had badly decayed and where the revenues and places attached to it were (as in Scotland) thoroughly sunk to be lay incomes snatched at by younger sons and the rest, the monastic institution survived. In England, where the monastic institution was strong, well-established and less corrupted by wealth and favouritism than, perhaps, in any other European major community, it was rooted out.

Now here we have one of those major problems an understanding and explanation of which are the very test of sound history. It is not easy of solution for the writing of sound history is not an easy thing. Among all forms of literary expression it is perhaps the most difficult. The reason of this is that the expression of apparent contradictions or defects in the story of the past have been addressed to moderns who have forgotten the past, or at the best have an erroneous, superficial idea of what it was like.

How came it that an institution so universally omnipresent, formed and taken for granted as the monastic institution disappeared from England " in a day and a night," so to speak ? I have debated that capital question with many contemporaries who were more or less qualified to understand the situation. (I say "more or less" because it is very rare to find among my contemporaries anyone with a full comprehension of what monasticism means, and still more rare to find anyone who can understand the Reformation past of England.)

I do not pretend to answer that most difficult of historical questions. I shall only suggest certain elements in the true answer to it. The first, of course, is the major factor that organised economic power was avid against the monasteries. It paid the whole of the English governing class to sweep them away. It paid nobody to maintain them in existence. This would have been true of pretty well any society in Western Europe at that moment, but it was specially true of England because the example had been set on every side. In every parish throughout that small agricultural England with its four or five million population the dissolution of the monasteries meant ultimately the enrichment of the men who had local power. That is not nearly enough to account for so sudden and so complete a change. You must also visualise, make real to yourself, that vital force of monarchy which has today in England been completely lost: the awful and conclusive authority of the sovereign. When Henry decided to defy the Holy See, to dissolve the communities amongst the nuns who claimed a defence against compensation from the centre of Christendom at Rome, he acted as King, and the word *King* meant more in the first half of the sixteenth century than is meant today by the words "capitalism," "army and navy," "police," "banks" all rolled together. It was a permanent attitude in men's minds that the monarch was the unquestioned director of the state. This did not mean that a monarch could do anything unquestioned. ' He could not for there was always the resource of rebellion against him, but the civic mind of those days was so steeped in the conception of royal authority that such authority formed, after economic power, the strongest power among men.

Here is another consideration : when the monastic institution was attacked for the benefit and with the support of the governing class it was socially in decay.

It is very difficult for the modern Englishman as he reads the story of his ancestors to understand what the decline of monasticism meant under the early Tudors. He has never known monasticism ; he has never formed part of a society wherein monasticism was a great social force. It seems to him a natural, an inevitable development, that the old mediæval monasticism should be replaced by the things and institutions which he knows. He comes into a modern English village, he finds the greater part of its land, as a rule, in the possession of one rich man. He sees no example of communal property anywhere. He naturally concludes that communal property is somehow an alien idea which Englishmen would not naturally support. Now Englishmen did naturally support communal monastic institutions everywhere throughout England during the Middle Ages. But that institution had already been undermined before Henry, with the support of the wealthier classes, battered it down.

There had been a most striking decline in its mere numbers. The great houses were down to something less than half their old establishment. This in itself would perhaps have not been fatal. The decline began at the Black Death, the losses then sustained had never been recovered, but had the institution remained vigorously alive it would have done what all institutions do, recuperated itself and built itself up again organically from recoupment. English monasticism failed to do this.

No doubt had English monasticism survived sufficiently during that generation to enjoy a new recoupment it would have been maintained. The blow fell upon it just when it was numerically at its worst.

Next we must remember that the Renaissance everywhere throughout Christendom and in England as much as anywhere else was in moral revolt against the monastic institution. That tradition was already held to be ridiculously outworn.

It was no longer the fashion and fashion governs men more than does any other goddess. Nobody had a good word to say any more for what had been the most vigorous of social institutions only two or three lifetimes earlier. All the stories of the time are stories ridiculing and taking for granted the corruption of the monasteries and of their inhabitants. It is the commonplace of sixteenth century literature, not only on its jocose side, but on its serious side. We have a parallel to the affair in our attitude towards capitalism today. Our intellectuals and all those whom they reflect take it for granted that capitalism is evil. Any movement against it, even so extreme a movement as anti-Jewish persecution, now for the moment so triumphant among the Prussians, is now received with a certain sympathy. The sympathy is not universal, but it is sufficiently widespread to be a symptom or index of the modern mind.

Again, nothing is more remarkable than the decline in our own day of the respect for the moral right to property. Now a mental revolution of this sort had taken place throughout Christendom at the end of the Middle Ages with regard to monasticism. When we undermine the moral basis of anything, the moral respect which it demands, you have gone far towards the destruction of that thing. Respect for the monastic institution had been seriously undermined even in England by the early sixteenth century.

Nor were the communities themselves content with their own traditions, still less enthusiastic for these institutions. When the monks and nuns were left free to repudiate their vows, they did so freely. There was a considerable proportion—what proportion we cannot tell, but one certainly large enough to affect the issue—who were members of the monastic communities without special vocation. Now to be a contented member of a monastic community, to be a contented monk or nun, requires what the ancient religion of the English calls a " vocation." If you are not called to that life in a special manner you will find it irksome indeed. To most people it would seem, not only irksome, but unnatural. In the decay of the Middle Ages there was hardly any religious community which had not a considerable fraction of men or women who would have been glad to escape from the discipline of conventual life (a discipline already badly relaxed) and it was mere danger of poverty which stood in the way of their release.

There were many other forces at work to disintegrate the monastic inheritance of the West though these forces were far weaker in England than in most parts of Christendom. They were here also and they worked in favour of the revolution which was taking place.

To all this must be added the very great effect on human affairs of a *military* tyranny. There had been a general rising throughout England against the new liturgy introduced by Seymour and his gang of harpies. Such a reaction was inevitable for, powerful though the landed interest was and universal as was its action throughout the country, you cannot attempt to reverse the domestic habits of a whole population without provoking resistance. Later, when the monasteries were attacked, there came the Pilgrimage of Grace supported mainly by the northern part of the country because resistance had been beaten down elsewhere with great ferocity by the interested beneficiaries of the Reformation and also because the north was further away from the centre of government.

But over that rebellion the forces of the Crown, ill-organised though they were, had gained *military* ascendancy. Such ascendancy would not have been achieved without the treachery of the Duke of Norfolk, but achieved it was and when the rebellion was suppressed the suppression had all the effect enjoyed in regular warfare by a victory in the field. Moreover the defeated rebels were hung all over

the place in very great numbers. You could not take a
long walk about England anywhere without seeing swinging
from some gibbet the wretched body of a man (or woman)
whom the authorities, that is to say the governing class,
had put to death for resisting the new interests of the
wealthy.

Nor had the popular resistance been of a simple and
religious kind. Had it been so it might have succeeded,
rather was it mixed up with all manner of confused griev-
ances. The new social order which had gradually and
imperceptibly developed through more than a century had
remembered a mass of discontent which had been focused on
nothing so simple as religious change. Rather were these
discontentments the product of a confused social memory.
Men wondered why a golden age which had not been so
golden after all should have disappeared and why they were
being exploited after a somewhat novel fashion which they
did not fully understand. They resented such oppression
far more than they resented the novel doctrinal points which
did not concern their ordinary lives and which, indeed, had
as yet hardly been raised. It has been very correctly pointed
out by such historians as Blunt (who has written in detail
upon this matter) that there was no sharp interruption of
ancient religious habits until the great social revolution
which is marked by the advent of Elizabeth Tudor to the
throne as the figurehead of the change of religion, still
more as the monarch in whose name the great transference
of property from communal bodies to wealthy landlords
had taken place.

There is a last element in the situation to be considered :
the presence of a new generation and the loss of older
experience. It was in some degree revolutionary to be
anti-Catholic in the later years of Henry, but it was also
to be novel, to be young, and to be doing what youth did
all around one. We must remember that there was no
general challenge to ordinary habits or inherited beliefs,

although the parish Mass had been elbowed out and a vernacular service substituted for it. There was nothing to prevent a man who preferred the older habit of life from taking Communion at the hands of a priest who might be regarded as orthodox ; and the habit of attending either service, that in the ancient tradition or in the new established form, seems to have been very widely prevalent. It was only after the great movement which came at the end of Elizabeth's first dozen years of reign that the suppression of Catholicism became at all vigorous or general.

There is a debate upon the point whether provocation came mainly from the state or from the old religious tradition which the state was now slowly eradicating. The debate is not germane to our issue for, indeed, neither party began the quarrel. To the reformers the vernacular liturgy in great part translated from the older forms and permitting of the widest interpretation seemed natural enough and no one can fail to remark that there was a lack of any strong reaction against it after the battle had been lost.

But the thing can be discussed indefinitely without our coming to a clear conclusion. The liturgical revolution was neither violent nor profound. It had no such effects as were to be found in the corresponding Scottish change.

One of the most illuminating terms commonly used in a later generation is the term " Tridentine." You will find it in the diarists and others of the succeeding century after the Reformation had done its most and Catholic reaction was organised under the authority of the general Council of Trent. Therefore although reaction was almost from its beginning attacked as a novelty we are told that the Catholic resistance was not itself a novel thing.

Popular phraseology which distinguishes generally between the Catholic and the Protestant sides of the great quarrel is not a sufficient criterion. The real point of the

H

great religious revolution which took place in the English mind during the reign of Elizabeth is *definition*. Those of orthodox tradition, those who desired the return of the ancient faith—only a minority desired it with any burning zeal—had no clear-cut programme nor any real leaders until the missionary priests began to come in, devoted to martyrdom. They failed ; and it behoves us to understand the nature of their failure, why they were defeated and how, if we are to understand the story of England under Elizabeth.

XI

THE CHURCH OF ENGLAND

IN the reign of Elizabeth Tudor can fairly be placed the rise and consolidation of that great national institution called " the Church of England." This is in general history the chief mark of that time and place : the establishment of the Established Church.

But of all historical statements this is the one which needs most careful approach and most modification, if we are to avoid ambiguity and falsehood ; for every single term used in connection with the life and character of that main national institution is subject to dispute, and the widest margin must be allowed for the play of that dispute, lest readers, unacquainted with the subject matter, should be misled—and, under modern conditions, very many readers of the English-speaking world are but partially acquainted with the subject matter.

To begin with, the word " Church " is in this connection used with very various meanings. It is used to connote very different functions : a teaching authority ; a repository of doctrine ; a special department of Christendom as a whole ; a local, purely national institution ; a much more extended institution which is alive and at work far outside the boundaries of the English State, all over the territories from which allegiance is claimed to the English throne. Before we can speak of the origin or progress, institution or development of the Church of England between the coronation of Elizabeth Tudor and her death, we must define the difficult, often uncertain, terms of our subject.

It is best perhaps to take the central historical fact to begin with ; and the central historical fact is this : that there exists a certain corporation, ecclesiastical in character but possessed of a regular organisation with regular officers, having public titles attached to their functions. This corporation is known as the Church of England or " The Established Church " in England itself; and those words obviously relate to the known thing, though they do not define its character (even where that thing exists outside the civil jurisdiction of the British Crown). The officers directing this corporation and, forming what may be called in general terms the governing body thereof, are bishops in communion with the archiepiscopal sees of Canterbury and York. Very nearly all these officers have a defined territorial limit to the exercise of their functions and these are, of course, at home, the English sees, and, abroad, such sees as may be in communion with these and attached to them in one general corporation. Below the order of bishops come the priests—to use the term legally attached to these officers—and the priests are supported by the lesser orders of deacons and subdeacons, from whom their own order is recruited. The total, including the laymen who accept the ecclesiastical authority of these officers, has a particular character, a special and unmistakable nature of its own, although controversy upon what the true bases of that character may be is endless. Most members of the Church of England affirm, one can even say that all active members would affirm, the continuity of this ecclesiastical corporation with everything that has been united from a remote past under an episcopalian system of Church government in these islands and the territories immediately subject to them. There are some of its members who would affirm so complete a change in the Church of England during the period of the Reformation that it became a new thing; and certainly there arose during that period a characteristic atmosphere generally called " Protestant," with which those who are not themselves members of the Church of England generally connect that institution. Roughly speaking, the foreigner, and the bulk of the natives as well, will tell you that the Church of England is a Protestant Church. But we must remember that such a proposition is vehemently denied by those who claim and vigorously maintain the continuity of the Church of England throughout the ages from the first establishment of Christian missions in these islands. We must use the term " these islands " and not the term " this island " alone, to be perfectly clear in our definition, lest we exclude the organised Episcopalian Christian communities planted in Ireland and claimed by the Church of England today as being part of the one body.

There is indeed one characteristic mark discoverable throughout the whole of that body, which is a repudiation of the Bishop of Rome, commonly called the Pope, and his jurisdiction. On that there is no doubt, though it is only accepted with reserve and qualification, as is everything else in connection with the title, " Church of England." Subject to such qualifications, the definition stands : an ecclesiastical corporation organised under an episcopate essentially national.

There is between a thing, a concrete real thing, whether that thing be an invisible corporation or a tangible object, a distinction which would be discovered everywhere in connection with all objects whatsoever : a distinction between the thing as we know it, a subject of experience, and the terms under which it may be defined. Of these two distinguishable things, the first is obviously the one of chief importance. We are concerned everywhere with the actual *things* under examination or discussion ; of that presence and reality we can entertain no doubt. On the underlying principles and definitions, controversy may be indefinitely extended. So it is with the Church of England. No one with the most elementary knowledge of the modern world can fail to recognise the *thing* when he comes across it. On how he would define it, which of its characters he would admit and which deny, there is no positive guide, no universally admitted element, save that it is national and possesses certain admitted formularies, creeds and canons, etc., patient of various interpretations.

At first when Elizabeth acceded, her realm was, as every-body knows, in communion with Rome. It had been " reconciled " (as the technical theological term goes) under her sister Mary. But this was only the last of several steps, each of which had marked sharply defined phases in the violent oscillation of opinion and legal definition which had covered forty years ; and in the course of which the public mind had become, especially towards the end of the process, appreciably confused even upon matters of doctrine, still more upon matters of practice and ritual habit.

It is customary to take the definite Lutheran movement originating in 1517 (more than sixteen years before Elizabeth was born), as the mainspring of the Reformation and the dividing-line between the preparation of a Protestant mentality and the open definite expression thereof. Indeed, the date 1517 (which is even earlier by more than seven years than Henry's first approach to that divorce from which his breach with the Papacy sprang) is the obvious boundary between the traditional ecclesiastical system of Western Europe and the positive reforming movement ; but, of course, that movement had been in process of incubation long before.

The real shock which launched active Protestantism was not Luther's original protest, but the publication of Calvin's book nearly ten years later, under the reign of his sovereign, Francis I, the King of France ; and this book which changed the history of Europe (it is called " The Institution of the Christian Religion ") came at a moment almost con-temporary with the attack of the Crown upon the monastic endowments of England. Both these capital things date from 1536, by which time the King of England had defied the jurisdiction of Rome for over three years (his marriage to Anne Bullen, Elizabeth's mother, may be taken as the breaking-point). The small but very eager body of anti-Catholic doctrinaires in England had been opposed by the King, but Henry had not long to live and meanwhile the enormous loot of monastic property had been launched. That loot had been consolidated when the revolt of the English people had been crushed immediately after. The natural determination of the new possessors to keep their new possessions inspired the effort to change the dynasty when little Edward VI was dying. That effort failed : Mary and the old orthodoxy were violently acclaimed by the English people as a whole, but the intense conviction of the reformers inspired a continued energetic attack and those who were devoted to that course were of great effect, through their zeal, eloquence and tenacity. It is debatable whether the numerous cruel executions of the next three years did really start any appreciable reaction in favour of the new doctrine. But the battle had already half exhausted the more violent of the assailants and the defenders when Mary Tudor died.

Put your mind back into the position of some fairly well-instructed man of fairly influential position among his fellows in some English countryside of that moment, at the end of 1558. Take such a man to have been at the time in the full vigour of middle life, say about fifty years of age. All his experience, like that of his neighbours, had been of sudden, sharp changes and attempted changes. Since his early boyhood and the boyhood of his contemporaries somewhat older than himself, those who were leaders by their energy and their talents were, for the most part, in reaction against the old traditional religion. The unity of religion under the accepted headship of the Pope had been denied during the years when his character was forming. The liturgy had remained the same ; he had heard the immemorial Mass at the parish church Sunday after Sunday (though not everyone attended, among a generally Catholic community of those days, any more than all will attend in such a community today. Precision in religion and the discipline of it belong rather to unpopular minorities than to the bulk of any population). All through his formative years he had heard and accepted or rejected the new speculations. He was still a young man, well under thirty, when that tidal wave, the loot of ecclesiastical property swept over England. The chances are that his family, perhaps his father, had been greatly benefited by the change. The manorial rights of the old monastic orders could be bought cheap and sometimes seized outright under the plea of an original foundation. Then came the years, for him the most vigorous of his life, the years of early maturity and manly energy, when dispute reached its height and almost anything seemed to be possible. He had had brief experience of the Mass translated into the English of his day and read out in that vernacular and chanted in that vernacular, an innovation which may have shocked or may have pleased him ; for many were shocked but some were pleased. After all that turmoil, accompanied by the intense unpopularity of upstart adventurers claiming the power of the throne, disturbing his patriotism and throwing his sense of allegiance into chaos, there comes the restoration of all the old things suddenly to the delight of the people, probably to his own belated satisfaction ; but it is accompanied by a proposal to destroy the new properties founded upon the loot of religion by his own class who had specially benefited. That class successfully opposes the change and the new distribution of property is maintained. That to which in all times men have been most attached, their wealth, is secured to him and his heirs, so long as there is no further reinforcement of the still well-rooted Catholicism of England ; but he and his family and all about him stand in some peril of loss. The newly established properties have hardly taken root. All those who enjoy them will instinctively combine to maintain their new advantages. They are the stronger by an alliance with older families of greater position who have also taken part in the loot wholesale. Your local Englishman of 1558-9, not only weary of a contest which seems interminable but already in some doubt whether a great mass of property recently acquired by him may not be threatened, sees security in a public settlement, without any active assault upon the doctrines he has inherited but for which he is no longer enthusiastic. A compromise following the line of least resistance seems natural to him and to many more inevitable. It is officially confirmed ; and he is now a fully accredited member of what we call the Church of England, but his vocabulary and social habits are still of the older world and carry with them still a savour of the old religion which had recently been the life of that world.

The growth, strengthening and final full formation of this institution " the Church of England " (in the form which we now know) was far more than the mere effect of a compromise between the various interests which divided men in this country in the last part of the sixteenth century. The Church of England, as we know it, was determined not only by the obvious interests of the landed class which had acquired so thoroughly such large additions of wealth on the dissolution of the monasteries, but also by a force which historians singularly neglect : the Power of the Word. Informing, quickening ; and at last welding the thing was a glorious use of the new English tongue.

The Church of England as we now know it was thus principally created by its liturgy, one of the finest things in the literature of Europe ; and also a thing unique.

Here let me recite a personal reminiscence which is indeed relevant to our subject.

I had occasion many years ago to advise upon a piece of satire—that rare but powerful instrument in social and political affairs—which piece of satire dealt with the life of a well-to-do obscure orthodox patriotic English merchant. He was but a figure of fiction ; but the author of that exercise desired to make him typical of his time, the last years of Queen Victoria ; and the disturbance of such a man's inherited ideals by the new movement called " Imperialism." It was the moment of the South African war.

A man who at that time was prominent—indeed the first amongst both the historical scholars of his age at Oxford and the appreciators of high English, being consulted upon the work in question, criticised adversely any satirical allusion to the ritual and what seem to many the merely conventional phrases of the Anglican liturgy. These phrases are at their finest in two famous documents : the Marriage Service and the Burial Service. This pre-eminent judge of what should and should not appear in a satire, strongly advised against the use of satire in connection with the liturgy, although strongly in sympathy with the agnostic side, indeed devoted to it. He said (and we must presume upon such credentials that he was right), " There is now such a sanctity attached to these rhythms in the public mind that any disrespectful treatment of them would mar the satirical effect of all the rest. The death of the merchant who formed the central figure in this piece of fiction must be left to the natural and profound emotions which are now inseparable from the English Burial Service."

Such is the Power of the Word.

It is to be remarked that foreigners unacquainted with the intimate and central forces of English life today, misapprehend this point altogether. No translation of that glorious prose into any modern contemporary language is adequate or can begin to be adequate. Such prose was forged in the white heat of the great controversy. Its main author was Cranmer ; but there is no signed manual, there is no accredited authorship. It is as though a great poem had been left not only unsigned but impersonal. The English Liturgy had appeared without generation, like a god. They are to be excused who profess towards it a sort of idolatry.

It is the prose of the English liturgy, far more than any other spiritual force at work in those violent days, which achieved the separation between the older England, inheriting from even the first centuries of Christendom, and the new England of the last three and a half centuries.

The thing is now accomplished : the casting, which had been poured into its mould when all was fluid is now fixed and permanent. It may be doubted whether it will ever be replaced, or whether the nation henceforward can seriously consider any other such influences. Attempts at revision may justly be called a failure, though they have been most honestly undertaken and most painstakingly. The liturgy of the Church of England, now ancient, traditional and sanctified by that emotion of patriotism which is the deepest feeling of the English, takes its permanent monumental place in the story of Europe. The echoes of it will continue to sound throughout the world which speaks or reads English ; but the core of it, the reality of it, will remain a peculiar possession to the citizens of this polity.

The translation from the Latin, from the immemorial liturgical Latin of Western Christendom ; " *Omnipotens misericors Deus* " is transmuted into " Almighty and everlasting God." Can any man conceive a stronger resurrection ?

DISSENT

COMPLEMENTARY to the conception of an Established National Church is the conception of dissent from such a Church.

In legal or constitutional theory, every subject of the British Crown is born a member of the Church of which the British Crown was called at first " The Supreme Head " and later " The Supreme Governor."

The original conception of a necessary, perfect religious unity among citizens was very strong at the beginning of Elizabeth's reign. It rapidly declined, for the reason that the religious revolution, during which the new establishment was arranged, had been Protestant in character. Therefore the New English Church was alive with the doctrine of private judgment. Therefore, also, it was full of those forces which made for separate Protestant sects.

Such sects did, as a fact, arise, but they were not fully organised until much later. Their rise, their character, their social tone and the rest of it is comprised among Englishmen under the general term " dissent." Dissent is thus the converse and complementary social and religious phenomenon which accompanies the newly established English state religion from the great sixteenth century change onwards.

We see the past through such a violent distorting medium of modern experience that the use of words with which we are familiar, and the meaning of which we take for granted, is often wholly misleading. A word which has a particular meaning at a certain period becomes, in modern times, vague and general—for instance, in the early seventeenth century the word " gentleman " had as particular a meaning as the word " hound " or the word " ox " or (to compare like with like) as the word " burgess," to which it stood in contrast at Oxford a hundred years ago. When we talk today of a man as a " Dissenter," the word connotes a certain measure of blame or contempt. It would be rude for us today to say to a man, " Are you a Dissenter ? " But you could legitimately say with proper courtesy, " Your family was Nonconformist, was it not ? " and even so you would have to handle the word " with hooks "—as the immortal Pitcher puts it.

A Dissenter from the establishment of the National Church early in the reign of Elizabeth, to at least the death of that monarch and beyond, meant a person who protested in some degree against the doctrine of the Established Church, and, nine times out of ten, " Dissent " connoted a denial of the real or supposed doctrine of the Established Church because it was not Protestant enough.

The words " Dissent " and " Dissenter " as a fact were very rarely used ; they became common only much later. But we must have names for things if we are to discuss them at all ; and the names " Dissent " and " Dissenter " are both convenient, well known and accurate.

In a sense, of course, the Catholic in communion with Rome who insisted upon following the Mass whenever he could get it and who would (at the very *end* of the process of Establishment) even refuse to communicate in the parish church was a Dissenter, and I myself have met old-fashioned people who have called me to my face a " Dissenter " because they could ride away on the excuse that the term was accurate : which indeed it is. A papist living in a Sussex village, as I did in my youth, and going to his own chapel, avoiding the established worship of the village church, was and is, technically, a " Dissenter."

But, as everyone knows, the word " Dissenter " has taken on a special meaning. It does not connote mere dissent from the doctrines of the Established Church (as expressed, say, in the Thirty-Nine Articles) but an implied protest that such doctrines are not sufficiently opposed to those of Rome.

Now Dissent, raising what its enemies call its " ugly head " but its friends " conscientious protest," was inevitably called into existence in England by the presence there, side by side with Dissent of an official Church, possessing and enunciating a certain measure of doctrine (though the definition of this last was never very strict), in the midst of a society wherein a very active minority was attached to religious definitions more precise and more directly hostile to the old religion.

The size of this anti-Catholic minority may be debated within very wide limits even up to the end of Elizabeth's reign. The Dissenting body was certainly quite small in the years before her accession. It was estimated, by careful contemporaries, at less than ten per cent. of the population (it was probably much less). Even those who counted almost anything as Protestant so long as it was not actively associated with the Roman Mass, would not at the end of Elizabeth's reign reckon the body of expressed Catholic allegiance at less than one-half of the nation. Without a clear comprehension of these proportions no one can understand the period.

The marks of dissent became, as Elizabeth's reign proceeded, clearer and clearer and were, at the very end of that reign, beginning to be generally defined. There were not a few bodies, especially among the middle classes of the towns, who openly accepted special new doctrines and the preference of such church government as would go with those doctrines.

The most important by far of these dissenting bodies was the Presbyterian. It had morally conquered north of the Border for even the Established Church in Scotland had adopted a Presbyterian air and manner, though it stopped short of allowing such an influence to transform the machinery of church government;

Now, though Scotland was much poorer than England and far smaller in population (perhaps not a quarter or a little more), two things gave influence to the national religious tone of the Scotch and made this in some degree an article for export. The first of these things was definition. The second was zeal : a zeal which was sufficient to produce in due time its crop of martyrs. Of a somewhat different complexion, but still wholeheartedly hostile to the ancient religion, was the Independent Body with which the name of Oliver Cromwell himself will always be associated. He was born but shortly before the death of Elizabeth Tudor, but his boyhood and the first formation of his character came so immediately upon the last influences of the Elizabethan reign that his religion is alive with the Dissenting vigour at work during the last years of Elizabeth.

There already existed, also, a certain small number of families wherein the divinity of Christ was denied. My own forebears, on the English side of my family, were attached to this capital mark differentiating them from the bulk of their fellow Protestants. They gave to themselves later the distinctive (and accurate) title of " Unitarians."

There arose, also, of course, a host of minor sects and sub-divisions, the principle inspiring which was the choice of religion by the individual and, therefore, the multiplication of separate bodies. It was this principle which weakened or destroyed the conception of an authoritative and teaching Church ; a conception originally native and even essential to the Reformers and maintained in vigour, until the eve of our own times, among English Protestants.

The main interest historically of the birth of the Dissenting Movement during the reign of Elizabeth is the after-effect of that movement upon the religion, and therefore the politics, of European men.

English Dissent produced a spiritual atmosphere—and therefore a political atmosphere—somewhat differentiated from the general Protestant atmosphere of Europe outside England. It did so for this reason : that elsewhere the quarrel between the Reformers and the ancient united religion of Europe was, in the main, clear-cut ; whereas here, in England (and, through England, in the English-speaking American world originally sprung from England) there was a sort of *diversity* in Protestantism which was not to be found elsewhere.

The English Nonconformist movement was rooted not in a new philosophy such as Calvinism was, but in that main revolution with which I have already wearied my readers (and shall continue to weary them) the looting of the Abbey Lands. It was the immense and sudden transfer of landed property, at one blow, in a thoroughly revolutionary manner, to a new set of owners, but still more to a new *kind* of ownership, which did the trick. The monasteries had lost their lands.

We have seen that the total transfer was anything from one-third to one-fifth of *all* the rentals of England ; and that vast mass of income changed hands *abruptly* between 1536 and 1540.

The ultimate effect was much wider than that : for the speculators who bought (and sold again) the new properties, enjoyed so immediate and, for the most part, so unexpected a piece of good fortune, that the whole habit of mind that man had inherited upon the possession (or rather *the over-lordship*) of land in this country became transformed.

It is true that the process was not over as early as 1540. The mass of the change was delayed for more than half a dozen years till the rapid dissolution of the whole fabric took place, through the Crown needing money for the French war.

On top of this came a further, slower, transformation of the landed system through the more gradual further loot of religion after Henry VIII's death. The gang of harpies, led by the Seymour brothers, which swooped down on

England while the nominal king was still a little boy, got rid of all manner of Church endowments to fill their own pockets. They sliced great fragments off the episcopal revenues. They captured tithes innumerable and got into their hands all manner of other property which had been hitherto a corporate and, in a way, sort of *public* use, until the great flood had broken loose.

The main period of this wild orgy in private enrichment at the expense of the English people continued during the whole reign of Queen Elizabeth—and that revolution was hardly completed at her death. Indeed those who would establish in history the main effect of Elizabeth's reign will emphasise particularly this huge economic upheaval.

As for Elizabeth herself, poor woman, she got little or no benefit by it; and the Crown, of which she was the precarious tenant, got still less, but in her day, following on a royal minority conducted for the benefit of the base Seymour brothers and their successors, and during the failure of Mary Tudor's desperate effort to save what could be saved, the snatching of religious endowments went on continually until the face of England was transformed.

We have also to remember in this connection the families who became millionaires at a jump by using the strange opportunity of the whole sweep of confiscation and still more the opportunities for buying cheap and either selling again dear or enjoying the increased value of the stolen land. Over and over again one finds land which would normally have sold at twenty years' purchase, or a little less, selling, or accounted for, at more like ten years' purchase.

The number of cases where land (and ecclesiastical endowment in general) was robbed out of hand and completely, are in a minority. Probably, if one could collect *all* the statistics (a thing today quite impossible) we should find that the cases of complete, cynical, and immediate theft came to a small minority on the whole. We have, indeed, stories (most of them only traditional, but one or

I

two authenticated and provable) which tell us of complete wholesale theft conducted in one operation. But when we examine in detail the transference of rental valuation during that prodigious upheaval which changed the face of England and began a new society, we naturally always go on figures of sales or valuation which, while showing the very advantageous means by which the looters got hold of their new wealth, still testify to the fact that the greater part of them did not get it for nothing.

The Crown, which was the chief agent in this vast robbery, raked in part of the valuation. Had some wise administration been present in the Central Government (instead of the reckless folly of Henry himself, with his utterly incalculable impetuous adventures) it might still have been that the looting of the ecclesiastical endowments would have ended by making the English Monarchy the richest in Europe. As it was, the storm left that Monarchy ruined for ever.

The common complaint against Elizabeth—or rather against Elizabeth's Government—that she and it were parsimonious, is a very false rating of history. They were not parsimonious : she was not niggardly. Queen and Government were ruined. Then there was this further factor : the purchasing power of money was going down the whole time, even after the currency had been reformed. Measured by the only accurate standard ; the purchasing value of the ounce of gold or its equivalent in silver was falling ; not indeed continuously but uninterruptedly, from the beginning of the great change and right on until the eighteenth century. The Crown received its revenue principally in *Customary* dues. It had to pay out wages and to purchase material at *Competitive* monetary rates, and that is the explanation of the economic breakdown of the Government which led at last to the Civil Wars and afterwards to the enslavement of the national executive by the wealthier classes.

Meanwhile, side by side with the ruin of the Central Government went the dissipation of religion.

The old fixed moral standards, inherited for generations, had disappeared under the shock of the economic revolution which had scattered not only the endowments of the old religion but its economic structure as a whole. The new generation which came on to a new England after the shock of that Gigantic Loot entered a society cut off from its past.

XIII

BUNYAN, WORDSWORTH AND OTHERS

I BEG to be excused for dragging in the name and fame of John Bunyan and adding them to pages which concern an earlier age, but no one will ever understand Bunyan, late as he was, who does not connect him with that earlier thing from which he derived : the dissenting fervour (which was already, in the case of a small minority, the *Puritan* fervour) appearing in the later days of Elizabeth's reign. And no one can understand that fervour and its special quality who has not grasped Bunyan and especially his most famous work, the " Pilgrim's Progress." It was despised by the collector of its time and is secretly, though I think unjustly, despised by very many cultivated men who claim a full appreciation of English literature. As with all those whose reputation is carried on the shoulders of religious enthusiasm rather than on their total technical performance as writers, Bunyan's manner has been given an inflated reputation. His matter is not open to debate in this connection. It was, of course, nothing deeper or wider than the Calvinism he had inherited. If that Calvinism is sympathetic to the reader the reader will praise Heaven for John Bunyan and the opportunities he has himself had of reading what is perhaps the most popular of the great English classics.

I approach the subject of John Bunyan and excuse myself for bringing it in thus belatedly long after that Elizabethan period (which is itself so commonly post-dated) through a certain personal experience which, at the risk of wearying the reader, I will now describe.

Just at the age when impressions are most vivid, at the moment when I was beginning to read but was still a child, " Pilgrim's Progress " became an active part of my life. It was read to me by the woman who brought me up and was in deep sympathy with its theme. Better still, she had, herself, had acquaintance with it from early childhood, and so had her family before her. That tradition takes one back to not more than a long lifetime after the famous book was written. Bunyan's *floruit* is from the middle of the seventeenth century onwards. He was born when Elizabeth, herself, had been dead for a quarter of a century, in 1628. The influence which moulded the humble circumstances of his early life were the influences of what was, upon one side of the English nation, and that the growing side, the very core of the national religion. And *that* is why he is so valuable to the historian and why those who find his manner repulsive, his creed absurd, and his emotional attachment to it puerile should make themselves especially acquainted with Bunyan's work if they would understand the heart of the English Protestant world. It is incumbent upon anyone who desires to grasp the inner and real quality of what was most intensely alive in the England of the later Reformation to make himself familiar with Bunyan's work, however much it may exasperate him or arouse his contempt, for it has moved very many and very great judges of English who are devoted to that work.

For what a personal judgment is worth (and a personal judgment hardly enters into the matter), I stand half-way. I do not deny the strength of his greater passages, though these are brief and often irrational, but I discover his interest to be mainly testimonial. Bunyan and his work are most vivid witnesses to a special moment and a special very important province of English political and social development. He not only wrote prose, some of it very striking, though most of it dull enough as far as style goes, he also wrote verse. It is jogtrot and passably ridiculous, but we do well to appreciate the fact that a proved writer who moved millions to enthusiasm was also a writer of verse which would move no one to anything but hearty ridicule. It is one of the best examples in literature of the peculiarity of verse, or to use a more sublime word, of poetry, that a man who was always dropping under the stress of his strong emotions into poetry wrote such absurd lines.

Bunyan's verse was an episode of which I suppose posterity will be a good deal ashamed—if indeed posterity preserves any memory of it—for it is quite on the cards that posterity will drop the whole thing.   It is quite on the cards that that strange episode of what some have called the " Puritan madness " will become to our successors not only dull, but meaningless.   It has no roots in the noble soil of European literature.   Whether it lives or survives the historian must not only notice it, but be actually conscious of it if he is to understand England, for the Puritan literature affected the future of this country more than did any other spiritual force.   Our appreciation of its value in history is nothing to do with our liking or disliking of it.   History is concerned with what was and in the relation of what was, so that today, however strange " what was " has become, we should still understand it and enter into some communion with it.

We may say, justly, what on earth was the motive of the excuse for these Puritan aberrations ?   We shall have some difficulty in answering that question, but at any rate the first point in the affair is to note the fact that the aberrations were *there*.   They took place.   They profoundly affected the English mind.   They had about them so much force that they affected even more profoundly the growth of a new society beyond the Atlantic and this new society having taken root produced in our own time that very remarkable and flourishing tree, an uncommonly large one, called the " United States."   The United States was produced by a rebellion against the connection of the colonies with England.   That rebellion was led principally by the Southern slave-owning gentry, but it was strongly supported by the commercial North.

It may be debated whether the United States of North America and their sharply differentiated culture would ever have arisen under other guidance than that of the Puritan tradition. The new nation beyond the Atlantic was not launched under the sole direction of the Puritan tradition. It derived from many other sources of which the most important was the Anglican gentry of the South, but the Puritan tradition has overshadowed the whole affair. It has produced political results peculiar to the United States : not to be discovered elsewhere. In our own time, for instance, it produced the to us extraordinary phenomenon called " prohibition " ; laws forbidding, in varying degrees, the manufacture and sale of intoxicating drink. This experiment for a time covered the whole community. It is now restricted to special districts. The characteristic of prohibition in these districts is that it there reposes upon public opinion and a public vote. To most men of a traditional European culture the prohibition of popular beverages, such as beer and wine, seems so abnormal as to be hardly sane, but it is to be remarked that where there has been popular excess in the consumption of ardent spirits rather than a common and temperate use of wine or beer the conception of prohibition can exist and can even flourish in the air of Europe.

There is in connection with the literary effect of English dissent a very interesting phenomenon which may be called Protestant Pantheism. The high priest and chief exponent of this frame of mind was William Wordsworth. It is most interesting to note how Wordsworth is treated with a sort of special reverence of exactly the sort which attaches to religious ideas. To call him names, to affirm with violence a detestation of his pantheist sentiments affects the hearer of such an attack in exactly the same manner as men are affected by an attack upon a transcendental creed which they have accepted.

Here is an element in English society and its derivatives

which the foreigner cannot understand. The Irishman, for instance, can make nothing of it. I have met many Frenchmen who labour most industriously at English literary history, but not one of them could I meet who had explained to himself the position of William Wordsworth's verse.

Here there comes in a question of high interest which may be put thus : Did the Protestant Movement in Europe advance or retard the literature of Europeans ?

Here is a question of particular, almost vital, interest to Englishmen because Englishmen stand in the very forefront of European literature and are also the special product of the Reformation. Protestantism gave not only impetus, but a sort of sanctity to emotion : not only to the religious emotion, but to pretty well all emotion. It had the converse effect of checking or destroying the classical spirit. It put a very high value on the rhetoric—on that form of human expression which the ancient philosopher described as being " not either verse nor prose, but a mean between the two." When a man tells you today that the Authorised Version of the Scriptures is written in very fine English (which it is) he means " in very fine rhetoric," and he will always be astonished upon hearing that the writing of Swift, for instance, may be called an example superior to the best passages in Isaiah or in the Book of Job. Yet the statement is accurate and valuable as criticism and as history. The essential of prose is the transference of thought from the mind of the writer to the mind of the reader, and prose is successful *as* prose in proportion as it is lucid, direct and effectual in establishing such transference.

English literature did, indeed, enjoy one brief phase of exact and sufficient prosaic expression. Roughly speaking this phase covered the early and middle eighteenth century, but the storm of the Romantic Movement blew that all away. With the Romantic Movement there passed a revolutionary wave over the English mind, and one very deplorable effect that wave has had is that it submerged,

probably for ever, the tradition of English prose work.
There are survivals and exceptions of which the great
Huxley is the best example, but for the most part when
the modern Englishman praises a piece of prose he praises
that character in it which is the least prosaic. He praises
its rhythms or its imagery or its appeal to some strong
sentiment such as patriotism. He does not praise it for
itself *as* prose. One might almost say, I think, that the
peculiar virtue of prose has been forgotten in England, and
for my part I cannot see by what influence it may be revived.

I have chosen the two examples in English letters,
Bunyan's work and William Wordsworth's, as tests of the
Protestant effect upon our literature, but the list might be
indefinitely extended for there are very few names of the
first rank which would not be included under that head.
Even those who thought themselves the most emancipated
were derived from a post-Reformation and not a pre-
Reformation England.

Indeed this is the most characteristic mark of English
letters as it is of all English social life. Modern English
literature and modern English social morals, social habit
and all pervading accepted philosophy takes Puritanism for
granted. To tell this truth does not mean that the Puritan
philosophy (which is a special department of European
Calvinism) is directly expressed, nor even that it is implied.
Rather do I mean that Calvinism which we know better
over here under the title of " Puritanism " colours and gives
its savour to the work of the English mind and does so more
and more as time proceeds.

The test is absence of gaiety which is the very stamp and
hallmark of the Calvinist mind.

By " absence of gaiety " I do not mean absence of
laughter, still less do I mean absence of joy for there may
be laughter of many kinds besides the spontaneous and
happy laughter of the unspoilt soul. There may be sardonic
laughter, cynical laughter and even ribald laughter and none

of these, least of all the last, is a spontaneous expression of joy through fun by an unspoilt mind. The enemies of Calvinism hated it with an intensity of feeling which can with difficulty be understood in a world which has been overrun by Calvinism as the English world has been over-run. The Manichean heresy of which Puritanism is our local example is not a mere excess nor a mere tendency to gloom. It is a positive expression of evil (or what its enemies call evil) by the free mind choosing such evil and preferring it to good. It has been wisely said that the saints are always gay which is true except for those moments when the saints are sad (and these are numerous enough), but there is nothing in greater contrast to the saint than the fool. Now in the eyes of those who feel the Calvinist influence to be a poison the Puritan is essentially a fool. He is a great deal more than a fool in their eyes, he is also a moral nuisance and a moral danger, but his characteristic is his lack of intelligence in the application of practical morals.

So much for the case against Calvinism, or rather for the adverse judgment of that philosophy, but this adverse judgment is mere affirmation. The enemy of Calvinism decries it as a destructive abomination, but to the supporter of Calvinism Calvinism appears as something constructive and solidifying, strengthening the society it fills, and strengthening individual souls which it supports with its rational sequences. No persuasion, through a man's experience or his reason or even his mere instinct of violence in the Manichean heresy can convey his persuasion to others by the mere statement of it. On the contrary he who detests the very approach of the Manichean air and who denounces it for what he feels it to be, a mortal peril, is regarded with horror by his Manichean hearer. The Manichean regards the anti-Manichean as an evil soul which demands conversion for its cure, or at the very best as an imperfect soul which requires completion by receiving the full information contained in the Manichean system.

The reader will note that I have used throughout these pages the term "Calvinism" as though it were equivalent to the term "Manichean," or the term "Puritan." For this many would criticise me as giving too great a position to Calvin in the history of European thought. But, frankly, I do not feel it is possible to exaggerate his importance and his influence. I am not speaking here of whether we are right to admire the skill on which that philosophy is built, still less whether we are right to rejoice in the very profound effect which it is the more important to emphasise, because it is unconsciously taken for granted, not as a discovery, but as a commonplace which the human mind accepts as a matter of course.

Those who have read Calvin's book, as I have, will marvel as I do at its prodigious results : for though it is rigidly thought out it is portentously dull—at least dull in our modern eyes. But it cannot have been dull to the Europe or to the England upon which it wrought as it did, though *why* it wrought as it did I am at a loss to discover.

I suppose it must have corresponded to something vivid and acute in the mood of the early sixteenth century throughout our civilisation, but what that something vivid was we have great difficulty in recalling today.

One must test the power and omnipresent effect of the Calvinist (or Manichean) innovation by observing how it has persuaded men to regard its successes as no more than the pushing of a good thing to an extreme. If you look around you will discover that by this time nearly all your contemporaries take it for granted that the Puritan rejection of the senses is a virtuous condition. Modern men will often speak of Puritanism with disgust yet at the same time speak of it as no more than an exaggeration of a respect for virtue.

To sum up : of all the effects arising from the Elizabethan turmoil the most lasting and the deepest has been this planting of the Manichean heresy ; and the irony of the position is that no men less desired such a result than the men of the Renaissance wherewith Elizabethan England was principally peopled, or at any rate, wherewith the life and creative spirits of Elizabethan England were informed. That is why Puritanism, a by-product of the Renaissance, in this country is not only strongly different from but almost contradictory to the thing from which it sprang. It is often so. The parent philosophy is the enemy of its child.

Have we got to the end of it yet? I am quite certain that we have not. On the contrary, the Puritan tide is in full flood and will presumably rise much higher before it subsides. It has, of course, one enemy which combats it continually and that enemy is the Catholic philosophy whereof the protagonists and disseminators are the Irish people throughout the world of English speech. He who is opposed to the Manichean (or Puritan) philosophy might be excused for regarding the Irish influence as one of those remedies which nature provides spontaneously for the poison which nature, itself, breeds. But whether we approve or disapprove of the Irish effect in the modern English-speaking world it is certain that this effect counts more as a corrective to the accepted morals and traditions of that world than does any other influence. The proof of this antagonism between the two is clear enough in the presence of boycott. Puritanism, or the Manichean spirit, sets up in defence of itself an undefined, but very active, affirmation which, without men's recognising it, is universally to be found in the anti-Catholic side of Europe and of the New World. That affirmation is essentially an affirmation not openly described, but accepted after the fashion which it is the modern habit to call "subconscious"; and, I repeat, it is not declining in strength, it is gaining in strength.

If you would have yet another proof of this you can see it in the obvious fact that those very men among our contemporaries who most sincerely boast of their own

exemption from the old Puritan limitations are most
thoroughly bound by those limitations ; for, in their struggle
against nature and joy, they postulate the excellence of such
a struggle. You never find among them the counter-
affirmation that joy is a duty, which is another way of
saying that the works of the Creator are good.

XIV

SCOTLAND

THE external story of Elizabeth Tudor is mainly the story of her relations with the Crown and people of Scotland. Those relations were fixed for much the most part—as was all policy—by William Cecil. But there was an exception to his power in this particular case, which came from Elizabeth's strong feeling upon the general institution of Monarchy and the particular case of sacred Monarchy, sacred, anointed Monarchy, attaching to Mary Stuart. The England whereon the earlier womanhood of Elizabeth Tudor rose had largely lost the sacramental emotion which had for so many centuries been the very note of Christian religion. Yet there was one strong sacramental feeling surviving throughout the country, and that was the feeling for Monarchy : the effective symbol of a crowned head : the identification of that symbol with reality—and such identification is the very essence of any sacramental system.

Now Elizabeth was, of all those whom the Renaissance with its strong core of scepticism had moulded, the least sacramentally inclined of public men and women. Yet she did feel the magic, the non-rational superhuman influence in the matter of Monarchy. It is one of the things which makes it most difficult for us today, who have entirely lost this sentiment, to get her exactly in focus.

It would be a shallow and false interpretation of Elizabeth which should regard her feeling on Monarchy as the mere product of her situation, or a mere reflection of her office as a Queen. It went much deeper than that. It went down to those roots whence also spring the great human affections (and patriotism is among these). It is true that she was fighting for her life and that without the sanction of Monarchy she was defenceless ; that in spite of her strong will, erudition and increasing knowledge of men, she would have been nobody but for kingship. Nevertheless, her feeling for kingship was real and deep.

It was this which made Scotland the largest matter in the foreign policy of her time. The great religious revolution which she was condemned to witness at work throughout Europe and particularly violently in these islands, had thrown the weight of the Scottish people ultimately into the English scale. For the predication and almost immeasurable influence of John Calvin, his French logic and drive, had taken over the Lowlands of Scotland a very firm grasp indeed. We must beware here, as in every other department, of transferring to the people of 400 years ago the notions which govern people now. Today we reckon influence by numbers and, as I have constantly repeated here and elsewhere, there is a sort of non-rational mystical attachment to mere majority (what our immediate fathers called counting noses). The sixteenth century knew nothing of that. Indeed it neglected the real strength which lies in any very considerable numerical superiority. For instance, the little Calvinist body, when it was but a tenth of England or more likely a twelfth and hardly appreciable outside London, had boldly set out to capture the whole government of England after the death of Henry VIII : and not a dozen years later a rather larger but still small minority of French nobles had attempted the same thing in France. And no one had thought it odd.

Whether there were a majority of Scotch families, even in the Lowlands, attached to or seriously influenced by Calvin as early as 1559, is doubtful. There is no doubt of the intensity with which they felt the religious emotions of the new creed. There is something almost Mohammedan about the fierce integrity of the Scottish religious movement, the like of which was quite absent from England. It is something which one foreign to Scottish national tradition finds it difficult to understand, but one which all observers of Scottish development must appreciate. Those who have not themselves enjoyed or suffered such intense sympathies with special philosophies will label the violent emotion " fanaticism." But that explains nothing ; it is no more than a name for strength of conviction, permeating the whole being and forcing it to action.

At any rate, this degree of religious feeling, which made Scottish enthusiasm so difficult towards anything south of the Border, produced active rebellion against the legitimate heiress of Scotland. Mary Stuart was born nine years after Elizabeth. Her father, the King of Scotland, James V, had died after a severe defeat in the field at the hands of irregular English troops when he was still a young man barely more than thirty years of age. He had married into the great French House of Guise ; for to counterbalance English influence by French was traditional with the Scotch.

The little child, his heiress, was thus already Queen of Scotland a few days after her birth. She was to live on under the heavy Stuart curse for more than forty-four years, the last eighteen and a half of which she was a prisoner in the hands of her chief enemy, William Cecil, determined upon killing her, an object which he ultimately achieved.

She would have been killed long before had Cecil been, as is sometimes pretended, completely the master of English policy, but though he was in the main the master thereof, his power was not unlimited, and it is the whole matter of this passage to insist that the Queen's influence was a counterweight.

This is the point which crops up again and again throughout the story of Elizabeth's active reign : the point of real power. The *real* power was with that small group who may fairly be called adventurers and were the sponsors for Elizabeth Tudor : who, with the help of Philip of Spain and under the strong title of her father's will, put her upon the throne, who in general controlled her. Had she attempted to escape from their control they would have got rid of her, for at their head was the most astute politician in Europe and after his fashion the most determined : William Cecil. He it was who saw so clearly and earlier than anyone else that the condition of stability for the Tudor reign of the new Protestant regime was the disappearance of Mary Stuart. Elizabeth saw that too, of course, but she was not single-minded in the matter, because she was divided between her interest, and the general interest of kingship and of crowns. To us, reading of the matter today here in England, this Scottish problem, arising in the early years of Elizabeth's reign and continuing till almost the end of it, seems by far the largest element in the whole situation, though today Scotland and England form one realm, long ago appearing as a unity in the eyes of the world. We cannot easily visualise a world in which Scotland and England were not only foreign to each other, but hostile. But that *was* the world into which Mary Stuart and Elizabeth were born, a dozen years apart, and in which they came to their separate thrones. In the eyes of contemporaries and in the general perspective of European history, the two main antagonists were the almost universal Empire and the French Monarchy now consolidated, though its territory was torn by religious war ; and the Hapsburg Emperor, King of Spain and Portugal, master of most of Italy and holding for trade and dominion the new world beyond the Atlantic. England and Scotland were but makeweights in that difficult balance ; England counting far the most of the two, but still much less than France and immensely less than the Hapsburg power, which had behind it not only the great free German cities but the wealth and commerce and seafaring of the Low Countries, the vast Spanish Empire, the Peninsula itself and the better part of Italy. It is also important to remember the scale of the actors

J

on that stage. We have, of course, no certain statistics, but we have rough means of judging and we can say that while the French Monarchy governed some three or four million families, the combined Hapsburg power much more than doubled that. England counted perhaps a million, or a little more ; but Scotland hardly a quarter of a million. It may be doubted whether the whole population north of the Border came in those days to as much as a million all told.

There is a further very important factor in the mixed policies of England and Scotland, which is matter both of total wealth and of disposable wealth. Tudor England, though so restricted in population—hardly a tenth of what it is today—though boasting only one really large town and though mainly agricultural, was a rich country, not relatively as the times then went but positively by any rational standard of measurement ; the basis of all wealth being then agriculture, and the next source of prosperity (on a far lesser scale) commerce, England had a large proportionate area of fertile land ; Scotland had little, and of commerce, in proportion, very much less. Further, Scotland was geographically divided ; it had a " waist," a tight-laced one at that, between the Firth of Clyde and the Firth of Forth. These were geographically two almost separate halves of the same realm, which halves met at Stirling. There were also two not exactly coincident provinces, but roughly similar divisions ; the Highland and Lowland Scotch world. There was even a pronounced division in speech, for the Highlands were then wholly Gaelic and though the Lowlands included Fife and a rather narrow coastal bit to the north and east along the sea, the bulk of such limited resources as the nation could boast lay in the Lowland part. The strongest moral force giving political unity to Scotland in this mid-sixteenth century was hostility to England.

Now this factor of unity had been badly and progressively damaged by the religious revolution, which had blazed up so fiercely in Lowland Scotland. In this we must count very high—though it may be exaggerated—the energy and intense conviction of John Knox. That cleric, for cleric he was, though he had never been a priest (he remained at the order of deacon) not only voiced the enthusiasm of the Reformation, but nourished and extended that enthusiasm. His hearers responded to the call of that violent cry, that trumpet of a voice, with a zeal which seemed extravagant for those who do not appreciate the fiery passionate new convictions of that day.

Now the Protestant party, so clearly in the ascendant morally, north of the Border, was inevitably the pro-England party and, though traditional hostility towards England was the moral force that united the nation, it had been this time nothing like the driving power of the religious force at variance with it.

I have just said that the pace at which the thing went was its most remarkable character. John Calvin's book, one of the few books that have changed the world, came out nearly ten years after Luther's original protest. It dates from 1536. We know how prodigious was its effect, though it is difficult for us moderns to understand why it should have had such power over the mind of that time. If anybody doubts the difficulty of answering that question, let him read for himself, as I have done, the original appeal of Calvin and ask himself whether in style or any other feature it could claim the right to do the very great work it did. Anyhow it did that work and started, with what was at first a very high momentum, the counter-Church which challenged everywhere the ancient Catholic tradition.

The Reformation was much more Calvin and Calvin's book than it was anything else. It had behind it the swords and the fighting spirit of the turbulent French nobility ; it captured whatever was most active in the world north of the Alps and the Pyrenees. There was even a moment when it bid fair to seize the whole culture of Poland. The storm blew over Christendom loud and long. It not only swept the French into the vortex of religious war but rapidly disintegrated the unstable mass of the Germanies, wherein, until the Hapsburg reaction began to gather strength, it threatened to extend universally.

There is another party to the business of Anglo-Scottish relations beside the religious forces at work ; and that other party is the body of Scottish nobles. Historians have often repeated, perhaps with some exaggeration, the statement that upon the greed of the nobles everything depended. We know what the vast loot of religion had meant in England ; one may say that in Scotland it counted even more. For it was working there in the midst of an impoverished people and the main lords of Scottish land were attracted invincibly towards the opportunity of added wealth. They were pulled towards loot as by a cord.

There is yet another factor which must be set down before we conclude the list : the peculiar corruption of the Scottish clerical personnel. Here we have a paradox which has been of profound effect upon European history everywhere : the corruption of the ecclesiastical system at the end of the Middle Ages was proportionate to the economic power of the Church, and yet was oddly enough more prominent in those that ultimately held fast to the unity of Christendom than in those who broke away. The Churchmen were in England less scandalous than elsewhere ; and the Church appointments were less scandalous. The most powerful of the French families could raise one of their lads to the Archbishopric of Rheims, which with Lyons was the chief Church matter of the Gauls. They waited till the boy had reached what was, ironically enough, the sufficient age of fourteen ; but the moment he had come to that stage of maturity, Archbishop of Rheims did he become. There is no parallel to an absurdity like that in contemporary England. The prelates who had hesitated upon the Article of Unity in the critical moment of Henry VIII's Supremacy

Law, or rather Decree, had done so with some reluctance ; and later, when the reign of Mary came, they were clear in their Catholic position. Nor did they abandon it with the advent of Elizabeth ; only two * of them consented to assist at her crowning. At the death of Mary the episcopal bench was already weakened in numbers by the death of members who were not replaced ; but even so their almost unanimous decision in favour of tradition is remarkable. The new Protestant prelates, gradually appearing in the place of the dispossessed men, were not of great moral worth. Most of them were worthy enough, but they were not zealous even for their new establishment. The typical figure is that of Parker, the new Archbishop, who was no more than Cecil's man, but sincere enough it seems and in tune with the innovation of the day. For the rest, the English Church was not as yet conspicuous in its personnel for learning or discussion, as it was later to become.

From the moment of Mary Stuart's defeat at the hands of rebels, the story is merely one of increasing pressure by the English power, which soon was holding the young Queen of Scots a prisoner.

That imprisonment began as something almost voluntary ; but it increased in rigour steadily until at last it became that of a condemned cell.

Perhaps the most important thing that happened in the whole of this triangular wrangle between England and Scotland, with the life of the Catholic Queen of Scotland forming the third issue, is the decision of Elizabeth Tudor to forbid the predication of John Knox in England.

It is the fashion today to belittle personal motives in the general story of Europe and to look on that story as a sort of inevitable process driven by blind forces. We shall come to truer conclusions if we reinstate somewhat that power she had : the power of personality. John Knox by

---

* It is commonly said that only one so lapsed, but that is an error, for we have record of one other bishop consenting to the change.

himself would have been nobody. That is true of every personal influence that ever acted on mankind. Had there not been a large body of highly inflamed opinion of which he was the *persona*, the mask or speaking tube, he would not have been heard of. A man today who should preach, however loudly, some truth with which our contemporaries are quite unacquainted, would be crying in the desert. It has always been so.

Moreover John Knox was not a rational personality. He was rather what is called in antiquity a " prophet " ; what is called today a " leader." But granted the circumstance of intense anti-Catholic enthusiasm, he made a vast difference. And if he had appeared in England in that crisis, he might well have lit a fire (as he did in his own country) which could not be extinguished.

That is why I say that Elizabeth's refusal to allow him to come in was of such importance. He was in every way obnoxious to her. He had bellowed against the influence of women in high politics, which, considering that it was the day of Mary Tudor, Catherine de Medicis and Mary Stuart and of Elizabeth herself, a whole clot of female monarchs at a moment when monarchs were three-quarters of the game, was daring anyhow, but particularly offensive to Elizabeth Tudor. Her whole point was that, though a woman, she was clothed through her Crown and her father's will and her Tudor inheritance with real central authority ; such as women very rarely exercise. Even so she did not in fact entirely govern. Far from it. Her minister counted more than herself. But still, to attack the power of women in authority was to attack Elizabeth personally and personal attack counts more with the sex than abstract principles. Among the not very numerous occasions on which Elizabeth was at sharp issue with those around her and yet got her own way, this veto on John Knox was the most important. Cecil was all for him : Elizabeth was all against him and Elizabeth won. In this connection, the importance of the monarch's sex during the essential years of the later English sixteenth century, one may note one or two other things. Because Elizabeth was a woman and yet exercised so much real power, her jealousies counted ; and, because she was a woman, there also counted largely the very transparent flattery of her appearance, with which she was surrounded. Let us get that point right. Women very naturally attach a high importance to looks in general. It is with them an essential matter as with men is a reputation for courage. There are few men who are really offended by being told that they are as ugly as monkeys ; but every man would be deeply moved against those who accused him of timidity. Now those men usually underestimate beauty ; they ought to understand that to belittle a woman's looks is not unlike belittling a man's courage.

Heaven knows that there was not much to praise in Elizabeth's looks. The mere fact that early in life she became as bald as an egg should settle *that* matter, for as Apuleius has well remarked, " No woman can be really attractive if she has no hair." But apart from that, the smallpox had ruined her complexion and on the top of that again her bad health had given her that pale yellow skin which all remarked. But, as is always the case with women, a certain measure of intelligence and vivacity was found pleasing in her, in spite of her ugliness. For ugly she was and how anyone can deny it in face of the portraits is more than I can understand.

There was a necessary rivalry between Elizabeth Tudor and Mary Stuart also, because Mary was natural heir to Elizabeth's throne. Mary had been brought up as a Frenchwoman at the French Court. That alone would have weighed very heavily against her claim ; but of more weight by far, and indeed decisive, was the English national feeling in favour of the dynasty, upstart though it was. There was in Elizabeth, growing upon her as the years proceeded, something vindictive, just as there was something capricious. One may put down the long seven years captivity of Catherine Grey wherein that unfortunate young wife and mother died, to political necessity and believe that this excessive rigour would be shown by Elizabeth's chief minister quite as much as by herself. But her callous persecution of women who crossed her path was excessive ; and her refusal to allow the wife of Dudley to appear at her Court was such an enormity that one wonders that it has not been more emphasised by those who describe the reign. She was not responsible for Amy Robsart's death as rumour accused Dudley of being and, therefore, indirectly accused her of being ; but she was responsible for the outrageous treatment of that lonely young heiress, without whose wealth Dudley could not have been launched. There is in this aspect of Elizabeth as a woman, with the most unpleasing frailties of a woman, a very long and large chapter of her sham or imperfect love affairs (using love in the conventional sense) to be set down.

The tangle and problem of the Anglo-Scottish relationship grew easier and easier with the combination of two things : the passage of time and the capture of the child and boy, James Stuart, by the reformers.

James Stuart, Mary Stuart's son by Darnley, had been proclaimed King of Scotland while he was still a baby. He had been born in June, 1566 ; his mother, Mary the Queen, had been compelled to abdicate the next year and the solemn proclamation of her infant was part of the machinery for rejecting her and, of course, for confirming the new owners in their possession of Church lands ; for in Scotland, as in England, all turned on that.   The child soon became the symbol of victory for the Reformation among his subjects ; that is, victory for those who had possessed themselves of the clerical endowments.

He was not yet a man, he was a boy of sixteen, when a party among the nobles kidnapped him.

In the next year another party counter-kidnapped him.

Nor did all this make for the dignity and power of the throne. But the point of the situation was not the boy's religion, which was settled naturally by the financial advisers to the Scottish nobles, but the fact that he was the most obvious heir to the throne of England; as Mary Queen of Scots had been before him. This is no place to discuss his insufficient and perhaps vicious character; nor the physical defects of this child of the impossible Darnley: his inability to stand up properly (his legs always sagging at the knees) and his walking by clinging to the nearest companion; nor to describe any of his characteristics, comic, evil or indifferent. The thing to remember about him is that the second of the Cecil dynasty, Robert Cecil, saw to it that James should become without shock or difficulty, monarch of England when Elizabeth died. By the ideas of the time Elizabeth should have had the decision in this and she would have done so had she faced, at the approach of death, her duty in the matter. But we shall see on a later page what that " approach of death " meant in the case of Elizabeth. The last of the Tudors let her succession go by default to the most obvious heir, who had for that matter been brought up for years in the expectation of the English throne and was certain to obtain it as a nominee of the Cecils. Preoccupation with Scotland, the Scottish claim to the throne and all the rest of it faded out with the declining years of the reign as it became all the more certain that the two crowns would be united in the person of the new monarch. The killing of Mary Stuart had achieved its end. It was the last and decisive act in the killing of their ancient faith among the English.

XV

THE QUEEN OF SCOTS

THE story of Mary Stuart, Queen regnant of Scotland, is commonly treated by historians as a whole tangle of problems : doubts as to whether this or that really happened, doubts as to motives, and doubts as to the actions.

There were, indeed, so many personalities involved in even the main policies of France, England and Scotland that the full analysis of their mutual relations might be an endless task. Moreover that task has been further elaborated by the violence of discussion and conjecture upon the period and main actors in it. Yet we have a clue to a certain simplicity in all the affairs and that clue is accepting the common motives of human actions and the common results of those motives.

For instance if we make of Elizabeth Tudor an exceptional diplomatic genius after the model of Bismarck we are certain to misjudge all she did. Many of her decisions were taken on impulse, many of them were so half-hearted as hardly to be decisions at all. In many she misjudged the situation, in many others her motives were so mixed that it is almost impossible to disentangle them. One student of the period will tell us that all her dealings with her cousin, the Queen of Scots, were thought out in detail and planned upon a fixed policy. Another, falling into the characteristic modern error of reading history backwards, will ascribe to Elizabeth motives of special English patriotism of which she certainly was not conscious. Others are even so old fashioned as to represent her as a convinced religious champion armed against Giant Pope and steadfastly resisting him and all his schemes.

Now the times were not of that sort, especially were they

not of that sort in the matter of those who governed. There was plenty of violent religious excitement on the side of the reformers and, even before the Jesuit effort was in full blast, there was plenty of more or less organised reaction against the reformers. But the individual actors in the drama were not principally concerned with the new doctrines or the old. They were principally concerned, as human beings nearly always are, with personal advantages and disadvantages. The chief advantage which everyone pursued was saving his or her own skin and that is as true or truer of Elizabeth than of any contemporary. She had lived in peril from babyhood. She was used to every form of outlawry, actual or potential. Her father had seen to it that she should be declared a bastard long before, with that irresponsible humour of his, he had designed her for the throne. That throne she obtained, but through what chances, after how many threats of disaster! Having attained the throne it was her principal business to preserve her personal power. Elizabeth was in a position where failure means death. She remained in that position all her life one may say. She was never really secure, but her chief chance of security lay in having her cause identified with the interests of the wealthier classes who had in part risen on the loot of religion and in part increased through the loot of religion fortunes already established.

There is further, in connection with Mary Stuart as the foil to Elizabeth and to her adviser, a most interesting problem which I recommend to the reader, though I do not pretend to have solved it. What was the nature of the charm which Mary Stuart undoubtedly exercised? It was through the exercise of charm that she maintained herself under conditions so adverse that her survival seemed impossible and reads to us today as something almost miraculous.

Now it is difficult indeed and perhaps impossible to recover, long after the physical presence of a human being which has disappeared, the character of the attraction that this being exercised. Mary Stuart has been explained, especially her influence has been explained, as a function of beauty : sometimes as a function of mere youth : but we have the portraits of her to guide us and we can affirm without fear of contradiction that beauty is not their special mark, at least not beauty of feature, for there may have been a beauty of expression and more likely still a beauty of intonation which nowadays, of course, we cannot recover. It has sometimes been said by acute observers that her influence was to be found in her gestures, the delicacy of those gestures and their subtlety. It may be so, but certain it is that the influence was there and one of the best proofs of it is the violent antagonism which she aroused in those of the other camp.

When people represent the duel as one between two women, Elizabeth Tudor and Mary Stuart, they are wide of the mark. It was rather a duel between John Knox and Mary Stuart.

There again we have a problem of influence. What was the secret of the dynamic effect which John Knox's prediction achieved ? Obviously the first and most powerful element therein was his sincerity. What has been called his fanaticism was an immediate product of his sincerity. He held himself to be a prophet. Such an attitude inspired all he did and thought and said. There is a story told, how on his death bed when he was past speech he lifted a hand and pointed to Heaven as giving testimony to the source of his strength. One might almost say that John Knox came only second to Calvin himself in the story of the Calvinist triumph. I have already pointed out that one of the most creative acts ascribed to Elizabeth herself was Elizabeth's refusal to admit John Knox into her kingdom. No doubt there was in this refusal a certain measure of statecraft, for although Elizabeth Tudor had neither the unity nor the simplicity of genius she did at any rate recognise better than most of those about her the danger of provoking a Catholic reaction. I shall on a later page consider why that Catholic reaction failed. Here it must be sufficient to emphasise the truth that everything was in its favour—or almost everything : but let us note that in that word " almost " we admit a certain element too often forgotten : the indifference of English Elizabethan society to doctrine. It was through this indifference that the Great Compromise was carried through. And how strong a quality that indifference was we may discover through the prolonged effect of it. That effect has continued to our own day and most powerfully inspires English men and women around us now. Even those men who are most attached to doctrinal indifference take such indifference for granted and regard such indifference as native to common intelligence ; they bear testimony to its power through the position they take up.

For, indeed, indifference to doctrine is an exceptional attitude. The human mind is more naturally attracted to positive statement than to the neglect of it. Yet it was neglected.

The indifference of which I speak has often been ascribed to the power of nationalism, but surely this came too late to account for the success of the compromise. It is true that men could easily be persuaded that the Counter-Reformation was something alien and therefore hateful, and certainly the Counter-Reformation approached England from abroad.

Its burning zeal (confined among men of English descent to a small number only) was not in itself alien, on the contrary, intensity of feeling is a specially English characteristic and if the Counter-Reformation had succeeded in England it would have succeeded through the vigour with which the English imagination works as also through the tenacity of the English character.

If the heroism of the Jesuit missionaries, intensely English by blood, were generally emphasised in our histories as it should be, we should understand the period much better. It has been *particularly* emphasised, of course, by special apologists, but it has not been generally emphasised and your average Englishman today knows little of it.

Yet consider what the emotion must have been which made men indifferent to the most acute sufferings of the body and to that greatest of spiritual sufferings, exile and separation from their own people. The missionary priests came from the seminaries abroad fully prepared not only for the agonies of martyrdom in its most horrible form, but for the chances of failure and with failure of rejection by their own people. This was the common trait in all their actions. Their enemies among modern writers think it sufficient to call them traitors and to label their whole political effort under the caption of " Treason." It was the main contention of Cecil who was the main author of this attitude that " No one was attacked under his rule for religion, only for treason." The trick is childishly simple and if it has succeeded it has succeeded only because modern men have forgotten what their ancestors felt like. The trick is to identify one party with the nation itself and the support of that party with loyalty to the nation, and therefore to identify resistance with disloyalty.

I conceive that a great part of this contention and a great element in its vitality was the antagonism existing in those days between the English and the Scottish nations.

That also is an element in the situation which modern men find it difficult to appreciate. It is true that Scotland and England are still very distinct. Even today it is something of an historical education and a most useful piece of travel to cross the border for the first time and especially to cross it in a leisurely fashion. I, myself, enjoyed that experience when I was still fairly young, in my early thirties, and I can recall after so many years the sharp sensation that north of the border I had come into another country.

Further (since we are upon the subject of personal experience) I enjoyed then acutely as I enjoy still what was then more common than it is now, the taste for theological discussion among the Scots. We got very little of that in England in the later part of the nineteenth century, but it was still actively alive in Scotland. My acquaintance among Scotsmen which has sometimes been intimate and has always been wide, has brought me against the repeated testimony of my own generation north of the border that indifference has succeeded to the old strength of theological debate. I cannot but believe that under the surface the old fires still smoulder—but perhaps that belief is rather due to my sympathy with theological debate than to a real recognition of inaction. One sees the effects of the old doctrines still strongly at work around us, but a direct statement of those doctrines is today rare. None the less they continue to inform the Scottish mind. You see this in that very important social relation the attitude towards wealth. The Scottish do not worship wealth as such, they do not pursue wealth (though they are often falsely accused of doing so) with any special zeal. They accumulate wealth because they are methodical and because they are intelligent in the use of method. Wealth has always been a dominant factor in society and is now by far the strongest factor. But the attitude towards wealth which you find among Scotsmen is of a special kind. It does not include a superstitious respect as it does elsewhere. It is rather the application of a test and a test certainly not of avarice, but of industry and application. If you take it for granted that the accumulation of wealth is the first of social activities, you will naturally look up to those who have succeeded therein as athletes look up to those who succeed in athletic competition.

It is to be remarked in the particular case of the struggle between Cecil and Mary Stuart that the woman was in no way attached to wealth. Cecil most undoubtedly was. The accumulation of a private fortune was the interest of his life and largely explains his political activity. He was betting on a result and he betted on the right side.

It is perhaps the chief element in the contrast between the two parties of that duel (I mean Mary Stuart and Cecil) that Cecil showed foresight where Mary Stuart lacked it. In a way Cecil, as it was he who led the affair and not Elizabeth, showed more foresight than Elizabeth did. There enters into this, of course, the element of personal feeling. He was personally inclined towards the Reformation and all its works. He was in no way fanatical, no man could be less so. But that side was the side to his taste. Elizabeth herself, in her little passing tiffs with her great minister, would emphasise this element in Cecil's character and convictions. Everyone remembers her rather bitter sneer at Cecil's support of his " Brethren in Christ." But there was a great element of sincerity therein. No doubt Cecil was mainly devoted to his own advancement and only after that as a consequence thereof devoted to the Protestant side of the great duel, but he was personally in reaction against the old religion. He had conformed under Mary as we all know and one story that he went about with a " fine pair of beads at his girdle " is quite possibly true. But that was in the nature of a politician, and William Cecil was not only a civil servant but also a politician, putting on an attitude suitable to his policy. A politician will of necessity conform to the policy he has adopted. But there is more than this in William Cecil's support of the Reformation which support became so continuous and so intense. After the advent of Elizabeth there was real reaction against the religion of his forefathers. It was not an intense reaction, but it was much stronger than any such feeling on the part of his sovereign.

I have said that the duel was rather between Cecil and Mary Stuart than between Mary Stuart and Elizabeth, but we must remember that Cecil was more of a free agent in the matter than was Elizabeth. Cecil could be a partisan without subjecting himself to any personal peril quite apart from his natural inclination to the reforming side rather than to the traditional side. During the first years of his political activity in its second phase (after the advent of Elizabeth) he insisted (not with full success) upon the extreme and the anti-Catholic policy both abroad and at home. He was the more free to do so because he was free to fly should the necessity for flight arise. Of course the new religion which he sponsored was not popular, but then neither was it greatly unpopular. It was an experiment which appealed to all those who, especially in early manhood, inclined towards novelty. The old faith was old-fashioned. The new arrangements which for the greater part of men were not a new faith at all, but only a new and not very definite set of political arrangements were fresh and the opposition to them old-fashioned. To be Protestant in those days was like wearing new clothes cut in a new style, and the younger men would usually be attracted to such change of garment.

William Cecil it was who in particular insisted upon treating Mary Stuart as a necessary victim. He was ready from very early in the business to have her put to death. It was, indeed, the logical consummation of his policy. She must be got rid of. She must be put out of the way. Elizabeth was, I think sincerely, opposed to that attitude or if not actually opposed reluctant to adopt it. We all know the judgment that she was thus reluctant on account of her feeling for the sanctity of monarchy and her hesitation to support rebellion against what the times called " their natural prince." This hesitation of hers has been called by some debaters no more than yet another piece of policy on her part. I think it was more. Elizabeth, herself, during all those earlier years and indeed right on almost to the end was subject to overthrow at the worst (though the danger of this grew less and less) but also subject, even at

K

the best, to organised resistance. Her throne was everything to her, and she could not rely upon the maintenance of her throne. Her very life depended at first, and even later when that life was more secure, upon the maintenance of her throne, which depended on the exercise of her character, the fulfilment of herself. If she was not a Queen she was nobody. Therefore her support of the principle of monarchy and in consequence her support of Mary Stuart's claims, at first, and her real disgust that the strength of rebellion north of the border had a large element of reality in them. It might even be said that the chief tragedy of Elizabeth's life, apart from her sterility—presumably through some mysterious mal-formation of which, as I have already said, we have not sufficient record—was the necessity, under which she felt herself to be more and more as time proceeded, of sacrificing Mary Stuart. This judgment may sound timorous. I know that most historians, especially foreign historians who see the situation better than we do here at home where we suffer under the weight of an inherited tradition, will not have it so. They would tell you that Mary Stuart was put to death, or rather murdered, by her cousin.

In the end this was true, but the Queen was slow to accept the responsibility and the burden. Elizabeth was never vindictive, except against individuals who had been insolent to her. She did not take pleasure in revenge, partly because she was too cold for that, but more I think because there was nothing to avenge. She had suffered gravely in youth from those who were opposed to her accession or who feared it, but she took no delight in relieving her feelings by counter-strokes against them ; and her moderation was not due to policy, but to character. For the reformed doctrines as such she could have had nothing but the contempt which intense religious emotion naturally aroused in the sceptical Renaissance temperament.

Let it be noted here that Mary Stuart had no corresponding enthusiasm for Catholicism. In a sense she laid down her life for it, but not with any permanent consistency. She said with great truth on the eve of her death that she died the victim of her religion, but when she had an opportunity for showing principle in the matter she did not show it.

One could get no better test than the Bothwell marriage. As a very young woman who had experienced the attraction she could exercise over men (and she certainly delighted in it), she had been thrown away upon worthless mates : men who were hardly men, vicious or puerile or both. There came in the most acute crisis of her life a man of strong, rough character, displeasing, indeed, and even disgusting, but still a man. To that man she yielded, nor did she yield with reluctance. It might almost be said (though such a phrase would offend her worshippers) that she yielded with enthusiasm. What a fate was that which overtook Bothwell when, after his seizure of the Queen, he was compelled to exile ! How his soul, though coarsened by experience and already coarse by nature, must have raged against the fate which sent him overseas ! The Bothwell marriage, I say, is not an episode in Mary Stuart's story, it is in a sense the pivot of it. That she should have been capable of such a marriage, that she should indeed have welcomed it (which I take to be the truth) explains at least one-half of her character. It is an error to use the word " strength " of brutality in any form, but brutality can masquerade as strength for the satisfaction of women who have lacked support during all their youth and who, being women, have been wasted upon alliances quite unworthy of them. It was an abominable piece of bad luck for such a woman that she should have missed a natural mating with someone who could have satisfied her appetite for strength : I mean not her appetite for power exercised by herself, but for strength in the man who should be her companion and even her natural leader. She tended to such a mating during all her youth and never came within a hundred miles of obtaining it.

It is not the least of Mary Stuart's evil fate that she was born immediately to be crowned. She was Queen and Queen regnant without dispute from the very first days of her life. The right to her title was fixed in her throughout. Had she had any apprenticeship, had she been a princess during her formative years, as her rival Elizabeth Tudor had been, she would have learnt ; as it was she had not the leisure nor the opportunity to learn. Isolation is the chief evil of human life and isolation was imposed upon this woman always and everywhere. When she made one desperate effort to be rid of it that effort was itself fatal to her.

XVI

THE CASKET LETTERS

I SUPPOSE nobody can write even the most elementary study of Elizabeth's period, even the most fragmentary commentary such as is this, without bringing in the " Mystery of the Casket Letters."
Yet the only mystery about them is the mystery of human credulity, the mystery of what is called nowadays (by a horrible neologism) " wishful thinking."
Men will believe anything that fits in with their bias, and no doubt there are a good many people left who still repeat that Mary Stuart was the authoress of those incriminating letters and of the verses which were put forth by her enemies under her name.   They were not written in a style which one can possibly connect with her.   They could not have been written for any motive which could be reconciled with her interests.   They are quite manifestly frauds.

One would have thought that, however high religious emotion ran it could never run so high as to support folly of this kind! But religious emotion will account for almost anything.

Surely the first question anybody would ask of a person presenting unlikely documents and ascribing them to an impossible origin would be, " Where are the originals ? Show me the originals so that I may judge whether they give any grounds for believing such nonsense."   To that obvious and primary question the bland reply is given, " We cannot show you the originals, they have been destroyed."   When you ask who destroyed them and what his or her motive can have been, you are told that they were destroyed by the very people for whom they would have been of first-class importance for establishing the guilt of Mary Stuart! The whole thing is such fantastic nonsense that it serves only one historical purpose.   It serves for an example of the length to which people will go in believing what they want to believe. I have indeed come across one case—and one only—of credulity in literary matters which can rival the credulity of those who like to believe, or to say they believe, that the Casket Letters are authentic. That is the case of the worthy don (of Oxford, I think), who proposed to set down the authorship of certain passages in Aeschylus to Euripides adding, as an excuse for his views, the stupefying sentence that the " Talent displayed would not be beyond the powers of a precocious southern boy already nine years old."

The most astonishing thing in the whole business is that anyone should have thought the silly lie worth telling. Was there not already a strong enough case against Mary Stuart, without any such addition ? Here is a young woman, the widow of a king, left undefended, surrounded by enemies, and having already committed the huge blunder of the Darnley marriage. She comes under the influence of a rough, coarse character : that of Bothwell. She yields to this influence. She yields to it so thoroughly that she consents to the new marriage with heretical rites which she must have disliked and her acceptance of which could do her nothing but harm with those who desired to support her. It needs no special skill in understanding human affairs to know what had happened. Mary Stuart took refuge from an intolerable strain. She clung to the first man she could find and was swept off her feet. Her action was certainly extravagant. But it was not more extravagant than many another action of those which we see going on all round us. Most of us could give examples of elopements as violent and odd, in explanation of which we can only say that the thing happened ; and must have been due (like any one of a hundred others) to sudden impulse. In this case the impulse is easily accounted for by the earlier misfortunes of the woman who yielded. Not content with giving the obvious explanation to a matter which is as clear as mud people must invent an impossible rigmarole rather than accept common sense !

It is not as though there were any well-established tradition here opposed to common sense, nor is it as though we were dealing with an example of miracle.

I confess that my own historical interest in the matter runs on lines which are disappointing ; for my interest in the matter is no more than this, " How do such enormities get accepted ? " Allowing for the full strength of religious and racial hatred combined, or rather religious and cultural *and* political hatred combined, it is still hardly possible to believe one's eyes when one reads the arguments still occasionally brought forward in support of the Casket Letters. One is reduced to Mr. Shaw's remark to the gentleman who is said to have accosted him in the street with the remark, " Mr. Lang, I believe ? " " If you can believe that you can believe anything."*

A religious frenzy so strong as to make anyone believe that the Casket Letters are true copies of originals written by Mary Stuart should move mountains ; it is perhaps enough to account for the kind of official history foisted upon us by the academies. But where else in human society does folly reach such a degree as it reaches here in England, on all and everything Catholic ?

In the course of a life already far too long I have heard it maintained, in the teeth of all history, that maritime supremacy was invariably victorious. I have heard it maintained that our professional politicians are overshadowed by so divine a grace that they are immune from corruption. I have heard it maintained that Americans are the same as Englishmen and that both Americans and Englishmen are really Germans. I have heard it maintained that sundry Hanoverians were models of political wisdom. I have heard it maintained that a society of many millions will change its hereditary religion in a day and a night and

* The same story is told of at least fifty other people.

come out at the end of the transformation utterly new. I have even heard it maintained that numbers are not a main element in war. But I never heard anything maintained to compare in folly with the assertion that the Casket Letters are authentic.

Suppose you were to be presented with letters purporting to be written by the late Queen Victoria expressing a high admiration for the French of the Second Empire in their capacity of Catholic apologists . . . but I won't go on! The whole hypothesis of the Casket Letters business is too grotesque to be worthy even of ridicule.

XVII

THE EPISODE OF THE ARMADA

THANKS to the work of a comparatively small group of sincere scholars, the episode of the Spanish Armada, which had already produced one of the best-rooted myths in the national history, is now more truthfully written upon and better understood than any part of English history during the great religious revolution.

There have been two sides to this excellent clearing up of illusion upon the past. One side of it has been the appreciation of what happened at the time upon the sea : the actual condition of the rival fleets and the actual story of the fighting. The other has been an appreciation of the economic condition, and especially the social part of it affecting Spain and its royal revenue and its public works.

As to the first of these departments of the subject, the general answer is that the failure of the Armada was due to the superiority at sea of the English. It is true, of course, that the defenders were nearer their bases and had to that extent a considerable natural advantage. But this advantage was slight compared with the advantage enjoyed by the English in every other aspect of the struggle. (I use the word " English " conventionally, for, of course, we must repeat at every turn that the position was much more complicated than a mere conflict between two nations ; it was only part of the general conflict between the ancient religion of Europe and the revolutionaries attacking that religion.) The ships fighting for the English government were better designed for service in their native seas, they were better manned, better gunned, quicker at manœuvre and of necessity, being unconnected with transport, both lighter and lying closer to the weather. Granted the unfavourable wind, which was what had rendered immediate invasion impossible, all the other maritime factors were also adverse to a Spanish success.

The second half of the situation shows a position just as definite. The Spanish monarchy had not the power to collect and distribute at the place and in the time required sufficient funds to support the effort, especially if that effort should be prolonged. And prolonged in the issue it had to be.

The one factor in the whole business where the attack was superior to the defence, was the possession of a single aim working with united centralised political power. This advantage was with the Spaniards.

It is true that an advantage of this kind should be, other things being equal, decisive. In war centralised power and simplicity of object should outweigh everything else, were everything else much the same with either combatant. The English ships were commanded in large measure by adventurers who were accustomed to consider nothing but private advantage. Most of the more conspicuous were no better than reformed buccaneers and reformed only for the moment. Their main object till now, during their active lifetime, had been not national, still less religious, but what is called today the " economic " motive ; what may more simply be termed " loot." The best known of them was John Hawkins. He was bred to that trade and to the slave trade with which it was inextricably entangled. What is true of him is true of his relative, Francis Drake. They were all on their own, though not all of them were so thoroughly independent as to propose the sale of the Queen's ships, for a consideration, to the enemy, as did Hawkins, when he tried to sell the English ships to the Spaniards. But the weakest element in the whole disorderly effort was the position of the Queen herself. Monarchy was the accepted and necessary principle of authority for all men in those days and the Queen did not command nor even support ; she waited upon the event.

And this attitude is as true of her in details as it is in the general scheme. Elizabeth was willing to risk a private gamble on the profit of a particular piece of piracy or more legitimate attack upon foreign craft ; but she did not act as the head of a nation determined to repel hostile invasion. Her reasons were simple enough and excellent—neither she nor anyone else could definitely call it hostile invasion. Many thought of it as foreign support for their own faction in the complex religious texture which England (not thirty years before almost homogeneously traditional), was now presenting.   To many more, perhaps to the mass of the inhabitants, the Spanish war was a mere confusion.   A most significant test for grasping the realities of that moment is the action of Elizabeth herself.   She lay low at the most critical moment of all, and got herself out of the way with Leicester when the invaders were actually entering the Straits of Dover, only appearing again when the uncertain situation had been settled.   The last heavy exchange between the two fleets was off Gravelines on July 29th (old style).   With the fairly heavy wind of the next two days all chance for the Spaniards of return through the Straits had completely disappeared, as had also all opportunity for awaiting the embarkation of enemy re- inforcements from the coast of the Low Countries.   Then, and not till then, the Queen made her speech at Tilbury to the assembled troops who were no longer called upon to meet the invader, as he could no longer be forthcoming.

It has been argued that when Elizabeth Tudor made this speech, which is one of the things most emphasised in our official textbooks, she could not have known that the Spaniards had passed Grisnez and were issuing from the Straits into the North Sea, whence they could not turn back against the wind.   They say she could not have heard that the Spanish ships (which everyone had seen leaving the Straits) had left until a post came in on the 10th and that the coming in of this post to Tilbury, where Elizabeth was dining with Leicester, prompted her to speak, because by that post arrived also a rumour that the invaders had already embarked and were on their way across. But they who argue thus forget the existence of an animal called the horse. It did not take forty-eight hours, let alone three or four days, for news to reach London that the Spanish convoys had been blown into the North Sea after having cut their cables. The news had to reach a point only fifty to fifty-five miles from the cliffs whence the failure of the Armada and its retirement northward were watched from both sides of the Straits of Dover.

* * * * *

A great deal of nonsense has been talked about the numbers in this crisis of Catholics and Protestants opposed to each other within the island. The reason that it is nonsense is that the terms are ill-chosen ; there was no clean-cut division as yet between the Catholic and the Protestant. An elementary acquaintance with the social conditions of the time ought to be enough to establish that. There was, as late as 1587-8 a remaining considerable body of opinion (not of individuals) which naturally desired a return of social customs, complicated, manifold, rooted in the habits of society. The Mass which had been the centre of the national religion was one of these and, of course, by all theological definition or rational consideration of men's habits, the Mass was by far the most important of the points at issue. The supremacy of the Pope was not one of them. It was taken for granted, indeed, just as we take for granted the function of government in taxation today ; but there was no special devotion to the Papacy among the general public. On the other hand, all Catholic habit had so long been rooted in society that the name of the Mass (and the Mass was the central, though unemphasised and fading institution) was still familiar to all.

There was, indeed, a considerable and a very ardent

minority which had begun a reaction against the unfamiliar habit of a new liturgy. This minority had begun to be enthusiastic for a restoration of traditional things. How numerous these reactionaries were no one can precisely tell, nor does it very much matter : for these things were not then a question of numbers but of enthusiasm. Anyhow, they were sufficiently numerous to form a solid basis for the effort to recover in England an organised Catholic worship and a return to the ancient national habits. If you add all those who vaguely regretted the topsy-turvy turmoil of the preceding thirty years, you may be certain that the people who were tired of it and wanted to get society on a solid basis again were the bulk of adult men and women then alive ; and obviously the bulk of the more elderly.

Opposed, however, to these intense nostalgic religionists, with their marked character, was a much smaller but still more intense body of Calvinistic reformers. Never forget that the heart of the whole affair was, throughout Europe, " Calvin versus the Catholic Church." For Calvin was the driving power and the underlying genius of the whole business. Long dead, he continued, his awful and determined ghost continued, to press the battle.

The third party to this hotch-potch of struggling ideals was something very different from either. It was the solid determination to enjoy the fruits of the great economic revolution : the material interest which I have summarised under the title of " The Abbey Lands."

Here we are, in the crisis of the Spanish War (so long postponed, so reluctantly entered, so still believed, hope against hope, to be avoidable). It was already half a life-time since the last of the monasteries had been swept into the money-bags of the new plutocracy. It was nearly thirty years since the advent of Cecil to power ; Cecil's use of Elizabeth Tudor had made the victory of the landlords (and of his own growing fortune) certain.

But cast your mind over your own time and ask yourself

whether so enormous a revolution registered in the last year of Queen Victoria could have been really firm by the year in which we live, 1941. Ask yourself whether the men who were between thirty and forty at the Dissolution, but by the time of the Armada were old, would have forgotten their past, or whether the traditions of their families would have disappeared. Of course they would not have done so. And the more certain is this from the fact that no one in England had dared to make a complete break with the past. That had happened in Scotland; it *might* have happened in England if the zeal and prophetic character of John Knox had appeared on English soil, either by his passing through England by Elizabeth's leave on his return to his native country from France, or by his coming here from Scotland to spread the gospel of the kirk. But Elizabeth had not allowed him to land and neither had he been allowed to come here to England from the north and set things alight. Here the fierce fire of the Reformation never blazed. The enthusiasm and the glow remained a separate, sectarian, minority thing, and has so remained : profoundly modifying English life, solidly erecting the mass of English middle-class opinion, making England most determinedly Protestant, steeping the English mind in Calvinistic ideas, which are everywhere predominant to this day ; but not going further ; not turning the average Englishman into a Calvinist.

Let us conclude then that the England upon which the threat of the Armada invasion fell was an England wherein, had the invasion succeeded, there would certainly have been a strong, and almost as certainly, a successful Catholic rising against the new-fangled alien liturgy of Cecil and his supporters. But let us conclude with equal certitude that such a rising would not have determined the national fate in any homogeneous fashion. It might have established a large, increasingly well-organised Catholic body, which should have remained an important exception within the

State, as did the Huguenots across the water in France. But times were already too late for it to do more ; a general pervasive influence of the abbey lands had done the trick and even at the moment at which I write, they still spread their influence over the English countryside ; the more so because they are abbey lands no longer. Let us return then to the retreat of the Armada.

There was nearly a week—six full days—between the first contact and the moment when it was clear that the Spanish effort had failed. That week has been generally described as one of a running fight between the attempted invasion and the maritime defence of the Channel carried out rather haphazard by individual actions between the English ships and their opponents. But a better picture of it is this : the division of the English armed forces by sea gave the Spaniards an opportunity for destroying those forces in detail. The opportunity was not seized because the Spanish political and military command was too centralised. When the Duke of Medina summoned his Council of War, lying off the Lizard, his captains, who had long experience of action at sea, advised immediate attack upon the English ships which were massed in Plymouth Sound. These ships formed only half the force available for defence. The other half was separated by more than the length of the Channel. The advice of the sailors who knew their trade was not taken. In its place the Duke of Medina determined to follow inflexibly the orders of his sovereign, which were, not to fight until he had established contact with the transports in the harbours of the Netherlands. These transports, having aboard them what we would call today a couple of divisions, were off Calais and anchored in those shallow waters on the 27th of July. There was no storm but there was a freshening wind from the south-west ; and there was something of a seaway in the Straits, as there usually is in these waters when the wind is in that quarter, especially after the tide has turned to ebb.

But it was not the weather which made the difference. It was not rough enough for that, nor did it blow hard enough; what made the difference was the superior seamanship of the English and the highly superior mobility of their smaller craft : smaller, that is, by far, than the huge Spanish vessels crowded with landsmen. With the wind round about south-west there could be no beating back against it in the face of opposition and, therefore, no chance of landing the enemy infantry on the convoys.

But meanwhile the wind backed further south, when, about midnight on the 28th of July, fireships released by the English bore down upon the enemy ships at anchor along the shoals from Calais to Dunkirk. These fireships had not only the wind behind them but the beginning of the flood-tide under them. There were only eight of them, but it was enough to give the impression of an awful advancing general conflagration. All the 29th the running fight continued, the English still showing their great superiority in gunnery, in the weight of metal delivered, but above all in the rapidity of their manœuvres. To this add a technical point which was of high importance to the issue : the smaller English ships were much stiffer than the far larger Spanish convoys, the latter leant over to the wind so sharply that shots to leeward were at once lost in the water ; and shots to windward went too high to cripple the English craft.

English shot, on the other hand, told continuously, especially as the defending force had the windward of the defensive. Though the English ships, like their much larger Spanish opponents, careened strongly to leeward from the south-west wind, they were not crank, as were the Spanish convoys. They stood up to it sufficiently. They had no occasion to fire to windward and the continuous fire to leeward against the Spaniards was at such low elevation as to be almost a plunging fire. The end of the action was a sort of rearguard fight ; about fifteen of the enemy still remaining clustered round their Admiral, and the rest tailing off eastward and northward before the wind and so up the North Sea and away.

There are one or two more myths to be got rid of before we leave the story of this first failure on the part of the invaders (for there was to be more than one other attempt before the hope of invasion was given up). One such myth is that Elizabeth had starved the supply of her ships through avarice. In point of fact, the English certainly delivered twice as many shots as the Spaniards and perhaps three times as many. And yet the supply of powder on the English side had been ample : so ample that, when the whole thing was over, the English magazines were less depleted than those of her opponents. The English Government was embarrassed for money continuously and inevitably during all the later sixteenth century and on into the seventeenth, without intermission. The reason for this is quite simple : the revenue was raised on traditional estimates, even the exceptional levies were reckoned in traditional figures and the expenditure was ceaselessly rising *because the value of money was changing for the worse :* that is, the ounce of gold or silver was buying less goods or services with every decade. We must multiply by at least twenty-five to get the purchasing value of money in the best part of Henry VIII's reign. We have only got to multiply by twelve in the later middle of Queen Elizabeth's reign ; we need only multiply by six under Charles the First, when England entered the Civil War or Great Rebellion. Before the end of the century we need hardly multiply by three. Elizabeth, that is to say the government, spent lavishly and spent all they could. It was the judgment of contemporaries and eye-witnesses that the heaviest actions fought in the narrow seas for the defence of England in those days exceeded in violence the great fight at Lepanto.

There is a very remarkable contrast, as might be expected,

L

between the number of guns and number of sailors, as also the number of soldiers, in the opposing fleets. When the Armada sailed from Lisbon towards the end of May, it counted 130 ships and rather less than 6,000 gross tonnage. There were just over 8,000 sailors on board, somewhat under 20,000 soldiers of a regular sort, and fifty per cent. more in the way of adventurers and servants and slaves. More than a third but less than half the Spanish ships were organised for an offensive war. When we say " organised for an offensive war, " this does not mean that the ships in that category were first-class fighting machines, as were the greater part of the small English vessels. It is an old and oft-repeated truth, remaining none the less true because it is hackneyed, that the invader could only hope for victory by grappling and fighting hand-to-hand ; and that he never got a chance to do.

XVIII

THE END OF THE ADVENTURE

A MERE recital of the sequence between 1560 and 1603, that is the last half of the sixteenth century and the long reign of William Cecil as the operative power (till his death) behind the throne of Elizabeth, is not sufficient to account for that capital event in the story of Europe : the transformation of English religion. We find, as we have found in these pages, that England entered that generation as a Catholic polity. English Society was an integral part of Christendom actively at work round the central institution of the Mass. We find, not indeed at the end of the forty years, but shortly *after* the end of that period, an England in which the centre of religious gravity had shifted from one side to another. England, some years after Elizabeth Tudor's death, was on the way to becoming an anti-Catholic society : one to which the Mass gradually became alien and abhorrent : one in which unity with Europe was no longer desired but disliked : one in which a strong-rooted and permanent reaction against the old Catholic unity was in full operation. This English change was the revolution that did most to transform Europe from a morally united to a disunited culture.

For it cannot be too often repeated that the English change was what made the difference. Not that England was copied elsewhere but that England afforded the first example of a national government opposed to the ancient traditions and, therefore, England presented the first example in Europe of a whole large society gradually reversing its attitude towards the past and adopting slowly, throughout its being, antagonism to that past.

The true cause of so prodigious a change was not the gradual growth within English society of new doctrines. There was only one new doctrine strongly at work in

173

Europe then : the doctrine of Geneva. There was only one prophet dominating and leading the moral revolution in Christendom and that prophet was Calvin, the Frenchman from Noyon, whose voice filled Geneva and made of it a rival to Rome. That voice had been hardly heard in England. Those who read the past in terms of the present —the commonest and most ignorant form of historical error—miss the crucial problem altogether. They imagine, because the England they know is opposed (one may say universally) to the older England, because the England they know is essentially and actively hostile to the older tradition, that therefore the England they have *not* known and cannot know, the England of their fathers in the active ferment of the Renaissance, was the same. But that is bad history, taught though it is in every text book and by every don. There came some accident whereby the England of 1600 was something radically different from the England of, say, 1625.

What was that accident ? We need to answer that question for, without an answer to it, so sharp a revolution and so profound a one is inexplicable. The negative forces are clear, the Mass was suppressed by official force. A generation which was not particularly devoted to the Mass grew up without that central institution to inform its mind. But merely negative forces can never account for these great changes in the history of a people. To account for this change we must find something more than mere loss of habit. Loss of habit would not have replaced a sort of indolent affection by an active dislike. Things of that sort are in the lives of individuals, as in those of societies, the effect of shock. It has been well said that though we talk of " falling in love," we use no phrase for that most evident of individual and social phenomena : falling out of love. Now what made the English people fall out of love with their past was the shock of growing Nationalism, reinforced by a particular political quarrel ; and this particular political

quarrel has not received the attention which is its due from
those who examine the story of their people.

The story of that shock does not properly belong to the
lifetime of Elizabeth Tudor, for it fell after her death. The
appetite for nationality, for the worship of one's own
society in particular and the consequent indifference to
Christendom as an ideal, was not peculiar to England ; it
was alive everywhere : in France, where it led, after the
typical French fashion, to civil war and the turmoil of a
revolution ; in Spain, where it led to a deification of the
Catholic throne. But what was peculiar to England was a
special dispute upon the claims of national loyalty in one
particular : the Act of Supremacy. The supremacy of the
Crown, in matters ecclesiastical as well as lay, was in the
atmosphere of the time. It was the air which all men
breathed. When Elizabeth was dead and, under the new
reign of an alien and unpopular cripple, there seemed an
opportunity for restoring in their fullness traditions which
were still strongly alive, the vast mass of Englishmen who
took the supremacy of the national Crown for granted,
included that other great majority of Englishmen who
would have been glad enough, though no longer in a very
active fashion, to return to those social and moral habits
which had governed the lives of their fathers and which
still in a diluted fashion permeated their own. They were
not enthusiastic for their return, but it would have suited
them well enough. But what did not suit them was foreign
interference. That interference was provided by the
quarrel which sprang up over the Supremacy of the Crown.
" Why not accept it ? " said the average Englishman, who
was not yet rooted in the new liturgy and only cared about
the violent Calvinist faction sufficiently to dislike it intensely.
To call a man a puritan was still at that moment of transition
an insult connoting a disgusting eccentricity, and most
astonished would the average Englishman of that day have
been to learn that after his old age and death the puritan,

through an accident of civil war, would exercise active power. When you ask the same average Englishman whether he was prepared to oppose the novel and not yet respected liturgy of the novel official Church, to be active against it, to attempt to replace it by something he had half forgotten and to do this at the expense of his national monarchy, he was reluctant indeed. Behind his reluctance lay, of course, the vast vested interest of the now established land system, the now traditional ownership by new proprietors of the abbey lands. But this was not in the forefront of political consciousness. That large majority—the bulk of the nation—which was still traditionally attached to Catholic things, had no desire for an immediate change after more than forty years—an active lifetime—of official habits which treated full Catholicism as a necessary opponent.

You get the whole thing epitomised and vividly emphasised in James Stuart's first address to the Parliament of his new kingdom. Read that speech and you will understand the opposing forces which faced each other in the crisis. James claims the name of Catholic ; he claims it vehemently. What he detests and combats is not general and Catholic doctrine, still less the Mass, but " the triple-headed beast," that Monster the Papacy. The number of Englishmen in this moment, which much more than any earlier moment determined the fate of English religion, who were ready to support the deposing power of the Pope was small indeed. Ridiculed and actually disliked as James Stuart was (and for good reason) by his reluctant subjects, he was at least a legitimate heir to the throne of England. There was a certain flavour of nationalism about him through his Tudor descent and it was this that turned the scale. Read our official histories and you might believe that there was a Catholic body on the one side and a Protestant body on the other, engaged in a clean-cut conflict. There was nothing of the sort. There was a general feeling for the Crown and a support of it because it stood for England, which had become an object of devotion. With those general sentiments the vague but almost ubiquitous Catholic tradition mingled and it was then henceforth impossible to dissociate the two. The average Englishman had made his choice.

XIX

TERRIBLE DEATH

THE awful passing of Elizabeth Tudor has repeatedly been described. My object in touching here upon that dreadful business is not to repeat what so many have quoted, but rather to put in their right proportions the tragic elements of her last days. Emphatically must it be reiterated that the dark cloud under which she left this life was not a judgment upon her apostasy or her contempt for Christian traditions. Properly speaking Elizabeth never apostatised because she never believed. Her private devotions are quoted as proving a certain sensibility to eternal ends. The proof has always seemed to me very thin. From childhood to the end of her old age the woman was a true Renaissance sceptic. And what else would you expect from such a character and at such a time. Could you look for any enthusiasm or any cognate emotion in a mind of that sort? Could you look for devotion of any kind? Our moderns in their desperate substitution of patriotism for religion have always desired to make out that Elizabeth was filled with a special patriotism. Neither she nor anyone of her time was so filled. The English man and woman of that day preferred their inherited habit of life to that of foreigners. In this they were merely human. The whole human race prefers its local habit of life to a foreign habit. But to our modern transports in the matter of patriotism you will find no parallel in those days. Patriotism *became* the religion of the English much later, and the later emotion grew, of course, from seeds sown before its time. But the effort to read into the Elizabethan world an emotion which was the special fruit of the struggle not with Spain, but with France is a crying sin against history. The segregation of special national types nourished upon a restricted and nearly always falsified national history is a modern thing, the product of modern conditions. Christendom in the days of Elizabeth was still one country. It was a country suffering from potential and often actual civil war because it was rent by violent disputes upon the ultimate philosophy of life. But it had not begun to fall into those quite separate worlds into which it has fallen today.

If Elizabeth had felt attraction to any human being in her sterile life she had felt such attraction for her contemporary Anjou, the brother of the French King. His departure provoked one of those very rare exhibitions of tenderness which are to be discovered in her life. She did not rant, rage, scream and roar as was her habit when she desired to " release her personality." She genuinely mourned. Yet Anjou was not only a fellow prince he was also a Frenchman and a Frenchman of a sort which a modern English woman would find particularly unattractive.

The fearful surroundings of the last royal Tudor deathbed were not, I say, the product of any special evil in Elizabeth Tudor herself—so far as one can judge. Her mental suffering was dreadful and the approach of her end was something she could hardly face. But which of us can boast that he will meet that challenge with serenity and courage. If he does so it will rather be his good fortune than an act of his will. Rather is that painful story of this woman's departure from this world an illustration of her real character than something from which we can draw a moral lesson. She felt that she was ceasing to be herself and that is what probably most of us will feel when the moment comes to reply to the summons of Azrael.

I can recall no two more poignant expressions in all the long collection of English anecdote than the cry, " Duke, Duke, it is a terrible thing to die," and the cry, " Things are changed with me." Both those cries were the cries of women. The one was the voice of James II's first wife in her agony. The second was the anguished cry of

Elizabeth Tudor when the reality of this world began to dissolve around her and leave her very self in the process of disillusion. St. Paul was right indeed when he pointed to death as something abnormal in the fate of humanity, nor shall our race ever be reconciled to the unnatural attack of that enemy.

She lay there not in a stupor, but in a sort of physical despair—if one may use the words. I have seen the same thing passing before my own eyes within my own experience particularly in the case of women who are of high culture and intelligence and a high experience.

Now although we must not exaggerate Elizabeth Tudor's culture she had certainly enjoyed erudition and maintained the fruits of it throughout her life. It was to this advantage that she owed, like most of her contemporaries, her lack of religion and her comparative indifference to the absence from her neighbourhood of the Catholic Church, its sacraments and its unfailing support.

That she did regret the absence is certain. So also it is certain that she felt strongly the contrast between a sovereign such as she could wish to have been, standing at the head of one of the great European states surrounded by its traditional prelates and its ancestral religion and her own position as a mere figurehead to a rapacious crew whose rapacity she joined, for we must never forget that Elizabeth herself sank to the grave indignity of sharing the loot. She was not above participating in certain " ventures." After the invention of the modern Elizabeth legend such an exceedingly undignified attitude on the part of a great European monarch is not well appreciated here. Men could see no loss of prestige in Elizabeth pocketing for herself what the buccaneers, her contemporaries, pocketed. But she must have felt her position false enough when she met the envoys of her equals.

There is not in all our history a more abnormal, a sharper finale than the last hours of the last Tudor. Those Tudors

who had come out of next to nothing socially ; stewards and
bailiffs, whose founder had been advanced by the very
undignified patronage extended to him by a lascivious
woman not quite sane. Those Tudors who had presided
over the earthquake of the Reformation in England and
over the complete recasting of English society by that
event ; those Tudors who were without great traditions in
themselves and without power to hand on similar traditions
to their posterity, who ended, fitly enough, without
posterity and having appeared, as it were, from nowhere,
went back as suddenly into nowhere to be succeeded by
the nobler Scottish line and by all the traditions of Stuart
chivalry.

Therefore is it that the death of Elizabeth Tudor, those
last days of hers, are so strong a symbol of the times.

I have sometimes wondered whether the spirit of Mary
Stuart, Queen of Scots, looked on with joy at the evil case
of Elizabeth's death. Mary, herself, had suffered death,
hardly at the hands of Elizabeth but by the very reluctant
consent of Elizabeth. In Mary's eyes, Elizabeth was
certainly guilty of murder, the murder of Mary's own
mother and guilty of base treachery therein, as also of a
certain weakness which we must hesitate to call cowardice
because cowardice was not native to the temperament of
the Queen.

The spirit of Mary Stuart could not have rejoiced in her
cousin's misery when she looked down on it from Heaven
and from Beatitude for though Heaven and Beatitude
rejoice in justice, and therefore in the execution of justice
by penalty, they take no personal revenge. But if Mary
Stuart could watch from some intermediate condition prior
to Beatitude the passing of that other Queen, she might
have experienced a certain sombre joy.

Of all the death beds—the official death beds—in English
history, that death bed is far the most fearful. Because it
was so fearful, a moral legend has been built around it by

those who deplore Elizabeth's life and such personal action as she had upon her time. Because it was so awful, it has been read as a moral lesson to warn men against doing what she did. But what did she do? Can she be blamed for having maintained her position? She had no choice. She had to maintain it or die.

Moreover it was not she that made the choice. The choice had been thrust upon her.

Yes, it was a fearful story, but the lesson to be learned from it is not the divine revenge that falls upon evil doing —for Elizabeth did nothing particularly evil in herself. It is rather that men will say anything to falsify history when religious passion has been aroused.

Had the history of England been adequately written with an impersonal desire to represent what the Germans call " Objective Truth " (and what sensible people call " Truth " without an objective) it would have been a commonplace with all English readers that the death of Elizabeth was one of the outstanding horrors of the story we have inherited from the past. She lay there for days refusing to move, plunged in utter despair. She had already lost all continuity with her vigorous past. She had collapsed. But such accidents are common to mortality at the close of its mortal life on this earth when the bodily frame which has been maintained by something spiritual breaks down on the approaching departure of the animated soul. The poignant, haunting horror of that death-bed should be cited, not in Elizabeth's accusation, but in truth of our own mortal weakness. I say again it might happen to any of us.

It is true that she did not attempt to cultivate during the days of her health (and that health was always precarious)— let us rather say during the days of her vitality—the business of religion, without which the last challenge of death can hardly be met. But in this there was nothing peculiar to herself. How many of us have cultivated the business of religion? Today hardly any do so. It is not for the people of our time to challenge in this matter our fathers of the former great agnostic wave which roused and submerged our ancestry of three centuries ago, but it is rather for us to contemplate the fruits of that abandonment which they also gave up : the abandonment of certitude and the search for certitude. The last phase of such abandonment when life has been fully lived out is such a phase as fell upon the last hours of Elizabeth Tudor.

We must remember her isolation, her lack of anything that could support her soul, her lack even of what people in her position have a right to demand, the security of the future.

Her famous cry on hearing of the birth of James, Mary Stuart's son, " I am a barren stock " reveals for a moment the depth of her despairing soul. Much more was its depth of despair revealed by that last spiritual agony of complete dereliction whereby she was introduced to the final thing. But her despair was not the result of ill-doing, it was the result of abandonment ; and loneliness has fallen upon far higher souls than hers.

XX

THE ARTS

CHANGES in social spirit produce changes in external forms throughout society and particularly in architectural forms. In nothing was the passing of the Middle Ages and the coming of the modern world more marked than in the almost violent transition from the Mediæval Architecture in the north to the modern. The gulf between two styles each of which represents and is produced by a separate spiritual atmosphere is deeper and wider in Britain than in any other province in Christendom. There was a revolution in taste the like of which is not to be found in any other country : so strong a belated reaction towards Gothic architecture as appeared in this island and will ever be honourably associated with the name of Pugin.

The reason that the contrast between the early architecture and the late is so very marked upon the face of English towns is, of course, the impact of the reformed religion. It was in the domain of religion that most care was expended and most money devoted to building ; only the claims of religion as a universal force in society were denied and decayed. The principal shock on building was, of course, the dissolution of the monasteries ; an action contemporary with Elizabeth Tudor's very early childhood. She, herself, might be taken as an example of a person exactly placed in time and space for the best observation of the change, for she did not live to see in her own life any new, great ecclesiastical building set up. It may be said with truth of Elizabeth Tudor that she had assisted at the death of the old Catholic architecture in her realm. There was no breach of continuity between the earliest arches of Roman brick and the last specimens of what we call today Gothic architecture. The one grew out of the other, and though the pointed arch and all the distinguishing marks

of the twelfth century change were very distinct in spirit
from the Romanesque (or, as it is called here, the Norman),
style, yet the least experienced traveller could see at once
that the pointed arch and the Norman which preceded it
belong to the same society, whereas all the later work harks
back to the classical pagan world.

There is, indeed, an exception to this general truth and
that exception is the cupola or dome.   It is true that pagan
antiquity was familiar with roofs formed from the segments
of spheres.   The Pantheon is a most obvious case.   But the
dome, or cupola, is not a common form until the close, or
past the close, of the pagan period.   It belongs particularly
to the earlier centuries of the Christian religion after its
political triumph, and is found especially in the eastern and
Greek half of the Empire whence also we inherited those
special forms which we still call "Byzantine."   But the
dome, or cupola, neither arose nor became common in
England during the reign of Elizabeth Tudor.   They arose
and became common only in the century after her death.

The characteristic of what is rightly called Elizabethan
Architecture is, as might be expected of that time and the
social revolution which marked it, the wealthy country
house.   The ruin of ecclesiastical building was almost
complete.   The exceptions are well known and have become
famous, the most famous of them being the Abbey of
Westminster which survived the destruction of the monastic
community after Mary Tudor's death : for it should never
be forgotten that Mary Tudor did make, to her honour, an
effort to revive Westminster : an effort the fruits of which
were destined, as were all those of that unhappy six years,
to be obliterated and destroyed.   Here and there up and
down the country an ecclesiastical building connected with
the monastic system was saved as Westminster had been
saved, and for the same use.   A noticeable example is the
Abbey of Romsey.

Wells also owes to the same process its bishopric and its

cathedral; but the very great majority of the abbeys were either pulled down or converted into dwelling houses for the new landlords, or fell into ruin. But, indeed, the latter fact is one of the strangest accidents in history and it would be interesting to prove, if it could be proved, the process whereby such a vast amount of handiwork was allowed to disappear without an effort to save it. As shelter alone these great vaults of the Middle Ages should have been worthy of survival, but with their ecclesiastical use the desire to maintain the mere material thing seems to have gone.

It has been suggested that a certain lingering superstitious habit made men respect the gradually crumbling walls, and that we look today upon those noble ruins through the favour of ancestors who feared if they despoiled to suffer the spiritual penalties of sacrilege.

This explanation will hardly fit in with what we know of the time. In certain districts, notably in the north, there was a strong devotion to the practice and tradition of the Catholic Church, but in most parts of the country, and particularly in the wealthier parts, men were growing indifferent to religion before they became hostile thereto.

It is remarkable that contemporary literature gives little clue to what men were feeling when the great monastic shrines of the Middle Ages were abandoned. Never has a revolution so drastic and so widespread passed over any society with so little immediate shock. There was, indeed, a rising in the North betrayed and destroyed by the Howards, and on the first introduction of the new Protestant liturgy in little Edward's reign there had been sporadic outbursts all over the country, but there was none sufficiently organised and above all there were no leaders because the accepted national leaders, English landed families, had now everywhere a very great vested interest in the new religious organisation. They had taken over the abbey lands. The splendour of the new great houses which rose upon the loot of religion was essentially the sunset of Mediæval England, although the Renaissance forms were everywhere among them. Thenceforward English architecture is the architecture of the rich. Houses are built to glorify one family or one owner. They have no communal purpose as the monasteries had had. And there is a side issue which has a great spiritual importance though difficult to define and more difficult to illustrate : popular pressure and popular judgment in the matter of building was denied because the religion of the populace had disappeared. No method of preserving that ancient tradition had been discovered or attempted. In its place you have zealous sectaries. What you do not get, and could never get again, was the whole-hearted spiritual support of the masses for the liturgy and doctrine presented to them. The liturgy, though written in the finest vernacular tongue, did not proceed from the people ; it was impressed upon them. It was impressed violently, against their will. All they could appreciate in the matter was a change of habit. If you read into the glorious liturgy of what was then the new service those emotions now aroused by the passage of time and sanctity which age always gives to any institution you misunderstand the emotions of the day. For us, Elizabethan English is classical. For those who first used it on their Sundays and Holy Days it was a novelty which had as yet no place in their hearts. The loss of beauty in the external forms of religious building was never recovered. Nothing specifical, nothing even specifically Christian, was to be found in the various innovations and experiments which followed in the succeeding century. Still less were any such to be discovered in the eighteenth century. Look around you today in London and ask yourself what are the marks of ecclesiastical architecture after the religious revolution. You can only reply that there are no marks. There is no one inspiration. There is no one style. Yet one of the greatest opportunities for new building appears in a lifetime, hardly more than

M

sixty years after Elizabeth's death : the Great Fire of
London. It could leave us nothing more original than
St. Paul's. The old Cathedral of London had been one of
the triumphs of mediæval architecture. The English
mediæval Great Church excelled especially in length, but
it also excelled in the height of its spires, a feature which
had arisen in the later Middle Ages. Old St. Paul's was an
example of both. It was the longest church in Christendom
and its spire rose into the air above any rival in any other
capital of Christendom. When it was destroyed in the
Great Fire of London nothing adequate, certainly nothing
popular, or national, replaced it. Sir Christopher Wren is a
very great figure in the national history. He stands at the
fountain head of the new Masonic organisation which
counts for so much in the new national life and is in power
everywhere today. He was very learned and very much
alive. But if you would test his sense of the past, his continuity with all that England had been for centuries, observe
how he handles the Gothic in the West Front of the Abbey.
It is a ridiculous parody of what Christian architecture had
been since its most typical living expression had arisen in
the Crusades.

The catastrophe was not peculiar to England or the
English change of religion. It fell with crushing force
everywhere throughout the west, even in Spain, where a
more living sense of glory in stone, and still more in the
carving of wood, had survived than anywhere else. When
after more than two centuries dried bones of dead architecture began to stir and to promise a quickening of a new
life, that new life came in no co-ordinated or universal
form. It came haphazard.

Here a man would build to the orders of some wealthy
patron in a manner imitating the classic, there he would
build with a very clumsy effort to continue the mediæval
inheritance which was now completely lost, and which the
architect misunderstood. In other places he would fall into

what was merely grotesque at the worst or at the best a personal experiment. To understand what had happened you may contemplate for your amazement any one of twenty monstrosities. Thus in Southwark as you approach London Bridge from the south-east you pass a steeple which is designed for a spire, but is cut off short before its terminal : a perfectly meaningless and offensive thing, typical of the time when tradition died.

Perhaps the mediæval architecture was continued more faithfully by local masons and builders than by any others. Oxford in particular preserved a remarkable tradition of its own. But though Oxford presented, as did Cambridge, the best examples of mediæval building in its later forms to be found anywhere in this island, those forms furnish no inspiration. It would not be an exaggeration to say that the sense and spirit of the Middle Ages and their inspiring flame of loveliness were lost until the remarkable revival of the early nineteenth century.*

The spirit of that revival, to the very great good fortune of England, was never allowed to fail. It went on from strength to strength and at this day by far the best revival of Gothic in Europe is to be found here. The French effort was certainly most inadequate. Chateauroux is sufficient to condemn it.

For the rest, apart from architecture, the arts were in danger of perishing. Sculpture had to wait long for any revival and when that revival came, its chief meaning had gone out of it, for the features had fallen dead. Painting, especially portraiture, was maintained, and we owe the respect for it (which happily survived strongly enough to prompt a resurrection) to Charles I as much as to any man. Surrounded by enemies who hated beauty and could not understand it, *he* selected with care and judgment the

* Perhaps the best example of how thoroughly the Gothic had died out and the whole spirit of it, even in those countries which had given it birth, is that afforded by the West Front of Orleans. It is even more startlingly out of tune with its ancestry than is the West Front of Westminster Abbey.

Royal Collection of pictures.   It was dispersed in the
Civil Wars.   That blow was the more severe because
after that dispersal there was to be no more active monarchy
in England ; and therefore no king with a revenue sufficient
for the collecting of a national gallery of painting.   Individual collectors among the rich helped to save the situation,
but they saved it slowly.   The Crown, the centre of the
nation in art as in everything else, was lost : for kingship
after the Reformation ceased to be kingship.   The king
after the full fruit of the Reformation had been gathered
was no more than the nominee of the new wealthy governing
class.

A man may well ask himself as he looks round modern
England, and indeed modern Europe as a whole, whether
the sense of beauty will ever revive.   Individual talent or
even genius has not been, and perhaps can never be
destroyed, but that collective spirit whereby the whole
community appreciates, supports and in a sense creates its
art, was no more to be found.   The destruction of Christian
unity had killed it.*

* It is remarkable that the military art, whether in fortification or offensive
weapons, was paralysed as thoroughly as any other.   It progressed somewhat,
of course, but it progressed haltingly.   Men seemed in this last phase of the
sixteenth century to be uncertain of their weapons and you see this particularly in the matter of artillery.   Italian science developed that arm and at its
beginnings the Germans had shown a special aptitude for it.   But artillery
did not begin to do its work until the succeeding century was well advanced.
Charles of Sweden understood its functions as well as any one, but even he
did not make such use of it as might have been made.   That Cromwell failed
to use it (save in siege work) is strange, for one would have thought that that
great cavalry leader would instinctively have developed the horse-drawn
offensive arm.   He did not do so.   Nor did any of his contemporaries.   Not
guns, but mounted troops decided actions in the Civil Wars.   This was due
in part to the effect that artillery had not learnt to be mobile.   Its traction
still depended, as a rule, upon chance men hired for the occasion, and therefore was clumsy throughout the period.   Not till the military efforts of
Louis XIV did artillery in the field begin to take its place which thenceforward was never to be lost, but to increase with each generation of gunners
until it became the decisive instrument of warfare in the last generation.

XXI

THE CATHOLIC SURVIVAL

S O far we have been considering the growth and strength
of that anti-Catholic movement which made modern
England and accounts for most of what we see round us
today. But the converse needs to be justly and carefully
appreciated. What was the nature of the resistance to the
change? What was the strength of that resistance? At
what point did the defence begin to fear it was defeated?
What were the factors of doubts and confusion on the
defending side which made the effort to restore religion
ultimately fail?

There is no doubt at all about the main cause of the
Catholic failure in England : it was due to the change in
government which, in its turn was based upon the enormous
economic revolution. But the surprising thing is that the
development was so very slow, the victory of the anti-
religious force so doubtful for so long, and the final rem-
nants of resistance so enduring and to the end so confident.

We have seen what it was if put in mere numbers. The
mass of the English community, Catholic in tone till well
after Elizabeth Tudor's death : a large and increasingly
conscious minority were still regarded by their fellow
citizens as adherents of the old religion, and therefore
maintainers of the English national tradition, to which the
Reformation was alien. This minority you find still very
large a hundred and fifty years after the first attack on unity.
They came, as we have seen, to one family in eight of the
English people, even if you only reckon the avowed and
admitted sympathisers with the older things. It was
certainly, if you admit in your calculations the large fringe
of doubtful men, a quarter.

The whole thing reminds one of the very slow melting
of ice in the Arctic seas in the early summer of the North,

surprisingly large fragments of the floes remain intact, the dissolution of the pack seems haphazard, and one might be certain that if the climatic conditions were only slightly to change the solid frost would return.

Yet unity was not restored. The strong instinctive demand for it bore no final fruit. The governmental pressure and the economic pressure combined, the official favour shown everywhere to the anti-Catholic were triumphant. Apart from the strength of the official machine, apart even from the violent pull of economic interest, there was something else, without which one can never account for the dislodgment of ancestral religion from the conservative English mind.

That something else was the growth of national feeling, allied to the Reformation tradition.

It is foolish to represent mere moods as though they were personalities or gods affecting and directing the fate of mankind. There is nothing divine about a mood, it is reason and experience which determine a man's attitude towards a new movement, especially if that movement be of very slow development as was the movement in England for abandoning tradition. There was an even stronger national enthusiasm under the united French monarchy of the day—that is of the seventeenth century—than there was in the distracted contemporary society in England, in which aristocracy was struggling to be born. Yet the French national movement, though it warped the religion of the French, did not break the continuity of that religion. The English national mood, slowly strengthening in the sixteenth century, had never demanded a revolt against Christendom and a breach with unity. It did not contain to a degree sufficient for the full purposes of religious revolution any great element of active heresy. The church was less corrupt here than elsewhere, there had not been here, as in Scotland, a shameless and universal capture of religious revenue for the benefit of individual rich men, until the attack on the monasteries, and we ought always to remember that the attack on the monasteries in England was not a general or popular movement ; it was dynastic ; it was undertaken by a king in order to enrich himself and to obtain for his uncertain dynasty the support of wealthy landowners.

Again, Englishmen had less appetite for civil war than any others in Europe. Now without civil war there could be no general destruction of the national religion. The Seymours had proved that. They could not get a following. They failed because the English temper was averse to violent change. Had it been France armies could at once have been raised from the gentry, upper and lower, to fight for increase of fortune at the expense of the national tradition in religion. But being England and not France there was no appearance of such armies.

Another point to be remembered is that the come and go of twenty years had left opinion jaded and bewildered. Elderly men in 1559, when the official change tentatively began, would be regretting the loss of the Mass as a domestic custom, groups of young enthusiasts would be welcoming the destruction of the Mass, or rather of the Catholic Church in this country ; the overwhelming mass in between would normally have done what the overwhelming mass in every society does, to wit, " carry on " : that is, behave as they had always behaved, regret change and resist it to the best of their power.

In other words, English society in 1559 was prepared for a continued rather lax acceptance of the old religious social custom. There would be numerous Masses, which by this time had become Low Masses, the celebrants thereof receiving various sums from endowments, often sums insufficient for the livelihood of the priest and therefore supplemented by school-teaching on his part or other duties. Side by side with this general rather lax habit of religion, there would be the major ceremonies, notably the daily High

Masses in the great Cathedral churches, but not the main body of endowed ritual which used to distinguish the Abbeys, for the Abbeys were no more. Here and there one survived as a newly established cathedral or was continued as a sort of national institution : but the vast bulk of these establishments had gone and their revenues had been pocketed by the new Reformation millionaires who are today the older and more respectable landed families.

It is probably at this point that we must fix the turnover. The common habit of religion changed—especially by the substitution of the vernacular liturgy for the Latin liturgy, not only for the first reason we gave, that men had grown bewildered and weary with shift and change, but also because the surrounding habit, the general atmosphere of the Mass had been starved into inanition by the disappearance of the hitherto omnipresent monastic houses, great and small. There were the parish churches but they did not represent the majority of places where the sacraments could be got, and the services of burial and of marriage and of baptism and all the rest of it.

No one can doubt who reads the literature of that day (especially in its common popular form, the play) that England remained a Catholic country, in general tradition and social convention right on till the death of Elizabeth. The only rival to the immemorial liturgical habit, enthusiasm for which had faded, was the intense Calvinist movement and body. But this body was small compared with the mass of the population. Unless we grasp that elementary fact we misunderstand altogether that England of which the religious change was imposed. Men were not going to fight any more to recover the Mass, the Latin Mass, and its various orthodox adjuncts. But they were not going to accept if they could help it the worry of being run by a minority of innovators. It is no wonder that in such a society the general Catholic tradition should not have survived. No one was really bothered during the first ten years of the Cecilian experiment so long as they did not interfere with or threaten the key points of the new settlement. You were interfered with and bothered if you ostentatiously avoided the new official worship. If you were rich such active obstinacy on your part offered a tempting bait to those who could make money out of your fines. But much the most of men especially of rich men would not run the risk of being fined at all. You were not asked to profess explicitly, continually and publicly a set of new doctrines which you might think newfangled nonsense at the best or at the worst exasperating ; all you had to do was to recite in your own language every week a form of prayer which had nothing offensive in it, most of which was a mere translation of the older Latin forms of prayer, and therefore quite consonant with your general mood inherited from family custom.

Under these conditions the sort of vague Catholic sentiment would presumably have long endured ; but, what is astonishing, is the fact that under conditions so adverse to the lively practice of the Faith that practice did survive.

Obviously the main factor in the maintenance and continuation of a religious system in its external, and therefore in its vital, framework is an unbroken continuance of performance. Now this was lacking to the Catholics of England after Cecil's rule began in 1559 ; save a few dependents upon the few rich houses the bulk of English families could neither hear Mass nor receive the Sacraments nor carry on any habit of what had hitherto been the rooted national religion ; yet that religion lived on. Men continued to say they were Catholic, in opposition to the Government and the whole official system, years and years after the actual physical presence of the Faith had been taken from them.

If any proof were needed of the strength with which Catholicism had rooted itself in the English mind this one fact would be sufficient proof. Elsewhere upon government acceptance or imposition of the new religion that new religion easily conquered its predecessor. Scandinavia is the great example. Scandinavia became Protestant very rapidly indeed and as a matter of course, not through any enthusiasm or predication, but because certain official orders had been given and those orders had been followed. In England such a transformation did not take place.

It is true that no one could predict the future fate of English religion during the earlier years of Elizabeth's reign. It is also true that some leader might have arisen to voice and to lead the popular will and that, even though no foreign influence were encouraged or even tolerated. The example of general European civilisation might have proved sufficient to save the Faith in England, after the first enthusiasms of the small Calvinist minority had died down, to launch a reaction towards that folly called society which all Englishmen still remembered and which the great bulk of Englishmen still desired. It is true also that such an incident as the Anjou marriage (had such a marriage been possible) might still have changed, in the long run, the religious fate of England. We moderns have difficulty in appreciating this because men always read history in the light of their own times and find it difficult or impossible to put themselves into the skins of their ancestors, to see things with their eyes and feel things with the senses of the long past generation. Though it sounds strange to modern ears it is an historical truth that England was essentially Catholic until the close of that long Elizabethan reign.

As the older men died out, however, as the new generation which had had no experience in youth of the Mass and all that went with the Mass grew into manhood something positive would be needed to replant that very positive and concrete thing the Catholic Church. It was this truth, the capital political truth of the time, which to the eternal honour of the Society of Jesus was grasped to the full, and vividly within its corporation. The Jesuits were prepared to provide the necessary impetus. It meant mortal risk for the individuals that should make the attempt; it meant torture and a terrible death. Yet the attempt was made. That it failed is ample testimony to the excellent organisation, under social conditions which made organisation difficult, of the governmental machine established by William Cecil. What gives this great man his title to greatness is the very presence and establishment of the Church of England. One cannot say of anything affecting a whole society gradually and organically that it is the work of one man, where mortals are concerned. It is true indeed of the Catholic Church throughout the world that it was the work of one Man; the more reason to be secure in the conclusion that this one Man was more than a man. But of particular external things one *can* say " One man was the main author of this " ; and the English establishment, the new Church of England had one man for its chief author.

He was a wizened pinchbeck little fellow. He had no presence ; he was not respected. But he did the trick. He gauged exactly the forces of his time ; he knew how devoted the English populace had become to the dynasty and he even understood the caprice of the woman whom he had helped to put at the head of the State, and in whose name and under whose official authority the great religious revolution of the English was ultimately accomplished. He knew that if she did not follow the directives which he had laid down he and his associates could get rid of her. He was able to estimate to the full her determination not only to survive but to remain a monarch. He felt completely, by something stronger than instinct, the necessary connection between the new religion and the new fortunes which had arisen from the confiscation of the Church endowments and their capture by a set of new millionaires and hosts of lesser men. It was his boast that no man in his day (after his grasp on the helm of state was fixed) had suffered for religion ; and that boast was essentially true ;

for to religion he was personally, we may presume, indifferent, though perhaps the habit of championing the Protestant cause had gradually coloured his mind. When he said that men under Elizabeth, that is under the general government of William Cecil, were put to death not for the expression of religious convictions but for treason, he said something which was objectively exact. But his statesmanship made it possible to make such an affirmation.

There attaches also to this very great man the further and most rare element of greatness, that he left his handiwork unsigned. He made the Church of England. The Church of England is a Cecilian thing ; yet he remained in the background of that creative act, and remains there still after nearly four centuries. Of such effect is concealment, silence and the indirect in human affairs.

*   *   *   *   *

How quickly did the old faith die and by what stages ? It died gradually if we measure the rate of its passing by years. If we count only in terms of time we might almost say rather that it " faded " than that it died ; but it died very thoroughly, for all that. It died more thoroughly in England than in any other province in Christendom, for no one except the Jesuits, who faced torture and death under William Cecil, actively defended it after the collapse of the northern revolt. Nowhere was the spiritual inheritance of Christendom (or, if you prefer a false phrase, of " Mediæval Christianity ") more thoroughly abandoned than here in England. There was no prolonged civil war and such civil war as did break out was confined to a restricted area. There was no vivid traditional legacy of the past vigorously maintained by the men who should have been its defenders. The excuse can be made, and *is* made, that the faith of the English was rather filched from them than destroyed by accident ; but the fact remains that the populace allowed it to be filched from them. There are plenty of excuses to be proffered and proffered they have duly been. There were no leaders because they who might have been leaders had all been bribed. There was no active and clear cut doctrinal issue which could give men something to bite into. Indeed to this day the issue is still left vague, but the broad truth cannot be escaped. The English people and their leaders abandoned the spiritual inheritance of their fathers. They became a new thing. It was a new thing of which most of them grew within a lifetime to be proud, and to which most of them grew also to feel a familiar affection, closely combined with patriotism. But a new thing it was. The old thing was not defended and it slowly died, abandoned. It was not fed.

Attempts have been made to estimate the process numerically. They have never been very successful. The enemies of the old religion have naturally put the figures of the new Protestant movement as high as possible. There has not been a corresponding effort made by the apologists of the old religion to belittle the numbers of those who accepted the faith. If we take as a text those who were willing to have their fellow citizens regard them as attached to the old religion and opposed in some degree to the new settlement, then we may say very tentatively and vaguely that something like half the families of England still retained the traditions of their fathers in sentiment during the whole of Elizabeth's reign ; there was nothing like half attempting the definite practice of Catholic religion (to which now was attached the official and invidious adjective " Roman ").

On a similar measurement one may say that by the beginning of the Civil Wars a quarter of the English population reckoned in families was still attached to the Thing which had set up the Church amid the ruins of which they lived. But that minority did not actually protest. It refused to accept the penalties of protest. By the end of a century after the great change which begins with William Cecil and is sharply marked by his establishment of Elizabeth

Tudor on the throne (it is a pretty irony that his zealous co-operator in that work was the chief of the Catholic forces in Europe, the young King of Spain, who was ambitious to marry his sister-in-law, the new Queen of England), the numbers of those who were still willing, had opportunity afforded, to practise the new religion of their forefathers was large.

When the final blow fell in what is called " The Revolution," when the organised effort of the wealthier classes drove out the last Stuart, there may have been an eighth of the English people who would still accept not indeed a reversal of the Reformation settlement, but the opportunity for practising the Faith as private individuals. It is probable that those who would actually have admitted, however vaguely, some attachment to the ceremonies and the airs of Catholicism might on the most general and indefinite computation have been stretched to a quarter. After 1688 resistance ceased.   There was no more sacrifice. There were no more heroics.   There was no more passionate protest.   The party which had been not defeated but spiritually starved out, went underground.   During the eighteenth century it may be that one family in a hundred retained its loyalty, but we can hardly put it higher than that.   When a revival did come it was not from within, but from without.   The main force working for that revival was the immigration into an England which had become thoroughly capitalist of Irish cheap labour, which immigration was powerfully reinforced by that main effect of alien government in Ireland, the Great Irish Famine. There was indeed a certain recoupment of Catholic numbers in England from converts, many of them distinguished. But the numerical effect of that effort was small and soon disappeared.   What the future holds in this capital matter we none of us know, but we can all testify that for the moment the battle for the Faith in England has been lost.

INDEX

Anjou, Duke of, 42-3, 83, 179, 196
Armada, The Spanish, 163-6, 169-72
Ascham, Roger, 43
Ashley, Catherine, 7, 25, 27, 28, 29

Bothwell, 157, 160
Bullen, Anne, 2, 10, 11, 20, 21, 22, 23, 25, 112
Bunyan, John, 126-8, 131

Calvin and Calvinism, 30, 69-71, 112, 122, 126, 131-5, 137, 141, 150, 167, 168, 174, 194
Cecil, Sir Robert, 147
Cecil, William Lord Burghley, 34, 40, 44, 49, 50, 74-83, 100, 101, 136, 138, 139, 143, 144, 152, 153-5, 167, 173, 197-8, 200
Charles I, King of England, 72-3, 189
Chaucer, 17
Church of England, The, 109-17, 118-25, 193-8
Courtney, Lord, 35
Cranmer, 6, 11-12, 116
Cromwell, Oliver, 98, 121, 190 note

Darnley, 146, 147, 160
Drake, Francis, 164
Dudley (see Leicester)

Edward VI, King of England, 4, 5, 6, 23, 24, 26, 30, 32, 34, 35, 61, 72, 113
Elizabeth, Queen of England,
Birth and parentage, 1-2, 9-16
Intrigue with Thomas Seymour, 2-3, 4-7, 19, 25-8, 29-30
Formative years, 19-24, 31, 38-9, 40-4, 48-9

and William Cecil, 40, 44, 49, 50, 75-7, 78, 80-3, 136, 138, 139, 144, 154-5, 167, 200
and Scotland, 29, 31, 136, 139, 143-7, 148-51, 154, 155, 156, 181
Ideas on Monarchy, 50, 57, 78, 136-7, 155, 156
and the Armada, 164-6, 171
Death, 178-83
Otherwise mentioned, 55, 60-1, 106, 109, 112, 123, 124, 168, 184, 200
Essex, Robert, Second Earl of, 43

Grey, Catherine, 146

Hawkins, John, 164
Henry VIII, King of England, 2, 3, 4, 10-13, 20, 21, 22, 23, 24, 39, 60, 112, 124
Hooper, John, Bishop of Gloucester, 36-7
Howard, Catherine, 22-3
Huxley, Thomas, 47, 131

James I of England and VI of Scotland, 146-7, 176, 183
James V of Scotland, 138
Jesuits, 74, 151-2, 196-7, 198

Katharine of Aragon, 2, 10, 11, 12, 13, 20, 21, 22
Katharine of Valois, 14, 15
Knox, John, 141, 143-4, 150-1, 168

Leicester, Robert Dudley, Earl of, 19-20, 146, 165, 166

Marlowe, Christopher, 41
Medina, Duke of, 169